W9-AUD-354

Senior Life Services of Morgan County
187 S. Green Street, Suite 5
Berkeley Springs, WV 25411

FIRST DAWN

JUDITH MILLER

FIRST DAWN

FREEDOM'S PATH • *book 1*

DOUBLEDAY LARGE PRINT HOME LIBRARY EDITION

BETHANYHOUSE
MINNEAPOLIS, MINNESOTA

This Large Print Edition, prepared especially for Doubleday Large Print Home Library, contains the complete, unabridged text of the original Publisher's Edition.

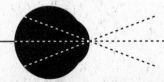

This Large Print Book carries the
Seal of Approval of N.A.V.H.

TO TRACIE PETERSON

For enduring friendship
and blessed sisterhood in Christ

A MESSAGE TO MY READERS

First Dawn is a novel based upon the settlement of two towns formed by a group of African-American and Caucasian men with a vision to settle western Kansas in the late nineteenth century. Their plan called for one city, Nicodemus, to be predominately settled by African-Americans and the other community, Hill City, to be predominately settled by Caucasians.

While grounded in fact, this book is a work of fiction and not a historical documentary. However, I have made every attempt to portray honestly the harsh circumstances these early settlers faced and the intense courage they displayed as they struggled to make a home on the western plains.

Both of these towns continue their crusades to survive. Nicodemus is the only African-American frontier town in existence today.

For additional information about these communities, visit the Kansas Historical Society Web site at *http://www.kshs.org* or the National Park Service Web site at *http://www.nps.gov/nico/*.

The path of the righteous is like the first gleam of dawn, shining ever brighter till the full light of day.

—PROVERBS 4:18 NIV

CHAPTER

1

Topeka, Kansas • July 1877

The iron behemoth punctuated the sizzling Kansas skies with a solitary high-pitched whistle as it belched and wheezed into the train yard. With a powerful burp, the locomotive jerked to a quaking stop that heaved the passengers to and fro like rag dolls.

A steely-eyed conductor with an official railroad cap pulled low on his forehead edged his way down the narrow center aisle. "Topeka!" His voice was curt as he enunciated the city's name.

Jarena Harban removed a folded handkerchief from the pocket of her frayed cotton skirt and rubbed the smudged train window. Vestiges of cinder and ash stubbornly clung to the outside of the glass, but she could see well enough to determine there were a multitude of people waiting at the train depot. They were mostly white folks, but she spied a few coloreds among the crowd. She swiped the window again, but to no avail. With a defeated shrug, she tucked the cotton square back into her pocket.

Across the aisle, her sisters giggled and whispered. Apparently, they found her useless ministrations a fine source of humor. Jarena leaned forward, prepared to launch a look of disdain toward the twins, but her worn straw bonnet slid forward to conceal her annoyed expression from everyone except her father.

"Don't pay them no mind. They ain't laughin' at you. They's jest excited to finally be here." Her father's rich bass voice soothed like rippling water.

Smoothing her skirt, Jarena stood and gave her father a tentative smile. "It's obvious they're not aware the train ride from Kentucky to Topeka was the *simple* portion of our journey."

"Now, don't you go borrowin' worries, gal. Ridin' across the prairie in a wagon is gonna be right excitin'."

Jarena raised her perfectly arched brows. "It's also going to be uncomfortable and *much* slower than riding in a train," she replied, making certain she spoke loudly enough for her sisters to hear.

Truth Harban locked arms with her twin sister, Grace, and directed a smug grin at her older sister. "There's gonna be plenty to see and do along the way."

"Indeed there will! I plan on you two helping with chores, so don't think you'll be running off to explore every hill and valley when we stop to eat the noonday meal or camp for the night."

"Tell Jarena she's not in charge, Pappy. She's only three years older than us, but she's always tellin' us what to do," Grace complained. She gave her father a bright, encouraging smile.

Ezekiel wiped his brow with the old kerchief that hung loosely around his thick neck and motioned the girls into the aisle with a swipe of his large hand. "Get on now and quit your arguing. I don't think none of us is gonna be taking charge of crossin' this here state. Massa Hill said we's to meet him on the platform, so get to movin'."

"*Mister* Hill, Pappy. There ain't nobody your master or boss no more—ceptin' maybe Jarena." Truth poked her sister in the side as she spoke. Once again the girls burst into a fit of giggles.

Jarena's father was frowning at the twins. "You two mind your manners," he admonished.

"And your grammar!"

Truth cast a sullen look at her older sister. "Jest 'cause *you* liked getting all educated don't mean *we* do."

Jarena sighed in exasperation. She had worked diligently to teach the girls proper grammar. Why they insisted upon ignoring their English lessons was beyond her.

As they stepped off the train, the twins peeked around either side of their father, each one beaming an impish grin in Jarena's direction. They were small for their fifteen years, and Jarena was certain their father often forgot the twins were no longer little girls, especially at times such as this, when they should be speaking proper English and acting like young ladies.

They'd been off the train only a moment

when Grace pointed toward a young man standing on the platform and banging a wooden mallet on an oversized brass gong. In between the incessant drumming, he cheerfully encouraged the passengers to partake of the fine food inside the depot dining room.

"You think we could get us somethin' to eat, Pappy?" Grace inquired in a wistful tone.

Their father shook his head and pointed to the basket Jarena had been carrying with her since they departed Kentucky. She had carefully planned what she hoped would be enough food to tide them over until they reached their destination. However, when they neared St. Louis, she had begun to grow uncertain. Fortunately, her father hadn't objected to the rationing Jarena had imposed, and they arrived in Topeka with some victuals to spare.

Grace tilted her head and raised her nose high. "It do smell good, though, don' it, Pappy?"

"That it do, chil'. You girls take your satchels and then stand outta the way." Ezekiel looked around for a moment and then pointed toward one end of the platform. "Go wait over there by that corner. Too many people rushin' around tryin' to get into dat fancy restaurant or find their bags."

Grace peered anxiously at the depot door. "Can't we go inside and see the depot?"

"There's lots more to see out here dan inside that train station. 'Sides, I wanna be able to find all three of you together once Mr. Hill gets all the folks gathered to leave for Nicodemus. Don't want none of you gettin' lost," their father warned.

Jarena strained to see through the crowd, hoping to pick out a familiar face. "There's Nellie and Calvin," she said, waving her handkerchief high in the air. "Nellie! Over here!"

Nellie waved in recognition before herding several other members of their group toward Jarena and the twins.

Calvin glanced about as they drew closer. "Where's your pappy?"

"He went off to find Mr. Hill," Truth replied. "You seen Mr. Hill since gettin' off the train?"

"Nope." With a swipe of his shirtsleeve, Calvin cleared the sweat from his brow. "Ain't seen Hill or Ivan Lovejoy. I thought they was both s'posed to meet us. Sure 'nuff is sweltering, ain't it? Don't recall it ever gettin' this hot in Kentucky."

Miss Hattie, Nellie's outspoken grandmother, stepped toward them and wagged her head back and forth. "That's purely 'cause you ain't old 'nuff to remember. I recall the summer of eighteen and forty—now, that there was one summer. Umm, umm! Why, it was so hot that the flies wouldn't even alight for fear of bein' fried when they come to rest. They'd just circle round and round 'til they dropped dead from the heat." The old woman drew circles in the air with one finger and gave a throaty laugh.

Nellie smiled gently at her grandmother. "Now, Granny, don' get started on dem stories 'bout the old days or we'll never get on our way."

Hattie limped toward a bench alongside the building and plopped down in the shady spot. "I sure is achy from all that sittin'. Don' look like we's goin' anywhere right now, nohow. Where's that Hill feller that's s'posed to be in charge?"

"Pappy's off lookin' for him," Truth repeated.

Hattie thumped the tip of her ancient

parasol on the wooden platform. "Ain't deaf, chil', jest got weary bones."

"Perhaps you should raise that parasol to help cool yourself," Jarena suggested kindly. "We may be here for a while yet."

"Don' think so. There's your pappy now. Looks like that Hill feller is with him." Miss Hattie used her umbrella as a pointer while raising one hand to shade her eyes. She put her hand on Jarena's arm and lowered her voice. "Ain't sure I trust that feller. He's got shifty eyes."

Jarena giggled and sat down beside the aging woman. Jarena had always felt close to her friend's grandmother and even more so since her mother had passed away. "You don't trust most folks until you've known them at least five years, Miss Hattie, but I believe you may be right about Mr. Hill."

Miss Hattie nodded knowingly, her head bobbing up and down in time with the foot-steps of the men as they drew closer. "Yep—his eyes is shifty *and* watery—that's a bad combination fer sure. Tell your pappy that man ain't worth his salt."

"It's probably better if you tell him. I said way more about Mr. Hill and this move to

Kansas than Pappy wanted to hear before we ever left Kentucky."

The woman gave Jarena a sidelong glance. "Nellie tol' me you was set on stayin' in Kentucky. How come you didn't want to give your ol' pappy a chance to get hisself outta them hemp fields?"

"I wasn't trying to keep him in the hemp fields. I asked him to wait awhile—until after some of the other families from Georgetown came west. So we could hear what things were truly like in Nicodemus before he made a final decision."

"Ain't got no sense of adventure, that it?" she asked with amusement as Mr. Hill approached.

Grace giggled and covered her mouth with one hand. "She didn't wanna leave her beau."

"Now I understand." Miss Hattie nodded as a sly smile curved her thick lips. "Yessuh, I surely do."

Jarena opened her mouth to issue a protest, but Miss Hattie and the other travelers were on their feet, moving toward her father and Mr. Hill. The two men stepped onto the platform and waved the small group forward. The hot summer breeze whipped at Mr. Hill's straggly blond hair, the thin tufts flying in all directions, while her father's wiry black curls remained motionless, totally unruffled by the wind. Mr. Hill straightened his shoulders and gave them a thin-lipped smile. His brown suit jacket and pants held several layers of the powdery dust that was swirling around them as they stood in the afternoon sun.

"Welcome to Kansas," Mr. Hill greeted halfheartedly as he surveyed the group.

"Pitiful welcome!"

Miss Hattie's whisper was a little too loud, and Jarena couldn't help but grin as she squeezed her hand.

Hill glanced in the old woman's direction. "I truly am pleased to see you. If my welcome seemed less than exuberant, it's because I must ask your further indulgence. There are several other folks interested in joining our group, and they're not yet prepared to begin the journey."

When no one else spoke up, Miss Hattie waved her umbrella in the air. "How long you 'spectin' us to sit here in this sun waitin' fer you to finish what oughta already been done? And where's Mr. Lovejoy? Ain't he s'posed to be meetin' us, too?"

"Mr. Lovejoy departed for Nicodemus last week," he replied as he loosened the collar of his once-white shirt. "As for the rest of your question, I should be prepared to leave in an hour or two, but for those of you who might be interested, I could take you into town in the wagon with me. That's where I'm to meet the remainder of our settlers. You could use the time to advantage—purchase any last-minute necessities and take a gander at the capitol building they're constructing. If everybody comes along, we won't be required to return to the train station."

Miss Hattie wagged her head back and forth and leaned toward Jarena. "Ain't fer certain I trust Ivan Lovejoy, neither. He ain't really one of us. He's been livin' out here in Topeka fer nigh onto three years now—least that's what your pappy tol' me."

"But he's from Kentucky," Grace said, "and Pappy says he's a good man."

Miss Hattie shaded her eyes as Ezekiel ambled toward them. "Your pappy don't think bad of no one 'til they prove they's no account."

"Can we go along to town, Pappy?"

Grace asked as she danced from foot to foot. "Please say yes."

Truth hurried to her sister's side. "This might be our only opportunity to see the capitol building, Pappy."

Ezekiel scratched the back of his head and then waved the girls onward. "I reckon won't hurt nothin'." When Jarena remained seated beside Miss Hattie, her father waved her forward, too. "You come along with us, Jarena."

"You two ain't foolin' me none at all," Nellie said to her friend and her grandmother. "I bet you's wantin' to go into town and have a look-see fer yourselves."

"Come on, Miss Hattie." Ezekiel walked to the older woman and assisted her up into the bed of Mr. Hill's wagon. "Might git to see something that'll put a sparkle in your eyes."

The old woman gave a disgusted grunt as she dropped down beside Nellie and Jarena. "I seen all the new and excitin' things I wanna see in this here lifetime, but don' look like I got much choice about seein' some more. Appears like all the rest of you is wantin' to ride along and take a look at this here big city of Topekee."

Ezekiel's stern look brought an immediate halt to the twins' giggling.

Jarena watched the girls momentarily squirm and then pivot their gaze upon the older woman. "We're sorry, Miss Hattie."

She nodded her acceptance of their joint apology before turning her attention back to Jarena. "Now let's get back to discussin' that boy you left in Kentucky. I thought I knowed everything goin' on back home. How'd this one get past me?"

"He's not my beau—just a friend." Her cheeks warmed at Miss Hattie's prying question. "The twins tend to exaggerate."

A glint shone in Truth's eyes. "Charles Francis."

"Is that right? Charlie Francis?" Miss Hattie's brow puckered. "I always thought that young man seemed a little bit sour—'specially for a gal with your sweet disposition."

Grace peeked around Nellie with a mischievous grin. "You won't be thinkin' Jarena's so sweet by the time we get to Nicodemus, Miss Hattie. She's got a mean streak. . . ."

"An' she's mighty bossy, too." Truth bobbed her head up and down.

The old woman leaned back against the

side of the wagon and guffawed. "I'd say a person would be needin' both of them things to keep the two of you behavin' on a regular basis."

Jarena beamed a self-satisfied grin at the twins as the wagon neared a bridge. "Pappy told Charles he could come callin'," she told Miss Hattie, "but that was about the same time Mr. Hill and Mr. Lovejoy came to Georgetown and got everyone fired up about moving to Kansas. We didn't have enough time to get to know each other very well."

Hattie patted Jarena's fingers with her gnarled, leathery hand. "Don't you be frettin', chil'. His mama tol' me they was comin' out here with the next group from back home. Not that Lula was wantin' to leave. She'd rather stay put in Georgetown, but I think she finally gave up arguin' against the move when Charlie said he was leaving no matter what his mammy and pappy decided."

"Charles said that? I didn't know. Thank you for telling me, Miss Hattie."

The thought of Charles's declaration caused a warm glow to tinge Jarena's cheeks. Even though he'd announced his intentions to travel west on numerous occasions, his words had fallen flat, always lacking the determined enthusiasm she had longed to hear. Now Miss Hattie's words caused her heart to quicken and restored her belief that Charles had been sincere—that he *would* journey to Kansas.

Miss Hattie grasped Jarena's arm as the wagon slowly rolled onto the narrow bridge that spanned the Kansas River. "This ol' bridge don't appear none too sturdy, and I never did figure out how to swim—ol' Massa never would let us learn. He told us there was a mighty deep river we'd have to cross if we run off, and we'd drown fer sure. Umm, umm. Dat man was a liar on top of being mean as a mad dog. I searched and searched after I got my freedom—never did find no river near thereabouts. Course ol' Massa got what he wanted. We was too afeared to run away."

"Well, you're free now, Miss Hattie, and there's no need to worry about swimming. The bridge is going to hold up, and we're all going to be just fine."

When the wagon finally rolled off the bridge and began to rumble down Kansas

Avenue, Jarena gave Miss Hattie a reassuring smile.

The old woman released her death grip on Jarena's arm and looked around. "These here folks in Topekee got themselves a lot of churches. Must have a disagreeable bunch living in this here town."

Truth leaned forward and looked at Miss Hattie. "I ain't seen nobody fightin'. Why you think they're disagreeable?"

"They got a Baptist church on one corner and a Methodist on the opposite corner, and right up the street they got three or four more churches. I figure they get their backs up 'bout something the preacher says and go huffing off to start 'em another church. Likely hopin' they'll get themselves a new preacher that'll say exactly what they're wantin' to hear. Um, hum, dat's what I'm thinkin'." Hattie's ample body swayed back and forth on the wagon seat as she pointed toward the various church buildings.

Mr. Hill glanced over his narrow shoulder and shook his head. "I can attest to the fact that folks aren't disagreeable, Miss Hattie. Topeka's a large city, and it needs more than one or two churches."

She pointed her parasol toward two men

staggering out of a saloon. "From the looks of those two, it appears you're right about this town needin' lots of churches."

The twins giggled and turned to watch the drunken men, but when Mr. Hill pulled back on the reins and the wagon slowed, they focused their attention on the noble limestone building looming before them.

Mr. Hill leaned back against the wooden seat and yanked hard on the reins. "Whoa!" The horses came to an immediate halt as the metal bits cut into their mouths.

Jarena cast an angry look in Mr. Hill's direction. "Pappy says animals are like people. They respond to kindness."

"I agree. Animals *are* like people. Some learn easily but some take a lot more convincing." He jumped down from the wagon.

"What'd I tell you? That man can't be trusted," Miss Hattie whispered to Jarena and Nellie.

"Come on, Granny. I'll help you down." Calvin grasped the old woman's hand, obviously wanting to quiet her.

Mr. Hill nodded toward the imposing building. "Guess you figured out that's the capitol—at least what they've completed so far. And as you can see, there are plenty of stores where you can make your purchases, but don't wait until time for our departure. I'll meet you back here in two hours. Don't be late!"

"Don' *you* be late," Hattie said, peering from beneath the floppy folds of her ancient parasol. "*You's* the one holdin' up our travels."

Jarena stifled her desire to giggle. Their small contingent had been required to overcome insuperable odds to make it this far. Miss Hattie was not going to be intimidated by the likes of William R. Hill. Jarena watched Mr. Hill skulk away without further instruction. He appeared to realize Miss Hattie planned to hold him accountable.

Truth and Grace rushed to their father's side, their eyes darting from place to place with an undeniable eagerness. "Can we go and take a closer look at the capitol?"

"And see inside the stores?" Grace added.

Their enthusiasm was contagious and quickly spread among the remaining members of the group. "We should take advantage of this opportunity," Nellie agreed while Miss Hattie dropped down on the wooden bench outside Peltham's Dry Goods Store.

"I'll be waitin' right here when ya'll come back. Too hot to be trekkin' around this here city." Miss Hattie pulled a worn handkerchief from her dress pocket and wiped the perspiration from her face.

Jarena hesitated, thinking Nellie would surely remain behind to watch after her grandmother. But Nellie hooked her arm through Calvin's, and the two of them hastened to gather with the others. Hurrying forward, Jarena stepped alongside Nellie. "Don't you think someone should stay here with Miss Hattie?"

"She's more than able ta fend fer herself. She'll use dat parasol to scare off anyone who comes near her."

"But we're not certain it's safe. This isn't Georgetown, Nellie. Besides, I'd think that given your condition, it might be better for you to remain behind and rest."

Nellie laughed at the remark. "You know it's only da wealthy white women who take to their beds when they's gonna have a baby. Why, I'll be workin' right up to the day I birth this chil'."

"And likely be up workin' the day after, too." Calvin's chest swelled as he gazed down at his wife.

"Why don't you stay and look after Miss Hattie, Calvin?" Jarena encouraged.

"She don' want nobody to stay with her. Now come on, Jarena. You're acting foolish," Nellie chided.

"Miss Hattie, are you sure you're going to be all right?" Jarena asked. "I'll stay with you if you want."

She waved her handkerchief. "You go on, chil'. I'm fine."

Jarena gave a doubtful nod, but she pushed any thoughts of the solitary old woman waiting in front of the store to the back of her mind. The hustle and bustle of the capital city with its throngs of people, variety of businesses, and tall buildings caused a rush of emotion. Topeka was truly amazing! Nothing like the frontier town she'd imagined. Why, this city even boasted *two* train stations—one for the Kansas Pacific Railroad and another for the Atchison, Topeka, and Santa Fe. Back home in Georgetown, they'd not yet enticed even one railroad to pass near the town.

Truth began to skip and swing her arms as the group made its way through town. "You think Nicodemus is gonna be anything like Topeka, Jarena?"

"Don't talk nonsense. And quit that skip-ping—you're kicking up dust. Nicodemus is a newly formed town. It's bound to be even smaller than Georgetown. We'll have a church or two and maybe a general store—perhaps a few little shops, if we're fortu-nate."

"You don't know fer sure. There may be some fine buildings jest like the ones here in Topeka," Truth declared with a firm nod.

Ezekiel patted Jarena's arm. "Don' dis-courage the chil'. This here's a fine-lookin' city, and if Nicodemus is only a smidgen as grand, I'll be happy. I know we done the right thing coming here. This here state is the freest and friendliest state for coloreds."

Jarena walked alongside her father, re-membering back several months ago when he'd rushed through the front door of their small house clutching a tattered handbill. He waved the paper in front of her and in-sisted she immediately stop cooking and read the words aloud. The broadside ex-plained that the largest colored town in America was being formed two hundred and fifty miles west of Topeka, Kansas. Her father nearly danced with delight when she read the line stating there were lots for sale—five dollars for a house and seventy-five dollars for a business.

Ezekiel Harban was immediately smitten with the idea of owning his own land. They attended meetings at their local church, where two colored men were introduced as the president and secretary of the Nicodemus Town Company, and William R. Hill was presented as the treasurer and the only white man who would be a member of the town company.

Life hadn't been the same since that day when Mr. Hill had smiled beguilingly at the members of the First Baptist Church and explained the wonders of the great Solomon Valley. He told them of fine acreage and a land that was much like Canaan, flowing with milk and honey for anyone willing to set his hand to the plow. They listened as he told of the rich black soil crying out to be tilled and planted, and of rolling hills that stretched as far as the eye could see. They harkened to his words of abundant wildlife, fine timber, coal deposits, and ample water available from plentiful springs and the south fork of the Solomon River that flowed nearby. And Jarena's father drank up the information like a man dying of thirst.

Her father was one of the first in line to hand over his life savings in exchange for four train tickets and a piece of paper. The paper was a deed declaring that he owned a piece of land in what he constantly reminded her was the freest and friendliest state for coloreds to settle: John Brown's former stomping grounds—Kansas.

Jarena gave her father a sidelong glance. "What are you going to do if Nicodemus *isn't* everything you expect?"

"You gotta have faith, gal. You's too young to always be lookin' fer the worst in things. Trust the good Lord. We's on the right path."

"We'll see, Pappy. We'll see."

CHAPTER

2

"There he is!" Grace pointed toward three wagons lumbering down Kansas Avenue. "Mr. Hill's in the first wagon!"

Jarena wished she could muster a bit of the twins' exuberance; instead she was filled with anger and frustration. As the minutes had ticked away, she'd grown increasingly vexed at Mr. Hill and his delays. A full three hours had passed since the small troupe had parted company with their leader. All nine families planning to go to Nicodemus waited restlessly in front of the dry goods store. And when the assigned time for Hill's return had come and gone, many of them had grown apprehensive. What if he didn't return and they were left to fend for themselves with their meager funds? How would they possibly survive? Jerome Holt, Herman Kemble, and John Beyer had spoken bravely of making arrangements to travel by themselves, while others had argued in favor of waiting for Hill's return. In the end, they had remained in their assigned location—all except the Tuttle family, who had decided to remain in Topeka instead of traveling on to Nicodemus.

Mr. Hill appeared somewhat contrite as he jumped down from the wagon. "Sorry for the wait."

Jarena thought it a meager apology but then realized his words weren't a request for forgiveness—or even an admission of guilt.

"I had more trouble arranging to rent the horses and wagons than I anticipated. However, I'm pleased to tell you that I managed to find three more fellows who want to come along and become a part of the new town."

Miss Hattie folded her plump arms across her chest. "Hmmph! That don' make up for the five you lost by being late."

Hill began counting on his fingers. "Five? That means we're down to thirty-one settlers making the journey. Who pulled out?"

"Walt Tuttle and his family decided they's gonna remain in Topeka," Ezekiel replied.

Hill glanced down the street as though he expected to see the Tuttle family waiting somewhere nearby. "Well, I'll go and find them. They've already purchased their land. Why would a short delay cause them to make such a rash decision?"

"Ain't no need to go lookin'. Walt sold his deed to Robert Fowler for half of what he paid you, and he's already got hisself a job working with the blacksmith down the street."

Mr. Hill frowned. "John Hanson?"

Ezekiel nodded. "Um, hum, dat's it. Anyways, Mr. Hanson done told Walt he needed help and they'd be better off stayin' in Topeka. Course, Walt's missus was all fer staying in the bigger city, too."

"And their daughter Dovie's gonna work as a housekeeper," Truth said.

Jarena secretly wished someone had offered her father a position in Topeka. She'd certainly rather remain in a large city with access to the railroad than continue westward. Yet if Charles was coming to Nicodemus, things would surely become more bearable.

The men Mr. Hill had said were joining the group jumped down from the covered wagons and approached the settlers. One of the men, a broad-shouldered, muscular man who appeared to be in his midtwenties, stepped up beside Hill. "You need us to hep load da wagons?" he inquired.

Mr. Hill nodded, and the three men transferred trunks and meager household furnishings from the freight wagons into the covered wagons they'd be using to travel to Nicodemus. "Doesn't appear you folks purchased many supplies," Hill remarked.

"We got enough ta get us to Nicodemus," Calvin replied. "Ain't no need loading down the wagons with supplies when we can buy 'em once we get to our new home."

Hill dug the toe of his boot into the dirt. "Might take us longer to get there than you're expecting. I can wait a little longer if you want to make some final purchases. We'll need to stop at the livery down the street for the other wagons. If you like, we could camp outside of town and depart in the morning."

"Iffen we run short of cornmeal, these here men will jest have to get out there and kill us somethin' to eat." Miss Hattie spoke for the group. "I'm all fer gettin' started, even if it is late in the day."

"Fine, if that's what all of you prefer. Let me introduce you to our newest recruits and then we'll load up. This is Percy Sharp, Henry Ralston, and Thomas Grayson." Mr. Hill pointed to each of the men as he announced their names.

"Still don' trust dat man," Miss Hattie said as she walked alongside Jarena toward the covered wagons. "And what we know 'bout them men he's adding on? Dey ain't got no womenfolk with 'em, and dat young one is the only one what looks like he kin pull his own weight. Dem other two is gonna be lazy—I can already tell. Don't get to be my age without bein' able to judge a man's worth."

"You think the young one, Thomas Grayson, appears to be of sound character?" Jarena eyed the muscular young man.

A quick jab from Miss Hattie's elbow regained Jarena's attention. "I thought you was pinin' after Charles Francis, and here you is already settin' your cap for that new feller."

A strong southerly wind whipped down the street, and Jarena clutched her bonnet.

"I have absolutely no interest in Thomas Grayson. I merely asked if you thought he was a reliable individual."

"You want me to go tell him you need a hand up gettin' into the wagon?" Truth sputtered.

With a warning glare, Jarena pointed a finger at her sister. "You'll do no such thing, young lady."

Miss Hattie laughed. "You surely got your hands full with them twins. Dey's about as ornery as the day is long—'specially Truth," she said. "I believe I'll jest walk down to the livery. Don' think I wanna crawl in and out of that wagon any more'n I have to. Besides, I been sittin' all afternoon."

"I'll tell Pappy that I'm going to walk along with you and we'll meet them at the livery," Jarena replied. "You want me to tell Calvin and Nellie?"

"If ya like. But tell 'em they don' need to walk. They's likely already in a wagon and ain't no need to climb back out."

Jarena hurried off to deliver the messages. By the time she and Miss Hattie had walked to the livery, the baggage had been rearranged and seats assigned. Jarena and her family had been allotted the fourth wagon, which would also carry Miss Hattie and the young man, Thomas Grayson.

Ezekiel explained that Mr. Hill had planned for only five conveyances. "But we tol' him eight was the least we'd agree to— one for each family. Even one of them new fellers tol' him that with our crates and baggage, there wouldn't be 'nuff room fer folks if we took only five. Don' think Mr. Hill was any too pleased, but it appears we're gonna be plenty crowded even with eight wagons."

Miss Hattie nodded her agreement. "Iffen I'da been here, I'da tol' him we needed at least ten. That woulda raised his hackles fer sure."

Thomas Grayson gave a hearty laugh at the older woman's remark. "Think you's a woman after my own heart, Miss Hattie."

"Don' you go tryin' to sweet-talk me. You's way too young fer the likes of me," she said, joining in his laughter. "Now give me a hand up into this wagon. Maybe we'll get out of town afore nightfall."

When the weary entourage finally departed Topeka, it was late afternoon, and Jarena had pushed aside all thought of working on her mending. All of her time was spent pushing crates back into place or catching a falling crock as it was jostled loose. There was little doubt they would need to rearrange their belongings when they finally stopped for the night. Nothing remained in place as the wagon shifted and pitched back and forth through the rutty grasslands.

The sun dropped behind a ripple of hills. Twilight was upon them when Mr. Hill finally declared they would make camp along the banks of a small creek.

"You'd best not spend much time with food preparation—better to get plenty of rest. We'll have a long day tomorrow."

Jarena set the twins to work rearranging and tying down their belongings in the wagon while she peeled and fried some yams over the open fire and Miss Hattie stirred together a batch of cornmeal mush.

"I'm afraid this won't be much of a meal," Jarena lamented.

"I bought a few things while the rest of you was off sightseeing," Hattie told her. "There's a slab of bacon in the wagon. Tell Grace to fetch it, and we'll fry up a little to go with the yams. It'll give 'em a little more flavor and seem more like a meal if we have us a little meat. And send Truth down to fetch some water. I's gonna need some coffee."

Jarena did as the older woman instructed, all the time wondering why she continued to remain with the Harban family when Nellie and Calvin were in the wagon behind Mr. Hill. Surely Miss Hattie would prefer to share her provisions and travel with her own relatives.

Grace handed her sister the bacon and peered into the frying pan. "I hope you're gonna fix more than that little bit. Pappy said Mr. Grayson's gonna be takin' his supper with us, too. That ain't enough food to fill all of us."

Jarena frowned and shooed her sister away from the fire. "It will have to be enough. We've got to make our supplies last until we get to Nicodemus."

Miss Hattie jovially slapped her bulky thigh. "Iffen you drink a lot of that water your sister's fetching for us, you can trick your belly into thinking it's full."

Grace asked, "You gonna travel all the way to Nicodemus with us, Miss Hattie?"

Miss Hattie tilted her head and peered out from beneath the wide-brimmed sunbonnet she'd donned when the wagon train departed Topeka. "You wanting to get shed of me?"

"No, ma'am. I'm glad to have both you an' your bacon! Just figured you'd wanna travel with Nellie and Calvin."

"Their wagon's already full. 'Sides, this is where Mr. Hill put me, so I figure I's gonna stay put." She gave Jarena a wide grin.

Jarena smiled in return. She was pleased to have the companionship of the older woman. The twins had each other to talk to, and now her father had Thomas Grayson. It would be nice to have an older woman with whom she could visit and share her concerns.

When the meal was ready, they gathered around the fire and clasped hands before offering thanks for their safety and provision on the journey—all of them except Thomas Grayson, who, Jarena noticed, had quietly slipped away the moment her father had mentioned prayer.

Truth turned to Jarena after her father had uttered the final amen. "Mary Beyer said her mama fixed plenty of food for them."

Jarena sighed. "Mary Beyer's only four

years old. She has no idea how much food her mother prepared."

Later, as they settled into their covers, Jarena lightly touched Miss Hattie's arm. "You think Mr. Hill has everything prepared the way it should be?"

"Don' be frettin', chil', 'cause it ain't gonna change a thing. Jest gotta trust the Lord. No need to lose sleep our first night in dis here new state."

Jarena considered the old woman's words. She knew worrying wouldn't change things, but she also knew remaining calm would prove a difficult task. She'd often attempted to cease worrying over her mother when she was lying on her sickbed. Even when the doctor had said that her mother wouldn't recover, Jarena had prayed and trusted God for a miracle. But a miracle didn't happen. Her mother died, just like old Doc Hardy had predicted.

On that night nearly two years ago, Jarena Harban's uncompromising trust in God had faltered. Oh, she still believed that Jesus was the Son of God and that He died on the cross to save her from her sins—that hadn't changed. But the issue of trust—that *had* changed. No longer did she cast all her cares upon the Lord, believing things would be fine. At her mother's deathbed, the issue of trust had changed. Instead of placing her unwavering confidence in God, she had reclaimed responsibility for her own well-being. God had fallen short of her expectations, so she no longer trusted in His provision.

Jarena turned first to one side and then the other, wiggling down into the blankets as she attempted to find a comfortable space. She could hear her father talking to Thomas Grayson. His words drifted up from beneath the wagon, and she listened to him assure Thomas that life would be grand once they reached Nicodemus. As Jarena slipped into a restless sleep, she wondered if Thomas believed her father's declaration.

CHAPTER

3

The smoky odor of burning wood filled Jarena's nostrils as she peeked out of the wagon before sunup the next morning. She could just barely see Thomas hunched over the small fire, feeding it with twigs while he fanned the flickering embers with his hand. The sky remained shaded with the dark, murky hues of night, with only a thread of orange etching the shadowy horizon. Daybreak would soon arrive.

Lifting her skirts, Jarena carefully hoisted herself down from the wagon and approached Thomas. "Have you been awake long?"

He startled at her question. "I didn' hear ya come up behind me." He nodded toward a fallen log. "Have a seat if ya like. I thought

I heard the horses stompin' about. Don' want to lose 'em to horse thieves."

She peered across the fire. "No, I suppose not. I may as well get breakfast started."

Thomas tilted his head and gave her a shy smile. "I brought a bucket of water up from the spring. Don' know if yer pappy told you, but I brought along food for the journey. Since we're all travelin' together, I told him I'd turn my supplies over to you in exchange for not havin' to do none of the cooking."

"No, he didn't tell me, but that's certainly good news."

"There's coffee and bacon, an' I got a dozen eggs packed in straw, and some flour and beans. There's even some cornmeal and molasses and some other things I can't remember, but I figure you can put 'em to good use."

"I'm sure I can, but I'll be careful to use your supplies wisely."

It didn't take long before the aroma of smoking bacon, frying batter, and boiling coffee awakened the remainder of their small group.

"Flapjacks!" Grace declared as she

neared the small cooking fire, her face alight with pleasure.

Jarena poured another dollop of batter into the frying pan and then pointed toward the small stream located a short distance from their campsite. "Down to the creek and wash up first."

Miss Hattie and Ezekiel settled near the fire and helped themselves to the bacon and flapjacks.

"You makin' more cornpone, Jarena?" Hattie asked.

She nodded and pointed at the molasses. "Help yourself. Thomas contributed the eggs, flour, and molasses. To tell you the truth, I didn't know if we'd stop long enough to cook the noonday meal, so I thought it best to cook extra this morning."

"You got you a smart gal, Ezekiel—and a good cook, too," Miss Hattie praised as she licked the molasses from her fingers.

"Bit headstrong, but she'll do." He sent Jarena a grin as he stood up. "You ladies take your time finishin' up breakfast. Thomas is gonna help me git the horses hitched up."

While Ezekiel and Thomas readied the wagon, the twins finished their breakfast and then scurried off to the creek to wash the breakfast dishes. A short time later, the tin plates and utensils had been repacked and the damp dishrag was hanging from the back of the wagon to dry in the morning breeze.

————

The days soon slipped into a routine, though occasionally their schedule was broken by the pleasure of stopping at a settler's cabin or visiting momentarily with other slow-moving wagons making their way westward. Like the rest of their group, Jarena would wave and shout hello, but she viewed the wagons closely as they passed. The other wagons appeared to be amply filled with beds and cupboards, plows, and other farm implements. She observed crated chickens, an occasional pig, and huge bags of grain among the other settlers' belongings. Women and children followed behind, herding cattle or horses, and she'd occasionally seen a dog nipping at the children's heels.

On one of those days when they'd passed several well-laden wagons, Jarena moved to the front of the wagon and sat beside her father. "Have you noticed that the settlers we've seen along the way appear more suitably prepared than our group?" she asked. "Do you wonder why they're carrying so many goods with them and we're taking so few?"

"They's likely coming from somewheres nearby—didn' have to travel on no train like us."

"Perhaps they traveled by train but purchased goods in Topeka or even St. Louis before beginning their journey by wagon."

"Why we need to do all that buying afore we leave Topeka? Anything we needs, we can buy fer ourselves when we get to our new town. Ain't no sense carting all them things when we can get 'em in Nicodemus. 'Sides, most of us didn't have money to buy all them goods. Once we gets to Nicodemus, I's thinkin' we's gonna be able to get our supplies on credit 'til our first crop comes in."

"I still haven't heard Mr. Hill say there's a mercantile or dry goods store in Nicodemus." Jarena turned to Thomas. "Have you?"

"No, he never did tell me nothing 'bout the town itself. He just said he was takin' folks out west to a town for colored folks and that there was still lots for sale if I wanted to buy one for five dollars. I gave him my five dollars, and he handed me a signed deed."

Jarena tucked a strand of hair behind her ear. "What if Mr. Hill isn't being completely truthful? Even Miss Hattie said she didn't believe he could be trusted."

"There ya go borrowin' trouble again, gal." Her father swatted away a fly. "If we'da needed to bring all them extra supplies, Mr. Hill woulda tol' us."

"Don't forget that he encouraged everyone to purchase additional provisions while we were in Topeka."

Her father shrugged and slapped the reins. "That there was merely a suggestion, daughter."

Apparently her father's trust had increased as much as hers had decreased throughout this wearisome journey. As far as she could tell, none of the men had taken time to seek out Mr. Hill and question him. Although there had been one evening when Jarena had convinced Thomas Grayson to discuss their concerns with Mr. Hill, the effort had gone unrewarded. Their leader had excused himself, saying he was ill and needed to rest. And so they had moved on, and Jarena decided she was the only one who was sparing energy to worry about what they would find when they reached their destination.

As their small column of wagons continued westward, the bluegrass and bluestem were replaced by thick, deep-rooted buffalo grass, and the trees grew more scarce and scrubby—except for the cottonwoods that dotted the riverbanks and shaded the occasional creeks. Intermittently they would spot the purple blooms of prairie clover or the delicate blossoms of wild blue flax peeking out through the shifting buffalo grass, but by and large Jarena found the scenery as tedious as their journey.

Thomas had pointed out the bleached bones of buffalos when they'd passed near the deep wallows used by the huge animals, but the twins had little interest in the skeletons or the barren pits. Instead, the girls directed a watchful eye for prairie dogs. They both delighted in the sight of the animals standing guard over their holes like tiny sentinels. It was Grace who decided the furry animals resembled small statues clothed in fur coats—at least until they emitted their high-pitched barks and darted downward into the mottled landscape.

As the settlers moved onward, the distance between farmsteads increased dramatically. The few houses they'd seen of late were soddies—at least that's what Mr. Hill had told the group they were called. They were squatty-looking homes he told them were constructed by cutting out large squares of sod and then stacking them like bricks on top of one another. Although it was a strange concept to Jarena's way of thinking, these settlers seemed to think their dirt homes adequate. She shivered to think of living in a house erected from hunks of earth. Who knew what might still be living in that sod.

Truth came running toward the wagon, her arms and legs flying. "Mr. Hill says to pass the word that we're gonna stop for nooning. I'll tell the others!"

When the wagons circled a short distance from the creek, Jarena glimpsed her first sight of a dugout. A family had burrowed into the hillside a short distance from the water's edge, where the bank was somewhat higher. Jarena and several others walked down to the river and gazed at the strange sight, startled when a young woman poked her head from behind the tattered canvas that covered the doorway. The moment the woman spied them, she hurried outside with a baby balanced on one hip and two toddlers clinging to her skirt.

"Welcome!" Her broad smile revealed a row of yellowed uneven teeth. "Come have a cup of coffee and set a spell."

Uncertain if they should accept the woman's offer, Jarena consulted Nellie and Mrs. Holt, who had been talking nearby. "Should we accept?"

"Of course," Mrs. Holt said. "We don' wanna appear rude. Come along!" She charged forward like a commander leading troops into battle.

Spending time with the stranger had been a battle—at least so far as Jarena was concerned. Forcing herself to remain in the burrowed-out hillock long enough to seem sociable had taken every ounce of endurance she could muster. The dark, dank dwelling made the soddies appear luxurious.

Returning to the campsite, Jarena related the entire experience to her father. "I felt like one of those prairie dogs we've seen out on the plains. It's not normal to burrow into the ground that way." She wiped the beads of perspiration off her forehead and shuddered involuntarily.

Her father patted her hand. "No need to worry, daughter. Mr. Hill already assured us dere's plenty of trees in Nicodemus. I'm sho' we gonna have a place that's at least as good as what we left in Kentucky."

Jarena stared at her father in disbelief. "I would hope for something better than the small cabin back in Kentucky. Otherwise, why did we leave?"

"Fer the *land,* chil'. No way I can make you understan', is there? It's fer the land. When we go to sleep at night, it's gonna be in a house that belongs to us, and when I harvest, it's gonna be crops that belong to us—no more sharecroppin'."

Jarena didn't attempt to say anything further, for her father was convinced their life would be grand so long as he held the deed to a piece of land. She completed her tasks, and when their nooning was complete, she rode along silently, with thoughts of the young family and the dugout fresh in her mind long after they had departed.

As the wagons rounded a steep hummock, Thomas pointed to the view ahead. "Look over dere."

Jarena followed his gaze and gasped at the sight. She clasped a hand to her chest, overcome by a deep sense of wonder. Beneath them lay a valley, a lush expanse of fertile-appearing land, with spans of rolling hills overlooking either side of the basin. Far above and to one side of the rolling hills, a magnificent outcropping of limestone rose at least three hundred feet above the valley floor.

She continued to stare, turning her head so as to enjoy every last glimpse of the beauty. "If we're going to live somewhere like this, then perhaps I will be able to adjust."

"Mr. Hill says we're gonna make camp at the Great Spirit Spring tonight," Truth called out to Thomas and her father as she scurried toward their wagon. "He says it ain't too far from here."

Ezekiel frowned. "Where you been, gal?"

"I was talking to Nellie and Calvin. It's not as dusty near the front of the wagon train," she replied with her usual bright smile. She hesitated for only a moment before excitedly asking, "What's the Great Spirit Spring?"

Thomas winked at Truth. "I don' know, but we gonna find out. Mr. Hill likely knows all about it."

"I hope you can get more answers about that spring than you've been able to pry out of him regarding our new town," Jarena muttered. "Instead of running to and fro between the wagons, you could help with some of this mending, Truth. Most of the holes that need darning are in either your stockings or your dresses. And you haven't finished your lessons for the past two days."

"I don't know what you'd do if you didn' have me to scold. And that's Grace's dress you're mendin', not mine," Truth retorted.

Jarena looked down at the dress. "Perhaps you're right, but Grace has already completed her lessons."

"I'll do 'em after we make camp. I can't read or write when the wagon is jostlin' back and forth."

"So long as you remember your promise when we stop for the night. I'll not be put off by your complaints or excuses."

Jarena watched Truth wave and skip off

toward the front of the wagon train. Had she ever been so carefree? Before she was fifteen, she'd been caring for their sick mother as well as performing the household duties and helping the twins with their schoolwork. She poked the threaded needle in and out of Grace's torn chemise, feeling much older than her eighteen years. Many girls her age were already married—or at least betrothed. But what with nursing her mother and taking responsibility for the house and care of the twins, there had been precious little time for herself, much less for a beau.

And lately her father had become more and more dependent upon her. There was little doubt he expected her to remain at home until the twins were out on their own. And certainly no one could forecast when that might occur, for neither one was willing to take on much responsibility. Not that they weren't capable. They both had adequate skills and abilities to perform most household duties, though Truth excelled in cooking while Grace proved herself to be an excellent gardener. However, both of them escaped cooking, cleaning, and sewing at every chance.

"Jarena! You daydreamin' again?" Nellie

Harris was walking near the back of the wagon, a layer of dust covering her calico skirt. "Jump on down and walk with me, Jarena. Let's have us a visit—that mendin' will still be there come evenin'."

She continued stitching. "But the daylight won't."

"Don't be so mulish. I ain't hardly seen you since we left Topeka."

Jarena gave Nellie a halfhearted grin as she stuck the needle and thread through the edge of the chemise. "Guess it won't hurt to stop for a while," she agreed. She tucked the mending into her worn sewing basket and jumped down from the wagon, running several steps to maintain her balance as she landed.

Nellie clapped her hands. "Good fer you! I thought you'd land on your backside, fer sure." Nellie gave her a broad smile and grasped Jarena's hand in her own. Soon they began to swing their arms back and forth as they walked off to the side of the wagon train. And for a moment Jarena felt as though they were little girls out for an afternoon romp.

"How are you feeling, Nellie?"

"Jest fine. I'm not sick, you know—jest gonna have a young'un."

Jarena nodded. "Guess I remember hearing how sick Mama was with the twins. Pappy said she could hardly get around for the last couple months before they were born. And her feet swelled up—almost looked like they'd burst if you stuck a pin in them."

"I still got a long time afore I have any of them complaints. Calvin says if I didn't tell, no one would even know we was gonna have a young'un. You think that's true?" She smoothed her skirt tight around her belly and awaited her friend's reply.

Jarena studied the barely rounded stomach as though she were an authority on expectant mothers. "Not much there now, but just you wait."

"That there Grayson feller's good-lookin'. I been watchin' him. I'm thinkin' he might be takin' a likin' to ya."

Jarena pulled her hand loose. "Don't be foolish, Nellie."

Nellie tilted her head back and laughed before reaching down to pull a nettle from her bare foot. "I think you could turn his head without even tryin' if you'd jest put

Charles out of your mind. I figure Charles will stay in Kentucky—that boy don't have no hankerin' to start a new life."

Jarena cast an accusatory glare in Nellie's direction. "What's come over you, Nellie Harris? If it was Calvin left behind, you'd not be thinking of another man—or would you?"

"Me and Calvin's married—Charles ain't even mentioned nothin' 'bout marrying you. Has he?" Nellie danced around to face Jarena. "Tell me, Jarena. Has Charles asked your pappy fer your hand?"

"Not exactly, but your grandma said he's coming to Nicodemus. Soon as his folks decide they're ready to leave Georgetown."

"You see? He ain't man enough to strike out on his own. Now, that Thomas Grayson, he appears to be more than ready."

Jarena was silent for several minutes, unwilling to continue bantering with Nellie. She had no interest in Thomas Grayson nor any other man except Charles Francis. And oh, how she missed seeing Charles. But even if he would have asked for her hand, Jarena knew she couldn't have remained behind while her father and sisters set out for unknown territory. They needed her—even more than she needed Charles. Unfortunately, Nellie had no way of understanding her loneliness. After all, Calvin was right alongside her, day and night.

Nellie reached down and grabbed Jarena's hand again. "Don't be mad at me, Jarena. I was jest pokin' fun."

She sighed. "Don't you miss being back home?"

"No, I can't say as I do. We're goin' to somethin' better, Jarena. We'll have land of our own and a town where we'll be free to make decisions instead of white folk making 'em for us. Won' have to worry 'bout nobody else tellin' us what we's s'posed to do."

"Things weren't so bad for you in Georgetown, Nellie. You could have gone to school as long as—"

"You know I don' like book learning. And workin' as a housekeeper fer them white folk wasn't much better than bein' a slave. They didn't treat me no better, and that's a fact. I never had a free minute fer myself. When I wasn't cleaning inside the house, they had me working in the yard, and in the evenin' they expected me to watch after their young'uns. Didn't pay me nothin' extra, neither. And the little bit of money they paid me I had to give back fer my room and board. I tell you, Jarena, I got mighty tired of working day and night and having nothin' to show fer it in the end. Me and Calvin is gonna have us a nice place to call our own in Nicodemus—same as you and your family."

"This move is what Pappy and the twins want, but it's not what I want."

Nellie bobbed her head up and down. "You want Charles, and you're thinkin' if your pappy would have stayed in Georgetown, maybe, jest maybe, he'd have asked you to marry him. That's it, ain't it?"

"Is that so wrong?"

She shrugged. "Ain't wrong, but you can't be fer sure he'd have asked even if you'd stayed behind. Charles seemed to take a likin' to Calvin's cousin Belle, as I recall. 'Sides, with all your book learnin', maybe you could teach the young'uns when we get to Nicodemus. We's sure to have us a fine schoolhouse, and you's the smartest person I know! You always said you liked helpin' the twins with their lessons. You need to think about the future instead of lookin' back."

Jarena gave her a feeble smile. "I've got the rest of my life to think about the future. Right now, I feel as though I've left too much behind. I'll likely never be able to put flowers on my mama's grave again."

"But your mama ain't in that grave, Jarena. She's in heaven. You know dat."

"Yes, but it gave me comfort to go sit by her grave and talk to her. I can't do that anymore."

"She can hear you jest as good in Nicodemus as she could in Kentucky. 'Sides, it's the Lord you need to be talkin' to, Jarena, and you know that's the truth."

"Look up yonder," Thomas hollered from the wagon's high seat.

They sped to catch up with the Harban wagon.

Nellie and Jarena craned their necks in the direction of a hill that rose about twenty feet above the valley of the Solomon River.

Jarena hurried to the front of the wagon. "Are we there? Is that the spring?"

"Looks that way. The wagons are slowing down."

Jarena stared off toward the rising mound. Water seemed to overflow from the top of the hill. It trickled downward in rivulets and then formed a stream that flowed into the river. The wagon stopped near the foot of the hill, and Thomas jumped down from the wagon. While her father tended to the horses, Thomas made his way up the mound and stooped down. He dipped one finger into the water and then stuck his finger in his mouth.

"It's salt water," Thomas announced in a loud voice.

"Mr. Hill says the Injuns believe the spring is sacred," Truth reported with excitement as she and Grace drew near, "but he says the trappers call it the devil's washbowl." Her eyes gleamed. "Kin we climb up and look, Jarena?"

"Ask Pappy. Mr. Grayson says it's salt water, so don't plan on drinking it." Moments later the two girls came running back to the foot of the hill. "Pappy says we can go if one of you goes with us," Grace panted.

"I have no interest," Jarena said before heading back toward the wagon. "I'm going down to the river. I need to wash some clothes before supper."

"I'll go with you," Thomas told the twins, "but it's jest a pool of water and nothin' more, so don't go up there expectin' too much."

"That's right. Don't expect much! That way you'll not be disappointed," Jarena whispered.

She gathered the soiled clothes and headed off toward the river, wondering if Nellie was right. Perhaps Charles wasn't ready to begin a new life. But how could she fault him if that were true? She didn't want a new life, either—at least not in Kansas.

CHAPTER

4

Thomas ambled down the hillside, pleased he'd taken time to accompany the Harban twins. They'd had a great time while exploring nature's wonders atop the mound. But the girls' astonishment also stirred memories that Thomas had buried long ago—memories of a time when he, too, had been filled with pure delight at the discovery of God's amazing creation.

Forcing the thoughts from his mind, Thomas turned toward the river. Sodden clothes had been spread across sturdy bushes or hung from the low-hanging branches of the cottonwood trees that flourished near the water's edge. Jarena had obviously been hard at work. He hesitated for a moment before walking in her direction.

"You might want to move dem clean clothes a mite nearer the wagon. If a wind comes up tonight, dey'll be scattered from here to Topeka," he said as he sidestepped close enough for Jarena to hear him.

She glanced over her shoulder and frowned. "I didn't plan to leave them here. I'm merely spreading them out until I finish the rest of the wash."

Raising a brow, Thomas gave her a half grin. "Merely a suggestion. No need to get yo' hackles up."

Jarena sighed as she rubbed a piece of hard lye soap into the collar of her father's shirt. "I have no interest in arguing, Mr. Grayson."

"Good! Then why don't I keep you company while you finish the wash? Maybe havin' someone to talk to will make your work easier."

"A little help is the only thing that's going to make my work any easier," she said, plunging the shirt into the water.

Thomas quickly moved to her side and knelt down. "Hand me that pair of britches and I'll soap 'em down."

Jarena sat back on her haunches and stared at him.

"Guess if you ain't gonna give 'em to me, I'll get 'em myself," he said, reaching around behind her.

Before Jarena could object, he had thoroughly doused the trousers and was taking the soap from her hand.

"I'm an old hand at washin' clothes. We'll have these done in no time. Why don't you tell me 'bout Kentucky? Your sisters say you didn't wanna leave."

"My sisters talk too much. Besides, that's only half true."

He grinned. "Which half?"

Jarena stared down at the wet shirt. "I asked Pappy to wait until some of the others came out here and settled—to make certain there were no problems before we left home."

"But he didn't listen."

"No. Pappy came home one afternoon all excited and waving a torn handbill over his head like it was the most important piece of paper he'd ever laid eyes on."

"An advertisement for Nicodemus?"

She nodded. "He already told you?"

"A little. But I'd like to hear what *you* have to say."

She tilted her head to one side and met his intense gaze. "Why?"

He shrugged a shoulder. "I guess 'cause you're the only person in the group that don' appear to be excited about goin' to live in dis new town. Your pappy says—"

"That it's the Promised Land, full of deer, buffalo, wild turkey, and other fowl—more good food than a man could ever eat? That there are herds of wild horses waiting to be caught and tamed? That because the soil is fertile and the weather so agreeable, crops will sprout from the ground almost unbidden? That because of John Brown, Kansas is the freest and friendliest state for coloreds to settle?" She groaned in exasperation. "I know what my pappy says, Mr. Grayson. I was sitting right alongside him in church when Mr. Hill and his partners gave their speeches. My pappy believes every word they said."

"And you think they were lyin'?"

"I think before a man drags his family across this country, he should be certain he's hearing the truth. But I'm not a man, and I didn't have a say in the matter. My pappy is set on owning a piece of land."

"Can't fault a man for takin' a chance at

seein' his dreams come true. Who knows? Your dreams might come true in Nicodemus, too, if you give the place half a chance," Thomas said, watching her.

Jarena stood up and dried her hands on the cotton apron that covered her faded blue skirt. "I believe that's the last of my wash."

"I'm sorry," he said, jumping to his feet. "I've made you mad, haven't I? Was it my comment about your pappy followin' his dream?"

"I'm not angry, Mr. Grayson. I hope Pappy and the twins will be happy in Nicodemus, but I find it difficult simply to rely upon everything we've been told. I suppose you could call it a . . . a lack of trust." Her final words were no more than a whisper quickly carried off by the warm evening breeze.

———

Thoughts of her visit with Thomas Grayson near the Great Spirit Spring were far from Jarena's mind two days later when Mr. Hill commanded that the wagons be brought to a standstill, and the thirty-one travelers clambered out of the wagons to see their promised land.

"This is it, folks. You're home!" Mr. Hill shouted.

Shock coursed through Jarena like lightning on a sultry summer night. "We're home? What does he mean? Pappy, what does he mean? There's nothing here." Her voice sounded hollow and desperate.

Jarena clutched her father's powerful arm in a death grip and squeezed her eyes shut. Surely everything would be different when she opened them—it *had* to be. Though she could feel her father tugging away, she tightened her grip on his arm. She needed an anchor.

"Ain't nothin' gonna change just 'cause you's not lookin'," he said in a soft voice.

She slowly lifted her eyelids. Her father was correct. Nothing had changed. The scrubby brush, the dry buffalo grass, and the flat, expansive prairie loomed before her like a bad dream.

"Where's the town, Pappy? There's nothing here." Once again she tightened her clawlike hold upon his arm.

"I see that, chil'. Now take them sharp nails outta my arm, and let's go take a look around."

Jarena knew there was an irritated look

on her face as her sisters ran up to her chattering excitedly.

"Ain't you glad we're finally here?" Grace asked.

"Have you taken leave of your senses? Take a look around you! There is *nothing*—absolutely *nothing* here!" Each word burst from her lips like an explosion of buckshot.

"*We're* here. And I reckon Mr. Lovejoy must be 'round here somewhere," Truth replied.

Jarena's jaw tightened. Her worst dreams were coming true. Why didn't her family understand how horrible this was? "Look at this place—both of you. Do you see *anything* that resembles a town? Any houses? Any church or school? Perhaps a livery stable or mercantile? Any evidence that a well's been sunk to provide water? Other than Mr. Hill's declaration, please tell me if you find even *one* thing that appears to be what we were promised."

With her hands on her hips and her chin jutted forward, Jarena defiantly awaited their answer. Before either of the twins could respond, Jarena heard heated words of protest from other members of the wagon party being directed at Mr. Hill. The protests caused satisfaction to wash over her like a spring rain.

At the sound of thunderous laughter from Herman Kemble, they all turned in unison. When his laughter finally ceased, he turned to Mr. Hill. "You's joshin' with us, right?"

William Hill's already pale complexion had turned a pasty white, and he tugged at his scraggly blond mustache. Jarena watched as he focused his unwavering gaze upon some indeterminate object on the horizon, obviously unable to look any of them in the eye. "We're . . . uh, we're a little behind schedule on our building projects," he lamely explained. "But soon we'll . . . uh, begin, and in the meantime, all of you can erect your own homes. You'll have the freedom to decide upon what type of shelter you want to build."

Jarena stared at him in disbelief. He made it sound as though they'd been granted some special privilege for which they should be grateful. Did he truly believe they were so foolish? And why did the other men remain silent? Were they so bewildered that they were rendered speechless, or was it their fear of contradicting Mr. Hill that caused them to suddenly become mute?

She looked for Thomas Grayson but couldn't find him in the crowd. Jarena turned to level a sharp glare at her pappy but stopped short. Was the dampness on his cheeks perspiration or tears? She couldn't be certain, but she softened her gaze and grasped his large, worn hand in her own.

"We're going to be all right, Pappy," she whispered with more confidence than she felt.

He glanced down at her, and another tear escaped his deep brown eyes. "You's right about that, chil'. The good Lord ain't gonna let nothin' bad happen. He delivered us to dis here promised land, and I know He's gonna be watchin' over us."

Jarena couldn't disagree aloud, for the older man's vulnerability was obvious. At this moment in his life, he needed encouragement, not harshness. Pushing aside the desire to remind him of her many admonitions, she squeezed his hand reassuringly.

Seemingly freed from his state of shock, Calvin Harris waved a fist in the air. "There ain't nothin' here! This is open prairie. There ain't no town!"

"He's right!" several others agreed, joining ranks behind Calvin.

Mr. Hill backed away from the angry crowd and quickly ascended a small grassy mound several feet away. "You're wrong!" he shouted. "There's opportunity all around you. Land! Freedom! The chance to make this town exactly what you want it to be."

A voice came from the crowd. "We want what you promised us. You took our money and done nothin'."

"Delays—merely delays," Hill replied as he loosened his collar. "You men know that nothing ever progresses as quickly as planned. Besides, we set September as the month we'd have everything completed, and it's only July."

Herman Kemble took several large steps toward the mound. "Even if we give you 'til the end of September, ain't no way you's gonna have this town built by then. Why, you ain't even got no supplies here to build with. Ain't no streets laid out or nothing else as far as I can tell. What'd you do wid our money? You sure didn' use it here. How you 'spectin' us to get by with no stores and no supplies, Mr. Hill?"

"Remember I was required to pay the filing fee for your land. And you should recall I encouraged you to purchase supplies before we left Topeka—and even at several of the small towns along the way."

"But you never told us there wasn't nothin' in Nicodemus ceptin' brush and dirt! You knowed we'da never come if you'da told us the truth, didn't ya?" Herman Kemble was nearly trembling with anger. "How we s'posed to survive out here? And where's Ivan Lovejoy?"

"The railhead's down in Ellis, but you can't make it there and back in one day, especially with supplies. As for Lovejoy, I'm not certain where he's camped, but I'm confident he's somewhere near here."

"He ain't gonna have enough supplies for all this group," Herman Kemble retorted.

Jarena looked at her father. Finally she saw the reaction she would have expected. His demeanor had changed from misery to anger. The vein in his neck throbbed, and his hands were clenched into tight fists. "We ain't even got horses and wagons," he accused. "You let us believe we could get everything we needed here in Nicodemus."

"I never actually said it would be possible," Hill replied.

"You's playin' with words—jest like you been doin' ever since you took our money back in Kentucky!" Herman Kemble hollered. "What you gonna do to make things right with us?"

Hill's hands shook as he flapped his arms up and down in an attempt to soothe the crowd. "If you have enough money to purchase these horses and wagons, I'll sell them to you and make it right with the livery in Topeka—all except my own wagon and team," he added hastily.

The men—Thomas Grayson among them—clustered together, and Jarena stood near the perimeter of the circle, anxious to hear the discussion. "We gotta figure how much money each of us can pitch in toward a couple teams of horses an' at least one wagon," John Beyer suggested. "Without horses, we gonna die out here."

After they added up their money, the men found they could afford only three horses and one wagon. The meager remaining funds would be needed for supplies.

"We oughta hang him," Jarena heard Jerome Holt whisper. "He's a liar and a cheat."

"Settle yerself, Jerome," another man

said. "Ain't gonna turn to no violence. Let's see what he says 'bout our offer on the horses."

Jerome pulled a cotton kerchief from his trouser pocket and wiped his forehead. "He'd best see it our way, or I'm all fer stringin' 'im up."

"Mr. Hill, we got an offer fer ya," Herman said as the group broke ranks. "We'll pay ya fifty dollars fer one team and a wagon. You give us one of your horses or pay the owner for one of dese others and make a gift of it to us."

"Fifty d-dollars? A g-gift?" Hill stammered.

"Call it a way to heal the wrong you done to these folks," Thomas Grayson put in, stepping toward William Hill.

Mr. Hill's skin now matched the whites of his watery eyes. He fumbled for words to defuse the growing anger of the crowd as pools of deathly gray settled inside the hollows of his sunken cheeks.

"Let the man speak," Ezekiel said as he stepped forward.

"Thank you, Mr. Harban. I feel terrible about the situation you're all facing out here, and you're right—you do need some horses and wagons. Here's what I'll do. I'll go and fetch the Peterson brothers—they live over near Hill City. They agreed to go with me and take all eight of the wagons to Topeka, but I'll tell them I'm only taking six wagons back. To prove my concern, I'm going to leave you folks with two wagons and two teams—but you only need to pay me for one."

Murmurs spread among the new settlers and finally Jerome Holt spoke out. "Don' be 'spectin' to hear me thankin' ya fer leavin' the wagons. It's the least ya can do after all the lies ya told us."

Mr. Hill's color improved as he inhaled deeply. He straightened his narrow shoulders before giving them a thin-lipped smirk. "I want you folks to take heart. I promised this town would be ready for you, and you're going to be amazed at what's been accomplished by the end of September. As soon as I return to Topeka, I'll be finalizing the arrangements. In no time you're going to have a fine little town that you'll be pleased to call home. Before winter sets in, this town will surpass all of your hopes and dreams."

"Let's hope it ain't our *bad* dreams, or

we'll be out lookin' fer you, Mr. Hill," Jerome replied. His voice remained edged with anger.

"You have my every assurance that you are going to have a school and churches and many shops bustling with business along the streets of Nicodemus before the first snow falls on the plains. Trust me! I am a man of honor."

"Don' appear we got much choice but to trust him," Calvin muttered.

Jarena glanced up at her father, wondering if he believed Mr. Hill's promises.

"Think we better be puttin' our trust in the Lord instead of Mr. Hill," her father said softly.

If only her father had listened to her back in Georgetown.

CHAPTER

5

The day Mr. Hill departed Nicodemus, a shroud of fear and foreboding settled over the encampment. Uneasiness reigned, especially among the women—and Effie Beyer in particular. Though Jarena had always considered Effie a bit flighty, the woman's behavior had grown more erratic since leaving Georgetown. Her ill-behaved children made life no easier for the woman. But most likely the recent odd behavior was caused by departing her home in Kentucky and then compounded when their small group had been deposited in the middle of the prairie to survive on their own. And who could blame poor Effie? The only things visible to remind them of what they'd been promised back in Georgetown were the Solomon River and one of Mr. Hill's line drawings depicting the layout of Nicodemus and the surrounding township.

So far as Jarena could understand from that drawing, they should have right now been in a community where the north and south streets were numbered First through Seventh and the intersecting streets patriotically bore the names of the first American presidents. But there were no streets or houses or any of the numerous businesses so artfully depicted on Mr. Hill's map. Worst of all, there was no place to purchase the supplies they so sorely needed. Surrounded by low-lying hills and a vast expanse of prairie, they could only surmise how Hill planned to build the town he envisioned. Little wonder Effie Beyer's behavior had become erratic. In fact, Jarena marveled that others had not become frenzied or inconsolable.

A vacant stare filled Effie's eyes as she approached Jarena. The twins had gathered a number of the children, Effie's brood included, and were leading them in a game of tag.

"You think Truth and Grace can make them young'uns behave?" Effie asked Jarena in a quivery voice. "If not, I'll get mine back over here beside me."

Jarena gazed into Effie's fearful eyes. "They'll be just fine, Effie. The twins will watch out for them. Both Truth and Grace are good with the younger children."

Effie dropped onto the flat-topped trunk Jarena now used as a small table. "I'm scared. I tol' John I didn't wanna leave Georgetown," she whispered, her focus flitting about as she spoke. "Don' go far!" Her eyes shone with fear as she yelled and waved at her children.

Jarena grasped the older woman's hand in a reassuring grip. "They'll be just fine."

"John's wantin' to take the wagon and go find our land. I don' wanna go off by ourselves. I told him we ain't got 'nuff supplies to last out there by ourselves, but I don' think he's gonna listen. What am I gonna do?" She raked her trembling fingers through a mass of unkempt thick hair.

Jarena pulled the woman into an embrace. "I'll see what I can do. I'll ask my pappy what the men are planning. You sit here and rest."

"Thank you, Jarena. You's gonna come back and tell me what he says, ain't you?"

Her eyes brimmed with unshed tears as she held fast to Jarena's sleeve.

"Of course I will. Just rest, Effie."

Jarena marched off toward the two wagons, where her father sat talking to several of the men. Whatever was wrong with these men? Did they not care what their wives desired? Was a woman's opinion deemed so useless that it was given no consideration? For they were now stranded in this unforgiving wasteland.

Jarena stooped down beside her father and waited until he turned to her. "Somethin' wrong, gal?"

She hesitated a moment, her gaze settling on Ivan Lovejoy. "When did Mr. Lovejoy arrive?" she whispered.

"Few minutes ago. He's been camped out on his acreage, but he's gonna move in here with the rest of us fer a spell. Like all of us, he says he was s'prised to find nothin' completed in the town. Is that why you come stompin' over here?"

"No, I was wondering if any decisions have been made—about where we'll stay until Mr. Hill returns."

Jerome Holt didn't hesitate to answer. "Best we all stay together."

The others nodded—all except John Beyer. "I was thinkin' to get on out to my land. Thought maybe ya'd let me take one of the wagons and maybe borrow a few tools. I'm anxious to get started on puttin' up some shelter for my family."

Percy Sharp, who had been pretty quiet thus far, shook his head. "You know I ain't one to speak against any man doin' as he sees best for hisself and his family, but we gotta think about the whole group—not just ourselves. Every man here is anxious to provide shelter for his family, I know dat, but rushin' off by ourselves is the worst thing we can do right now. There's safety in numbers. I think we should stick together right here at the townsite."

"I agree," Robert Fowler stated. "If you take off with one of the teams and a wagon *and* the few tools we got amongst us, how's the rest of us gonna get anything done 'round here?"

John's jaw tightened. He yanked his hat from his head and threw it to the ground. "Appears you think I'm selfish, Robert. Who was it that loaned you the fi' dollars to pay the land company so's you could come out here?"

Robert glanced toward heaven and then shook his head. "I ain't saying you's selfish—jest saying we ain't got much in the way of supplies and we best keep the little we got in one place. And jest in case you forgot, I paid back the money I owed you—plus a quarter for interest."

"Is all of you agreein' with Robert?" John asked angrily as he surveyed the group.

His answer was a chorus of *um-hums* and nodding heads.

A puff of powdery dust billowed from John's side as he picked up his hat and slapped it on his pant leg. "Guess if that's how all of ya feel, I got no choice but to stay. But I'm telling all of ya that when Mr. Hill gets back here with our supplies, I'm headin' out to my place."

Jarena sighed. At least she would be able to carry good news to Effie. Perhaps the woman would settle herself once she knew that her family would be remaining with the group.

She made her way back to where the harried woman was seated and gave her an encouraging smile as she drew near. "You can rest easy, Effie. He's agreed to stay with the rest of us until Mr. Hill returns."

Effie's forehead creased with worry lines, but she thanked Jarena. "I best get back over there. I was watchin' John. He's mad as a hornet—won't be no pleasin' him tonight."

"That may be true, but it's the other men he's angry with, not you. In his heart, he knows it's best to remain with the group. He'll come around soon enough."

Effie jumped up and skittered across the small encampment, her billowing skirt whipping about her legs. Jarena tsked as she stared after the woman. She almost thought about saying a prayer for Effie Beyer, but there was no need to bother, for Jarena and God weren't on speaking terms. In fact, they hadn't been communicating much since before she left Georgetown. Her prayers had grown sporadic after her mother's death, had increased when her father announced they would leave Georgetown, and had stopped completely when they boarded the train destined for Kansas. Oh, she still uttered the perfunctory prayers before meals and at bedtime, but the intimate chats had ceased. There was no use praying if God never answered.

"You sure is lookin' sour today." Miss Hattie chuckled as she plopped her ample body onto the trunk Effie had vacated.

Jarena gave her a halfhearted smile. "I was talking to Effie. She's getting more unpredictable with each passing day. I worry about her—and her children."

The older woman attempted to fan herself with a limp handkerchief. "Best we be prayin' for her. Outside of helpin' with the young'uns, ain't nothin' gonna help her 'cept our prayers."

Jarena sat down beside the older woman. "You pray for her, Miss Hattie. God doesn't hear my prayers."

"Don't be talking nonsense, chil'. God listens to *everything.* He answers *all* our prayers."

"Well, if that's true, why did my mother die? And why am I sitting out here in the middle of this desolate place?" she asked crossly.

"Now, hold on—I said God *answers.* I never said He answers the way we *want.* There's a big difference 'tween the two."

"That's the response I get from everyone. That's not an answer, just an excuse."

"You listen here, gal. God don't need nobody making excuses for Him. You think jest 'cause you don' get the answer you want that God's not listenin' to you? Does your pappy always answer the way you want?"

"No! We wouldn't be here if he did."

"Does that mean he didn't listen to you or that he didn't understand what you wanted?"

"No. But it does mean he didn't care what I wanted—just like God doesn't care."

"Your pappy cares and God cares. Thing is, they got more control over your life than you do, and that's what you're not likin'. You think you know what's good for you better'n God does, but that ain't the truth of it. Whether you wanna believe it or not, God's got plans for you, Jarena, and He ain't gonna give in to your whims. It ain't fer us to know everything, gal. If you's as smart as I think you is, you'll get down on your knees and start prayin' again. It's time you started trusting God."

Trust. She was beginning to hate that word. She jumped up when she noticed the men's meeting breaking up. "Looks as if they've finished talking. Think I'll go and find out what they decided."

Miss Hattie grinned. "You can run from me, but you cain't run from God."

Jarena ignored the remark and hurried off to meet her father. "Any other decisions been made?"

"We gonna stay here and live the best we can, just like we did on the trail. I asked Thomas to throw in with us."

Jarena's eyes widened at her father's casual announcement. Myriad rejoinders immediately came to mind, but she bit her lip and looked skyward for a moment before returning her father's gaze.

He reached up under his wide-brimmed hat and scratched his head. "Is that there look s'posed to tell me you don' like my idea?"

"We don't know anything about him. He's a stranger. Besides, it seems he'd be more at ease with the other single men."

"Thomas is a good man, and he's willin' to help me when the time comes to start buildin' our house. I don't recall you complainin' about eatin' the food he gave us out on the trail."

Jarena knew there was no sense in arguing any further. Thomas Grayson would remain a part of their family; her father had already decided.

"We all picked out spots where we'll make our camps 'til Mr. Hill returns. Ours is gonna be over dere," he said, pointing toward a flat, grassy area protected on one side by a low-lying hill. Her father turned to leave and then glanced back over his shoulder. "Gonna be hard 'nuff gettin' along out here. Best we's kind to one another."

Jarena tried to smile, but she figured it looked more like a grimace. "I'll do the best I can, Pappy."

He nodded. "I know you will, chil'. I always been able to count on you."

Several days later Jarena hunched over the small fire. Grasping the fabric of her skirt for protection, she lifted the iron skillet of cornmeal mush from the fire. Rationing food was a necessity, and the gnawing in their bellies had become a pervasive, unwelcome companion. All of them longed for a hearty meal, yet the abundant animal life they'd been promised was not the reality. She wondered what would happen when winter set in and the jackrabbits and prairie hens disappeared completely. She'd attempted to discuss the matter with her father on more than one occasion—especially when the men were lamenting their lack of hunting weapons. But he had discouraged such talk, telling her they would be fine— God would take care of their needs. Jarena had wanted to angrily rebut his words, but she remained silent. Only time would tell who was correct.

She had joined her family as they'd laid out the campsite that would be their home until Mr. Hill returned. The other families had staked out their makeshift camps nearby, each wanting the protection of the group, yet seeking a small modicum of privacy for their families. Members of the group had equally divided the canvas and shared their few tools in order to construct the small lean-tos that now dotted the prairie land-scape. The worn white canvas, held over-head by fallen cottonwood branches found near the river's edge, provided their only shelter. The unrelenting winds would daily swat the flimsy roofs to the ground, and daily they would console themselves by saying it wouldn't be long until Mr. Hill re-turned. Each time they spoke of Mr. Hill's re-turn, Jarena wondered what would become of them in this desolate place if Mr. Hill did not return.

Jarena leaned across the fire and stirred the paltry skillet of mush. At the sound of approaching footsteps, she jerked around to see Thomas walking toward her.

"Mornin'. Didn' mean to scare you." He leaned down, lifted the coffeepot from atop the glowing embers, and poured a small portion of the brew into his tin cup. He looked at the thin layer of mush. "Not much left in the way of supplies?"

She remained crouched by the fire. "No, not even enough to cook a decent breakfast. What are we going to do? Have the men talked about our future out here?"

Thomas squatted down and looked at her with kind, deep brown eyes. "Not that I've heard—unless they made some plans last evening. I didn't join 'em. Took the twins fishin'."

She nodded. Neither he nor the twins had snagged a single fish.

"I'm headin' down there again right now," he said. "There's gotta be at least a few fish in that river."

"If you catch any, I'll be happy to cook them."

"And eat 'em?"

"*And* eat them!" She watched Thomas stride off with his makeshift fishing pole in one hand and her father's pitchfork in the other before she turned back to the fire.

Her father's long shadow stretched across the flames. "That Thomas?"

"Yes. He's gone off in hopes of catching a few fish. He says they bite better early in the morning or in the evening when it's not so hot, but I'm not certain he truly knows. After all, he didn't bring any back with him last night. I do hope he's successful this morning. We've got next to nothing to keep us going. Do you think we can continue waiting on Mr. Hill?"

Her father poured himself a cup of coffee and sat down by the fire. "Decided last night—we can't wait no longer. We's put our little bit of money together and we're sendin' one wagon down to the railhead in Ellis today. We'll get what we can. Maybe a few more tools and some food to keep us goin'. 'Cept for prayin', ain't much else we can think to do."

Jarena wanted to offer her suggestion, but it would serve no purpose. Her words would fall on deaf ears. She thought they should all pile into the wagons and head off for Ellis. Maybe they could hire out and earn enough money to purchase train tickets back to Georgetown.

"Will everyone go?"

Her father looked at her as though she'd lost her senses. "It's thirty miles each way, and we gots to stay here and protect our belongin's from thieves and claim jumpers."

Jarena glanced about the camp at the smattering of household goods, the few tools, and the partially empty trunks. She saw little that needed protection.

"Who's going?"

"We decided to send Thomas."

"Why Thomas?"

"Why *not* Thomas?" her father countered. "He's good with the horses, he's young an' strong, and he's been in the West longer'n any of us ceptin' Ivan Lovejoy. And Ivan made it real plain that he ain't goin'. We agreed Thomas is the best choice."

"He's never been *this* far west, has he? And who knows how long he's been in Kansas. Has anyone even asked him?"

"Stop your frettin', Jarena. Thomas is a good choice. The women won't want their husbands leavin' without 'em, and that's a fact. Most of 'em are still expectin' Injuns to come ridin' over one of them yonder hills."

"And who's to say they won't—the Indians, I mean."

"Mr. Hill tol' us we wouldn't have no trouble with Injuns."

"And we can believe everything *he* told us!" The words gushed forth unbidden. All her plans to remain silent had gone up in smoke, just like the smoldering brushwood she'd thrown on the fire.

"Now, don' you go gettin' uppity with me. Ain't no call for that sharp tongue of yours. We all know we's got problems—don' need to be reminded all the time."

"I'm sorry, Pappy." She nodded toward the river. "Appears as though Thomas caught himself some fish."

Thomas was running across the prairie, holding several fish high in the air. "Look what I got," he called out.

Grace sat up from her sleeping blanket under the canvas, rubbed her eyes, and poked her sister. "Look!" Without a word, both girls jumped to their feet and ran over to greet him.

Truth returned to the fire carrying the three large fish that Thomas had strung onto a heavy piece of twine. "Look at these! Ain't they somethin'?"

"Yes, they *are* something," Jarena corrected.

Obviously annoyed, Truth dropped the line of fish in front of her sister. A few inches further and the smelly catch would have landed in Jarena's lap.

"You want me to clean 'em, Pappy?" Truth asked.

"No, I'll clean the fish. You can help yo' sister with some of the chores. I'm thinkin' maybe you and Grace could spend some time down at the river doin' the washin'. No reason Jarena should be the only one doin' laundry."

The excitement in Truth's eyes faded as she plopped down nearby.

Thomas met Jarena's gaze. "Think you can manage to eat some of dem fish?"

"I'll do my best."

He grinned. "I know you will. Sure gonna be good to have some fish, ain't it, Mr. Harban?"

"Sure will. Come on with me over here a

ways, and we'll get 'em cleaned. I'm needin' to have a word with you."

———

Thomas followed along with a sense of uneasiness churning in his belly. Surely Mr. Harban hadn't somehow found out about his past. He swallowed hard and chided himself. There was no possible way word could have reached this desolate place. Except for Ivan Lovejoy, these people had had no contact with the outside world—and Ivan couldn't truly be considered the outside world. Nobody in this small group knew where he came from or why he was on the run. In fact, they didn't even realize he was on the run. Best he settle down and let Mr. Harban speak first.

Ezekiel dropped the catch on the ground. "These here fish is gonna taste mighty good. You done a fine job, but I still ain't fer certain why you took my pitchfork."

Thomas laughed. "I set a couple of lines afore the sun was up. Once it got to be daylight, I used the pitchfork to stab at the fish that got near the bank. Caught that one with the pitchfork," he said, pointing at one of the larger fish. "Woulda had another, but it slipped off when I lifted it outta the water. Didn' make that mistake again. The next time I stabbed one, I swooped it up toward the bank. Worked pretty good."

"Right smart of ya," Ezekiel commended as he began cleaning the fish. "We had a meetin' last night—while you was down at the river."

Thomas nodded and waited.

"Ain't no way we's gonna survive iffen we don' get more supplies. We put our money together and decided to send a man down to the railhead at Ellis to get what he can with the money we scraped together."

Thomas nearly sighed aloud as he grabbed one of the fish and slit it open. "Sounds like a good idea. I got a few dollars I'd be happy to give. Is that all you wanted to ask me?"

Ezekiel hesitated for a moment. "No. As a matter of fact, we decided you'd be the best choice to make the trip down to Ellis."

"Why? Wouldn' it make more sense for one of you to go? I'm not truly a member of your group."

"You sound just like Jarena. Why, you's as much a part of this group as the rest of us. We need someone that ain't got women-folks dependin' on 'im. You's young and strong, and ain't no doubt you can handle that team and wagon long enough to get yerself down to Ellis and back again."

"What about Percy Sharp and Henry Ralston? They's both single and know how to handle a team."

Mr. Harban gave him a questioning look. "Ain't nobody gotten to know either one of dem very well. I vouched for you, said you was a good choice. Now you's sounding like you don' wanna help out."

"No, I'm willin' to go. I'm willin'." He didn't want the others to think him unappreciative of the trust and acceptance they'd given him.

"Good! We got us a list all made up. Now, let's go have us some fish and corn mush. Once we finish breakfast, you can be on yer way."

"All right. I'll go hitch up the wagon while Jarena's fryin' the fish. Be sure and save me some." He forced a smile before he turned and headed off toward the field where the horses had been hobbled for the night.

How he wished the men hadn't entrusted him with this task. He mumbled to himself as he walked. "If they knew 'bout the bounty on my head, they wouldn't be so quick to hand me their money. Or a team of horses an' a wagon. How'd I get myself into this?"

CHAPTER

6

Georgetown, Kentucky • August 1877

Macia Boyle soundlessly hurried down the hallway in a pair of new white leather slippers. Her blond curls bobbed up and down in a chaotic rhythm as she came to a halt at the bottom of the stairway. "Father! I wasn't expecting to see you."

Dr. Samuel Boyle stood inside the front door of their home. "I just now arrived. Why don't you join me in the parlor?"

Her bow-shaped pink lips turned upward into a demure smile. "Must we talk now? I'm expecting Jackson Kincaid at any moment."

Samuel placed his physician's bag on the

elaborately carved receiving table beside the staircase, removed a folded paper, and met Macia's eyes. "Why don't you join me in the parlor until he arrives? We both know Jackson is notoriously tardy. It may be another hour before he appears. Turn around and let me see your dress."

His appeal pleased her, and she pivoted slowly.

"Emerald green looks particularly lovely on you, Macia. You and your mother should both wear more green. Is that a new gown? I don't believe I've seen it before, have I?"

"No. Mrs. Langford delivered it just last week."

"So that fishtail at the back of ladies' dresses is still in fashion, is it?" he teased.

She emitted an exasperated sigh. "Mermaid's tail, Father, not fishtail."

Samuel laughed heartily as he patted her shoulder. "Mermaid tail, fishtail—I don't know how you ladies manage to keep abreast of these important fashion trends.

"Margaret! Where are you?" he called while taking hold of Macia's hand and leading her into the lavishly decorated front room of the house.

"I'm right here, my dear. No need to raise

your voice." His wife walked into the parlor and placed a fleeting kiss on his stubbled cheek. "You look tired. Let me have Cook bring you a cup of tea."

Samuel sat down heavily on the brocade settee. "I'm no more tired than usual, and I truly don't want any tea, but thank you for your concern, my dear. Is Harvey close at hand?" He patted his hand on the cushioned divan.

Taking her husband's cue, Margaret sat down beside him. "I don't believe so. I haven't seen him since earlier this afternoon. Is something wrong?"

"No. I had hoped to talk to the entire family at one time, but perhaps this is best after all. I'll talk to the two women in my life and get your reactions first." He smoothed the wrinkles from his trousers. "Do sit down, Macia. Pacing in front of the window won't cause Jackson to arrive any more quickly than if you're seated."

She plopped down. Both women watched intently as he carefully unfolded the large piece of paper he'd carried into the parlor.

"I want both of you to look at this broadside."

Macia quickly scanned the page. "Why did you want us to read this?" Her words were spoken in a nearly inaudible whisper.

"What do you think?" he asked, a look of exhilaration on his face.

"You aren't planning on *us* moving to this place, are you? What's the name of it?" Macia asked, pulling the circular closer. "*Hill City.* You aren't planning on our family leaving Georgetown and going to Hill City, Kansas, are you?" Her voice was trembling by the time she completed the question.

Margaret leaned forward and patted her daughter's hand. "Now, don't upset yourself, darling. Father merely brought this home to keep us informed of the latest news about town. Isn't that right, Samuel?"

Macia could hear the urgency in her mother's words. She waited, hoping to hear her father's immediate agreement. Instead, he inhaled deeply, settled back into the cushion, and gave them a pronounced frown.

"No, that's not at all what I intended. However, before either of you becomes unduly distressed, let me speak my piece. The only thing I'd ask is that you maintain a modicum of objectivity as you listen," he urged. "Will you do that?"

Macia simply stared at him. Apparently her mother had nodded in agreement, for her father smiled and began to speak.

"Margaret, you know I've long desired to move away from Georgetown—get out of the South. I've remained in Kentucky because it's always been your home, but you know I'm not happy in the South. I've always been an outsider in these parts. If it weren't for the fact that folks in Georgetown need medical care, they'd shun me altogether."

Margaret edged forward on the settee. "Only because of your attitude about slavery and the coloreds. If you'd kept your opinions to yourself, folks would have taken to you just fine."

He gave his wife a lopsided grin. "Well, we both know *that's* never going to happen. Why should I lead people to believe I agree with them when I don't? Fact is, things around Georgetown haven't changed all that much. Unfortunately, a lot of good men, both colored and white, died in the war, but I don't see the Negroes around here making much progress. Most of them haven't been able to break away from the hemp fields, and I certainly don't see a change of attitude in most Southerners."

Macia's mother appeared completely baffled. "Why, what do you mean, Samuel? The Negroes are free. They can come and go as they please, the same as you and I."

"Exactly my point, Margaret. We freed them to a dusty road with only the rags on their backs. How can they live unless they continue working for their same masters?"

"They're paid wages and given a place to live."

"Oh, Margaret, do pull off your blinders. Most of them live in the same old ramshackle dwellings they've always occupied, but now they must consider those hovels a part of their pay. The meager wage they're paid is barely enough to buy food for their table."

Macia sighed. "What has any of this to do with this Hill City place?"

"It would be an excellent place for our family to begin a fresh, new life," Samuel replied. "Think of the adventure, the excitement—"

"The lack of civility," Margaret interjected.

"There's ample civility out west. I spent

the afternoon with the founder of Hill City, and he tells me we would be a most welcome addition to the town. From what he said, Hill City is a prospering little community that will grow by leaps and bounds in the future. Besides giving us a fresh start, purchasing land in the West is a wise investment. Mr. Hill tells me there's plenty of farmland for sale, and purchasing acreage now, while the prices are cheap, makes good sense."

"If it's such a prospering town, why is he in Kentucky advertising for folks to move there?" Macia smugly inquired.

Her father didn't flinch at the question. "If you'll look at the date located at the bottom of the page, you'll see that this broadside was printed several years ago. Mr. Hill merely had it along with him and showed it to me. I asked if I could have it. To tell you the truth, he didn't come here seeking prospective citizens for Hill City. He's arrived with several colored gentlemen in order to encourage additional Negroes to move west, to a town that's being formed exclusively for coloreds. There's already one small group that's settled in Nicodemus. In fact, he told me most of them are from this part of Kentucky."

Macia folded her arms across her waist. "I say we forget about Mr. Hill and his namesake city. Let him do what he came here to do: find more settlers for his colored community."

Margaret nodded in agreement. "She does make a sound point, Samuel. It seems as though this Hill City is already a thriving little community, and we're well established in Georgetown."

"Have you heard nothing I said earlier? I've never felt settled in this town. And putting that fact aside, I believe this would be an excellent means to require more of Harvey—force him to take responsibility for his life. He doesn't feel an iota of guilt about his lack of contribution to this household."

Margaret pulled a dainty lace handkerchief from her sleeve, a precursor to her habitual tearful displays.

"There's no need for tears, Margaret. We're merely having a discussion, and you know as well as I do that it's time Harvey took on the responsibilities of a man."

"Harvey's still very young," she defended, dabbing the corner of one eye.

"He is nineteen. I wouldn't say a word if he had continued with his education or if he spent his time learning a trade. I've encouraged him to continue his education just as I encouraged Carlisle."

"Just last week Harvey told me he was giving serious thought to reading the law."

"In the meantime, his behavior is abhorrent. I hear him come stumbling in at all hours of the night. He spends his evenings playing cards and socializing, and then he sleeps most of the day—trading daylight for dark. Moving out west will take him away from his revelry here in Georgetown and force him to grow up."

"I suppose that's true," Margaret conceded.

"*What?* How can you agree to such a thing, Mother? What kind of work could Harvey possibly find in Kansas? He's more suited to life in Georgetown or some large eastern city."

"Harvey is currently suited to not working at all, and that is what I plan to change," her father said with a definitive tone. "If I invest in land, there's no reason why he can't farm for a living."

Macia and Margaret gasped in unison.

"What's wrong with farming? It's good, honest work. If he doesn't want to go to school, he must discover a way to support himself. I can think of nothing better for him than hard physical labor."

"You'll never get him to agree to such a thing," Macia stated.

"That's fine. If we decide to move west and he doesn't want to farm, he can remain in Georgetown and support himself in any manner he chooses."

"He will starve to death." Margaret frantically moved her handkerchief from one eye to the other and back again.

Samuel nodded. "Exactly my point."

A knock sounded at the front door, and Macia jumped from her chair as though she'd been projected by a tightly coiled spring. "That's Jackson. Please promise me that you and Mother won't make a decision until we have more time to talk. I can't begin to tell you how distressed I am over this entire topic."

Her father patted her hand. "We won't make a decision this evening, and I'll listen to everything you have to say before coming to a final determination."

"Thank you. I've been invited to the Kincaids' for supper, but I should be home by ten o'clock."

"I never did like any of those Kincaids," Samuel muttered as she walked from the room.

Macia turned when she reached the hallway. "I heard your remark, Father, and it wasn't what I'd expect to hear from a kind Christian man such as you."

She tied her feather-trimmed straw bonnet under her chin and opened the front door, careful to block Jackson's entrance.

His eyebrows furrowed slightly as he took her arm and walked to the street. "I had planned to greet your parents," he commented while helping her up into his carriage.

"Forgive me. I didn't mean to appear rude, but they were in the midst of a discussion."

He gave her a knowing look. "I understand. My parents have arguments from time to time, also."

"They weren't arguing, merely discussing," she defended. She didn't want Jackson believing that her parents were unhappily married. However, truth be known, she doubted whether he cared one way or the other.

Jackson ignored her reply and flicked the reins. "Mother is looking forward to your visit. I believe she'd like your opinion on a piece of needlework she's been stitching. Or is it a dress she mentioned? I'm not certain, but there's some item that she's anxious to show you," he said as they neared the edge of town. "Is that your brother?" he asked, nodding toward a carriage careening in their direction.

"Indeed it is. Signal him to stop," she said while frantically waving at the coach.

Macia watched intently, uncertain whether Harvey could bring the buggy to a halt without causing it to overturn. She breathed a sigh of relief as he slowed the coach and came alongside Jackson's carriage. Always the jokester, he waved his hat in a grand flourish.

"Hello, Macia. How are you, Jackson? Something amiss?"

"I thought I had best warn you that Father came home proposing that we all move to some town out west."

Harvey gave a hearty laugh. "Mother will

soon change his mind. And if she doesn't, I will."

"I'm not confident you'll succeed. *You* are part of the reason he's talking about making this move," she disclosed. "You'd best come up with some excellent arguments, because I don't think he'll be easily dissuaded. When I left the house, he had Mother nearly convinced."

Her words appeared to shock him into sobriety. "I'll go straight home and talk to him," he replied.

Jackson eyed her suspiciously as they moved onward. "You *were* playing a joke on him, weren't you?"

"No. Unfortunately, what I told him is true. My father has decided our family should move to the western frontier and become one with the savages," she uttered dramatically.

He guffawed and waved one hand in a dismissive gesture. "I don't think you need worry about savages. I understand the cavalry has them under control—at least throughout *most* of Kansas."

His cavalier attitude annoyed her, and she sent him an icy glare. "This isn't funny, Jackson. How would you feel if your father suddenly announced that he was moving to the frontier?"

"Now, now, Macia, there's no need to work yourself into a state of apoplexy. I'm certain this whole idea will leave your father's mind as quickly as it arrived."

"Don't speak to me in that placating tone, Jackson. I'm not a child. The fact is that if my father decides to move west, it will radically alter my future."

He sighed deeply as he tugged back on the reins and the carriage came to a halt in the circular driveway that fronted his parents' white-pillared manse. He jumped down from the carriage and hurried around to assist her. "Perhaps Mother will have some words of advice for you," he suggested as a young colored boy appeared out of nowhere and led the horses and carriage off toward the barn.

The front door swung open as they approached. A regal-looking colored woman attired in a black dress with white collar and cuffs greeted them and took their wraps. The servant smiled when Macia expressed her thanks, but the woman's smile quickly faded when Jackson rebuffed her friendly behavior. As they walked down the hallway,

Jackson chided Macia for thanking the servant. In a condescending tone he stated her conduct was unacceptable and would only serve to send mixed messages to the servants regarding their proper place within the household. Not wanting to argue, Macia nodded as she took his arm.

They'd barely crossed the threshold into the sitting room when Jackson smugly announced to his parents that the entire Boyle family would likely be moving to the western frontier. He ignored her pleading looks to cease his diatribe, seemingly taking great delight in relating every detail—including their earlier discussion with Harvey along the roadside. Had they not been sitting in clear view of his parents, she would have kicked his shin.

To make matters worse, when Jackson finally completed his tale, Mr. Kincaid took up the attack against her father. Macia wanted to run from the room. She had expected a fine supper and an evening of pleasant conversation. Instead, she was being forced to listen as her father was relentlessly insulted. She longed to tell all of them she found their behavior boorish and that she wasn't at all interested in their opinions. However, she forced her lips into a pleasant expression and said neither.

Booth Kincaid was only too happy to expound upon Samuel Boyle's many faults and failures—primary among them, the fact that he was a Northerner who sided with the coloreds and looked down his nose at the southern gentry. Mrs. Kincaid was exceedingly pleased to add her disdain over the fact that Carlisle, Macia's older brother, was attending theological seminary in Maine rather than at one of the fine schools located in the South. Then there was a discussion between Mr. and Mrs. Kincaid concerning the many trials and tribulations Macia's poor mother had been forced to bear because she'd married an outsider. They spoke as though her father had been reared in some foreign land rather than the northern United States.

When they finally were seated around the dining room table, the conversation turned to the weather, and as Mr. Kincaid began expressing his deep concerns over the lack of rain and crop yields, Macia sighed with relief. However, her reprieve was short-lived. The moment the conversation lagged,

Mrs. Kincaid began to inquire about Harvey and his future plans.

Before Macia could reply, Jackson laughed boisterously and said, "Seems his indecisive behavior is one of the primary reasons Dr. Boyle is looking to move out west."

"Is that so? Samuel having trouble getting the boy to take hold and assume responsibility?"

"I think my father is hoping to give Harvey the same opportunity you've given Jackson," Macia astutely replied.

Mr. Kincaid gave her a quizzical look. "And what opportunity is that?"

"Why, to become a farmer."

Jackson sputtered, and several drops of coffee dribbled down his chin. "I am *not* a farmer." He absently wiped his face with one of the starched linen napkins. "The coloreds do the farming."

"Oh, I momentarily forgot. *We* wouldn't have any coloreds to farm our land, so I suppose Harvey would actually be required to perform the work—get his hands dirty. Besides, I suppose the coloreds will be busy enough farming their own land."

Mrs. Kincaid appeared puzzled. "Whatever are you talking about, Macia?"

"Why, didn't you know? Mr. Hill and his friends have been recruiting Negroes from Georgetown for their new all-colored town in Kansas. Some have already settled out there."

Mrs. Kincaid began to fan herself. "Have you ever heard tell of such a thing, Booth? Coloreds starting up their own towns? Do you think our sharecroppers might consider leaving?"

"Our Negroes aren't about to go anywhere." Mr. Kincaid stabbed a piece of pork roast. "They know they're better off sharecropping on the land they've lived on all their lives. Besides, there's not one of them that would have the means to leave. It takes money to move west and buy land."

Macia tilted her head to one side and met Mr. Kincaid's pompous gaze with a sweet smile. "My father says the small farms cost only five dollars. Do you truly believe it would be impossible for your sharecroppers to save that amount?"

"Not long ago you mentioned a couple of families had pulled up stakes and disappeared." There was a note of panic in Mrs.

Kincaid's voice. "Do you suppose they're among some of the settlers this Mr. Hill has recruited?"

"Absolutely not. There's no way our field hands could accumulate enough funds to purchase land and outfit themselves for a journey west. Except for the Negroes working in town as tradesmen, I don't think Mr. Hill is going to have much luck finding coloreds who have the necessary funds to settle their town. Takes a good deal of money to join such a venture—and we'll be certain to let our coloreds know that, won't we, Jackson?"

CHAPTER

7

Ellis, Kansas • August 1877

The hot August sun was unrelenting. Beads of perspiration trickled down the sides of Thomas's head and formed a wet band inside his wide-brimmed hat. He wiped his forehead with an already damp kerchief and settled back against the wagon seat. Though he would have enjoyed having a companion on his journey to Ellis, he hadn't forced the issue. Ezekiel had said they needed the men to remain in case of trouble with Indians or claim robbers.

Thomas slapped the reins and clucked at the horses. "Come on, now, you can move a little faster," he urged, anxious to arrive in Ellis before nightfall.

Even if he pushed the team, the stores would likely be closed when he got to town, but he'd make his purchases first thing in the morning. Surely he could be back in Nicodemus with only one final night on the trail. Shoving one hand into his pants pocket, he wrapped his fingers around the leather pouch that contained the settlers' money. Right now, Thomas wanted nothing more than to be relieved of the cash that filled his pocket. Instead of his worries ending when he'd entered Kansas, they'd been increased. Once this task was completed, he would not accept another undertaking for the settlers—at least not one that could bear devastating consequences. The entire settlement was relying on him, hoping he could bargain with the storekeepers for unrealistic prices and return with their wagon loaded with goods. What if he couldn't fulfill their expectations?

He passed only one rider along the way, and that man had merely waved his hat overhead as he continued onward. After hours of journeying through brush and empty prairie, the sun descended beneath the western horizon in a blaze of glowing magenta and orange, but Thomas continued onward. When he finally located the livery in Ellis, it was well past dark.

Pleased he had reached his destination without incident, Thomas pulled on the reins and brought the horses to a halt. With any luck, there would be someone sleeping inside who could assist him with his horses and rig. He banged on the heavy wooden door several times, but when his knocking failed to rouse anyone, he yanked the rope attached to an iron bell hanging over the door. The noisy clapper gonged several times. Thomas glanced about and hoped the noise wouldn't awaken the whole town. When he finally heard the door latch being raised, he sighed in relief. A young towheaded fellow rubbed his eyes as the door creaked open.

"I's sorry to break up your sleep, but I'm needin' to board my horses. I been travelin' since early yesterday mornin' and—"

The young man waved him forward. "No need to apologize. Caring for horses is what I get paid for, no matter the time of day or night. If you'd like to leave the wagon alongside the barn, we can unhitch your team over there." He pointed at the far side of the building.

Thomas nodded. "That'd be fine."

"Will Southard's my name," the young man said as he adeptly unhitched the team from the wagon and led them to the livery doors.

"Thomas Grayson."

"Grain or hay?"

Thomas hesitated for a moment. The money in his pocket was needed for supplies, yet if they didn't have horses, they couldn't possibly survive. He watched Will run his hand down one of the horses' flanks.

"Looks like they could use some grain," the young man offered. "Where'd you come from?"

"Thirty miles north. A new townsite named Nicodemus."

"That the town William Hill started up for colored folks?"

"That's the one."

"Odd name, Nicodemus. You choose that name from the Bible?"

Thomas chuckled. "No. Nicodemus was an African prince brought to dis country in chains back in the days when slave ships was makin' their voyages back and forth across the ocean. Nicodemus is s'posed to be the first slave to ever buy his freedom; it's him the town's named fer."

A look of admiration crossed Will's face. "He must have been quite a man."

"I don' know for certain if the story's a true account, but dere's plenty of folks who say it is."

Will raked his fingers through his rumpled blond hair. "So what brings you to Ellis?"

Thomas picked up a cloth and began to wipe down one of the animals. "We need supplies—of just about ever' kind you can imagine."

The young man nodded as he filled a bucket with oats. "Well, the shopkeepers will be mighty happy to hear the news. They're always pleased to make a sale—especially a large one. How many folks you got settled up there?"

He snorted. "There's about thirty of us, but ain't nobody settled. I joined up with the group in Topeka, but most of the folks that's up there came from Kentucky. Mr. Hill told 'em the town would be ready and waitin' for 'em, but when we arrived, there wasn't one thing ready for us. Not a house or a school or even a place to buy supplies."

"How long you been there?"

"Not exactly certain. Nigh on to a month not countin' our travel time from Topeka," Thomas replied. "Hill promised he'd be back and the town would be ready by September. I reckon September's gonna be here long afore Hill ever returns. He said he'd come back with supplies, but he still ain't returned. And now we done used up all our food."

Will's jaw went slack as he looked at Thomas with incredulity. "No disrespect, but folks moving west generally come loaded with tools and supplies, even a couple cows and maybe some pigs and chickens. Didn't Hill warn ya to bring more provisions?"

Thomas shook his head. "Most of dese folks wouldn'ta had much to bring anyway."

Will nodded. "You're welcome to bed down in here for the night if you don't mind sleeping in a barn."

"That's the best offer I've had since leavin' Topeka. Believe I'll take you up on it." Thomas thanked the man for his generosity.

Will's freckled face shone in the flickering lantern light. "Find yourself a spot before I blow out the lantern. Gets mighty dark in here."

Finding a corner that was well padded with hay, Thomas threw his blanket on top and instantly dropped off into a sound sleep. Sunlight was flooding the livery when he awakened the next morning, and Will was up and moving among the stalls.

"General store should be opening in another hour. The restaurant down the street is open and serving breakfast. I'm going down to get some bacon and eggs. Care to join me?"

Thomas placed his hand over the lump of coins in his pocket. He was tempted. The taste of bacon and eggs would be mighty fine right now. He hadn't eaten anything but cold cornpone since leaving Nicodemus. Surely they realized he'd have to purchase some food for himself, he reasoned. Of course, they wouldn't expect him to eat anything so costly as bacon and eggs while they were making due on hoecakes and mush.

"Naw, I'll get me somethin' later," he finally replied.

"Anybody comes by, tell 'em I'm down at Millie's having breakfast, would ya?"

"I'll do that." Thomas walked out the door into the bright morning sunlight. A warm squall of wind stirred the dusty street, and he wondered how long it had been since rain had last fallen in western Kansas. They hadn't encountered even a drop since leaving Topeka, though Will hadn't complained of drought, and they hadn't seen any dry creeks along the way.

Poking a piece of straw between his teeth, Thomas stood just outside the livery until he saw a short bald man and a middle-aged woman pause in front of the general store. The man withdrew a key from his pocket and unlocked the door. Apparently the general store was now open for business. With any luck, Will would soon return so Thomas could go make his purchases. No doubt the residents of Nicodemus would be concerned about his whereabouts if he was gone for much more than two nights.

Thomas was pacing in front of the doorway when Will eventually returned. "Sorry I was gone so long. Started talking and forgot the time," he said. "I brought you some of Millie's buttered biscuits for your trouble."

The smell of the warm biscuits seeped from the napkin-wrapped bundle, and all thoughts of the general store escaped Thomas's mind. He cradled the warm bread in his hands, enjoying the buttery aroma for a moment longer. When he could wait no more, he opened the napkin, lifted a biscuit to his mouth, and greedily sank his teeth into the flaky creation. With forced restraint, he chewed slowly and savored each delectable morsel.

"Believe I'll save this other one for later. Appreciate your kindness," he said while retrieving a tiny piece of biscuit from his shirtfront and popping it into his mouth. He gave his fingers a final lick and then grinned at Will. "I best get over to the general store and see how many supplies I'm gonna be able to afford."

"Tell Mr. Hepple you've got your wagon over here and you'll drive over to load the supplies. That way he can just set them out in front of the store," Will instructed.

He nodded and set off for the mercantile. A small bell jingled as he pushed open the front door. Thomas glanced up at the small metal contraption that had announced his arrival. The woman he'd seen earlier appeared out of nowhere to greet him.

"May I help you?" she politely asked.

"I'm needin' to purchase supplies for about thirty people, but I ain't got too much money. I've got a list here." He noted the sparsely supplied shelves as he pulled the neatly folded paper from his pocket.

The woman quickly scanned the list. "How much money do you have?"

He reached into his pocket and removed the pouch.

The woman carefully counted his funds. "I think we're going to need Mr. Hepple's assistance. You've some difficult decisions to make."

For the next half hour Thomas answered Mr. Hepple's innumerable questions regarding Nicodemus and the plight of the small band of settlers camped thirty miles to the north.

George Hepple studied the list and recounted the coins—several times. And then he rubbed his bald head. "You don't have near enough money for all the items on this list. You need to decide which ones are most important. But before you decide, I want to tell you that Mr. Hill isn't going to be returning to Nicodemus—at least not any time soon."

Thomas gaped at the man. "How do ya know that?"

"Because he was in my store about a month ago. He was traveling with the Peterson brothers. He told me he was having them return the wagons to Topeka, and he was heading back east by train—to Kentucky, I think. Said he was going to locate some more settlers for Nicodemus and that he'd be sending them out here on the train. You could ask Will or Chester. I reckon Mr. Hill would have talked to one of them about furnishing wagons to the new settlers when they arrive in Ellis."

"He might be back soon, then. It don' take all that long to get back and forth on the train, do it?" Thomas asked in a hopeful voice.

Mr. Hepple shook his head back and forth. "He talked like he was planning to stay in Kentucky or Tennessee for a while and just send folks out on the train. I could be wrong, but . . ."

"But you're likely right," Thomas said. "Sure don't sound like he's sendin' supplies or anyone to help build the town."

The storeowner appeared as deflated as Thomas felt. "I'm sorry to be the one giving you the bad news, but at least you know you can't depend on him. The truth is, you folks need to get yourselves prepared for winter."

"I think I'm gonna need some help decidin' what's most important. Like I told your missus, we ain't got a whole lot of money."

"I can't help you much at the moment. As you can see, my shelves are about empty. But the train will be coming through with our supplies the day after tomorrow, and then I can fill your order."

"Not 'til Thursday? I can't wait 'til then. The folks up in Nicodemus are expectin' me to load up and be on my way today."

Mr. Hepple placed the list atop the shiny walnut countertop and pushed it across. "You have no choice. I'm the only store in town that carries most of these items. Better to wait than to go home and return again next week. Once the supplies are unloaded, we can figure out exactly what you want to purchase."

"I reckon you's right. Thanks for your help. I'll be back on Thursday." Thomas hung his head as he walked through the doorway. The tiny metal bell gave a farewell jingle as he closed the door behind him.

Although he hadn't wanted to make this journey, he thought it would be simple enough: drive the wagon to Ellis, load up with as many supplies as possible, and return to Nicodemus. But it was not working out that way. As usual, things had taken a turn for the worse. Seemed as though that was the way of things in his life. Nothing ever worked out the way it was supposed to.

Spying a small stone, he took aim with the toe of his shoe and kicked the rock with a deliberate force that sent it sailing into the air. He watched as the nugget came to a bouncing halt in front of the livery.

His hat was pulled low and his shoulders slouched when he entered the barn a few minutes later. He ambled toward his horses, wondering why things couldn't just go as planned once in a while.

"Hey, Thomas," Will called. "This here is Chester Goddard. He owns this place."

Thomas nodded at the burly, be-whiskered man who was rubbing lotion on the galled skin of a roan mare. "Pleased to meet ya."

"Will tells me you're in Ellis to purchase supplies—says you've settled in Nicodemus," Chester commented as he continued his ministrations.

"Yep, but it don' appear I'm gonna get those supplies 'til the train comes in on Thursday."

"That a fact? Hepple can't seem to get his ordering to match up with what folks need. Seems as though he's always low on the supplies folks are wanting to buy," Chester remarked. "If you want to earn a little money while you're in town, there's a fellow who needs help with his dugout not far from here. I think he'll pay you a fair wage. Besides, you can learn how much work it is to dig one of those things," he added with a broad grin.

Will ceased mucking one of the stalls and leaned on his pitchfork. "Might be some folks needing an extra hand in the fields, too, maybe doing some haying."

"Yeah, I'm sure there's plenty of folks around here that'd be glad to have you swing a cradle for them, but a man gets weary of that work in a hurry. If I was you, I'd check on the dugout. Never hurts to see firsthand how things are done, especially out here on the prairie."

Thomas contemplated his prospects. If Chester was right about Mr. Hill not coming back, they'd sure need to figure out some kind of shelter before winter set in. Though he'd been inside a couple of dugouts on their trip west from Topeka, Thomas had no idea how to craft a dwelling in the side of a hill. There were surely some instructions that would aid in making the dwelling secure from the elements—and he wouldn't mind a hint or two on the easiest method of digging out space enough to accommodate a family. Given the fact that they would need more than simple lean-tos if they were to suitably shelter thirty people throughout the winter, Thomas heeded Chester's advice and drove the team to a piece of land three miles northeast of Ellis. Not far from a narrow creek, he spotted a man swinging his pick into a hillside.

"Ho there!" Thomas called out as he neared the diggings.

The man turned at the sound and waved vigorously. "Welcome! Are you looking for work?"

"Mr. Goddard at the livery tol' me you

were lookin' to hire on someone to help with your house. But I can work only today and tomorrow."

"Two days is better than none. Jump on down and I'll put you to digging if you'll accept a dollar a day and board."

"And some grain fer the horses?" Thomas asked, hoping the man wouldn't think him greedy.

"So long as I can use them and the wagon to haul off some of this dirt."

Thomas grinned and nodded as he shook hands with the man. "Thomas Grayson," he said as the man pumped his arm up and down.

"Jeremiah Horton," the man replied. "You can grab that shovel over there." He pointed to a pile of tools and farm implements.

Thomas scanned the items before picking up the heavy shovel. If a man could judge by the number of tools, it appeared Mr. Horton was well prepared to begin home-steading—and obviously lonely, for he either lectured or questioned Thomas the entire day. By the time evening arrived, Thomas was pleased to lead the horses the short distance to the creek bordering Mr. Horton's property.

"Bring some water back for coffee," the man hollered.

Thomas held the bucket high and continued onward, anxious for a few minutes of solitude. While the horses drank their fill, he walked a short distance upstream and dipped the pail into the clear, cool water, filling it to the brim. With nothing but the sound of the trickling stream and the occasional warble of a meadowlark, Thomas relaxed and wished he could remain in this quiet place.

Instead, he picked up the bucket and doggedly returned to the camp, where Mr. Horton served another meal of leftover beans and ham. But Thomas cared little. He was hungry. Even more, he was tired. After a day of cutting through the tough buffalo grass and tunneling into the hard, dry hillside, every muscle in his body quivered and ached. He had already closed his eyes when he heard the fire sizzle. His host had likely spit a stream of tobacco juice into the dying embers.

"Hard work, ain't it?" Mr. Horton's booming voice jarred Thomas from his reverie.

"Yeah," Thomas said before turning his

back toward Horton and tugging his hat down over his face.

The man took the hint and said no more, but before the sun had risen the next morning, he was up and moving. Bacon was sizzling in an iron skillet and the aroma of boiling coffee filled the air, yet Thomas didn't move until Mr. Horton nudged him with the toe of his boot. The man was obviously intent upon getting a full day's work out of Thomas before he departed.

"Got your breakfast ready," Horton said. "Thought I'd make use of your team and we could both cut up sod since I got two breaking plows. My old plow ain't as good, but they'll both work."

Thomas sat up and took the tin plate of food Mr. Horton offered. "No biscuits?" Thomas asked with a wry smile.

Mr. Horton gave a hearty chuckle. "Ain't figured out how to make biscuits, but if you promise to come back and work again, I'll learn how. Or maybe by then I'll have my missus out here."

After they washed up the dishes, Thomas listened carefully to Mr. Horton's instructions. Although he'd never used a breaking plow before, by early afternoon he and the horses had mastered the task well enough to turn the sod in a reasonably acceptable fashion. The work would make Horton's planting much easier come next spring.

While Thomas worked on the field where Jeremiah Horton would plant his corn, the older man used his own team of horses and the better of the two plows to break sod for the bricks that he would use to extend the front opening and to form part of the roof for his dugout. With a wood frame and the sod bricks, he could erect an entry that would permit more light into the shelter, which, he told Thomas, was an important detail to remember when you're considering women- folk. They want as much natural light as possible, he'd explained, though he didn't say why.

"Let that go for now and come help me," Mr. Horton called to Thomas around mid-afternoon. "I want to get this cut into bricks. Grab an axe," he instructed.

For the remainder of the day, the men worked to form the sod bricks, with Thomas carefully heeding the man's instruction. What he learned from Mr. Horton could mean the difference between life and death when he returned to Nicodemus. "If you didn' have this plow, how would you go 'bout cuttin' the bricks?" he asked as the two worked alongside each other.

"Chop 'em out with an axe. Hard work, though, and a man wouldn't get much accomplished with only an axe to cut through the buffalo grass."

"Reckon you're right 'bout that. I was wonderin' if maybe you could see your way clear to let me borrow that old plow."

"You mean take it thirty miles north? How would you be paying me, and when would I get it back?" he asked, his eyes alight with the prospect of a deal.

Thomas pushed his hat back on his head. "I'll take only one day's wages for my work, and I can send the plow back down with Mr. Goddard's wagons. Mr. Hepple over at the general store said dere's another group of settlers comin' from Kentucky real soon, and Mr. Goddard is bringing 'em up north with his wagons. He could bring the plow back with him when he returns to Ellis. And I'd work another two days for you come spring."

Jeremiah stared off toward the north as if to envision the possibility. "Them settlers might never show up, and that means my plow would be sitting in Nicodemus until spring. Next thing you know, you'd decide to keep it until after spring planting. Who knows? I might never get it back."

"You can use only one plow at a time— you're only *one* person with *one* team of horses. But I s'pose you gotta do as you see fit. It's your plow to keep or loan out."

"You say you'll give me two full days of work come spring?" Jeremiah asked as he swung his axe into a broad chunk of sod.

Thomas grinned. Once Jeremiah Horton realized that Thomas would bargain no further, the older man was willing to give in. "I did."

"And I gotta pay you only a dollar for your work the past two days?"

"As well as grain for the horses."

Jeremiah extended his hand. "You've got a deal. When you leave, I'll ride with you to the Rooks' farm so you're sure to find his place. He'll sell you butter, potatoes, eggs, and molasses cheaper than you can get it in town—maybe flour and cornmeal, too. Beans, sugar, and rice you'll have to get from Hepple at the general store."

Thomas hesitated, thinking of the small

pouch of coins. "How much fer potatoes and molasses?"

"Last time I was over to his place I paid two dollars and fifty cents for ten bushels of potatoes and forty cents for a gallon of molasses. Eggs was sixteen cents for two dozen, but you'll have to ask him about bacon and ham. Seems he's always changing the price on them items."

"I'll get some of the molasses, but I think I'll settle on rice, beans, and cornmeal instead of the potatoes. I need to use some of the money for a few tools."

"Suit yourself, but be sure you buy some shoe nails from Hepple. This prairie grass is hard on sole leather, and it's cheaper to fix your shoes than buy new ones—and they'll keep the snow and water out a lot better if you keep 'em greased with skunk fat."

Thomas thanked him for the advice. How would he ever decide the best way to spend the little money in his pocket? What purchases would be most necessary to meet the needs of thirty strangers out in a desolate land?

Once again they worked until after sunset, but the next morning, Horton was good to his word. He loaded the plow into

Thomas's wagon and paid him a dollar and fifty cents.

As Jeremiah hoisted an extra sack of grain into the wagon, Thomas gave him a puzzled look. "I know you don't have much money," the settler said, "and you likely don't want to spend any of what you've got on grain, but those horses are going to need feed to keep 'em going through the winter."

"But you paid me an extra fifty cents."

"You more than earned it—you're a hard worker. A man ought to be paid a fair wage for his work," he replied as he placed his foot in a stirrup and mounted his horse.

Jeremiah rode alongside the wagon until they arrived at the Rooks' farm, where Thomas carefully chose several items.

"I'll be heading back home now. And I'm expecting to get that breaking plow back as promised," Jeremiah said as the men parted company a short time later.

"No need to worry. And thank you for teaching me—I appreciate your patience."

Horton guffawed. "I think it was you that had the patience. The wife says I talk too much, and I figure you got tired of hearing me ramble on, but I hope some of it will help you. Have a safe journey." He turned the horse and rode back toward his homestead.

By the time Thomas reached Ellis, the train had arrived, the supplies were unloaded, and Mr. and Mrs. Hepple were filling their shelves with the much-anticipated merchandise. Thomas weighed the suggestions he'd received from both Mr. Hepple and Mr. Horton and walked out of the store hoping that he'd made the proper decisions. He longed to be on his way home. However, there was one final stop he must make. He needed to tell Chester Goddard of the agreement he'd made with Jeremiah Horton.

"I'll be glad to help you out. You must have made a good impression on Jeremiah. I've never known him to be generous with his tools—or anything else, for that matter," Mr. Goddard remarked after Thomas had explained their arrangement.

"He treated me more than fair and taught me a lot. I's grateful for the work and 'preciate ya sendin' me out to his place," Thomas said. "I best be on my way. Hope to see you with those new settlers real soon. And tell 'em to bring lots of supplies," he added as he walked out of the livery.

"I'll do that," Mr. Goddard yelled after him.

It was close to noon before he pulled out of town. Though he had hoped to make it home as soon as possible, Thomas knew he'd be forced to stay out at least one night. Pushing the horses any harder in the hot August sun would be cruel.

As he rolled up his blanket before sunup the next morning and then hitched the team, he wondered how he would be received when he finally arrived in Nicodemus.

Late in the second day he saw the white canvas roofs flapping in the breeze and smoke rising from campfires in their small settlement. "There it be, boys. Nicodemus!" Thomas said to the horses. He slapped the reins and urged the team to step up their pace.

He could now see what appeared to be the entire group of settlers gathering near the largest of the fires. An unexpected sense of exhilaration overcame him as he rode the wagon into the townsite and brought the horses to a halt near the assembled residents. He had expected shouts of exhilaration but instead was greeted with an eerie silence. He scanned the group, surprised by the angry faces.

"Where you been?" Herman Kemble hollered. "You shoulda been back days ago. I tol' Ezekiel if you took off with our money, I was gonna track you down and see to it you was hung."

Thomas flinched at the words. He had expected the folks to be concerned, but the thought that the settlers had actually discussed hanging him was more than a little disturbing.

"I tol' Ezekiel I didn' wanna be the one to go. Wasn't my idea—none of it. You'll find what supplies your money would buy in the back of the wagon." He gathered his bedroll and a box of supplies he'd purchased with the money Jeremiah Horton had paid him. "You can unload and fight amongst yourselves about who gets what. I'm through with all of it 'cept for that breaking plow. Don' nobody touch that, 'cause it's here only on a loan to me. I'll unload it myself."

"What's that you're carryin' off?" Herman Kemble called out.

"These here is supplies I bought with money I earned workin' in Ellis. I had to wait 'til the train arrived with supplies for the general store. Ain't none of you got cause to think I'm shortchangin' you. There's a list I had the storekeeper write out that shows what I bought and the cost. You'll find every penny you gave me's accounted for." He angrily strode away from the group.

CHAPTER

8

Georgetown, Kentucky • September 1877

Samuel Boyle lifted a medical book from one of the glass-fronted bookcases in his office and began flipping through the pages. Surely he could find something between the covers of one of these tomes to help him diagnose Mr. Stavely's illness.

"No patients to see?"

Samuel looked up from his reading. "Carlisle!" He dropped the book onto his desktop and jumped to his feet. "What an unexpected surprise! When did you arrive?" He pulled his son into a warm embrace.

"Only minutes ago. I thought you'd be

here at your office, so I decided to stop before going to the house."

Samuel held his eldest child at arm's length and surveyed his lanky frame. "You appear to have lost some weight. And I believe you're at least an inch taller."

Carlisle laughed at his father's assessment. "You're correct that I've grown taller, but I've not lost any weight. They feed us well enough—not nearly as good as the meals Cook serves, but filling enough."

Samuel fondly patted his son's shoulder. "Sit down, sit down," he said, pointing to a chair. "So tell me what brings you home from seminary without so much as a letter telling us to expect you? Some problem with your studies?"

"No. Quite the contrary. My grades are excellent, and I'll soon complete my courses. This matter is a bit more serious, and I thought it best to sit down and talk with you and Mother rather than merely send a letter."

Samuel grasped the leather arms of his chair for leverage as he rose to his feet. "Then we best be on our way home, for if we remain here, I'll badger you until you've divulged your news. Besides, I'm weary of poring over these medical books."

Samuel walked alongside Carlisle, tucking his reading glasses into his jacket pocket. Once they were seated in the buggy, Samuel handed the reins to Carlisle. It was good to have his son sitting beside him. Yet, try as he did, Samuel could not imagine the cause for Carlisle's return. Surely he wasn't planning to embark upon some madcap plan for his future. Carlisle had always been the sensible child, the one most like himself—at least that's what Samuel had always thought.

Of course, how could he condemn his son for choosing a diverse path when he, a staunch opponent of slavery, had married a southern woman and settled in a state that had embraced slavery as a civilized way of life? He shook his head at the thought of the foolishness of his youthful decision. But he had been deeply in love with Margaret—still was for that matter—and he'd told himself he could make a difference if he lived in the South. Of course that hadn't proved out. Oh, he'd been able to covertly lend medical care to a number of slaves, but not enough to make any great difference. In the process, he'd managed to anger and alienate most of the prestigious southern gentry while causing his wife a good deal of embarrassment. And now he was making plans to move the family to Kansas. Likely nothing Carlisle had to tell them would compare to that piece of news. Otherwise, Margaret would dissolve into a fit of apoplexy and take to her bed.

Samuel gave his son an encouraging nudge on the shoulder as they stepped out of the carriage and walked up the front steps of the house. Though the cause of his son's return remained a mystery, Samuel knew Carlisle would need his support.

"Margaret! Come see who sauntered into my office only minutes ago," Samuel called.

The two men grinned at each other when they heard Margaret's footsteps click across the wooden floor in the hallway.

"No need to shout as if—" She stopped in midstep and clutched one hand to the bodice of her dress. "Carlisle! Do my eyes deceive me?"

He leaned down into her open arms. "Not at all, Mother."

When Margaret finally loosened her embrace and moved back a step, Samuel could see her eyes were brimming with tears.

"Look how much taller you are—but it appears you've lost weight." Her voice was filled with motherly concern.

"Exactly what I told him only a few minutes ago. He says he's hungry as a bear, so I trust we'll soon be eating supper. A hearty meal will provide you with the opportunity to put some additional weight on his frame." Samuel turned to raise a sly eyebrow at Carlisle.

"Fortunately for you, I had planned an early supper for this evening. Macia has plans to attend a concert at the lyceum, though I hope she'll change her plans when she sees you've arrived home for a visit. And Harvey cares little what time we dine." Margaret emitted an exasperated sigh.

Carlisle's cheerful laugh brought a smile to Margaret's lips. "You fret overly much, Mother. Harvey is young—he'll mature in good time."

The flounce of Margaret's skirt swayed gracefully as she paced back and forth in front of the fireplace. "I fear your father doesn't think Harvey will ever become a man." She turned and directed an accusatory gaze at her husband.

Samuel unbuttoned his jacket and sat down on the divan. "Carlisle is merely being kind. We *all* know Harvey is going to require an additional push if he's ever going to grow up and become a responsible adult. The difference is that I'm willing to both state the truth and seek a solution. And please do sit down, my dear. All that pacing is making me weary."

Carlisle looked from one parent to the other. "It appears some things haven't changed around here—at least where Harvey is concerned."

"Enough about Harvey!" Margaret declared. "I want to know why I didn't have a letter advising me you were coming home for a visit. Something is amiss, isn't it?"

"You and Father always assume the worst. I have a short break before my classes resume and thought it a good time to make the journey home. I'm not ill, and I've not been booted out of school. I thought you'd be pleased to see me."

"Of course I'm pleased. I'm more delighted than words permit. But it's just so . . . so . . ."

"Unexpected?" Samuel completed his wife's statement.

"Well, yes—and unlike you. You've never been one to throw caution to the wind," she added. "At least not until you decided to attend school in Maine!"

"I suppose I have been the least impulsive of your children. But I don't believe I'd characterize my decision to attend school in Bangor as throwing caution to the wind." Carlisle's tone had grown defensive, and Margaret settled back into her chair.

" 'Tis true you've never been so foolhardy as Harvey," she stated.

"Did I hear my name?"

Margaret shuddered at the crash of the front door as it closed. "How many times must I ask you—"

"Not to slam the door?" Harvey asked with a boisterous laugh. "I truly don't know, Mother. I believe I lost count after a thousand. And look who's here! Nobody bothered to tell me you were coming for a visit, Carlisle. It's good to see you."

There was an edge to Harvey's voice that Samuel didn't fail to notice. "Carlisle's visit was totally unexpected. *None* of us knew he was arriving."

Harvey dropped onto the divan beside his father. "So what brings you home, dear brother?"

"The remembrance of an excellent meal and the desire to spend time with my family."

Harvey gave his brother a sly grin. "You've never returned home unannounced before."

The statement hung in the air, begging a response. When Carlisle said nothing, Samuel glanced at his wife. "Where's Macia?"

Harvey leaned forward and rested his forearms across his thighs. "You can be certain she's not in the kitchen learning how to prepare supper, though it seems she should begin spending some time with Cook if she's going to adapt to life on the frontier. Don't you think?"

Carlisle raised his eyebrows and gave Harvey his full attention. "Life on the frontier? Whatever are you talking about, Harvey?"

"You mean Father hasn't told you of his latest idea?"

Margaret wagged her right index finger back and forth. "Your father's decision isn't firm yet, is it, dear?"

"Barring unforeseen circumstances, I would say I've made a final determination. I've signed papers to purchase the land, and I'm meeting with Mr. Hill tomorrow," Samuel replied before glancing at his older son.

Carlisle looked concerned. "I wish you had told me."

Samuel understood. Obviously Carlisle feared his mysterious news was going to cause his mother some sort of distress. Having her upset before he delivered his news would make the announcement all the more difficult. Samuel shrugged and gave the boy a sympathetic look. There was little else he could do except hope that Margaret would maintain a sense of decorum when Carlisle finally took them into his confidence.

"Ah, here's Macia now," Samuel said. "Macia, come and see who's here."

Macia hurried into the parlor, holding the train of her candy-striped frock in one hand while patting her perfectly coifed blond curls into place with the other. There was no denying Macia's beauty. In fact, she looked as though she'd stepped directly from the pages of *The Ladies' Treasury.* Her gaze settled upon Carlisle, and a smile immediately illuminated her features.

"Why didn't anyone tell me Carlisle was coming home?" Her simpering voice sounded like a spoiled child's rather than a young woman anticipating marriage.

Margaret patted her daughter's arm. "None of us knew, my dear."

"I smell something wonderful cooking," Samuel said before Macia could ask any further questions. He hoped to complete the evening meal before Carlisle divulged his news. Otherwise, they might never reach the dining table, and his stomach was growling for food. "Margaret, would you see if Cook is ready to put supper on the table?"

Moments later, at his wife's signal, Samuel jumped to his feet and began motioning his family toward the dining room. He herded his family through the doorway and began saying grace before Harvey had even seated himself. The moment the prayer ended, Samuel grasped the platter of roasted beef and browned potatoes, helping himself to a healthy portion of each.

Harvey reached for a biscuit. "Let me tell you about Father's plans for the rest of us,

Carlisle. I'm certain you'll find them most interesting."

Samuel frowned at Harvey and quickly shook his head. "No need to go into detail while we're eating. You've already said enough."

"Right! Wouldn't want to upset our digestion. No need to worry, Father. Your decision isn't going to upset Carlisle, and the rest of us have already expressed our distress over the whole thing," Harvey said before addressing Carlisle. "You see, dear brother, our father believes I should embrace farming as my life's calling. Do you not find his notion bewildering?"

Carlisle shifted in his chair and glanced around the table. "I'm not certain it matters what I think, but I will say this much: you should keep an open mind. Great opportunities can present themselves in places where we least expect to find them."

"I'm not interested in hearing such banality, Carlisle. I had hoped you would be man enough to inject a modicum of sanity into this discussion. But I should have realized you'd take the path of least resistance and say whatever Father wants to hear." Harvey thrust the serving fork onto the platter of beef with a force that cracked the serving plate and sent small shards of china flying into the air.

"Harvey! What's gotten into you? Your behavior is insufferable! You will clean up the mess that you've created and then return to the table." Samuel struggled to keep his temper in check.

Macia glanced down at her brother, who was crawling on the floor hunting for the remains of the broken platter, and then turned her attention toward Carlisle. "Do tell me how things are progressing with your studies, Carlisle. Are you still enjoying Maine? I would think you'd dislike being so far from home—and all those months of cold weather must be horrid," she ventured.

"I don't mind the climate, and I do believe you'd love the huge snowfalls. To tell you the truth, it's great fun bundling up in blankets and going on sleigh rides. Of course, I still miss the family," he hastened to add.

"You are returning to Georgetown when you complete seminary, aren't you? I wouldn't think you'd want to remain up north. Do tell me you'll be coming back home," Macia persisted.

Carlisle gave his father a sidelong glance. "I plan to settle where I'm most needed."

Harvey got up from the floor and carefully placed the broken pieces of china on the sideboard before once again taking a seat beside his brother. "That remark tells me you're returning to Georgetown, because we all know this place needs all the help it can get."

"Harvey! You stop those boorish remarks right now," his mother commanded.

"I'm only speaking the truth, Mother. Don't you think Georgetown could use help from one of God's anointed?"

"Well, I think you should come back to Georgetown," Margaret said to Carlisle. "Perhaps then your father would rethink his decision to move west."

Samuel spread a dollop of rhubarb jam on his biscuit. "I believe I've already said that the decision has been made, my dear."

"Not so far as *I'm* concerned," Harvey rebutted. "I'll not be a part of moving out to the frontier, nor will I take up farming as my occupation."

Samuel wiped his mouth with the linen napkin before placing it on the table alongside his plate. "Then you may want to think about how you'll support yourself here in Georgetown once the family is gone, Harvey, for I'll not be supplying you with any funds. You'll need to find some way to earn a living, since you've obviously become accustomed to living indoors and eating three meals each day."

Without awaiting a reply from Harvey, Samuel shifted his weight and sat up a little straighter. "Now, Carlisle, do tell us about your studies."

Samuel's intent had been clear, for Carlisle didn't hesitate to monopolize the conversation from that point forward. He regaled them with details about the theological material he'd been studying, and then he told them of the weather, his new instructors, and the friends he'd made at the nearby church, as well as his classmates' many comical antics. Surprisingly, they finished the meal on a harmonious note, and for that Samuel was thankful.

Margaret appeared relaxed as she placed her napkin on the table. "Would you prefer to have coffee in the parlor, Samuel?"

"That would be most enjoyable."

Macia grasped Carlisle's arm. "I hope you'll excuse me. Jackson will be calling for me shortly. Had I known you'd be visiting, I would have planned to remain home."

He arched his eyebrows. "Jackson Kincaid?"

She smiled and nodded before hurrying from the room.

Carlisle joined his parents as they settled in the parlor. "How long have Macia and Jackson been seeing each other, Mother?"

She pursed her lips. "Several months now, isn't it, dear?"

"Too long, as far as I'm concerned," Samuel said. "I don't like those Kincaids."

Harvey laughed as he dropped onto the settee beside his brother. "Seems as though Father doesn't like anyone who hails from the South anymore—with the exception of Mother, of course."

"I don't think that's quite true, Harvey," Carlisle said. "Besides, I concur with Father. Unless Jackson has gone through a dramatic change in his life, he's a poor choice for Macia."

Samuel crossed his legs and rested his cup and saucer on one knee. "Too much like his father. Booth Kincaid doesn't know how to treat others with respect, and neither does his son. Little doubt in my mind that

Booth married a woman of means so he'd never have to earn a living using his own abilities—he'd starve to death!"

When a knock sounded, Harvey trudged off toward the front door with no more than a grunt.

"There are times when I believe Harvey's lack of respect nearly matches that of the Kincaids," Samuel said, feeling an overwhelming sadness as he uttered the words. "I truly believe moving west will be the remedy to his reluctance to take responsibility for his future."

"Did you listen to his statement at supper, Samuel? He said he will not go. I believe he means it," Margaret whispered to her husband.

"And you heard my response. I will not continue to support his indolent habits."

Jackson Kincaid strutted into the room with his usual pomposity. Samuel stared at the young man, wondering how his daughter could possibly be interested in a man such as him. There was no substance to him. Yet, just like his father, Jackson carried himself through life with a cavalier attitude that never failed to set Samuel on edge.

"Well, look who's here!" Jackson exclaimed. "I'm surprised Macia didn't tell me you were coming home for a visit. Mother was asking about you not long ago, Carlisle. And what's this I hear about moving west to become a farmer, Dr. Boyle?"

Macia slipped into the room and immediately linked arms with Jackson. "I'm hoping we can come home early and spend some time visiting with Carlisle after leaving the lyceum," she said, giving Jackson a doe-eyed look and fluttering her eyelashes.

Samuel ignored Macia's comment and her behavior. "Personally, *I* plan to continue my medical practice. However, our family may take up farming."

"If it's farming that interests you, there's land to be purchased without leaving civilization," Jackson said.

Samuel gave him a crooked smile. "Civilization is one of those words that can be interpreted in many different ways. I don't consider holding folks in bondage by paying them minuscule wages for sharecropping to be civilized behavior. Of course, there are folks like you and your father who find the practice perfectly acceptable—even civilized."

Macia's face registered horror. "Father!"

Jackson glowered at Samuel and then grasped Macia's elbow.

"Have my daughter home by nine o'clock," Samuel called after the couple as they left the room.

Harvey sat down beside his father and smirked. "It would appear I'm not the only one in Georgetown who believes your anticipated venture into the wilderness is ill-conceived."

"The difference between us is that you care what those people think, but I mind not at all. I might add that if you're going to take sides in this matter, it would be wise if you deferred to me. After all, *I'm* the one supporting you—a matter you might want to ponder."

"I've already said that I have absolutely no desire to farm. Even more, I don't wish to make my home amongst the savages. Since there are three of us who prefer living in Georgetown and only one of us wants to leave, I'm wondering why you continue to insist upon this move."

"Because *I* want to live somewhere other than Kentucky for the remainder of my life. I have willingly remained in Georgetown until you children completed your basic education—or, in your case, Harvey, the amount of education we could force upon you. There is nothing to hold us here. I can open a medical office and treat patients anywhere."

"And what if I choose to remain here?"

"Suit yourself—but I meant what I told you earlier. I'll not send you a stipend, and you'll not live in this house. I plan to sell it."

Margaret's fan snapped open. The tiny curls that framed her face were bouncing in rhythm to the fluttering air currents being produced by her fan. "Why sell the house? I think you should reconsider that decision. What if the West doesn't prove to our liking?"

Samuel shook his head. "We'll work more diligently and try harder to adapt to our new surroundings if we've sold the house. With all ties severed to Georgetown, we'll not be easily tempted to give up."

Margaret placed her coffee cup on the walnut side table. "Should Harvey remain behind or Carlisle return to Georgetown, we would still have ties to Kentucky."

Samuel turned an apologetic gaze toward Carlisle. Their discussion had gone completely awry, and Samuel had been as much to blame as the rest. Rather than helping to maintain calm and order, he had fanned the fires of discontent. And for that he was sorry.

Carlisle tugged at his shirt collar. "You had best not rely on me, Mother. In fact, I know I will not be returning to Georgetown. That's one of the reasons I came home—to tell you I have made a decision about my future."

She began to wring her handkerchief. "Is this news going to make me unhappy?"

Samuel noted the quiver in his wife's voice and immediately came to Carlisle's aid. "Now, now, my dear, no need upsetting yourself. Carlisle is a sensible young man. Remember, you have always told the children to pray fervently when they must make a choice and then follow where God leads. Isn't that so?"

Margaret eyed him suspiciously and gave a token nod. "Yes. Although the last time Carlisle prayed about his future, he left for Maine."

"I've decided to become an Army chaplain," Carlisle announced.

Margaret stared at her son as though he'd

spoken in a foreign tongue. Harvey looked surprised, as well.

"That means he'll join the military and be a preacher for the soldiers," Samuel explained.

Samuel's words seemed to shatter Margaret's trance, and she frowned at her husband. "I *understand* the duties of an Army chaplain, Samuel." Before he could reply, his wife directed her full attention toward their older son. "I am completely perplexed, Carlisle. Why would you even consider such a profession? When you left home, you said you wanted to become a preacher. You insisted you could better serve God if you attended theological school and received proper training. Aside from voicing my displeasure, I made no attempt to dissuade you. And now look what has happened. Those Northerners have filled your head with outlandish ideas of becoming a soldier. *Soldiers die, Carlisle.*"

She whispered the final words as though confiding a secret to which only she was privy.

Carlisle patted his mother's hand. "Rest assured I shall finish my schooling before entering the Army, Mother."

"I think it sounds quite exciting," Samuel said, "and patriotic."

"Oh, do stop, Samuel! How did you ever decide upon this foolhardy scheme, Carlisle?"

"Several officers from West Point came to the seminary and told of the need for chaplains—especially on the western frontier. I didn't make this decision lightly. I've prayed about it for months now, and I continue to believe this is what I'm supposed to do."

Samuel nodded. "You'll get no argument from me, son. I realize there's danger involved in the military, but I admire your willingness to follow God's leading."

Margaret glared at her husband before dabbing the tears from her eyes. "So you agree to go traipsing off to be mortally wounded? It was only last summer when General Custer and all of his soldiers died at the hands of those ruthless Indians. Is the fact that you're going to finish your education supposed to ease my mind?"

"I believe you're overstating the danger, my dear. After all, much will depend upon Carlisle's assignment," Samuel offered.

His wife's tears stopped, and her eyes filled with anger. "Quit taking his side in this,

Samuel! Where is your concern for your son's well-being? Have all the men in this household taken leave of their senses?"

Harvey moved to his mother's side and squeezed her hand. "I certainly haven't. I couldn't agree with you more, Mother."

"Oh, pshaw! You're not concerned about Carlisle's welfare. You're merely taking my side because you're afraid you may have to change your ways."

Harvey drew his arm away as though she'd slapped it. "Nothing I say is correct. If I agree, I'm incorrect, and if I disagree, I'm incorrect," he whined.

"You'll evoke no sympathy from me," Samuel stated.

With that, Harvey marched from the room with his shoulders rigid and head held high. "I'm going to visit my friends," he mumbled.

"I fear I've caused you much more distress than I imagined," Carlisle ventured after the front door slammed.

Margaret tucked her handkerchief into her pocket. "I'm concerned, Carlisle. I won't deny that. But you're no longer a child. I've stated my opinion. The ultimate decision is yours."

"Thank you, Mother."

She shrugged her shoulders with an air of resignation. "It appears as if we will all begin life anew—you in the Army and the rest of us out west. Let us hope that at least you and your father will be happy and fulfilled."

"There's one good thing to be said for your move west," Carlisle said. "It will get Macia away from Jackson Kincaid."

Samuel covertly watched his wife. He wanted to believe she would eventually come around about his plans for a new life in the west. As her features began to soften, he felt a tiny glimmer of hope.

CHAPTER

9

Nicodemus, Kansas • September 1877

A cool, gentle wind breathed across the prairie during the month of September and imbued the struggling settlers with new-found energy. There was little doubt winter's hardships would soon besiege them, so they staunchly set aside their fears and labored with a renewed zeal.

Ezekiel and Thomas continued their arduous work with the breaking plow, knowing the precious tool must soon be returned to Jeremiah Horton. Before that time arrived, they prayed the weather and the horses would cooperate, for they must cut sod bricks for each of the dugout entrances as well as bricks enough to help insulate and support the roofs. The ongoing labor of the other men and boys had resulted in completion of at least the digging portion of a dugout that would accommodate a small family, though the fireplace and entrance both remained incomplete. Once all the sod bricks were cut and the breaking plow was returned to Mr. Horton, Ezekiel and Thomas would begin erecting the front of their new homes.

The group of settlers had agreed the first dwelling should be inhabited by the Harris family—due both to Miss Hattie's age and ailments as well as the anticipated birth of Nellie and Calvin's baby. An old woman and an infant would, after all, require more protection from the elements than would the rest of them.

The days melted into one other with little to distinguish time, place, or responsibilities—unless the weather was uncooperative. Yet today had dawned cool and bright, and Jarena sighed with satisfaction—her clothes would dry, but it wouldn't be overly warm as she stood over the fire. She and the twins had filled the caldron with water the night before, and she was pleased to see the fire already burning and the water beginning to bubble. Likely her father or Thomas had started the fire well before sunup. She shaded her eyes and looked around the small camp. She could hear Miss Hattie's scolding voice in the distance.

"Wilbur Holt, you git yerself over there and git to work!"

Jarena grinned at the sight of the old woman prodding the tall fourteen-year-old with one end of her walking stick while soundly rebuking him. She'd exchanged her parasol for the walking stick, though she vowed the parasol would be called back into use come springtime. "You's plenty old enough to be helpin' cut dat sod. Lazy! That's what ya are, 'cept when it comes to eatin'."

Wilbur yelped at Miss Hattie's jab, which brought Caroline Holt on a run. "What's wrong with you, Wilbur?" his mother hollered.

"Miss Hattie's a-pokin' me with her stick," he wailed.

"Good for her! I tol' you to get over there and help yo' pappy a half hour ago. Now get to moving, or I'll tell Miss Hattie to use dat stick on your backside 'stead of jest pokin' at ya."

Shoulders slumped, Wilbur mumbled his displeasure as he shuffled toward the hillside where his father was digging.

"You can move faster'n that! Straighten up dem shoulders, and don' you be sassin' yo' mama, neither," Miss Hattie reprimanded. The diatribe continued until the boy was well out of earshot.

Jarena watched Wilbur glance over his shoulder at Miss Hattie, his features forming a scowl. She knew that the boy had best do as he'd been told. If he argued, Miss Hattie wouldn't hesitate to use her walking stick on his backside. None of the children were exempt from Miss Hattie's correction, and none of the adults questioned the old woman's authority to wield her justice. Miss Hattie had seen more of life than most, and they believed in her sound judgment.

To Jarena, she was also a mother figure. "Miss Hattie! Come sit and visit with me," she called.

The old woman waved her stick in recognition of Jarena's request but patiently waited until Wilbur reached his prescribed destination. Now certain the boy would not escape the vigilance of his father and the other men, she turned and, with a halting gait, walked toward the Harban lean-to. Jarena fetched a chair her father had fashioned from an empty nail keg and scraps of wood and placed it nearby. "I'd sure enjoy a little company while I do the washing," she requested when Miss Hattie drew near.

Hattie dropped onto the hard wooden seat and nodded toward the caldron. "Your day to use the kettle, I see."

"Yes. Seems as though my turn never comes often enough. I'm truly thankful it's not raining today," she said, remembering the storm that had come upon them the last time she'd attempted to launder clothes. "How many times has it rained since we arrived in this place? Only two! And whose turn was it to use the wash kettle both times? Mine!"

Miss Hattie leaned back and laughed heartily. "You been spendin' too much time alone, chil'. You's taken to answerin' your own questions, even when you got someone to do it for ya."

Jarena responded with a feeble smile.

" 'Sides, I thought Mildred let you bring your wash over and throw in wid her."

"She did."

"Then what you so riled up about? You got your washin' done and got to visit with Mildred while you done it. Instead of feeling sorry fer yerself, you should be thankin' the good Lord that He gave you a reason to spend time visitin'. Ain't a soul in this place that don' know you's unhappy to be here, Jarena. But it's 'bout time you quit sulkin' around and start offerin' thanks for what you got."

"Which isn't much, as I see it. Look at this place, Miss Hattie. We're either living under torn pieces of canvas or burrowed into the sides of these hills like animals. There's not enough food and no way to prepare for winter. We'll likely all be dead come spring."

Miss Hattie thumped her stick into the thick buffalo grass. "God willing, we'll make due. Dere's still some rice and cornmeal Thomas bought down in Ellis—and them jackrabbits ain't half bad."

Jarena wanted to tell Miss Hattie the remaining supplies, along with most all the jackrabbits, would be gone come winter. Instead, she heeded Miss Hattie's admonition and mumbled her halfhearted agreement while she stirred the boiling clothes with a long wooden paddle. The water churned and bubbled while the steamy heat drifted upward to dampen Jarena's face. Thankful for the cooling breeze, she turned toward the south. Could her eyes be playing tricks on her, or had she truly spied a wagon in the waving expanse of prairie grass?

Hurrying around the fire, Jarena shaded her eyes with one hand and focused upon the flowing wall of grass. Had her sighting been a mirage? Nothing more than smoke and sunlight mixed with a strong desire to see old friends from Georgetown?

"Wagons!" she shouted. She reached down and gripped Hattie's shoulder. "Look, Miss Hattie! It's wagons, and they're coming our way!"

"Quit dat hollerin' and loosen your grip, chil', else I'm gonna lose both my hearin' and the use of my arm."

Jarena loosened her white-knuckled grasp but feared the older woman would be bruised come morning. "I'm sorry, Miss Hattie. I didn't realize."

"Go on and see who's comin'. Think it might be some of the folks from back home?"

The thump of her feet striking the hard

earth pounded in Jarena's ears as she sprinted toward the string of approaching wagons. A brief glimpse of the Francis family caused her to run even faster, and her arms flailed in giant circles as she continued onward.

"Is that Charles Francis?" Truth hollered as she and Grace came running alongside Jarena.

"I think so." Jarena's lungs felt as though they would explode, yet she was unable to slow the pace. Knowing the Francis family—particularly Charles—was among the group fueled her onward.

Truth and Grace bolted ahead, their lithe bodies more accustomed to the exertion. "It's him!" Truth yelled as she waved Jarena forward.

Jarena continued running, but her gait slowed, her breathing becoming more labored. Tired and winded, she bent forward, inhaled deeply, and then straightened her body. It was then that she saw him. He was running toward her with a smile that stretched from ear to ear and waving a worn felt hat above his head.

She waved her arms in return. Before she could catch her breath, he was swooping her high into the air, all thought of propriety lost in the moment. She stared into his dark brown eyes, unable to comprehend that he was finally standing before her.

"Charles!" She could think of nothing more to say.

He touched her left cheek and then looked into the distance. She followed his gaze. "How much farther to the townsite?" he asked.

"This *is* the town."

"You always did know how to make me laugh." He tilted his head back, and Jarena waited until the sound of his laughter drifted off with the wind.

"I'm speaking the truth, Charles. What you see lying before you is Nicodemus—wretched as it is."

He stared at her, his expression mirroring the same disbelief that had enveloped their small group only two months earlier. She knew what he was thinking—the denial and disbelief. The refusal to admit this place could be their Promised Land—yet the frightening realization that it was. Like a tiny root inching downward to strengthen itself in the earth, the truth had begun to take hold—the pain and horror shone in his eyes.

"Yes," she whispered, nodding her head in final confirmation. "This *is* Nicodemus."

Charles grasped her hand with a ferocity that caused her fingers to tingle and then grow numb. "I don't think my folks will soon forgive me for this," he finally said.

"But it was *their* choice to come. You didn't force them."

"I knew they wouldn't remain in Kentucky if I came west—not after losing Arthur. None of us would have come had we known it was like this. Why didn't you write?"

His accusation stung. "This isn't Georgetown, Charles. We have no post office—we don't even have a general store. What you see before you is the town. Nothing but eight small campsites with lean-tos our only means of protection against the elements. But I did write one letter. I sent it with some folks heading back east. They promised to mail it for me, but I doubted they would. I had no money for postage, and I suspect they were embarrassed to tell me they hadn't the funds to spare."

Jarena nodded toward the approaching line of wagons. "How many folks are in those wagons?"

"About three hundred of us left Kentucky,

but we had an outbreak of measles down near Ellis and some of the families were forced to stay there. I reckon we have about eighty families in this wagon train. The others were planning to follow as soon as possible, though I'm guessing most will turn and head for home once they hear the truth about this place."

"Eighty more families," Jarena marveled.

The settlers cheered as the wagons pulled into the townsite, and Jarena thrilled at the unfolding scene. There was pure pleasure in seeing the familiar faces. And, she decided, increasing their numbers would be good for Nicodemus and certainly lift the spirits of the current residents. Jarena surveyed the wagons, praying they were stocked with supplies—that unlike their group, these settlers had come well prepared.

"This is all dere is to the town?" Mr. Francis inquired as he drew nearer Jarena and Charles.

"I'm afraid so, but there's more than when we set foot on the townsite in late July. See the sod dugouts the men have been constructing? It was too late to plant when we arrived."

Mr. Francis stared at her with the same disbelieving look that she'd seen on Charles's face only moments earlier. With obvious concern, Mr. Francis and the other new arrivals listened while their friends and former neighbors recounted stories about their struggle to survive during the past two months.

Herman Kemble pushed his hat back on his head. "I cain't say as our introduction to the West has been easy, but we's mighty glad to have the rest of you arrive. Dere's safety and comfort in numbers."

Reverend Mason, who had just arrived, stepped forward. "But what 'bout Mr. Hill? Hasn't he returned at all?"

Ivan Lovejoy frowned. "We planned to ask you folks if you'd seen 'im. Last news we had 'bout him was that he had headed back to Kentucky to sell more land. You heard or seen anything of Mr. Hill, Wilbur?"

Wilbur Rawlins swept his eyes despondently around the barren townsite. "He was back in Georgetown and told us things was grand. He told me all of you was livin' off the fat of the land."

As each question was answered, the anger and dissatisfaction of the new arrivals seemed to increase. In fact, most of the group continued talking until well into the night. Jarena sat beside Charles, with their only protection the lean-to that her father and Thomas had constructed when they first arrived. The canvas canopy was now no more than waving strips of fabric that had been shredded by the incessant prairie winds.

Charles glanced at the sky. "You have quite a view of the stars from your bed each night."

She nodded. "The lean-to provides little shelter, but with the arrival of more men, surely enough dugouts can be prepared before winter."

"More people also means that more shelter is needed. Besides, I think many of these families will depart come morning."

Jarena startled to attention. "Why? Do they care so little for our well-being that they will run off and leave?"

"They have to do what's best for their own families, and if they believe they should return to Kentucky, who are we to argue? To be honest, I think they would all leave if they had sufficient funds to make the return journey," he confided.

"So those who will remain have no money? Did they purchase supplies in Ellis?"

"Not much. Most of us spent our savings to purchase the land and pay for the train fare. We thought there would be supplies available in Nicodemus."

"Didn't anyone in Ellis tell you about our troubles?"

"They said we should purchase our supplies from them and that there were no stores in Nicodemus where we could buy anything. We figured they were trying to frighten us off so we'd go back to Kentucky. Then the owner of the general store said a fellow named Thomas Grayson could vouch that he was telling the truth. But none of us had ever heard of anyone by that name."

"This isn't the South, Charles. Folks around here aren't going to lie to run you off. In fact, most of them have been kind to us. Maybe you can talk more people into staying." She tried to camouflage her desperation with cheerfulness, but Charles's countenance made her doubt she'd accomplished it.

"It would take a tongue more eloquent than mine to convince these folks."

"Then you'll be leaving, also?" she asked in a hoarse whisper.

"No, but I'm certain I'll meet resistance from my parents. If they think we should go back to Kentucky, I'll encourage them to do so, though I won't leave with them. Their funds are limited, so they may have no choice but to stay."

"The little money Pappy brought has long since been spent on supplies and food. Yet he's happier than I've ever seen him—the twins, too. They appear to find this all a grand adventure. But when the winter snows arrive, I fear we'll all starve to death."

Charles hunched forward and patted her hand. "There's always the chance winter won't be as bad as you've imagined."

"We've talked to folks who know this area, and they say the winters are hard. The people down in Ellis will tell you the same thing."

"With all these frightful tales of winter, I can't decide if you're trying to convince me to stay or depart."

"Oh, I *do* want you to remain. But I must be honest and tell you all that I know of this place so you won't later be angry with me."

She looked deep into his eyes, wanting him to see the truth of her words.

He smiled and placed his palm along her cheek. "I believe you, Jarena."

When Charles left to help his parents set up camp, Ezekiel approached Jarena. "Charles plannin' to stay or is he gonna skedaddle back to Kentucky with his mammy and pappy?"

"They're leaving?"

"That's what they said. And I think the Wilsons be leavin', too. Truth and Grace bedded down under a wagon with the Wilson girls. They truly was excited to see their friends."

"Those girls will probably giggle and talk all night," Jarena said.

Her father leaned down and poked at the waning fire just outside their lean-to. The wood crackled, and a host of dying embers sparked to life and cast a wiggling shadow of her father's brawny figure. "What about Charles? He leavin'?"

"No—at least that's what he told me. I think he's expecting his folks to return home, but he says he's staying no matter what they decide."

Her father heaved his muscular body onto

the ground. "All them that's got money is leavin'. I talked long and hard—tol' 'em we could make it through the winter a lot easier if dey'd throw in with us. Guess it's gonna take more than talkin' to convince 'em."

"How many do you think will leave?"

"I heard that sixty families will be pullin' out."

"That's more than half of them!"

"And them ones down in Ellis'll prob'ly never come when they hear what it's like here."

"They're feeling the same as we did when we saw this place—betrayed."

"That's true enough, but we got more important things to worry about right now. We's needin' to get these dugouts built, and Thomas promised to send the breaking plow back to Ellis with Mr. Goddard's wagons."

"Nobody brought tools?"

"A few axes and the like—same as the rest of us. The ones that was gonna farm figured they'd be able to borrow from us when the time came for plantin'. The rest figured the town was already up and runnin' and they'd just move into their new businesses—that's what they paid that extra money fer. Didn't nobody figure on building a dugout or soddy the minute they got here." Ezekiel kissed her good night. "You go ahead and bed down. I'm gonna spend some time prayin'."

Jarena didn't argue. She knew where her father would go. The day after they'd arrived in Nicodemus, he'd found a secluded place where a large, smooth rock jutted out of the ground. He'd gone there every night to lean against that rock and pray. Sometimes he'd be gone only a few minutes, sometimes he'd be there half the night. She wasn't certain what filled his prayers on those long nights—probably their fragile existence in this harsh and unforgiving land. She wound herself inside the thin blanket and wondered how long her father would pray this night.

She wasn't certain how long she'd slept, but the sun was over the horizon when she awakened to the sounds of horses being hitched to wagons. Rubbing her eyes, Jarena shook off her blanket and stood gazing toward where the new colonists had bedded down for the night. Her father had been correct. In fact, even more of the recent arrivals than he'd anticipated were preparing to depart. She frantically scanned the area, hoping to gain sight of Charles or his parents.

Shifting to her left, she saw him waving his hat in the air, just as he had when she'd first seen him yesterday.

She gestured in return and hurried toward him, excited yet fearful what he might say. "Good morning!"

"Good morning to you." His wide smile warmed her heart.

She gave a quick nod toward the wagons. "It appears they're preparing to leave."

"Yes." He rubbed the back of his neck.

She waited, and when he said nothing, she was compelled to ask, "And your parents, what have they decided?"

"They'll remain. But only because of me. They argued the folly of my decision, but I told them I want a fresh beginning—a new life."

A new life. She wondered if his new life would include her. She cared for Charles, and the thought of marriage intrigued her—more so in Georgetown than Nicodemus, however. Life was too unsettled and uncertain in Nicodemus. Then too, she wasn't clear how people in love were supposed to feel. She had missed Charles, but she had also yearned for all of the friends she'd left behind. Being in his presence was enjoyable, and sometimes he made her heart pound—perhaps that meant she was in love. Once or twice she'd thought of asking Nellie but feared her friend would laugh at such questions—or worse, that she'd tell the twins. Maybe the next time she was alone with Miss Hattie, she'd ask her about love, but for now she was content to know Charles was going to remain in Nicodemus. For now her thoughts of love and marriage were likely unnecessary. After all, Charles hadn't yet spoken of marriage.

Charles grasped her hand. "Come have some breakfast with us."

Jarena glanced over her shoulder. "I haven't seen my father yet this morning, and he'll need to eat."

"He's already out in that far field with that Thomas fellow. They've been out there since before sunup. My mama sent me out there, and I asked your father to breakfast, but he refused. Said they had to return that plow they're using and they wanted to get as much sod broken as they could before the last wagon pulled out for Ellis. I took him some cornbread and a couple biscuits."

"I know he's thankful for your kindness, Charles."

"I offered to spell Thomas for a while with the plow, but he said nobody could use it but him. Probably just as well, since I don't know anything about plowing. Now, if he needed a silversmith, that would be different."

Jarena looked around the open prairie. "I don't imagine there's going to be much need for a silversmith in Nicodemus. At least not any time soon."

"Then it's good I didn't plan to continue in the trade. I'm anxious to try my hand at farming, where I can take charge. Mr. Henry was a good man, but that business back in Georgetown belonged to him. I would have been his apprentice until the day he died."

"And his son's after that 'cause you'd never have the money to buy such a fine business," Jarena said as she neared the fire, where Charles's mother was engrossed in cooking breakfast.

"Good morning, Mrs. Francis," Jarena greeted.

Mrs. Francis looked up, and it took only a

fleeting glance for Jarena to see the pain in the older woman's eyes. "How are you, Jarena?"

"Much better now that I'm surrounded by so many familiar faces." She took the tin plate of corn mush and syrup Mrs. Francis offered.

"Best enjoy it while you can. What about you, Jarena? Would *you* leave iffen you had a train ticket back home?"

Charles jumped to his feet. "Mama! I told you I'm going to stay here regardless of what anyone else does. Owning my own place is what I want to do, and my decision has *nothing* to do with Jarena."

His words cut to the quick, and Jarena stopped eating in midbite and slumped like a wilted flower thirsting for a drop of water. "Even if I had a ticket, I couldn't leave. My family is here, and I have nothing left in Georgetown except my mama's grave." She handed the empty tin plate back to the older woman. "If you'll excuse me, I must see about the twins. They spent the night with the Wilsons. Thank you for the breakfast," she added, nearly forgetting her manners.

Hiking her skirt, she strode off toward the

wagons with Charles's words ringing in her ears. *"My decision has nothing to do with Jarena."*

She rounded the wagon and spotted her father and Thomas moving toward the townsite. Jarena watched as the two men exchanged words. Thomas was hauling the plow, and her father looked weary from the early-morning work. The wagons began to pull out of their circle and form into a straight line. Most of the departing families were already seated inside the wagons, obviously anxious to begin their journey home—and Jarena couldn't fault them, for she, too, longed to leave. Had Charles asked her to be his wife and return to Kentucky, she would have gladly joined the departing wagons. But he hadn't, and so both she and Mrs. Francis would remain in Nicodemus against their own desires.

"Hold up!" Thomas hollered as he approached the last wagon. He bent over, gasping for air, and when he'd finally gained his breath, he straightened and walked toward the front of the line.

"Find a space and jump aboard if yer wantin' to leave," the driver called.

"The breaking plow—I promised Mr. Horton I'd return it with the wagons goin' back to Ellis. Mr. Goddard said dere'd be no problem sendin' it back with you."

The man shoved his hat to the back of his head. "Ain't room in none of dese wagons for dat plow."

The driver flicked the reins and signaled for the wagons to pull out as Ezekiel stepped alongside Thomas.

"There's no room for the plow," Thomas said. "I gave Mr. Horton my word—what if he sends the law after me?"

There was a deep fear in Thomas Grayson's eyes. Jarena could see it take hold as he spoke to her father. They all feared lawmen—and for good reason. The law never appeared to be on the side of the colored man. But with Thomas there seemed to be something more.

CHAPTER

10

The group of settlers—old and new together—sat in a large ring, much like the circle formed by the recently departed wagons. Once again a plea to contribute funds was issued. Believing the appeal unfair, the new arrivals objected strongly. Bitter words soon peppered the quarrel and required more than a few wise words from Ivan Lovejoy, Wilbur Rawlins, Jerome Holt, and Ezekiel, who attempted to defuse the increasing hostility. Before peace was finally restored, Reverend Mason had pointed to Scripture for the answer. He reminded them they were members of the family of God, and rather than withholding their meager funds, they should be seeking out ways to help one another. The shamefaced group finally approved a journey to Ellis to purchase supplies and return the plow.

In the meantime, they decided to cut as many sod bricks as possible to provide frontage for the dugouts. They would dig with every tool available and into any nearby hillock. Desperate for shelter, the new arrivals began their work at a feverish pitch.

"If they continue at dat speed, they gonna wear themselves out afore noon," Thomas commented as he and Ezekiel passed several families frantically digging into the hillside.

"Dey'll learn," Ezekiel replied with a slight smile. "You been givin' any more thought to what I asked you?"

"Nosuh, and I don't plan to, neither. You're gonna have to find someone else t' make that trip to Ellis, 'cause it won't be me. After hearing that folks was talkin' about hangin' me when I was late gettin' back from that trip I made afore—well, that's 'nuff to tell me I won' be in charge of their money again. If it was jest to return the plow, I'd consider makin' the journey."

"I unnerstand, but I think they learnt their

lesson. Nobody wants to take time to make the trip."

"Well, I won't change my mind."

"Then I s'pose I'll be the one to go."

"Once you're on yer way, I'll begin diggin' out the shelter for you and your women-folk."

"No need for you to bother yourself," Charles Francis said as the two approached. "I'll take care of helping Mr. Harban with his dugout." Charles stood with his axe propped on one shoulder. "Thought I'd cut some of this sod into bricks for our place," he added.

"Mighty nice of ya to offer yer help, Charles," Ezekiel said, beaming in the new arrival's direction.

"You gonna have plenty to do gettin' your own place ready for winter. I'm better able to hep the Harbans," Thomas interjected.

"Probably best you work on your own shelter." Charles swung his axe into the sod, where it stuck without completely severing the thick grass.

Thomas directed a self-satisfied smile at Charles. "That buffalo grass is stronger than you might think."

Charles tugged the axe out of the ground

and then took another hefty swing, this time cutting through the sod. "There isn't anything out here on the prairie that I can't handle as well as the next fellow."

Charles swung the axe into the strip of sod again with a noisy grunt. "Mr. Harban, I'll keep an eye out for Jarena while you're down in Ellis." He had evidently overheard their conversation as they had approached.

"Jarena and the twins will be fine. Thomas will sleep nearby, and dere's 'nuff folks aroun' that no harm is gonna come to them. You look after your own folks. I know your mama ain't happy 'bout bein' here, so you best be doin' all you can to please her."

"Yes, sir, whatever you say. Whereabouts are you planning to build your dugout, Thomas?" Charles turned a menacing glare on Thomas.

Thomas hesitated, and Ezekiel slapped him on the shoulder. "He ain't gonna dig no shelter for hisself. I tol' him ain't no sense in it."

Charles took a step toward Thomas. "You're going to *live* with them? In their dugout? All winter?" His voice was loud.

"Well, it ain't as though we're gonna be hibernatin' like the bears," Ezekiel put in.

"Me and Thomas agreed to share a place afore the rest of you came. Come spring, he's gonna help me build a soddy out on my farmstead, and we'll put in crops together. Then I'll help him with his soddy. Works out good since our acres adjoin each other," Ezekiel explained.

Charles nodded as though he understood, yet his eyes were filled with anger. "Seems as though you just moved right in and made yourself a part of the family."

"Not without an invitation," Thomas replied curtly. "Best I be going. I need to get busy with this plow." He stalked off.

Charles thrust his axe deep into the ground and then met Ezekiel's puzzled gaze. "I don't trust him, Mr. Harban."

"He's been a mighty big help to me since we got here."

"I don't think you should leave him alone with Jarena—I think he's sweet on her."

Ezekiel rubbed the back of his neck. "We ain't got time for no arguin' or pinin' over the womenfolk. There's too much work needs done 'fore winter sets in."

The sun had barely begun to peek over the horizon the next morning when Thomas loosed a hobbled team of horses and led them to the wagon. With a quick precision, he hitched the team and then hoisted the plow into the wagon bed. Ezekiel had finished a warm bowl of mush when Thomas approached the lean-to.

"The wagon be ready when you is."

Ezekiel nodded and waited until Jarena wrapped several chunks of corn bread in a piece of cloth and handed the package to him. "Gotta have me a little somethin' to eat along the way," he said before giving Jarena a hug. "Tell the twins I said to behave—and make 'em help you."

"You told them last night, Pappy, but I'll remind them."

Thomas walked alongside Ezekiel to the wagon. "I'm feeling a mite guilty 'bout sending you off by yerself."

"No need. Think I might enjoy the time alone—just me and the Lord."

"And the horses. You might check with Mr. Goddard at the livery and see if he gots any cheap feed for the horses. We're gonna need to find some way to nourish them this winter. I know the people come first, but I's worried 'bout dem animals."

"I know, boy. I'll see what I can do. Try to

find enough to keep yerself busy." Ezekiel laughed heartily, for he knew Thomas would have little time for rest.

"I'll have a go at it. And don' you worry 'bout things back here. We be fine."

Ezekiel gently slapped the reins, and the horses stepped out. The wooden freight wagon gently swayed back and forth as it rolled through the thick buffalo grass. Thomas watched until the wagon was out of sight before returning to the lean-to.

He picked up the axe and rested the wooden shovel handle across his shoulder. "I'll be on the other side of the hill. I plan to start diggin' today," he told Jarena.

She looked up from her mending. "I'm going to send the girls down to the river to fetch water so I can wash. If you have any-thing that needs laundering, you can put it in that pile." She indicated an overflowing basket of clothes.

"Looks like you've already got more'n enough."

"Few more shirts and overalls won't make much difference. Besides, it doesn't appear you'll have much time for doing laundry."

A smile creased Thomas's lips, and he hesitated only a moment longer before gathering his dirty clothes and adding them to the basket. "Thank you," he said before heading off.

"I'll bring your dinner out to you."

He glanced over his shoulder and met her bright chocolate brown eyes. "That be nice. Maybe the twins could come along an' we could eat together."

"I'll see how far my washing and the twins' chores have progressed by then."

Thomas nodded and trod off to the hillside Ezekiel had chosen for their temporary dugout. Even though Thomas and Ezekiel would begin their soddies out on their own land claims next spring, Thomas agreed with the older man: remaining near the other settlers throughout this first winter was prudent, even if it meant digging out a home they'd use for only a short time—at least that was their hope. The two men reasoned that they would salvage any sod bricks for later use in their new homes.

Though he'd worked with the horses and breaking plow and had used an axe to cut sod bricks over the past month, this would be Thomas's first day of digging into the hillside. Angling the shovel, he thrust it into the deep-rooted grass without success. Using his full weight, he pushed on the shovel and emitted a loud grunt when the spade finally wedged into the hardened earth that lay beneath the thick, grassy roots. He didn't recall the work being quite so strenuous when he helped Mr. Horton down in Ellis.

Perspiration soon dripped from his forehead, and the warm breeze did little to cool his sweaty body. He should have carried a jug of water with him, but perhaps Jarena would bring extra at noonday. If not, he'd go down to the spring himself. He swiped his shirtsleeve across his forehead and then gauged his progress. Digging out a hovel that would accommodate the Harban family might prove more difficult than he'd expected.

The morning hours wore on, and the sound of axes and shovels being plunged into the ground fell into a rhythmic pattern that could be heard throughout the townsite. By the time noonday arrived, Thomas was anxious for Jarena's arrival. When she finally rounded the hill carrying a cloth-covered basket, he heaved a weary sigh and dropped to the ground.

She smiled as she lifted the basket off her

arm. "You look tired. Are you thirsty?" she asked, offering an earthenware jug of water.

He nodded and lifted the bottle to his mouth with shaking hands. She likely thought him ill-mannered, but he continued to take great gulping swallows until he could hold no more.

"You nearly downed the entire jug," she said before turning to leave.

"You're not gonna stay and eat with me?"

"I left Truth and Grace rinsing the clothes. I best return. You can bring the basket back this evening."

"Please stay—jest for a few minutes. Did you eat yet?"

She hesitated, and he quickly spread out the tattered cloth that had covered the basket before pointing to a spot where she could sit.

"I suppose it won't hurt to sit down for a few minutes, but I'll eat with the twins when I return."

He scooted up beside her and looked inside the basket.

"There's some fish in there. Mrs. Wilson brought it over. I think Mr. Wilson would rather fish than dig," she said with a giggle.

"Cain't say as I blame 'im. This dirt is hard as a rock. I been at it all mornin', and dere's all the progress I made." He jerked his thumb toward the small mound of unyielding earth he'd dug out of the hillside.

"Appears to be going slow for everyone," she said. "Where's your family, Thomas?"

Her question was tossed at him with a nonchalant innocence that caught him unaware. He opened his mouth to tell her the truth but stopped short. "Here and there. Never stayed too long in one place, but iffen things go all right, I may just stay in Nicodemus. You ever lived anyplace 'sides Kentucky?"

"No, Georgetown's the only place I ever lived. Do you have friends or family in Kansas?" she persisted.

"No, I don'. It's excitin' getting to see new places, don't you think?"

Jarena picked a tall blade of buffalo grass and began to wind it around her finger. "I would have been happy to live and die in Georgetown."

"Even with Charles Francis out here in Nicodemus?" His dark eyes twinkled as he watched for her response.

She continued to wrap the blade of grass around her finger. "I doubt whether Charles would have left Georgetown if I was still there."

"I see. Well, Charles *appears* to be a nice enough fella, I s'pose."

The blade of grass fell to the ground. "And what does that mean?"

"Don't mean nothing 'cept I don' know him well enough to say much more'n that."

"Charles is a *fine* man—just ask anybody."

"No need. I ain't lookin' to make Charles my friend, so it don' matter what I think of him." Thomas bit into a piece of the fried fish.

"You think Charles isn't worthy of your friendship?"

Clearly she was upset. Thomas broke off a piece of corn bread while he considered his reply. "I ain't lookin' for an argument, Jarena. I'll take your word that Charles is a good man—ain't got nothin' to do with him being *worthy* of my friendship. For now, I'm not lookin' to make any friends—'cept maybe you."

Her eyebrows arched. "Don't forget the basket." She rose to her feet and hurried off.

Thomas swiped his shirtsleeve across his mouth. "Now, why I'd go and say that aloud?" he muttered to himself. "Shoulda kept my big mouth shut!"

CHAPTER

11

Word of Ezekiel's return spread among the Nicodemus settlers like wildfire across the prairie on a windy day. They gathered together at a surprising pace and focused their attention toward the approaching wagon. Jarena waved a threadbare handkerchief high in the air while the twins raced pell-mell to the wagon. Their father smiled broadly, leaned back, and reined the horses to a halt long enough for both girls to clamber up alongside him.

"Looks like he's happy. Let's hope dat's a good sign," Thomas commented as he walked next to Jarena.

"Good sign of *what*?" Charles asked as he approached Jarena from the opposite side.

"That he was able to bargain for a decent price on the supplies."

"If you were worried, maybe you should have gone along instead of spending your time trying to impress Jarena," Charles said brusquely.

The look of surprise on Thomas's face didn't escape Jarena—nor did the scowl that followed.

"How would *you* know what I was doin'? I thought you was busy with yer own diggin'."

Jarena stood nearby as her father and the twins scrambled down from the wagon. "Any difficulty on the journey?"

Ezekiel gathered her into a quick embrace and brushed a fleeting kiss upon her cheek. "Ever'thing went jest fine, daughter. Thought maybe I'd win over some of the Georgetown folks that's recovered from the measles and they'd come and give the town a look, but that's not gonna happen. They's all made up their minds to go back to Kentucky. I *was* able to convince a few of them to loan me some extra money—not much, but enough to hep get some extra feed fer the horses."

"I'm worried 'bout food fer my fambly, not dem animals," one of the new arrivals said.

Ezekiel gave the man a warning look. "You best remember that dem horses is worth their weight in gold. They more than earned their feed when we was cutting sod, and it's the horses that hauled our supplies back from Ellis. Without horses, we be in trouble for sho'."

———

While Jarena and the twins joined the other folks gathered around the wagon, Thomas grasped Ezekiel's arm and pulled him aside. "Ya returned the plow?"

Ezekiel nodded. "Mr. Goddard said he'd see it wuz returned to the owner."

"You didn't take it to Mr. Horton?"

"Didn't have time fer goin' to Mr. Horton's place. 'Sides, you tol' me Mr. Goddard's an honest man. Why you actin' so edgy 'bout that plow?"

"I wanna be sure it gets back. I gave my word."

"Well, it got back to the livery, and that's as much as you promised. Now quit yer worryin'. How'd things go 'round here while I was gone?"

Thomas tugged on the frayed cuff of his shirtsleeve. "Charles been sniffin' around where he's not wanted. Otherwise, dere's been no problem what I know of."

Ezekiel pulled off his hat and slapped it across his knee. "I knowed dis was gonna happen. Charles is sweet on Jarena, and you's not likin' it, are ya?" he asked with a chuckle.

"No such thing. I's not interested in Jarena. I was jest tryin' to look out for her while you was gone," he insisted.

"Ha! Ya think I believe that nonsense? Don't ferget that I was once young myself. I know how you young'uns think. Come on now and let's get this wagon unloaded 'fore dark sets in."

Thomas scanned the contents of the wagon. "Looks like Mr. Hepple was well supplied."

"Sure 'nuff. The train got there with his supplies the day afore I did. Never seen so much fancy furniture sittin' in a store. He tol' me there's a doctor comin' to live in Hill City, and he shipped his belongings by train. Mr. Hepple agreed to keep the doctor's belongings at his store 'til he arrives. Said the doctor even special-ordered farmin' tools.

Seems he's bought a house, but he's gonna do some farmin', too."

Thomas scratched his head. "I never knowed a doctor to take up farmin'."

Ezekiel grinned. "I tol' Mr. Hepple it pleased me a heap to know there might be someone tryin' their hand at farmin' that knew even less than we do."

"You know about farmin', Pappy," Truth said.

"I knows 'bout growin' hemp, and this here land ain't good fer growin' hemp."

"Can't eat hemp, neither," Truth said with a girlish giggle as she lifted a burlap sack of cornmeal from the wagon.

Ezekiel was bone tired, and his back ached as he unhitched the team. He wanted nothing more than a hot meal and a night of sleep. However, his suggestion that they wait until morning to divide the supplies was met with a host of angry protests. Waving as much as his weary arms would permit, he finally silenced the crowd. "Do whatever you see fit," he relented. "I'm too tired to argue. Jest remember that this here food's gotta last us all winter—best be careful and use it wisely," he admonished.

Shoulders sagging, he grasped the reins and began to lead the horses away.

"You go and rest," Thomas offered. "I'll take care of the team an' then bring our portion of the supplies to the lean-to."

Ezekiel nodded. "Believe I'll take ya up on that offer."

Grace's eyes were shining with excitement as each bag of beans or rice was opened. "Can we stay and watch?"

"If it pleases ya," Ezekiel agreed.

Jarena linked arms with her father and matched his stride. "I'll come with you. I've got a pot of rye coffee boiling. Mrs. Wilson said a farmer's wife told her how to make it when they were in Ellis. It's not like real coffee, but it's better than no coffee at all."

"Where'd ya get the rye?"

"Mrs. Wilson. She said the farmer and his wife gave them some. Said they considered it an act of mercy. The Wilsons didn't understand the comment until they saw this place. Then they knew why the couple had taken pity on them."

Ezekiel laughed wearily. "I bought some coffee, but it sho' won't be lastin' all winter."

"Tell me what else you saw when you

were in Ellis, Pappy. Is it a big town like Topeka?"

"Ain't nowheres near as big as Topeka. Only one street lined with stores, but there's lots more folks livin' 'round 'bout that area—farmers and the like. They got a good livery and blacksmith—and they was all nice to me. Didn't seem to have no dislike 'bout doin' business with a colored. They was all excited 'bout that doctor—all of 'em comin' into the store to look over his furniture and making guesses about how much each piece cost. Mr. Hepple seemed to be enjoyin' all the fuss."

Jarena's brows furrowed. She couldn't imagine why a doctor who could have a fine home and a normal life in any large city would want to move west. What could possibly entice an educated man who had been living in Kentucky to uproot his family and move to Kansas? She wondered if this doctor was like her father—trying to fulfill some distant dream. Did he have children? Were they like Truth and Grace, excited over the prospect of a new adventure, or were they like her—opposed to change?

Ezekiel handed her his empty coffee cup when they got to the lean-to. "Some of the folks down in Ellis is hopin' the doc will change his mind and settle in Ellis. Guess they ain't got no doctor in their town, neither."

"But if he's already bought land in Hill City . . ."

"That's what I said. Ain't no way he'd be able to farm all them acres iffen they live in Ellis."

"If they're wise, they'll turn around and go back to Kentucky," Jarena muttered as she balanced the coffeepot atop the hot ashes of the fire she'd been using to boil the wash water.

CHAPTER

12

Georgetown, Kentucky • October 1877

With a thud, Macia Boyle plopped onto the train seat and folded her arms across her chest. She molded her features into a glowering frown. It was the same unpleasant look she had been directing at her father for the past several weeks—or had it been even longer? At this point Samuel was uncertain, but he forced himself to smile graciously while settling beside his wife.

No doubt this was going to be a long journey. Samuel looked about at his family members and momentarily questioned his decision to uproot them from all they held dear. He was uncertain who appeared more angry, Macia or Harvey. And his dear wife, Margaret, seemed completely forlorn.

"Lovely day for traveling, don't you agree?"

Margaret gave a faint nod while Harvey and Macia continued to focus their icy glares in his direction. Perhaps he'd try again. "Our accommodations are quite acceptable, don't you think?"

Another nod and enduring cold stares were all Samuel received in reply. He leaned back in his seat and decided he'd wait until the frosty environment thawed before attempting any further conversation. Surely someone would soon have a question and be forced to speak. Macia opened a book and began to read while Harvey closed his eyes—likely hoping this was all a bad dream, Samuel decided.

They had traveled only a short distance when Margaret shifted toward him. "I do hope our furniture has arrived. I won't be able to keep a decent house without my own things surrounding me. I realize that such a concept is difficult for a man to understand, Samuel, but it's true. Attempting to roll a piecrust or make biscuits is nearly impossible without your own bowls and utensils."

Samuel smiled and patted her hand. It had been years since his wife had prepared her own biscuits or piecrust, but this wasn't the time to remind her of that fact. Such a comment would likely send her into another diatribe about Cook and the maid being unwilling to make the move west with them. He had promised to hire someone to help with the household duties, though he remained uncertain how or when he'd be able to accomplish that particular feat. At the moment, however, he needed only to allay his wife's concerns over their household goods.

"I received a letter from the owner of the Ellis mercantile earlier this week. He advised me our shipment has arrived. In fact, even the new items I ordered have been delivered to his store."

"You ordered new furniture?" Margaret's face registered disbelief.

"No, not furniture. But I did order farm implements, a wagon, additional medical supplies, a buggy, and runners to replace the wagon wheels when the winter snows arrive—and livestock, of course."

She grimaced at the news. "I fear you're spending all of our savings on items we won't even need if we return to Kentucky."

He jerked around in his seat. "We are *not* returning to Kentucky, Margaret. If anything happens so that we're unhappy in Hill City, we will decide upon another place to live, but it will *not* be in the South. If this doesn't work out, I'll think of something."

"No need to raise your voice, Father," Macia said, arching her brows. "I'm certain the people in the next coach aren't interested in your nebulous plans for the future."

He met his daughter's cold stare. "You may recall that on many occasions, I've attempted to discuss our move in a civil manner. Unfortunately, it seems the only way I'm able to convince any of you that I am earnest is when I speak in a harsh manner."

"There's never been any discussion." Harvey slouched down into the seat. "Whenever any of us voiced an objection, you immediately rejected our arguments. You made yourself abundantly clear from the beginning: we're being forced to live wherever *you* decide. I never considered your declaration an invitation to discussion."

Samuel stared at his son and daughter. Though only a few feet separated him from his children, it seemed as if the narrow space had grown into a yawning abyss.

Samuel leaned back and rested his head upon the cushioned seat in their private compartment. He'd spared no expense in travel accommodations. It had been a meager attempt to mollify his family, though he should have known it wouldn't help. For a brief moment he considered once again voicing his genuine need to live somewhere other than in the South. Dare he tell them how desperately unhappy he'd been all these years, how he'd yearned to live anywhere but among those who had embraced slavery as a way of life before the war?

Samuel closed his eyes and knew he should remain silent. What good would more words accomplish? After all, to truly explain the depth of his feelings would likely cause wounds that would never heal—especially with Margaret. Oh, she knew of his unhappiness, but she had tucked away any thoughts of his discontent in the same manner she packed the children's outgrown clothes—hidden out of sight and far from mind.

Perhaps his decision *had* been unfair. He'd been wrestling with that thought since purchasing the acreage in Hill City. However, he truly believed that years of deference to the children's desires had caused their undeniably selfish behavior. Perhaps if he had told them *no* more often during their formative years, they would have accepted his decision to leave Kentucky without fanfare. Both Macia and Harvey had been willful from an early age. They should have been reared with a strong hand, but that hadn't occurred—nor had their conduct changed. All of this left Samuel to wonder whether he had failed miserably as a parent. But then there was Carlisle, who was neither spoiled nor selfish.

Samuel bent forward and rested his forearms across his thighs as if to close the chasm dividing him from the children. "You are both very young with your entire lives spread out before you. This is an opportunity for you to see what God has created beyond the borders of Kentucky. You may be pleasantly surprised. And if you are intrinsically unhappy in the West, you should explore other places before rushing back and settling in Kentucky," he urged.

"I didn't realize the depth of your distaste for the place of my birth," Margaret said, her voice barely audible above the train's clacking sounds.

Pain reflected in her eyes, and Samuel realized that his short discourse had done exactly what he had wanted to avoid. "Please don't misconstrue what I've said, Margaret. I find Kentucky a beautiful place, but like the other southern states, its beauty is tainted by bigotry. I know in my heart that it is time to leave. I believe there is a God-given purpose for this move."

When he looked at his family, he saw that his explanation had not helped. The children stared through him as though he hadn't spoken at all, and Margaret's pained look remained. He closed his eyes and silently prayed that his family would eventually come to love their new home and that he had truly understood God's leading.

Throughout the remainder of their journey, the family exchanged only necessary information as they switched trains or when they stopped for meals at a depot. Even shopping and an overnight stay at a fine hotel in St. Louis did not help breach the gulf. For the most part, each one silently watched the passing scenery and remained lost in private thought.

CHAPTER

13

Samuel flagged the weary-looking conductor as he entered the car to validate their tickets. "How far to Ellis?" he inquired.

The trainman pointed toward the north side of the rails. A smattering of small wood and limestone buildings was partially visible through the smudged train windows. "That's it coming up."

Samuel straightened, tugged his suit jacket into place, and did his best to look enthusiastic. "Not much longer now."

Macia stared at the flat, desolate prairie and then gave her father a dour look. "It's good that I hadn't raised my expectations."

The train screeched to a stop, and Samuel stood to assist his wife along the aisle. As they stepped down from the train, a stiff

wind whipped their clothing, and they hastened inside the train station without
prompting.

"Quite a wind stirring out there," Samuel
commented to one of the men seated inside
the train station.

The haggard old man laughed and, with
amazing precision, spit a stream of tobacco
juice into a brass spittoon near the counter.
"This ain't nothing. Jest you wait until we
get us a real windstorm."

Samuel glanced at the billowing dirt cas-
cading down the street and then peered at
his wife from beneath the narrow brim of his
felt bowler. It was obvious she'd heard the
old man's comment—they all had. "Sounds
as though we're in for some new experi-
ences." His attempt at cheerfulness fell flat.
"No need to look so grim. It appears as
though this good man has survived the elements."

The man gave a hearty nod. "There's
plenty of us that have survived. Course,
there's them that ain't, too."

Samuel turned his attention to Harvey.
"Why don't you see if you can locate our
luggage while I set about finding the livery
and general store."

"There's only one street," Harvey mumbled under his breath as he trudged off toward the station platform.

"Wait here," Samuel instructed Margaret and Macia before making his way to the ticket counter, where a railroad employee was busy counting money and tickets. "Excuse me, could you tell me how far it is to the livery and the general store—the one owned by Mr. Hepple."

The clerk placed one hand atop the pile of money and looked Samuel up and down before actually meeting his gaze. "Hepple owns the *only* general store in Ellis, and it's down the street thataway." He pointed his thumb to the right. "The livery's directly across the street," he added.

"Thank you," Samuel replied.

The man continued to examine Samuel before his eyes drifted to Margaret and Macia, who had followed him and now stood a few feet away. "By any chance are you the new doctor moving up to Hill City?"

Samuel smiled and extended his hand. "Yes. Samuel Boyle. And this is my wife, Mrs. Boyle, and our daughter, Macia. That's our son Harvey bringing in the baggage."

The man shook Samuel's hand. "Pleased

to meet you. I'm Jim Benson. You sure have had a lot of goods arriving here lately. My wife made a special trip over to Hepple's just to have a looksee at your furniture. She said she'd never seen anything quite so fancy."

Samuel nodded politely, uncertain how he should respond to such a comment. "I'm . . . I'm glad you've been enjoying it."

"Oh, she didn't sit on it or nothin', just looked. My missus said she was particularly fond of a velvet corner chair."

Once again, Samuel smiled and nodded. "Well, we had best get over to the livery and pick up our wagon. We'll need to get loaded up so we can head out to Hill City."

"Mr. Hepple took most of your furniture up there last week, though from the looks of things, you got plenty of other goods to haul. You ought to consider living here in El-lis. Ain't no train service up in Hill City—ain't much of nothing in Hill City, as a matter of fact. I think you'd be much happier in Ellis, and we could use a doctor."

Macia immediately stepped forward and tapped her fingers on the counter. "You mean Hill City is even more desolate than this place?"

"Far as I know, though there's more in Hill City than Nicodemus. Both them towns was platted out by W. R. Hill, but I don't know as he's done any more than sell the land. Only a few weeks ago there was maybe three hundred coloreds come out here from Kentucky and Tennessee—all of 'em fixing to make their homes in Nicodemus. Few days later, more than half of 'em were on the train headed back home. Can't say as I blame 'em, neither."

"Surely you're wrong! Coloreds wouldn't want to head back to the South, where they were so poorly treated," Macia sarcastically countered, her eyebrows raised in a questioning arch directed at her father.

"They were afraid they couldn't make it through the winter—didn't come prepared. Now, you folks, you've done the right thing. You ordered your supplies and shipped your belongings ahead of time. You'll do mighty fine through the winter. Mr. Goddard said you even had the forethought to order a sleigh."

"Well, a doctor must be able to travel in all types of weather. It's been nice to make your acquaintance, Mr. Benson. I'm certain

we'll see you again when we're in Ellis."
Samuel directed his family toward the door.

"Hope you won't be buying tickets home
the next time we meet up," Mr. Benson said
as he waved good-bye.

————

Loading the wagon had taken time, patience, and the assistance of Will Southard
and Chester Goddard. Though her father
had helped the men, Macia and Harvey had
been quite content to sit and watch. By the
time they actually departed Ellis, her father
appeared strangely invigorated. Macia was
now certain her father was attempting to
live out some pathetic dream; had she not
been forced to participate, she wouldn't
have cared. However, her father's dream
had now become her nightmare!

Citing the family's inexperience at traveling by wagon, Mr. Goddard suggested her
father hire Thurlow Wilson to act as their
guide to Hill City. Mr. Wilson supposedly
possessed all of the necessary abilities to
assist the small family with their thirty-five
mile trek to the north and west of Ellis. And
although Macia doubted whether the
scruffy-looking man would be of any assis-

tance, her father immediately offered him the job. He appeared even less energetic than Harvey.

Mr. Wilson led out on his large bay mare while her mother rode in the buggy with Harvey; Macia sat wedged near her father in the covered wagon with a crate of squawking chickens tied near her side. Though she had repeatedly begged her father to leave the noisy birds behind, he had argued they would all be pleased to have eggs once they arrived in their new home. Mrs. Hepple had been no help—she'd readily agreed with everything her father said. In fact, the storekeeper and his wife had even convinced her father to purchase four cows. But when her father had requested that Macia walk behind with the cows and keep them moving, she had adamantly refused.

Harvey guided the buggy alongside Mr. Wilson's mare while Macia and her father followed behind in the lumbering wagon. They'd traveled only a few miles when Macia waved to Mr. Wilson. "When will we arrive?"

He slowed his horse until the wagon caught up with him and then spit a stream of tobacco juice across the grass. "Ain't gonna be today, sis."

Her father slapped the reins and gave her a sidelong glance as they continued onward. "We'll sleep out in the open tonight and arrive sometime tomorrow. Quite an adventure, don't you think?"

Her voice caught in her throat as she gasped at his reply. "You're jesting."

"No. It's more than thirty miles to Hill City. We have a loaded wagon and four cows. In fact, as slow as we're traveling, we'll be fortunate if we're there by tomorrow."

"Then move more rapidly. I don't want to sleep out here," she said, waving at the expansive prairie that surrounded them.

"It's impossible to complete the journey today. We'll be out at least one night, Macia. As for tomorrow, time will tell. With our frequent stops to keep the cows moving, it's bound to take much longer than I anticipated."

Once again she waved and hollered to Mr. Wilson. "You need to keep those cows moving," she admonished as he reined his horse alongside the wagon. "They're straying and slowing us down. Make your horse do something to keep the cows moving."

Mr. Wilson laughed at her command and patted the gun holstered at his hip. "I was hired to direct you to Hill City and protect you, if need be. If you want those cows kept together, you get down and do it yourself."

Her face turned bright red, and she glared at Mr. Wilson's back as he resumed his position ahead of their wagon. "Aren't you going to make him move those cows along, Father?"

He shrugged. "He's right. I hired him for protection and to lead us to Hill City. I don't think a few coins will convince him to herd the cattle."

"Stop the wagon and give me a stick! I'll do it myself." Macia jumped down, and with the use of threatening yelps and an occasional slap to one of the cows' rumps, she managed to force the animals into a somewhat consistent pace throughout the afternoon.

Her only satisfaction was Thurlow Wilson's look of surprise when she began to herd the wayward cows. The hours passed in slow monotony until at last the countryside unfolded into the grandeur of a rose-tinged prairie twilight. Macia sighed in relief as they approached a small meandering creek, toward which she and the cows began to move with well-defined purpose. The thirsty animals were anxious to drink their fill, and Macia was eager to soak her blistered, aching feet. By now, one thing was absolutely certain: she detested the lumbering cows as much as the squawking chickens.

Mr. Wilson waved his hat high in the air. "We'll stop here for the night."

Much as she disliked the idea of sleeping outdoors, Macia didn't argue. Her entire body longed for rest, and her throat was sore from shouting at the lumbering cows. She soaked her feet while the animals lapped the water. They would need no encouragement to drink or graze this night. While her father unhitched the horses, Harvey gathered wood from near the creek, and though Mr. Wilson laid and started the fire, he did little else except care for his horse.

A short time later the smoky aroma of frying bacon filled Macia's nostrils. Although she would not admit it aloud, she was thankful her father had insisted upon stopping to purchase the bacon, ham, and eggs from a farmer outside Ellis who had been recommended by Mr. Hepple.

Her mother turned away from the fire and gestured with a fork. "Dry off your feet, put on your shoes and stockings, and unpack some of those eggs. They're packed in straw in a small crate near the back of the wagon, so be careful as you work. We don't want to break any," she warned.

Unwilling to force her swollen feet back into the shoes, Macia ignored the first part of her mother's instructions and walked barefoot to the wagon. She carefully unwrapped the eggs and placed them in her bonnet.

"Is this enough?" She held her sunbonnet at arm's length.

Her mother nodded but noticed Macia's bare feet. "You should wear your shoes, Macia. You'll step on a nettle or a sharp stone."

"Or a snake," Harvey added.

Macia glared at him as she hobbled off, anxious to sit down again. Her father hunkered down beside her and examined her feet. "You shouldn't scowl—it causes wrinkles. Why are you so annoyed at Harvey?"

"Because he sat in the buggy all day. Perhaps I should drive the buggy tomorrow and he can herd the cows. We'll then see how much he likes his new life."

"We could try that," her father agreed.

"Truly? You'll actually make Harvey herd the cows? And I can drive the buggy?"

"If that will make you happy."

She hesitated. "It won't make me happy to be here, for I will never be happy to live in this desolate place, but it will at least make the day more bearable."

She continued rubbing her feet as her father strode off toward the buggy. Moments later he returned with a small jar of ointment. "Try rubbing this on your blisters. It will help."

She dipped her finger into the salve. "Where will you and Harvey sleep?"

"We'll sleep near the fire with Mr. Wilson so we can hear if anyone approaches. Mr. Wilson warned that there could be horse thieves lurking about. He's going to hobble the animals for the night. We don't want to take any chances."

"Horse thieves? We've seen only two other riders and one wagon all day. And they were both anxious to return east."

"Perhaps. But Mr. Wilson says sometimes riders scour the countryside watching for settlers they judge to be easy prey. He tells me a team of horses is worth its weight in gold out here on the prairie. Now, let's go have our supper." He offered his hand and helped her up.

Macia hobbled alongside her father, remembering Mr. Wilson's refusal to help with the cows earlier in the day. "I think Mr. Wilson is likely spinning tales in order to make you believe he is truly worthy of the money you've paid him."

Her father smiled, but he didn't acknowledge she might be correct. And though the hired man had done little around camp, Macia was quick to note he was first in line for supper. The simple fare of bacon and eggs tasted better to Macia than anything she'd eaten in ages—including the fancy farewell meal she'd been served at the Kincaid home the evening before they departed Georgetown. Even the coarse rye bread spread with butter that her mother had purchased from Mrs. Hepple tasted better than the buttermilk biscuits prepared at home by their old cook.

It had grown dark by the time Macia washed the dishes in the creek water and dried them with an old linen towel. She hooked the wet towel onto a nail at the rear of the wagon before crawling inside and wedging herself into the small space beside her mother.

"How will we ever survive this ordeal, Mother?" she whispered.

"I don't know, but we will. God will protect us."

Macia stared upward. The star-filled sky was hidden by the rough piece of canvas that covered the wagon. She was at least thankful she wasn't forced to sleep on the ground like Harvey and her father. Soon her mother's soft snores mingled with the hoots of owls perched in the cottonwoods along the creek. A coyote howled in the distance, and she wondered if her father and Harvey feared for their lives or trusted that Mr. Wilson would protect them. She pictured wild animals circling their wagon, slinking low with their stealthy bodies blending into the shadowy darkness that surrounded them, and wondered if they could jump inside the wagon. The thought of being attacked by one of the drooling fang-toothed animals caused her to shudder. With a quick yank, she pulled the blanket until it covered her head. Her lips quivered as she prayed they would all be alive come morning. If God truly wanted their family to survive in this barren land, He surely had His work cut out for Him!

Weary from a full day of travel with no more than a brief stop at a settler's dugout, Macia shaded her eyes and gazed across the plains. Now void of its lush springtime greenery and occasional summer blooms, the prairie had cloaked itself in the dull shades of ecru and brown—a sign that winter would soon be upon them.

Macia shifted her weight. She was tired from sitting in the buggy, although she was certain that Harvey would gladly exchange places with her. As the day had worn on, her mother had become quiet and withdrawn, and Macia wondered what she must be thinking.

"At least we won't be forced to live in one of those awful dugout dwellings we saw near that last creek," Macia commented.

Her mother merely nodded as the buggy jostled along the rutted path. She sat up straighter and stared to the west. "That must be it."

"Where?" Macia asked. "I don't see anything."

Her mother pointed. "There! Near that ridge!"

Macia reined in the horses until the wagon had come alongside them. "Is *that* it, Father? Is *that* Hill City?"

Before he could answer, Mr. Wilson hollered over his shoulder and announced Hill City was in the distance. "I'm going to ride ahead to the livery. I'll meet you there." And with that, he spurred his horse to a trot.

A broad smile curved her father's lips, and Macia wondered how he could be happy. From what she could see, there was little cause for joy. In fact, there didn't appear to be much of anything except a few houses and several sad-looking buildings that appeared as if they might be part house, part shop. Surely this couldn't be the town.

"Perhaps Mr. Wilson has never been here before. Perhaps we've turned the wrong direction." *Please don't let this be our final destination.*

Her father jumped down from the wagon and surveyed their surroundings as a woman with a child resting on one hip stepped outside a small soddy. "Welcome!"

Without waiting for her father to take charge, Macia greeted the woman and said, "We're looking for Hill City."

"You've found it. This is Hill City." She turned away and directed her attention to Macia's father. "Are you the new doctor?"

"Indeed," he replied.

"I been watching after your place ever since Mr. Hepple brought your furniture up here last week. Feeding the pigs, too." She tilted her head at the crates of chickens tied to the sides of the wagon. "He should've brought the chickens when he brung the pigs. I would have been glad to take care of 'em for you."

"That's very kind of you. I'm Dr. Samuel Boyle, and this is my wife, Margaret, and daughter, Macia," he said while helping them down from the wagon. "And that's Harvey back there with the cows."

"I'm Betsy Turnbull. My husband Levi's gone to help the Bentleys. They got a place about five miles to the north—problems with a young'un that was bit by a skunk. You folks have come well prepared. Not like the rest of us." There was a forlorn look in her eyes.

Macia truly did not want to stand around conversing. She was anxious to get settled into her own room as soon as possible. "Do you know where our house is located?"

The girl gave her a queer look and pointed down the street. "Why, that's it right there. The only wood house anywhere nearby—unless you count the few made of logs. Ain't many of those, either—not many trees in this part of the country."

Macia watched her father and was certain he was guarding his reaction. No doubt he was as stupefied by this place as the rest of them. And yet he said nothing. When she could bear the silence no longer, Macia addressed Betsy Turnbull. "That *can't* be the house. Mr. Hill told my father the house was a grand two-story home with spacious rooms—more modern and lovely than any home in these parts."

Betsy bobbed her head up and down with enthusiasm. "And it *is*! Why, you have wood floors and glass windows, and there's a sod barn out back for your animals. That barn is bigger than my house. And your furniture will look ever so grand once you get it all arranged. Mr. Hepple said he placed all of it in the parlor and dining room, and I'd be proud to help you."

"How kind you are," Mrs. Boyle said. "And what a sweet little girl. Your first?"

"My third. The other two died shortly after birth, but Sarah's a healthy little girl." The baby grinned in spite of the flea bites that covered her chubby arms and legs.

Seemingly not knowing how to respond to Betsy's sad revelation, Mrs. Boyle turned to her husband. "I suppose we should go and take a look inside the house."

"You folks gonna want to take over the post office duties? Me and Levi's been doing it since Doc Smith's widow left town, but Levi said not to count on the money 'cause you folks would likely want the extra income for yourselves." The weight of poverty was obvious in her tone.

"If you and Levi want to continue with the post office duties, I'm certain you'll hear no complaints from anyone in my family," Dr. Boyle replied kindly. "Why don't you come along with us and you can tell us about your life here in Hill City."

Betsy appeared overjoyed by the invitation and headed down the street alongside

Macia. "I suppose you grow lonely out here, don't you?" Macia asked.

"Sometimes, but the town's building up, and there's usually folks around if I want some company. Ain't like the Bentleys—living so far out with no one around for miles and miles."

Macia didn't argue, though she wondered how this woman could possibly remain optimistic: she lived in a flea-ridden soddy, had endured the death of two babies, and was clothed in a tattered calico dress. "So you're happy living in Hill City?"

"Why, of course. Who wouldn't be? Levi's got a quarter section of land near the river, and we've had some decent crops the past two years. And now it appears I get to keep tending the post office duties. You'll like it fine once you get used to it. Winters get mighty cold and the summers are hot, but this here is fine country."

Macia gave the woman a pitying smile. There was little doubt Betsy Turnbull was completely daft—obviously driven insane by the uncivilized surroundings.

CHAPTER

14

Nicodemus, Kansas • October 1877

The hours of daylight on the prairie decreased as fall set in, and most of those hours were filled with a continuous wearying labor. And though the digging and lifting, the hauling dirt and cutting sod required enormous physical stamina, none of it required much intellect. As his body toiled, Thomas found himself lost in his own private thoughts—rehashing the decisions he'd made in early September. Should he have left Nicodemus back when those first settlers had grown angry with him over his late return from Ellis? And should he have struck a bargain with Ezekiel Harban? Both could have proven to be dangerous choices—and still could!—for a man unwilling to divulge his past.

There had been opportunities—he could have joined up with one of those wagon trains that had passed through. Not that he was looking to find anything more than what he'd already found in Nicodemus. Truth be told, he wasn't looking to *find* anything. Instead, he wanted to lose himself among this small group of settlers, to fit in as snugly as a hand fits into a glove. So comfortably that no one would ever guess he wasn't one of them.

But it didn't appear as if his acceptance would come easily, for as time marched on, Charles Francis made it abundantly clear he would oppose Thomas at every turn. Charles approached each task as a competition. If Thomas borrowed Herman Kemble's shotgun and returned with a jackrabbit, Charles remained on the prairie until he could bring back two. When Thomas returned with two birds and a snake, Charles stayed out until he came back to camp with three birds and two prairie dogs.

Though Ezekiel had earlier admonished

Charles for his childish behavior, the older man now appeared somewhat amused by the antics; occasionally, he would even encourage the competitive behavior. Thomas had spent many hours weighing out Ezekiel's change of attitude. And after much thought, he had decided the older man was using the competition as a means to evaluate Charles and his ability to suitably provide for Jarena—testing the young man's mettle before consenting to their marriage. This moment of clarity had come to Thomas only two days earlier. That was when Thomas had reentered the competition. Although he wasn't vying for Jarena's hand, he had decided he would assist Ezekiel anyway. After all, he, too, wanted to be certain Charles was a worthy choice for Jarena. At least that's what he told himself.

"Gettin' colder every day," Ezekiel said as he stepped outside and leaned down to warm his hands over the fire he'd kindled early that morning. He and Thomas would continue to work on the sod brick extension to their dugout this morning, and if bad weather would hold off just a little longer, they'd be done by the time winter was upon them.

"But we's made good progress," Thomas replied. "If Charles keeps helpin', we be done in no time." He gave the older man a sidelong glance.

"I don' think Charles cottons to the idea that you gets to be around Jarena all the time. He still thinks it'd be more fittin' if you went and lived with a couple of them other single men."

"Guess he needs to remember it was *you* what struck this bargain for me to live with you and your fambly."

Ezekiel gave him a toothy grin. "Oh, he knows that—don't change his thinkin' none, though. He tol' me last night he'd be over here to hep today. Think he's worried Jarena will see we can get along without 'im."

Thomas nodded and decided he wouldn't object to Charles's assistance today. Moving the sod bricks from the field to Ezekiel's dugout was heavy, tiresome work, and he would encourage Charles to help him. "I's goin' on over to the field. Tell Charles ya've noticed I've been deliverin' six sod bricks at one time." Thomas hoped Charles would accept the challenge.

"Charles ain't built quite so sturdy as you—don' think he'll be able to tote six of 'em at one time. But he did fetch a big load of buffalo chips jest yesterday. Said he didn' want Jarena gettin' cold this winter. Course, I don' think one load's gonna be enough to keep us warm all winter." There was a gleam in the older man's eye as he mentioned the load of buffalo chips.

"So you're thinkin' if I go out and fetch two loads, Charles'll go back out and haul even more."

"Could be." Ezekiel leaned down to pick up one of the sod bricks.

Thomas spied Charles walking toward them a few moments later.

"These things is *mighty* heavy," Ezekiel commented as the young man approached. Thomas detected a hint of a smile as Ezekiel massaged his lower back.

Charles dropped the hand barrow to the ground and rushed forward. "Let me help you, Mr. Harban."

"Why, thank ya, Charles. I was thinkin' maybe you could haul some dirt in that barrow of yours and help me ta fill in between these sod bricks—unless you'd rather go out to the field and fetch more bricks. Thomas has been hauling 'em the last few days, and I gotta admit he's doin' a mighty fine job."

Just then, Jarena appeared from inside the cave-like dugout with a basket of laundry. "I'm going down to the river and fetch water. Thought I'd wash some clothes since you've already got a good fire going."

Charles nearly fell over his feet as he hastened to pick up the two buckets sitting beside the entrance to the dugout. "I'd be pleased to fetch the water for you."

Ezekiel frowned at the young man's offer. "I thought you was gonna help with the sod bricks. Jarena's able to carry a couple buckets of water from the river. And so are the twins! Where are they, anyhow?" Deep creases furrowed Ezekiel's weathered forehead. There was little doubt that he was unhappy to lose Charles's assistance. Before Thomas could say a word, Ezekiel turned a steely gaze in his direction. "Don't *you* even think of offering to go after water. We got more important things to do 'round here."

While Thomas carted the heavy pads of soil throughout the morning, Charles remained at the dugout. And although Charles had indicated a preference for helping pack dirt between the sod bricks,

Thomas noted he was spending more time near Jarena and the boiling kettle of clothes than working at the dugout.

Thomas grunted as he unloaded another pile of sod bricks in front of the dugout. "Don't appear like you're gettin' much help from Charles—might do better to have him work farther away from Jarena."

Ezekiel smiled slyly. "You jest might be right on that account. Charles! Why don' you get on out to that field and pick up some more bricks. Thomas is gonna stay and help me pack dirt. Believe his back's getting the best of him. You's likely stronger than him."

Charles whispered something to Jarena before grabbing the handles of the wheelbarrow. "Never was any doubt in my mind that I'm stronger than him." He directed a look of disdain at Thomas as he rushed off to prove his point.

But Thomas didn't nibble at the bait. Instead of hurrying off to compete with Charles, he moved toward Jarena with a self-satisfied grin, pleased with the recent turn of events. "Anything I can help you with?"

Jarena gave him a surprisingly sweet

smile as she looked up at him from beneath her thick dark lashes. "If you wouldn't mind stirring the clothes for a short time"—she pushed the wooden paddle in his direction—"my arms are growing mighty weary."

Her hand brushed across his arm, and the pleasure of her touch surprised him. He looked at her and wondered if she had sensed the same delight. But she avoided his eyes, and soon his vision was completely blurred by the steam that rose from the kettle and mingled with the crisp autumn air. While he stirred the boiling water, Thomas surveyed the small community. It consisted of nothing more than burrowed-out dugouts furnished with the rudimentary belongings the settlers had been able to bring with them or had pieced together since their arrival. To the distant traveler, the smoke curling from atop the scattered hillocks was the only evidence a town existed. Thomas wondered how long it would be until Nicodemus actually looked like the town that had been promised to the settlers.

Jarena plunged several pairs of work pants into the water, causing a foggy barrier to momentarily divide them. "Why is it you avoid my questions about your past, Thomas?"

He tensed at her question, thankful she couldn't see him through the misty vapor. After exhaling a long breath, he struggled to relax his rigid features. "You exaggerate. I don' avoid yer questions. I don' have nothin' to tell. My family is dead, and I don' like to talk about them. Even you've said it's hard to talk about your mammy since her death."

His words appeared to give her momentary pause, but still she persisted. "You could at least tell me where you call home. You know we're from Kentucky, and I have little difficulty speaking of my home."

Why did she keep pressing him for information? He glanced at the field, where Charles was loading bricks. Was Charles encouraging Jarena to ask these questions? Was he hoping to plant seeds of doubt in Jarena's mind in order to gain an advantage—hoping she would mistrust Thomas and think he wasn't worthy of her affection? For a moment he wanted to rush to the field and confront Charles Francis. Yet he knew Charles was right. He didn't deserve a girl like Jarena. He didn't deserve *any* girl. In fact, he was lucky to be alive. Pursuing Jarena was pure foolishness that would only put her in harm's way.

He clenched his hands into two tight knots. "There's nothin' I wanna talk about!"

Her eyes widened and she appeared hurt by his angry outburst, but he didn't apologize. Instead, he strode off without looking back. Better that she think him rude and abrasive now than someday suffer the pain of losing another loved one.

CHAPTER

15

Hill City, Kansas • October 1877

Macia bent over one of the many open trunks in the dining room and ruffled through the stacked blankets and clothing. Finally, she touched upon a piece of stitched cotton fabric. Her quilt! She pulled on the cloth as a knock sounded at the front door.

The metal hasp scraped her head as she jumped to attention. "Ouch!"

Rubbing her scalp, she hurried toward the door, completely forgetting the assorted warped floorboards throughout the house—until the toe of her leather slipper wedged beneath one of the misshapen planks and caused her to stumble. Macia flapped her arms like a goose taking flight as she attempted to reach the front door in an upright position.

She kicked at yet another bent floorboard before yanking on the doorknob. There before her stood Betsy Turnbull, jostling baby Sarah on one hip, and an unkempt man standing close by her side.

"Good morning. Hope you folks slept well. Me and Levi thought we'd come by and see if there's anything we can help ya with." The baby was bouncing up and down at such a feverish pitch that Macia marveled when the child didn't protest. Truth be told, Macia thought the action appeared more suited to churning butter than comforting a child.

Betsy's cheerfulness was as annoying as the puckered floorboards, and Macia breathed a sigh of relief when she heard her father approach. She stepped aside and flicked her hand as though shooing a fly toward the open door. "The Turnbulls wondered if you would like some help setting *your* new home aright."

Macia winced as her father invited the eager neighbors inside. The thought of being forced to entertain Betsy Turnbull at this early hour—or at any time of day, for that matter—was daunting. During their encounter yesterday, Macia had furtively scrutinized Betsy's hygiene and personal appearance, and the woman appeared no better today. Her clothing remained rumpled, her fingernails were encrusted with dirt, and her hair hadn't been properly combed and styled for much too long. As for her husband and child—well, they were equally disheveled. Furthermore, Betsy Turnbull was altogether too cheery, particularly for the morning hours.

Macia quietly made her way back into the oddly shaped room her mother had designated as the dining room and began unwrapping the china, carefully wiping each piece before placing it in the walnut buffet.

The sound of footsteps drew near, but Macia remained silent and pretended she was still alone in the room. Betsy leaned closer, refusing to be ignored. "Mighty nice having wood floors, ain't it? I can tell ya from experience that getting rid of fleas when ya have dirt floors is near impossible.

And you're fortunate to have a cellar—helps keep the critters out."

"These are a poor excuse for floors—there's not one room where they're not completely warped. A person can't walk through this house without tripping."

Betsy nodded. "Cottonwood. Ain't no way to keep it from warping. Doc Smith's widow was gonna put down pine floors, but when he died, she changed her mind and decided to get rid of the place and move back east to be near her family."

"Little wonder," Macia muttered, keeping her back to the intruders. She wished they'd move on and leave her to her thoughts.

"You want me to help you unpack those trunks?"

Macia directed a pleading look at her father. "No. I'm fine. Perhaps my mother could use some assistance in the kitchen."

"Indeed," Samuel said, taking his daughter's cue, "let's step into the kitchen."

Macia sighed as she listened to introductions and then heard her mother offer the visitors a cup of tea. Of course, the Turnbulls eagerly accepted. Above the sounds of her mother preparing tea, Macia heard her father inquiring about the young boy with a skunk bite. A strange curiosity caused Macia to rise and move closer to the doorway.

"A sad thing to watch," Levi Turnbull said. "The boy was out in the woods hunting and got hisself bit by a skunk a while back. His folks was terrible worried—even took him on the train to see a doctor in Kansas City. The doc said he'd be fine, but a few hours after they got home, he commenced to having spasms. No need to go into all the horror of what that boy and his folks went through, but that's sure enough a terrible way to die. We buried the boy last evening."

"A mad stone would have done him more good than a trip to some Kansas City doctor. He'd probably be right as rain if they woulda jest bought a stone instead of spendin' good money on them doctors. No offense, Dr. Boyle," Betsy quickly added.

"*Whatever* is a mad stone, my dear?" Macia's mother asked.

Macia peeked around the corner just enough to see that Betsy appeared astonished by the question. "It's a hard clump of matted hair and mucus—comes from the belly of an animal," Betsy explained. "Only thing is, the stone's gotta be big enough to cover the whole wound. When you get one that's the right size, they work real good—least most of the time. Right, Levi?"

Levi glanced at Mrs. Boyle, whose complexion had faded to the shade of pie dough. "Ain't no need saying what shoulda been, Betsy. They lost their boy, and they're suffering hard for it."

Macia didn't hear Betsy's reply. She couldn't bear listening to any more of the fearsome tale. Her mind roiled with thoughts of the lad thrashing about uncontrollably as seizures slowly conquered his body and mind. She wished the Turnbulls would quit talking—better yet, she wished they would go home.

Macia finished unpacking a crate of china and had begun to empty one of the many trunks deposited in the parlor when her parents, along with Harvey and the Turnbulls, besieged her.

Her father called from the dining room. "Come along, Macia. Levi and Betsy have graciously agreed to take us through town and introduce us to all of our neighbors."

She continued unpacking the trunk, her gaze fixed upon the blankets and tablecloths as though they were spun of gold.

"You go on without me. I prefer to remain here."

Her father approached her and touched her shoulder. Macia twisted her head and saw the determination in his eyes when he said, "I insist."

She knew that look and tone of voice. It would do no good to argue. She grabbed her bonnet from a peg in the hallway, once again tripping before she reached the front door. How had the rest of them managed to avoid that irksome floorboard?

Macia hiked her skirt off the ground and marched down the dusty street behind the others. How long had it been since rain had fallen in this desolate place? Each time she opened her mouth, the unremitting wind coated her tongue with a layer of grit. She tugged at the brim of her bonnet, caring little that the hat was now tilted at an unseemly angle. In fact, her chapeau more closely resembled a mask than a hat, but so long as it protected her eyes, she cared little. She suddenly wondered if this need to survive the elements had caused the demise of what Betsy Turnbull had once been. Worse yet, was it a precursor of what she would soon become? Macia shivered at the thought.

Harvey took her arm. "Are you cold?"

She tipped the brim of her hat just enough to meet his inquiring gaze. "My trembling has nothing to do with cold weather; it's this place. What is Father thinking?"

"We can only hope Mother will convince him that he's made a mistake," he said, bending his head against the wind. "I'd even be willing to live up north. Anything other than remaining here."

Macia grasped her brother's arm. "Perhaps *that's* his plan. He's brought us out here so that we'll be pleased to move to Massachusetts or Pennsylvania or one of those other northern states. Oh, I do hope I'm right, Harvey, for even if Northerners are inhospitable and lacking in gentility, we could adjust. I fear we will perish out here. Even God has forsaken this desolate land."

"Here we are," Betsy said as they came to a halt in front of a small frame building. "We have only a few businesses, but each one is constructed of either wood or stone."

She made the statement with obvious pride as she led them into the general store operated by Mr. and Mrs. Johnson. The shelves held few supplies, though Mrs. Johnson was quick to advise another shipment would soon arrive. Macia certainly hoped so. There was little on any of the shelves, and certainly nothing she would ever purchase.

"And this was Mr. Jacoby's newspaper office. But he died and his widow returned to Ohio. And this here's the Kramer place," Betsy said as they started toward the next establishment. "As you can see, it's a soddy. They live here, too. Mrs. Kramer's a seamstress and he's a tailor, but they mostly farm." She rattled off the information as though she'd been charged with leading them on a tour of genuine significance.

Harvey raised an eyebrow. "Appears he'd starve to death if he had to depend upon his tailoring to support himself."

"That's true for everyone living here," Levi said. "I'm a cooper, but I spend more time out in the fields than anywhere. But once the town gets bigger, me and Jeb Malone are gonna throw in together. Jeb's a blacksmith, and we're going to start our own business. Jeb's single."

Harvey poked Macia in the side. "Sounds

as though you're going to have a beau come calling on you before you ever have a chance to miss Jackson Kincaid."

"Maybe Jeb has a sister that would enjoy meeting you," she hissed as they drew near the Kramers' sod house.

Mrs. Boyle stepped between her children and gave them a disapproving frown. "Please stop whispering. It's impolite."

Mrs. Kramer greeted the group and explained that her husband had gone to deliver a new wool suit to the president of the Stockton bank. "He says my Virgil does better tailoring than anyone else in these parts—and he's right. If you ever need a new suit, Dr. Boyle, you come and talk to Virgil. There's no one any better, not even in St. Joe or Kansas City. And I've availed myself of the latest catalogs from *Godey's Lady's Book* and can imitate almost any gown they offer." Her voice was filled with pride.

"We'll bear that in mind. I'm certain my wife and daughter will be availing themselves of your services in the future. Mrs. Turnbull tells us that you're quite a seamstress."

Macia was agape. What had her father

said? In the *future* she might need Mrs. Kramer's services? Macia moved closer to Harvey and grasped his arm. "It sounds as though he's planning on staying."

"He's merely being polite."

Before Macia could refute his comment, her mother stepped between them. "I believe I asked you two to refrain from whispering. Must I treat you as children and keep you separated?"

Macia shook her head. "Sorry, Mother."

Macia knew what was expected of her. After all, southern civility had been daily ingrained in her upbringing. Yet she could not engage in these meaningless exchanges, for she truly did not care whether grasshoppers might eat next year's crops or that the lack of rain this year could affect next year's growth. Quite frankly, Macia cared little if the water level in the river was up or down, or if these people had sufficient food or fuel stored for winter. She toyed with her bonnet ribbons and absently gazed about, wishing they'd return to their house—for even that seemed more appealing than being subjected to this endless drivel.

Levi led them to a small outbuilding that appeared more a shed than a barn or livery.

"This here is where Jeb's doing his smithy work—at least for the time being."

"You folks chose a poor time to be settlin' in," Jeb Malone commented after his introduction to the family.

His eyes lingered on Macia, and she hastily turned her attention toward Harvey, who smirked and cocked one eyebrow while their father hastened to explain they had purchased provisions enough for the winter.

Macia waited patiently until her father had completed his reply and then turned to Jeb Malone. "Have you a sister, Mr. Malone?"

"How did you know? Betsy told you, didn't she?" Jeb grinned at his neighbor.

Macia beamed a satisfied grin at her brother. "No, she didn't mention your sister, but I believe one of my brother's greatest concerns regarding our move to Hill City was the possible absence of single young ladies. Thankfully, you've set our minds at ease."

Jeb rubbed the day's growth of stubble that shadowed his jaw and frowned. "I'm afraid Lucy can't improve that situation for your brother since she's only ten years old, but if you harbor some of those same concerns for yourself, please set your mind at rest. I'd be honored to come calling on you."

Her plan had gone awry. Harvey was grinning like a Cheshire cat, and Betsy Turnbull's jubilant reaction was downright embarrassing. She acted as though they'd announced a wedding date. "Thank you, Mr. Malone, but I've given my heart to another."

He looked disappointed. "You're betrothed?"

"Now, Macia—tell the truth," Harvey said as though instructing a young child to confess. "Jackson Kincaid hasn't asked for your hand. In fact, he didn't even say he'd write to you."

Macia forced a smile and, tilting her head ever so slightly, twisted her heel back and forth with gusto atop Harvey's shoe. "Mr. Kincaid has not asked for my hand, but I have deep feelings for him," she stated while enjoying Harvey's pained countenance.

The color heightened in Jeb's cheeks, and he looked down at his dust-covered boots. "Well, if you ever decide you want to see some of the countryside, or maybe learn to fish, I'll be happy to oblige. I know Lucy would enjoy your company, too. She gets lonely—misses having a woman around to teach her things."

Macia's mother stepped closer to Jeb. "Your parents? Where are *they*?"

He looked off toward the horizon. "Cholera. It's just the two of us."

"How sad for such a young girl to be without her mother's influence. You must send her to our house so we can meet her." Mrs. Boyle patted Jeb's arm as she scanned the barn. Macia wondered if her mother expected young Lucy to suddenly appear from inside one of the stalls or perhaps drop from the hayloft.

"That's kind of you, ma'am. I may do just that. There's little I can teach her when it comes to cooking and sewing."

There was a haunted look in his eyes, and Macia wondered if Jeb was still not over his own grief.

Her mother gave a consoling nod. "Macia enjoys young girls, though I doubt she'd be much help teaching Lucy to cook or sew. She's done little enough of that herself."

Jeb and the Turnbulls rotated toward Macia in unison, their faces filled with astonishment. Obviously they thought her an absolute oddity.

Betsy Turnbull was the first to speak. "You can't cook or sew?"

Macia squared her shoulders like a soldier ready to meet the challenge of battle. "I don't enjoy fancy work, and I've never had a need to cook. Though I imagine I could do so if required."

Harvey doubled over in laughter, and Jeb Malone looked at her as though she were a pitiable excuse for a woman. The entire incident was more than Macia cared to endure. With a quick turn, she stormed outside.

"How *dare* they treat me in such a rude manner?" She stomped her foot on the dusty street and resolutely folded her arms across her chest.

"Who are you talking to?" a small voice inquired.

Macia turned toward the sound and was met by a pair of cornflower blue eyes. Nothing had gone well all day—why should it begin to do so now? There had been nobody in sight when she walked outside. Where had this girl come from?

Macia hesitated for a moment as she stared at the child. "I'm talking to myself. What's your name and where do you live?" she demanded.

"I'm Lucy Malone, and me and my brother live here."

"My brother and *I* live here."

Lucy's eyebrows furrowed as she scowled. "No you don't! This is *our* house."

Macia laughed and nodded. "You're right—it is your house. I was correcting your grammar."

"Oh. Are you a schoolteacher? Jeb said maybe someone would be moving here before long to help me with my lessons. He's not so good at school learning." Wisps of hair had escaped the uneven braids that rested upon Lucy's shoulders, and she tucked the loose strands behind her ears.

"You certainly have pretty hair, Lucy. You should let me help you braid it one day." Before the child had an opportunity to respond, Macia censured herself. What was she thinking? She ought not encourage the child's friendship. If Macia had her way, the entire Boyle family would be gone before winter.

"Oh, that would be lovely. I have some of

my mama's combs. Could you show me how to use them? She wore them when she married my pa."

Lucy's eyes were sparkling like precious gems. Denying her now would be impossible. Lifting one of the braids between her fingers, Macia nodded. "I'll show you how to use hair combs, but let's not use your mother's good ones. You wouldn't want to lose them. I have some you can practice with. Besides, you don't need combs if we braid your hair."

Lucy pursed her lips into a slight pout. "I like to wear it down for Sunday meetings."

"Then I shall find you some of my combs to use on Sundays so that you may save your mother's combs for very special occasions. Would that be agreeable?"

Lucy's reply was cut short as her brother rounded the side of the barn. "There you are, Lucy! I've been worried about you. Where have you been? Didn't I tell you to come directly home from the general store? And where are the parcels you were to pick up? Did you lose the money I sent with you?"

Lucy's pleading look was enough to spur Macia to action. "Stop! If you expect her to answer any of your questions, please cease this barrage and give her a moment to reply, Mr. Malone."

Jeb Malone turned his heated features upon Macia, who caught her breath and took a quick step back. Anger had darkened his blue eyes to the deep purple shade of the iris blooms that dotted her mother's flower garden each spring.

"Please don't interfere, Miss Boyle." Jeb's tall, lean body cast an ominous shadow that seemed to block out the sun. "Where were you, Lucy?"

"I was right here talking to Miss Boyle." The little girl's voice was no more than a whisper. "I'm sorry I disobeyed."

He pulled her close and kissed the top of her disheveled hair. "You know how I worry."

"I know." Lucy wrapped her arms around Jeb and buried her face in his wrinkled shirt.

He held the girl away from him and looked down at her as though no one else were present. "I'm sorry. I spoke in anger. I shouldn't do that."

Lucy grinned and stretched her arms around him. "You're forgiven." She leaned back to look up into his face. "Guess what?"

"What?"

"Miss Boyle's going to teach me how to use combs in my hair so I can fix it just like Mama used to!"

Jeb peered above Lucy's head and held Macia's gaze with his steely blue eyes. There was something in his stare, something she couldn't quite make out, something he intended to convey with that moody look. She glanced away and then turned back. What was it he was trying to tell her? Suddenly she knew. He was flashing a warning. But why?

As they prepared to depart a short time later, Jeb bent his head, his lips nearly touching her ear. "Lucy's already lost too much in her young life. Don't add to her pain by making promises you won't keep."

CHAPTER

16

Nicodemus, Kansas • November 1877

The impassioned prayer meeting ended with a loud chorus of *amens.* Now they would set about making hard choices, for on this cold morning, the residents of Nicodemus had assembled for two reasons: prayer and decisions.

Truth and Grace huddled together on one of the wobbly benches positioned along one wall of the dugout. Truth snuggled closer to her twin, hoping to absorb additional body heat. "Why we gotta stay here? Can't we jest go home?"

Jarena leaned around Grace. "Because I

want to hear what's said, and it won't hurt for the two of you to listen, also. You need to understand how difficult it's going to be for us to make it through the winter. The men are hoping they can come up with a plan."

"Afore we left Kentucky, Pappy said God was gonna provide," Grace said, her eyes filled with a doe-eyed look of innocence. "Don' see what the men need ta discuss."

Jarena couldn't be angry with Grace. Her sweet, soft-spoken nature made it impossible. "That doesn't mean we're not supposed to do our part, too. We need to make plans and take some action on our own. We can't merely sit and wait on God to provide."

"Why not?" Grace's eyebrows knit together in studious contemplation. "God sent manna to the Israelites, didn' He? They didn't do nothin' but complain."

Jarena leaned to the side and hugged her sister. "Yes, He did. But we don't know how many of those Israelites died before they received manna. If our actions can keep anyone from freezing or starving to death, we should do it. Don't you think?"

"That makes sense," Grace said, bobbing

her head up and down. "I'd feel terrible if someone died when I coulda done somethin'. We best stay and hear what we can do to help."

Truth gave her twin an exaggerated frown. "You sho' do shift with the wind, Grace."

"I'm sorry. But this be mo important dan goin' home. We'll still have time ta do something fun later today."

"And what did you have planned for this afternoon, young lady?" Jarena asked Truth.

"I tol' some of the younger kids I'd lead 'em in a game of hide the handkerchief if it ain't too cold out."

"You need to quit playing games and learn responsibility," Jarena asserted. "If you want to go home, I'll give you permission—but not to lead the children in their games. Instead, you must promise to get busy on that basket of mending."

Truth gave her older sister a smug look. "It's Sunday. Mama never did nothin' but cook and read da Bible on Sunday."

"Mama didn't live out here on the prairie, and I'm telling you that if you go home, I'll expect to see a pile of mending completed.

However, you're welcome to stay here with us if you don't want to sew."

"You know I don' like to mend. I always stick myself with the needle." Truth looked at her finger as though she'd already been stuck and was beginning to bleed.

"Not so," Jarena insisted. "That's merely the excuse you use. You can sew a finer row of stitches than either Grace or I. You may have Pappy fooled, but I know you can sew *and* cook. You burn the food or stick yourself with a needle so you won't be required to do either. And don't even begin to defy my words. I figured out your tricks a long time ago."

After a number of the women and all of the small children had exited the dugout, several men who had been listening from outside filed indoors, appearing thankful for a modicum of warmth. The small space was filled to capacity, yet many of their number were still required to brave the cold if they were to hear any of the discussion.

"Listen up, folks!" Jerome Holt stood in the open doorway holding his hat in the air to signal the group. "I say we all move outside. How can we reach an agreement when we can' hear everybody speak?"

Mary Fowler pulled her coat more closely around her shoulders and frowned. "It's too cold to meet outdoors."

Miss Hattie stood up and began walking toward the door. "If I kin put up with a little cold weather, then so kin the rest of ya," she said in her usual challenging manner.

One by one, the group rose to their feet and followed the old woman's lead and then clustered together, trying to avoid the chilly wind. Heavy gray clouds that appeared laden with sleet or snow hung low in the sky as they moved outdoors. Though Thomas assured the twins that it was not yet cold enough for either of those events, the girls maintained a watchful eye and hoped the weather would bring an early conclusion to the meeting.

Jarena stood behind her sisters with Thomas and her father on either side, and Miss Hattie, Nellie, and Calvin close by. Reverend Mason moved to the center of the group and looked about as though unsure where to begin.

"I'm not certain I'm the one to be leadin' this meetin', so if anyone else wants to step forward, I'll be happy to turn over control." He waited a minute, and when no one offered, he continued. "Well, I s'pose the first thing we need to acknowledge is that we's not gonna make it through the winter on the supplies we have. They's jest not gonna last. Even though some of da men have hired out and made some mo money, dere's little work to be found now that winter has begun to set in. There's no denyin' we's in dire straits. Widout supplies, we's gonna die. It's as simple as that."

Miss Hattie thumped her walking stick into the tough buffalo grass, which had lost all of its summer coloration. "Now, dem ain't very comfortin' words, Preacher."

"I'd like to be encouraging, Miss Hattie, but I cain't build false hope. We's all seen with our own eyes what's happenin' out here. There never was the animal life we was promised. With dis cold weather and winter settin' in, the few small animals we been able to hunt is all but disappeared."

"Maybe that's what *we* should do: disappear," Jarena muttered. Miss Hattie's light touch caused Jarena to look in the older woman's direction.

The corners of Miss Hattie's lips curved up slightly, and Jarena detected a hint of sympathy in the old woman's rheumy brown eyes. "You're beginnin' to sound like a bitter ol' lady 'stead of a sweet young woman, Jarena. Don't let dat happen," she cautioned.

"I'll try. Are you feeling poorly, Miss Hattie?"

"No worse'n anyone else my age— course, ain't nobody else my age 'round here, is dere?" She chuckled quietly, and the sparkle returned to her eyes.

"You should be in front of a fire instead of out here in this cold wind," Jarena whispered.

"You got any suggestions 'bout what we oughta do, Preacher?" Jerome Holt asked. "Don't seem to be too many choices."

"Well, some of us what came out wid the second group has been talkin'." The preacher waved toward Wilbur Rawlins. "Wilbur has agreed to go out on behalf of the town and look fer aid. We think it'd be best if he tried to first get some hep from folks in eastern Kansas. We're hopin' when people realize how bad off we is, they be willin' to lend a hand."

Wilbur was well-known to everyone. After all, he was an officer of the town company and had been highly instrumental in bringing the second group of settlers west. Had

Jarena been a member of the second group, those facts alone would have turned her against the man. Yet, for some unknown reason, the group continued to hold him in high esteem—even value his opinions.

The gathering turned their attention to Wilbur, who puffed his chest into a prideful swell. "I'd be honored to go out on behalf of our colony. I believe dis is the only alternative left to us. We's all heard that the Kansas winters can be brutal, and we's jest not prepared to survive without help. I believe the good people of Kansas will be pleased to lend a hand when dey hear of our plight."

"I don' like the idea of beggin' for a handout." The words were shouted by someone near the back of the group.

"There's no shame in askin' for help when it's truly needed," Reverend Mason replied.

"Maybe so, but it don' speak well for our settlement," Jerome Holt remarked. "It's one thing to try to git work from the farmers 'round here, but it's another matter to go to the big cities and ask fer money from strangers."

Wilbur's features pinched into a tight frown. "We're not in no position to let pride stand in our way."

A smattering of *amens* could be heard among the group, and Reverend Mason nodded enthusiastically. "Pride can be a sin, Jerome."

"So kin slothfulness, but I ain't accusin' nobody here of that particular sin," Jerome said while leveling a cold stare at Wilbur. "Ain't fair to be sayin' those that disagree are filled with pride, Preacher. I ain't being prideful when I say I think askin' for help is a mistake—just statin' a fact. An' I got a right to my opinion, too. The ones that should be helpin' us are the town companies that told all their lies."

"Too late for placin' blame. That won't do us no good, either," Ezekiel commented. " 'Sides, Wilbur weren't no better informed than the rest of us, or he woulda come better prepared."

"Or stayed in Georgetown," Jarena added in a whisper.

Ivan Lovejoy edged his way through the crowd. "I disagree with the idea of goin' from town to town lookin' for help. If we gonna get adequate aid, I think we should have a representative go directly to the governor. If we got the governor's endorsement, we could make a plea ta Congress for

assistance. I think if this is properly presented, we could set up a joint plan with
Congress to hep us until we's all self-sufficient."

John Beyer resettled his hat on his head.
"I don' think we oughta be doin' that."

Herman Kemble nodded in agreement as
he moved to stand alongside John Beyer.
"That's right! The last thing we need to be
doin' is gettin' the gov'nor and the Congress involved. They'll be takin' this acreage
away from us, sayin' we ain't fit to own land
iffen we need the government to help us."

"You both need to quit thinkin' like runaway slaves," Ivan Lovejoy said. "Nobody's
gonna take your land away from ya. Just
because we need a little help don't mean
the government is gonna try to remove us."

Herman snorted loudly. "I ain't so sure
you're right on that account. There's plenty
of white settlers that couldn' prove up their
claims—we seen 'em with their wagons
packed up headin' back east. The government didn' come to *their* aid. Why you think
they're gonna be willin' to help *us*?"

" 'Cause we've come here to establish a
whole community. We're not just one or two
homesteaders hopin' to stake a claim.

Won't bode well fer the governor or Kansas if folks get word of a whole town dyin' one winter."

Wilbur raised his hand. "All them that think we're better off findin' support by goin' to the cities and towns and askin' for help rather than goin' to the government, raise your hands."

Ivan flapped his arms up and down. "Put your hands down! We're not ready to make a decision just yet!" He scanned the crowd, pointing to a couple of men who continued to signal their agreement with Wilbur. "I said we're not ready to vote yet."

Herman marched forward and faced off with Lovejoy. "Who are you to say when we're ready to make a decision? Last I knew, we was all equal."

Reverend Mason pushed his way through the crowd and stepped between the two men. "Let's don' lose our tempers and come to blows over dis. We're reasonable men and we's gonna find a practical solution. I say we take a vote in order to see if we need more discussion."

Ivan Lovejoy's hands were rolled into tight fists, and his jaw had begun to twitch. However, he seemed to know he'd lose even more support if he went against the preacher.

"Raise yo' hand if you agree with Wilbur Rawlins." Reverend Mason's lips formed numbers as he silently counted. When he had finished his count, he motioned the people to lower their arms. "Those in favor of Lovejoy's proposal, raise yo' hand."

Jarena watched while the preacher tallied the votes in favor of Mr. Lovejoy. It didn't take long: not many agreed with his position.

Ivan looked disgusted. "This is a mistake."

"Wilbur, I think you should leave t'morrow at first light," Reverend Mason said. "We'll pray you come back wid a full load of supplies."

"We need the wagons and horses. Wilbur oughta take the train," Herman Kemble suggested.

"You got da money for train fare?" someone asked.

Herman kicked his boot at a clump of buffalo grass.

"No need to be hard on yerself," Ezekiel said, patting Herman on the back. "I was thinkin' the very same thing. Kind of frightenin' to let loose of one of our teams and a wagon."

An appreciative smile curved Herman's lips and he nodded. "Guess we gotta take a chance or we'll starve to death fer certain— and that's a terrible hard way to die."

In the gray light of daybreak the next morning, a small group gathered to bid Wilbur farewell and pray for his safety. Ezekiel and Jarena were among those present.

"Things is gonna be jest fine," Ezekiel whispered to his daughter. Wrapping his arm around her narrow shoulders, he looked into her eyes and gave her arm a gentle squeeze. She longed to share his confidence; instead, her heart was filled with apprehension of what lay ahead.

CHAPTER

17

A sharp scream pierced the still countryside and shattered the silent beauty of the bright white snowfall that blanketed the town of Nicodemus. Jarena startled awake and sat up in bed with her eyes opened wide. She held her breath and listened.

"Pappy! Did you hear that?" Her voice was ragged. Trembling, she yanked her blanket up around her neck.

"Coyote," her father mumbled in response.

In his bed across the room, Thomas rolled to his side. "That weren't no coyote. Sounded human to me." His voice was low and filled with worry.

Before Jarena could answer, another shrill cry cracked through the still December night. Thomas jumped up from his pallet and hurried to the makeshift door of their dugout while Jarena waited in her bed. When Thomas said nothing, she wrapped the worn blanket around her shoulders and padded across the cold dirt floor to join him.

"You see anything?" Jarena stood by his side and stared into the mantle of snow shrouding the small community. The stark white coverlet sparkled in the moonlight and shed an unexpected brightness upon the mounded dwellings. She shivered as a blast of frigid air brushed her cheeks with a frosty kiss.

"No, but I'm sure that noise wasn't no animal howlin'. Wait! Look over toward Calvin and Nellie's place. Is the door open?" They waited and watched, straining to see any sign of movement. "It's Calvin. He's comin' outside."

"Miss Hattie ailing?" Jarena called out, her voice carrying on the cold night air like a clanging bell.

Calvin lifted his lantern higher. "That you, Jarena?"

"Yes. Is something wrong over to your place?"

Calvin ran toward them with the lantern

dangling from his hand. "It's Nellie. The baby's comin', and she's havin' trouble."

"What's goin' on?" Ezekiel called from his bed. "A man can't get no sleep in this here place. Close that door—you's lettin' this little bit of heat get outside."

"It's Nellie—she's having the baby, Pappy. Calvin's on his way over here."

Truth sat up in bed and rubbed her eyes. "Why's Jarena and Thomas at the door, Pappy?"

Calvin's eyes were filled with fear as he stomped the snow off his feet. "Sorry for the mess—and for wakin' up everybody, but Nellie's doing poorly and Miss Hattie's plumb wore out. Can you come and spell her for a while, Jarena?"

She flashed a questioning look at her father.

"Jarena don' know nothin' 'bout birthing a child, Calvin. Best to get Mildred Kemble. She's a good midwife. Won't hurt none for Jarena to go along and lend a hand with boiling water and such, if she be needed."

Calvin wrung his hands. "I think having Jarena there would give Nellie some comfort. She's in an awful lot of pain. Miss Hattie said she don' think the baby's turned right."

"Now, don't go borrowin' no trouble. Wait and see what Mildred has to say. She's brought more babies into this world than Miss Hattie has. You get on over to the Kemble place and fetch her back to your dugout. If Mildred can't come, then fetch Caroline Holt. Jarena will be over shortly." There was a calmness to her father's voice that appeared to strengthen Calvin.

Once Calvin was out the door, Grace and Truth settled back under their blankets, and Ezekiel sat on the edge of his narrow bed. "You go over and help out for a while, Jarena. They's likely worryin' when there ain't no cause, but if having you around will ease Nellie a bit, then that's the least you can do fer your friend."

"What about breakfast?"

"Truth and Grace can both cook jest fine. 'Sides, soon as you leave, we're all goin' back to sleep. It'll be at least an hour 'til sunup."

Jarena pulled an old blanket along the rope that separated her bed from the men and quickly donned her dress and stockings before pulling on her worn leather shoes. She hastily pulled the blanket down from the rope and tucked it across her lumpy bed, all the time hoping Nellie wasn't suffering overly much. Her stomach lurched at the thought.

Her father laced his fingers together. "You want me to walk ya over dere?"

He hadn't made a move to get into his boots or coat. Jarena's lips formed a gentle smile. Although it was far from warm in their dugout, she knew her father didn't want to venture out into the frosty night air. It wasn't far to the Harris dugout, and the moonlight would radiate light off the snow to brighten her path. "You go on back to sleep, Pappy; you too, Thomas. I can see just fine. There's no need for anyone else to get out in this cold."

"Tell Nellie we be prayin' for her," her father said.

Jarena shrugged into her coat and grabbed a folded blanket from the foot of the bed before brushing her father's cheek with a kiss. "I'll tell her."

As she walked across the crusted snow, Jarena wondered if her father's prayers would do any more for Nellie than they had done for her mother when she lay dying. Another scream disturbed the nighttime silence. She quickened her pace. If they had still been living in Georgetown, Nellie would have had a doctor available. But out in this wilderness, there would be no one but a midwife and God. And Jarena wasn't certain He would be paying attention.

She knocked on the wobbly door and then pushed it open without waiting. Nellie's moans filled the one-room dugout, and Jarena's pulse quickened as she glanced about. Miss Hattie was sitting on her bed while Calvin paced back and forth in front of her. Mildred Kemble had arrived and was sitting on a wooden box beside Nellie and Calvin's bed.

Jarena hung her coat on a peg inside the door and hastily stomped the snow from her shoes. "How's she doing?" she whispered to Miss Hattie. Her friend's eyes were closed and her moans had stopped.

Miss Hattie crooked her finger, and Jarena went and sat down beside the old woman. "Mildred jest checked Nellie, and she says the baby ain't turned right. She's gonna try and force it around, but it'll be painful—least that's what Mildred said."

Jarena gave an involuntary shudder and then leaned closer to Miss Hattie. "How's she going to do that?"

"Don' know. Sounds as though she's gonna do some kind of twisting on her belly. She said Nellie needs to stay relaxed while she works on her. From what she said, I don' think Mildred's had much luck with it in the past, but she's gotta try somethin'."

Mildred motioned to Jarena. "Come on over here, gal. You talk to Nellie and try to keep her calm while I set to workin' on her."

Jarena truly didn't want to be nearby while the woman inflicted pain upon her friend, but she did as she was told.

Mrs. Kemble stood up and pointed to the box where she'd been sitting. "Go ahead and sit down there. Hold her hand and talk to her for a few minutes."

Jarena appraised Mrs. Kemble, uncertain whether she wanted to play a role in the older woman's ministrations. "You won't hurt her, will you?"

"Jest do as you're told," Mildred sternly replied.

For what seemed an eternity, Jarena sat

beside Nellie babbling about the cold weather and the celebration they'd had when Thomas had killed a jackrabbit a few days earlier. "That rabbit was the first meat we've had in a long time, and I boiled the bones for soup. I'm going to bring some over for you later today."

Mrs. Kemble placed her hands on Nellie's swollen belly and began her attempt to turn the baby. Nellie screamed, arched her back, and then grasped Jarena's hand with such force she was certain her fingers must be broken.

"Try to calm her! She needs to relax!" Mrs. Kemble hollered above Nellie's piercing squeal.

"How's she supposed to relax when you're hurting her?" Jarena shouted in return. Calvin took his pacing straight out the door. Obviously, he could endure the cold weather more easily than watching his wife suffer any longer.

The older woman ignored Jarena's question as easily as she ignored Nellie's plaintive cries. While Jarena kept her gaze focused upon Nellie's contorted face, Mrs. Kemble continued twisting and manipulating Nellie's belly. Jarena tried everything she could think of, but nothing seemed to ease the pain.

A rush of cold air signaled Calvin's return. "You've gotta stop—she can't take no more of dis."

Mrs. Kemble nodded in agreement. "You's right. I don' think I moved the baby much, and she needs to save her energy for when da pain gets worse."

Nellie's eyes fluttered open. "*Worse!* It's gonna get *worse*?"

"She's just talking, Nellie. Nobody can feel your pain, so there's no way of knowing whether it will get any worse, but it sure isn't going to do any good to worry." Jarena tried hard to believe her own words. "Try to relax before the next pain comes. I'm going to run back over to the dugout and tell one of the twins to heat up some soup for you. You need to eat something that will give you some strength."

Jarena looked at Mrs. Kemble for some sign of reassurance, but the older woman had already moved away from the bed and was slipping into her coat. "I'll be back after I see to a few chores at home. Gotta make sure my young'uns is fed, and it don't look like Nellie's gonna be givin' birth any time soon."

"What about Mrs. Holt? Do you think she'd have some advice?" Jarena asked before Mrs. Kemble could escape.

There was no doubt the suggestion offended Mrs. Kemble. "Caroline ain't been midwifin' anywhere near as long as me. Next best thing to me is gonna be a doctor, and I ain't seen one of them wanderin' about this town, have you?"

Jarena wagged her head back and forth. "I didn't mean to insult you, Mrs. Kemble. I'm just worried about Nellie."

"Truth! Grace! I need to take some soup to Nellie," Jarena called out the minute she entered the dugout. "Can you heat up some of that soup we were planning for the noon-day meal?"

Grace's eyes shone with excitement. "Did she have a boy or a girl?"

"Neither—she's not given birth yet."

The twins looked disappointed. "I'll set the soup over da fire," Truth said, "but it'll be some time afore it's hot enough for eatin'."

Jarena grasped her sister's hand. "If you put some in the small pan, it will heat faster and then I can get back right away." She grabbed a small pot and handed it to her sister before turning her attention to her father. "Things aren't going well, and Mrs. Kemble hasn't been able to get the baby turned. She said the best thing would be a doctor. I'm afraid Nellie's going to die, Pappy. She's in terrible pain, and I don't know how long she can go on like this. On the way home, Mrs. Kemble said if the baby didn't turn, it would die."

Ezekiel rubbed the stubble that covered his jaw. "There's a doctor in Hill City—leastwise that's what Mr. Hepple tol' me when I was down in Ellis. Sounds as though I oughtta take the horse and see if I can make it over dere."

Shaking her head, Jarena sat down opposite her father. "It's begun to snow again, Pappy. I don't know if you should go. What would we do if something happened to you?"

"I'll go," Thomas volunteered. Everyone turned toward him as he entered the dugout. "Only thing I'm worried about is takin' a horse with me. If something should happen and we'd lose another horse . . . S'pose we oughtta see how folks will feel about that?" There was a hint of fear in Thomas's voice.

"I ain't gonna waste time tryin' to get everyone's agreement," Ezekiel said. "You best dress as warm as you kin. You'll be lucky if you can make it by nightfall in these conditions. Jest keep yourself headed due west. You best eat a good meal and take along some of dat cornpone afore you leave—and stop by the Harris place. Tell Calvin you're goin' to fetch the doctor and that you need to borrow his shotgun."

A short time later Jarena lifted the small pan of soup from the fire and then walked alongside Thomas toward the Harris dugout. "Have you been in snowstorms like this before?" she asked, her teeth chattering from the cold.

"I spent one winter in Massachusetts 'fore headin' west the nex' spring. It's mighty cold up north, and they have more'n their share of snow in dem parts."

"Did you go there when you were very young?"

He stopped in his tracks. "I don' like

talkin' about my past. Ain't nothing there I wanna remember."

"Not even your mammy and pappy?"

He frowned. "No, Jarena, not even them. They's dead and gone. In a better place than this—least that's what dey believed."

"You don't believe in heaven or that you'll see them again—when you die?"

"I'm not sure." He shrugged. "I don' spend much time worryin' 'bout death. Figure when it's my time, I'll die, and iffen dere's a heaven, maybe I'll be good enough to get in."

"Fortunately for all of us, being good isn't how we gain entry into heaven. If that were the case, no one would ever get in—we could never be good enough to deserve an eternity in heaven. You know that, don't you? The Bible tells us the only way into heaven is by accepting Christ as our personal Savior. Have you done that, Thomas? Accepted Jesus as your personal Savior?"

Silence.

"Thomas? Did you hear me?"

He grasped her elbow and hurried her along. "It's too cold to be standin' out here talkin' 'bout the hereafter. Let's get inside." His evasive words formed frosty plumes that hung between them like a frozen obstacle.

Long after Thomas departed for Hill City, Nellie remained in a sleep induced by the laudanum Mildred had given her. Miss Hattie dozed in the old rocking chair—the one piece of furniture she'd insisted upon bringing to Nicodemus. With the two women sleeping, Calvin mumbled his thanks to Jarena and made a hasty departure to check the traps he had set the previous day. He'd said he was certain he would return with a rabbit or squirrel—or perhaps a prairie chicken—so he should go check before the snow got any worse. Although Jarena didn't share Calvin's confidence, escaping the dugout for a brief time might ease his worries, and so she had smiled and agreed.

Jarena covered Nellie with an extra blanket before she moved a chair closer to the fireplace. She stared into the flames and considered the last six months of her life. It seemed years since they'd left Georgetown. Could it truly be only five months ago that the four of them had boarded the train for Topeka? On the one hand, so much had happened; on the other, so very little.

The Christmas holiday would soon be evident in the Georgetown stores, where the merchants would be displaying their latest wares. Mr. Finnery at the general store would be telling all who ventured inside of the fruits, nuts, and special candies that were arriving for the holiday celebrations throughout the town. The preacher would be speaking of Christ's birth, and there would be a palpable sense of excitement and joy during church services.

Jarena cast a casual glance around the Harris dugout and knew she'd not experience such pleasure this Christmas. Though their life as sharecroppers had been sparse and their Christmas holidays lean, they'd always had a fine dinner with at least a piece of fruit and perhaps a new hair ribbon or pair of gloves. This Christmas there would be no fine dinner. They'd not be patting their overfull stomachs or loosening too-tight clothing. This year there would be no table laden with food, no gifts to exchange or visits with cheery friends. This Christmas, hunger would be their unwelcome visitor—and likely would remain throughout the winter. Already their clothes hung too loosely on ever-thinning frames, and if food did not soon arrive, their bodies would appear more skeletal than human by winter's end—if they survived at all. The thought caused Jarena to shudder.

The fire momentarily jumped to life as a small sheaf of sunflower stalks sizzled and then dropped atop the gray embers. Jarena leaned forward and warmed her hands, wondering how her father continued to maintain his staunch resolve amidst their dire circumstances. Even when his belly growled from hunger or his body ached for rest, he smiled and showed her the piece of paper that proved he owned a piece of this prairie. Perhaps because he'd suffered through slavery and had experienced indignities Jarena couldn't begin to imagine, owning a piece of land made his freedom all the sweeter. How could she not cheer him on? Did he not deserve at least that much from his children? She would do better in the future—at least she would try.

Miss Hattie's soft snores mingled with Nellie's occasional moans, and Jarena wondered how Thomas was faring on his journey to Hill City. She pulled her chair away from the fireplace. It seemed inappropriate to be savoring the fire's warmth while

Thomas traveled through a blizzard to save her friend.

Jarena bowed her head. The time had come once again to pray.

CHAPTER

18

Wet snow trickled down Thomas's neck. He pulled his coat collar close and tucked it under his chin. Since leaving the Harris dugout, the weather had continued to worsen; he now feared the storm was reaching blizzard proportions. He rode onward, but the blinding force of the storm made it nearly impossible for him to gauge his direction. Before leaving Nicodemus, he and Ezekiel had discussed the storm's movement. The blizzard had come in from the north, and Thomas had been making every attempt to keep the blowing wind to his right, using it as a guide. Now, however, the blinding snow was swirling around him in circular patterns that made it impossible to determine direction.

The weary horse plodded forward while Thomas remembered the warm fire he'd left behind in Nicodemus. Why had he volunteered to make this journey? He knew why—the loss of his life would mean nothing to the settlers in Nicodemus, while any of the other men would leave families mourning their death. Better that he should die than one of them, he decided as a huge gust of wind encircled and held him hostage in its whirling grip.

Suddenly the horse dug in like a tenacious mule and refused to move. What if he didn't arrive at his destination by nightfall? He kicked the animal's flanks, but the mare would not budge. Perhaps he would die sitting atop this old workhorse—an ice-covered statue in the vast wilderness. Had the thought been less credible, he would have laughed aloud. The intensity of the storm continued to increase by the minute, yet the horse remained motionless. He doubted there was any shelter to be found in these flatlands, yet how could he tell? He couldn't see more than a few feet in front of the horse. An outcropping or hillock might be nearby, but likely he would unwittingly ride past it, unaware that protection was close at hand. He reached down and patted the horse's neck. Ice and snow draped the animal's mane, and Thomas wondered if they both would succumb to the harshness of the elements before reaching their destination.

"Not the way I'd choose to die," he murmured while urging the horse onward. The mare finally relented and once again began slogging through the heavy snow. He'd heard stories about folks becoming so disoriented in snowstorms they became overpowered by the cold; eventually their despair and weariness caused them to lose hope and surrender to their urge to sleep. And it was at that very moment when they would condemn themselves to death—or so he'd been told. He harkened back to those tales he had heard, longing to remember some small detail that might assist him on this dangerous trek—a tiny recollection that might give him an advantage over the forces of nature. But he could think of nothing.

The pelting snow stung his face, and Thomas bowed his head against the unremitting storm. "Is this how you're plannin' to end my life?" he asked aloud while attempting to hold the reins between freezing fingers that now refused to tighten. "You know I ain't one to put much stock in prayin'—never have liked to ask favors from no one, but I'd be much obliged if ya'd let me live long enough to get to Hill City. Ain't so much fer me that I'm askin', but for that woman and her young'un what ain't even been born yet. Maybe you could consider it an early Christmas gift to Calvin an' his fambly."

Thomas had hoped to look into the distance and see Hill City before him, for surely he'd been traveling long enough to have arrived at his destination. Instead, the harshness of the blizzard increased to proportions that he'd never before experienced. When nightfall could no longer be denied, he spied a crevice in a nearby hillside. He pulled back on the reins and slid off the horse's back, certain this would be the best protection that he could find before he was completely enveloped by darkness.

Hopeful the cut would provide enough shelter to keep the animal alive, he led her close to where he hoped to tunnel into the hillside. At least the weather-worn bluff would provide shelter from the wind. "Wish

I had somethin' to feed you, girl, but you're gonna have to hang on 'til we get to Hill City." The mare gave a soft whinny, and Thomas patted her side before turning his attention to the hillock.

He longed to fall over into the deepening snow and escape this cold torture, but he willed himself to use his freezing hands and begin shoveling into the hillside. Though his body rebelled, Thomas used every ounce of strength he could muster. Like the prairie dogs, he hoped to burrow out a safe haven to protect himself against the elements. Desperate, he told himself he needed to create a shelter only big enough to protect his body from the freezing wind. If he could complete that one task, he might make it through the night.

And so he dug at a fever pitch until, with his muscles aching and his strength completely spent, he dropped into the opening and permitted himself a reward—a piece of Jarena's cornpone. How he longed for a cup of hot coffee and a fire to warm his hands, but at least he was sheltered from the wind. Surely the storm would pass during the night. The mare stood nearby with her backside positioned toward the wind, and Thomas suddenly remembered one of the stories he'd heard back in Massachusetts—a tale of a man killing his own horse and using its body as a shelter in order to survive.

The thought gave him pause. If tomorrow brought no relief, would he be forced to make such a decision? Could he kill the mare to save himself? Such action would surely breed a firestorm in Nicodemus, for the horse was far more valuable to the survival of the town than one man—especially one who was a stranger among them. He didn't need to decide tonight. He would remain awake as long as he could, but if sleep came and he never awakened, so be it.

The sound of laughing voices and jingling bells skittered through Thomas's head like mice chasing through the rafters. He drifted in and out of consciousness, the peacefulness of sleep drawing him back into its loving embrace. The jingling returned; his mare snorted and stomped and he awakened. Stillness blanketed the pure white countryside. Again he heard it. Jingling bells—and boisterous laughter. Forcing his aching, frozen limbs to move, he lunged forward and propelled himself out of the snow-packed enclosure.

"Ho! Over here!" he called. He stood completely still and strained to listen.

"Helloooo," a voice returned.

"Here! I's over here!" Thomas shouted as he hurried to release the hobbles from the mare. He stood up, and in the distance, he saw a team pulling a box sleigh. With a determined yank, he pulled off his stiff hat and waved it high above his head. "Looks like we's gonna make it, old girl," he told the horse, unable to believe his own eyes.

There were two men in the sleigh. Both of them appeared to be young—and white. For a moment, Thomas wondered if they'd help or leave him to die. "This ain't the South—they's gonna help you," he muttered aloud, hoping the words would fortify him.

He waved as the sleigh came alongside. "You lost out here?" the driver asked.

"I's from over in Nicodemus—tryin' to make it to Hill City. We need a doctor real bad. We's told there's a doctor in Hill City." His teeth continued to chatter long after he'd completed his reply.

"My father's the doctor. I'm Harvey Boyle."

The other man extended his hand. "I'm Jeb Malone, the blacksmith over in Hill City."

Thomas reached up to shake hands. "Thomas Grayson. Any chance you could haul me back to Hill City so's I could talk to the doctor?"

"Sure thing. Best tie your horse on the back of the sleigh. Looks like she could use some grain. Jeb's the fellow who can help you out with that."

"That horse ain't the only one hungry in Nicodemus," he said as he tied the horse and then hoisted himself into the wagon. "I'm thankful fer your help. I hope I'm not causin' you too much trouble."

Harvey emitted a boisterous laugh. "Jeb's been trying to get me to take him back to town for a half hour, but this is quite a snow. I've been enjoying myself too much, so I refused. We don't get snows like this one at home."

Thomas tensed at Harvey's remark. "You from down south?"

"Kentucky. We don't get much in the way of heavy snow, and I wanted to come out here and enjoy a sleigh ride. Jeb is used to cold weather—he's originally from up north, and he'd rather stay close to a fire."

"Is there more than one person sick over in Nicodemus?" Jeb asked Thomas.

"No, and I wouldn' truly say Nellie's sick. It's her time, and the baby won't come. We got us a good midwife, but she ain't had no luck gettin' the baby to turn. You think your pappy's gonna be willin' to tend to a colored woman?"

Harvey laughed and slapped his knee. "My father will be more than pleased to help. He took great pleasure in providing clandestine medical treatment to slaves before the war—much to the vexation of their owners. He cares little about the color of a man's skin."

"Then ya think he'd be willin' to make the trip to Nicodemus?"

"Once he hears there's a need, you won't be able to keep him away."

Jeb turned on the seat and faced Thomas. "Did you sleep out in the storm all night—alone?"

He nodded. "Just me an' the horse."

A couple of miles farther on, they came to a community with several small structures

and one large house. Thomas quickly surveyed his surroundings. From what he'd
seen thus far, Hill City had progressed more
than Nicodemus, but still, it wasn't the town
he'd expected to see rising out of the
prairie.

"You go in with Harvey and talk to Dr.
Boyle," Jeb said. "I'll take your horse over to
my place. I can rub her down and feed her
for you."

Thomas wagged his head back and forth.
"Don' give that horse no feed. I ain't got no
money to pay ya."

"Give him some of our feed," Harvey said
before turning toward Thomas. "We've got
plenty, and that horse is nothing but bones.
Come on and we'll talk to my father."

Thomas tipped his hat. "I thank you fer
your kindness."

Harvey smiled and nodded. "Here in
Kansas, folks have to look out for one an-
other. Otherwise, most of us would perish.
Jeb taught me that."

"Well, I know Jeb is right on that account
'cause we got us a whole passel of folks
ready to perish over in Nicodemus—jest
ain't found no one to help look out for us."
Thomas followed Harvey up the few steps

to the house and stopped on the front porch. "You tell your pappy. I'll jest be waitin' out here, and you can let me know what he says."

Harvey tugged Thomas by the coat sleeve. "No, of course not. It's far too cold to wait outdoors. Come in."

Thomas glanced at the floor as they stepped inside the foyer. Their boots were dripping snow onto the carpet, and he wanted to go back outside. What if the mistress saw the mess he was making on her rug?

"I thought I heard the front—Well, who have we here?" an older man inquired as he approached Harvey and Thomas.

"This is Thomas . . ."

"Grayson. Thomas Grayson. Is you the doctor?"

"Indeed I am."

"I come to see if I could fetch you back to Nicodemus, Dr. Boyle. We got us a situation and we need help. One of our women, Nellie Harris . . . well, it's her time, but the baby ain't turned right and she's in terrible pain, and the midwife ain't been doin' nothing to help and they sent me to get you and then—"

Dr. Boyle held out his hands, palms forward. "Slow down and catch your breath. Here, come sit by the fire."

"I . . . I can't. My britches is wet an' dirty an' . . ."

Ignoring his protests, the man led him to a high-backed wooden chair. Once he'd warmed a little, Thomas told his story with clarity and speed, stopping only to take sips of the coffee and bites of the biscuit and ham Dr. Boyle's daughter had brought him. When he was finished, he stood and walked anxiously toward the door. "You ready to head out?"

The doctor grabbed his black medical bag as Harvey brought the sleigh up next to the front steps.

"I hope my father is able to help your wife," the doctor's daughter said.

"Oh . . . no, it . . . uh, ain't my wife what's having the baby. I jest volunteered to come get the doctor so's Nellie's husband could stay with her. I ain't got no wife."

The girl gave him a gentle smile. "Then it was most kind of you to come out in this terrible weather to help someone else. Not many folks would be willing to place their life in danger for another. The Bible says that's the greatest of all gifts—to lay down your life for another."

Thomas held the collar of his jacket closed and mumbled hasty words of thanks, but he silently wondered how she'd gotten the wrong idea about him. He hadn't been trying to die for anybody, and he didn't want this lady to think he was some kind of saint. He surely wasn't.

CHAPTER

19

While the sleigh moved toward Nicodemus, Harvey talked nonstop. He told Thomas about Georgetown and their move to Hill City, and he even repentantly related a few instances of his disorderly behavior while living in Kentucky. Thomas was stunned by Harvey's revelations. Harvey didn't seem the type of young man who shirked responsibility or disobeyed his parents. He had swiftly offered his assistance out in the blizzard and had even insisted upon feeding Thomas's horse. Harvey admitted he was a changed man. While Harvey attributed the influence of Jeb Malone for the changes in his life, Dr. Boyle gave full credit to God. Either way, Thomas was thankful he'd met

Harvey Boyle after he'd moved to Kansas rather than before.

As they reached the outskirts of Nicodemus, they could see smoke rising from the low-lying hillocks that made up the small settlement.

Thomas pointed to the right, and Dr. Boyle turned the horses without hesitation. "That's the Harris place over there," Thomas directed.

Harvey edged forward on the seat. "I thought you said they lived in town."

"This here *is* the town. It's all we got right now. Over dere is Zach King's place." The words *King's Emporium* had been carved into a thin piece of wood that was attached to the door. "Zach put up some shelves right inside his dugout door—calls it a general store, but it's the home where he lives with his fambly. He ain't got nothin' on the shelves ceptin' a few jugs of molasses and a little cornmeal he brought from Kentucky, but he says he's gonna have the finest general store in town one day. I figure he'll be usin' that molasses and cornmeal to feed his young'uns afore much longer—if he ain't already. Miss Hattie says Zach's got him a general store that's generally out of everything." Thomas laughed. "But there ain't nobody in Nicodemus doubting that ol' Zach's gonna have him a fine business one day."

Dr. Boyle pulled back on the reins, and the horses came to a halt in front of the Harris dugout. Thomas jumped down from the sleigh. "This here is Calvin and Nellie's place. I'll take ya in and introduce ya, Dr. Boyle, and then I'll be on my way. I don' wanna be in there, what with the baby coming and such."

Harvey's eyes widened at the remark. "Me neither. I'll wait out here in the sleigh."

"You can come over to the Harban dugout with me 'til after the birthing if ya like," Thomas told him with a grin. "Jest wait right here."

Harvey propelled his head up and down as if he were priming a pump and settled back in the wagon while Thomas knocked on the door of the dugout. Calvin opened the door, his eyes shining with fear as he waved Dr. Boyle forward. Jarena stood up to greet the two men.

"How's the patient doing?" Dr. Boyle asked Jarena.

"Not so good. I'm scared she might not

make it. She's weak, and Miss Hattie here is afraid the baby might be dead." She tilted her head toward the old woman, who sat on a rocking chair near Nellie's bed. "Oh, Thomas, it's been horrible waiting for the doctor to get here."

His head dropped to his chest. "I did my best to get back as fast as I could, but the blizzard slowed me down more'n you can imagine."

"I know you did everything possible, Thomas," she said, grasping his sleeve. "Please don't think I was condemning you. We're all grateful you went—truly."

He nodded. "I best be gettin' out of here so the doctor can tend to Nellie. I'm takin' his son Harvey over to your place until his pappy's done here. Ya might point the way when he's ready to leave."

"Of course. And thank you for everything, Thomas. You'll have to tell me about your journey this evening."

———

Samuel Boyle neared Nellie Harris's bedside. The girl had obviously been drugged, for she remained in a semi-conscious state during his preliminary examination. He turned toward Miss Hattie and arched his brows. "Laudanum?"

"Midwife give it to her—had to do somethin' to ease the pain. Only thing we got."

He nodded. He wouldn't condemn. Folks had to do whatever they could in dire circumstances such as these. And there was little doubt Nellie needed relief from the pain. Thomas had told him the girl was young and strong, but she couldn't physically endure days of birthing pains without something to relieve the agony. However, he hoped the dosage hadn't been enough to harm the infant. The midwife's assessment had been correct. Although Nellie was in labor, the baby hadn't turned properly. The infant's shoulder had lodged and now blocked the birth canal.

With Nellie relaxed from the drug, Samuel knew what he must do. He cast an apologetic gaze at Calvin and then placed his large hands across Nellie's abdomen. Using enough brute strength to force the child into position, he manipulated with a twisting motion that transported Nellie into a screaming wakefulness. Her earsplitting pleas shattered the room and sent Calvin racing outdoors.

Dr. Boyle leaned over Nellie and took her face between his hands. "I'm not going to do that again, Nellie. The baby is turned, but you must now push as hard as you can. Your baby's life depends upon you. Can you hear me?"

She panted for breath. Beads of perspiration dotted her upper lip. "I'll do my best."

Dr. Boyle smiled. "I know you will. I'm likely going to have to use forceps to help the baby down the birth canal. I apologize, but it's going to hurt. The thing is, we've got to move quickly."

Samuel was correct. The birth was painful, but the baby boy gave a lusty cry as he entered the world. It was a good sign that the child would survive; he could only hope Nellie would do the same. The girl had suffered terribly, and she would need time to recuperate.

Jarena handed Dr. Boyle a cup of weak coffee as the family began to discuss a proper name for the infant. The tenseness in his shoulders eased as he finally relaxed in a chair by the fireplace and took in his surroundings. He couldn't be absolutely certain in the dim light, but the interior of the dugout appeared to be no more than sixteen by twenty feet. From what he could see, it looked as if the dwelling had been thoughtfully constructed using as much of the hillside as possible and then building up the sides with sod bricks so that under the eaves the height was about six feet. The fireplace took up one end of the room, and the remainder was filled to capacity with two beds, Miss Hattie's rocker, a makeshift table and chairs, and several trunks. Shelves and pegs had been lodged into the walls and were laden with clothing and sundry belongings. The room was tidy, though Samuel wondered where the baby would find room to play once he began to toddle about. They'll enlarge their dwelling by that time, he told himself as he downed the last of his coffee.

He stood up and handed his empty cup to Jarena. "Decided upon a name?"

Nellie gave him a weary smile. "We decided on Nathan Samuel Harris. We don' want him to ever ferget the man who helped bring him into dis world."

"I'm honored. Now, you must all promise that Nellie will stay in bed and rest. I plan to return and check on both her and little

Nathan very soon. However, I believe I best find my own son and head home."

Jarena jumped to her feet. "He's gone to our house. I'll show you the way, Dr. Boyle."

After leaving further instructions for Nellie's care, Samuel donned his coat. He knew the family would do their best, but with so little food, Samuel wondered if Nellie would gain enough strength to rebound from her ordeal. She'd lost a great deal of blood, and he worried she might not recover. He'd have to find some way to help.

Harvey's silence was unsettling. Though the boy wasn't given to intellectual conversation, he had remained unusually quiet throughout their return to Hill City. "Feels good to be home, doesn't it?" Samuel asked as they pulled up in front of the house.

Harvey gave a somber nod. "Never thought I'd be glad to see this house, but I am."

Samuel patted his son on the back and chuckled. "Amazing how much more we appreciate what we have once we realize there are others with much less, isn't it?"

"I'm not certain that's the answer," he

said, his brow furrowed. "I knew most of the coloreds in Kentucky didn't live as well as we did, but it didn't bother me. Why is *this* so different?"

"I don't know. Perhaps because you've never before been confronted by so many people in dire circumstances. Or perhaps because you're beginning to mature and think of others rather than yourself."

"They need help, Father."

Samuel nodded as he opened the front door. "You're right, but the matter needs more thought than I care to give it out here in the cold. Let's go inside."

Margaret fluttered to greet them and immediately announced supper was waiting, though Samuel noted she was massaging the back of her neck. Likely she was suffering another of her headaches, which would probably lead to several days in bed. He wondered if his wife sometimes used her headaches and melancholy to escape dealing with life. She'd certainly taken to her bed more frequently since settling in Kansas. The thought caused him a twinge of guilt, especially since he was a doctor and had been able to do nothing to ease her spells.

"Take off your coats and come sit down. I've a hearty stew and freshly baked bread. Both Macia and I are anxious to hear all the details of your mission of mercy. We can eat as soon as I dish up the stew."

While they ate their supper, Samuel detailed their journey and the birth of the child, stopping to answer his wife's occasional questions and listen to her words of praise for his ministrations. Once he'd answered all her questions concerning the birth, Margaret insisted upon details about the small community.

Harvey wiped his mouth and placed his napkin by his plate. "They don't even have enough food to feed themselves."

"It's a tragic situation," Samuel agreed. "I don't know how those folks are going to make it through the winter. Unfortunately, the information we received at the Ellis train station proved to be correct. The town they were promised is not there."

Leaning forward in his chair, Harvey captured his mother's attention. "Many of them have feelings of deep hostility toward Mr. Hill."

Samuel took a sip of his coffee and thought of the weak brew he'd been served in the Harris dugout. "And rightfully so. He deceived all of them and has left their group in a situation that would test even the most adept frontiersman."

"It appears Mr. Hill is not a man to be trusted, yet I would like to believe he will return and give some justification for his behavior." Margaret poured a dollop of cream into her coffee and began to stir. "I don't want to believe that he would callously leave people in dire straits merely to promote his own financial gain."

"He didn't exactly tell *us* the truth about Hill City, either," Macia remarked. "At least I *hope* Father didn't bring us to this desolate place knowing in advance what we would find here."

"Rest assured that I expected much more. However, I think your brother will attest to the fact that you would be most happy with this house once you saw the conditions in Nicodemus."

Margaret gave her husband a look of concern. "Tell me, what can we do to help?"

Samuel brightened at the question. Perhaps Margaret would take hold out here in the West if she had something other than housework to pique her interest. After all, she had maintained a busy schedule of charity and church work back in Kentucky.

He patted her hand. "I plan to return to Nicodemus in the next week or two to see about Nellie's progress. Perhaps we could go to the general store and purchase a few provisions that I could take along. The men did tell me they have sent out a representative to seek assistance from larger cities back east. They're holding out hope they'll receive at least some supplies through that process. When I return, I'll ask if there's any specific help that we can provide."

Once again, Margaret began to massage the back of her neck. "Well, it's just all too horrid! For the life of me, I don't understand why any of you men think living out on the frontier is such a wondrous concept. And those poor women over in Nicodemus are likely wondering the same thing!"

Macia scooted to the edge of her chair. "Could I go with you when you return to Nicodemus?"

"I believe you'll find the conditions far worse than I have described, Macia. I've offered to examine any of the settlers who need medical treatment, and I fear you'll immediately want to leave. It's probably best you remain at home."

"Harvey's no more accustomed to seeing such conditions than I, and *he* appears to have survived the ordeal. Perhaps there's some way I could be of help, too. I truly want to go with you, Father. I promise I'll not utter a single complaint if you will please permit me this one concession."

Samuel knew Macia's request wasn't unreasonable, yet he wanted assurance he wouldn't be forced to leave Nicodemus before administering aid to those in need. He had to admit that when difficult situations arose, Macia wasn't always one to remember her promises.

Macia gave her father a wary look. "You aren't planning to stay the night, are you?"

He laughed and shook his head. "No. Unless the weather should take an unexpected turn, we should be home in time for supper."

"Then I shall go," Macia said and placed a kiss on her father's cheek.

CHAPTER

20

Macia selected two reading primers from a small bookshelf in her room and carried them downstairs to find Harvey waiting by the door. She had used both books while learning to read as a young girl. Although she'd been quick to chide her mother for loading their trunks with such items, she was now pleased the older woman hadn't relented. Without a school in Hill City, it was obvious that parents would be the ones relegated to the task of educating their children. And in Lucy's case, that would mean no instruction at all, at least so far as Macia could ascertain. Given her assessment of Jeb, it was unlikely he could read very well—if at all. And even if he could, she doubted that he would devote any time to such a chore. Macia was pleased she could at least supply Lucy with some additional reading material and spend a small portion of time helping the girl.

When they arrived at the Malones' a short time later, Lucy joyfully embraced Macia and tugged her inside by the hand but merely nodded at Harvey. "Jeb's over at the barn. He said for you to go over there." Without waiting for a response, she firmly closed the door.

Macia grinned at the girl's forthright behavior. Anyone who could stand her ground with Harvey was certainly an ally to be cultivated. "I've brought some books we can use for your reading lessons." Macia handed the books to Lucy and then removed her coat and gloves. She watched with delight as Lucy began leafing through the primers.

An infectious smile played on Lucy's pale pink lips. "Where did you get such fine books?"

"They were mine when I was a young girl, and my mother has kept them for all these years. Shall we begin?"

Lucy bobbed her head up and down. "Let's sit over by the fire where it's warmer."

Macia picked up one of the straight-backed chairs and moved it closer to the fire. "Why don't we begin with this book? You can start out by reading to me; then I can see where you need help."

Lucy began to read haltingly from the first page. However, with a bit of coaching, she became more confident and soon required little assistance. It didn't take long until Macia found herself focused upon her surroundings rather than Lucy's reading, her gaze flitting from place to place as she attempted to fathom what it would be like to live in such a hovel as this. Certainly Jeb had done much to make the dwelling habitable—much more than Harvey could have accomplished in the same circumstances—or any of the other young men she knew. He had plastered the inside walls to cover the sod bricks, and the furniture, though sparse, was arranged in a pleasing manner. There were even two windows flanked by neatly hemmed curtains. She wondered how long their parents had been dead. By Macia's standards, the house was uninhabitable, yet there were many feminine touches showing someone had attempted to make the soddy livable.

Lucy tapped on the page with her finger. "Do I read the next page?"

"First I want you to tell me what you read."

"What?"

"Tell me the story—in your own words. I want to be certain you truly understand what you've read."

"Why? I thought you said this was a *reading* lesson."

"It *is* a reading lesson, but if you don't understand what you've read, then reading isn't much help."

Lucy shrugged her shoulders and proceeded to explain the story in great detail. When she had finished, she gave Macia a whimsical smile. "How did I do?"

"You did very well!" Macia complimented. "That's likely enough reading for today, unless you'd *like* to do more."

"Would you help me fix my hair with the combs you gave me?"

"Yes, of course. I was just noticing the pretty curtains. Did you hem them by yourself?"

Lucy giggled. "No. I can't sew, but I think they look very nice, too." She began digging through a drawer and soon retrieved the combs, along with a silver filigree hairbrush. "This was my mama's." The child reverently stared at the brush.

Macia's eyes widened at the sight. "It is quite lovely." There was no need to stretch the truth. The brush was obviously part of an expensive dresser set and seemed strangely out of place in these surroundings.

"I have the matching pieces, too. Jeb says they're mine to keep forever," she confided as Macia brushed through her fine golden brown hair.

"They are a wonderful keepsake. One day you can pass them on to *your* daughter."

"That's what Jeb said, too." Lucy's lips curled into an impish grin. "I think he likes you."

"Did he say something about me?" Macia asked as she continued brushing.

Jeb hadn't said more than a few words to her since their first meeting, when she had rebuffed his invitation to go fishing. Granted, she had no interest in him, but knowing of his continuing attraction stimulated her ego. After all, she hadn't heard from Jackson Kincaid since leaving Georgetown, and there was little to boost her self-esteem in this place. The few people in Hill City were too busy attempting to survive.

"He thinks you're pretty, and so do I. If you and Jeb got married, you could be my sister. Wouldn't that be grand?"

Macia needed to change the subject. "Do you have a mirror you can look in while I arrange your hair?"

Lucy jumped up from the chair. "There's one that matches the brush." Once again, she dug through the drawer. "We have Mama's wedding dress, too. It's beautiful, and you could wear it if you and Jeb get married. This is a picture of Mama and Papa on their wedding day." She held the brush in one hand and a framed picture in the other.

The child was correct. The dress was quite stunning, and Macia wondered if Lucy's mother had come from a wealthy family. Though why would anyone of affluence come to this place? She nearly laughed aloud at her thought. After all, her father was considered prosperous, and *they* had come west. Yet this small, poorly furnished soddy didn't suggest a family of means. Perhaps Mrs. Malone's family had disapproved of her husband and had disowned her when she married him. But surely they wouldn't have purchased an expensive wedding dress for their daughter if they hadn't approved.

"Let's finish my hair." Lucy's request startled Macia back to the present, and she picked up the brush.

"Hold the mirror so you can watch how I twist your hair before inserting the comb." Macia carefully twisted the child's hair and then used the comb to secure her handiwork. "Now let's do the other side. If you were going to a special party, you'd want to heat your curling iron on the stove and use it to turn up the ends of your hair, but we won't do that today."

Lucy covered her mouth with one hand and chuckled. "We can't anyway, 'cause I don't have a curling iron."

Macia brushed Lucy's remaining hair into place as Jeb and Harvey entered the soddy. The frigid air followed the two men into the room, and Macia shivered.

"Well, doesn't your hair look pretty," Jeb told his sister as he pulled off his coat.

A slight blush tinted Lucy's cheeks. "Thank you. You think Mama would have liked it?"

He nodded. "She would think you're the

most beautiful girl in all of the world. What's this picture doing out?" he gently inquired, picking up the framed wedding photograph.

"I was showing Mama's pretty wedding gown to Miss Macia. I told her the dress is all packed away and if she married you, she could wear it and she'd be my sister. Isn't that right?"

"That's right," Jeb agreed. "All she needs to do is tell me when and where." His lips formed an ornery grin. "But I don't think she's gonna agree. She's got her a beau back east, remember?"

Lucy looked across her shoulder at Macia. "But you *could* change your mind, couldn't you?"

Harvey winked. "Of course. She *could.*"

"Please don't listen to Harvey," Macia said. "I hope to wed Jackson Kincaid. It would be best for you to plan on someone else wearing your mama's wedding dress, Lucy." She handed the girl her hairbrush. "I think we should be going home before the weather turns any colder, Harvey."

"Notice she said *hope.* Jackson's probably found two or three girls to court since we left home," Harvey teased.

Macia pulled her coat from the wooden

peg near the door. "Come along, Harvey. We need to be getting home."

Lucy directed an admiring gaze at Macia. "But he'd never find *anyone* prettier than you."

"Thank you, Lucy. You practice your reading, and if Jeb gives you permission, you can come to the house and let me check your progress. Why don't you come on Sunday afternoon, and we can have tea?"

"Can Jeb come, too?"

"I don't think Jeb would be interested in coming to tea. I'm sure he has other more important things to do."

Much to her dismay, Jeb shook his head. "Not at all. Sunday afternoon would be just fine. We'll see you then."

"Thank you for fixing my hair and for the books. I'll practice hard," Lucy promised as Macia and Harvey bade them good-bye.

Macia bit her lip until they were several yards away from the house. Then she doubled her fist and punched Harvey in the arm. "Why did you do that, Harvey? You think your behavior is amusing, but it's not. *I* know you're teasing me, but *Lucy* doesn't. You're giving the child false hope by telling her exactly what she wants to hear. She longs to have a woman live in that little house and become her big sister, and you've told her I might consider that option."

Harvey rubbed his arm as he walked alongside Macia. "I don't know what you're getting all riled up about. Jeb's surely told Lucy he doesn't stand a chance with you. But Jeb would be a better choice for you than Jackson—especially living out in these parts. Jackson would be even more useless than I am."

"Well, I don't intend to live in Hill City. When Jackson and I wed, we'll be living in Kentucky, so I'd appreciate it if you'd refrain from encouraging Lucy to think I'll marry her brother. And Jeb would *not* be a better match for me. Jackson and I are perfectly suited."

"Well, I wouldn't count on Jackson. You know he's got a wandering eye. Do you truly believe he's sitting at home pining for you?"

"Yes, of course I do." But she knew neither she nor Harvey believed her reply.

CHAPTER

21

Ten days later, with the gifts and supplies loaded into the wagon, Macia and her father headed off toward Nicodemus. The provisions would not be enough to help the fledgling community to any great extent, but the Johnsons were not scheduled to replenish their shelves until later in the month—and perhaps even until January or February if the weather didn't cooperate enough to permit a journey to Ellis. Had the Johnsons been agreeable, Macia believed her parents would have purchased everything in the store. And though the Johnsons wanted to help the settlers in Nicodemus, they also needed to maintain stock for the local residents.

Macia snuggled under a layer of blankets

and thought back to their trip to purchase goods at the Johnsons' general store. Mrs. Boyle had embraced their shopping venture with an enthusiasm that had surprised Macia. "We've been given the opportunity to bestow special gifts during the holiday season," her mother had declared as they had entered the mercantile. Though her mother had attempted to equate the shopping endeavor with some of their family's previous Christmas adventures, Macia had thought the comparison preposterous. After all, how could purchasing goods in the poorly stocked general store measure up to their yearly Christmas excursions and shopping in Lexington and Frankfort? However, Macia had tried to match her mother's enthusiasm. After all, outside of attending church services on Christmas Eve, purchasing these necessities would likely be the height of their holiday celebration.

At her mother's insistence, Macia had located several pieces of ribbon and tied them around a few of the packages. "A bit of festivity is good for everyone," Mrs. Boyle had declared.

And likely she is correct on that account, Macia thought as the horses came to a halt in front of what appeared to be a burrowed hill fronted by sod bricks. "What kind of dwelling is this?"

"It's a dugout, but the hills are low, so they've added sod bricks to form the front of the house, along with rafters and thatching topped by more bricks to form part of the roof. Having this type of front allows them a window for more light, and they can use wood doors."

That "door" was no more than several wood planks nailed together, but she didn't correct her father's assessment. The town appeared much like Harvey had described: nothing more than a number of sod projections jutting outward from the hills. Macia shivered at the sight and wondered how anyone could survive the winter living in one of the gloomy dugouts.

"Are they as terrible inside as they appear from the outside?"

Her father shrugged. "They provide no more than shelter—you'll find nothing luxurious about these accommodations."

Macia rubbed her hands to ward off the cold while her father knocked on the dugout door. "I don't find our own home luxurious."

The door opened, and a broad-shouldered young colored man of about Harvey's age greeted them. "Dr. Boyle! Didn' 'spect to see you standin' there when I opened the door."

Macia's father shook hands with the young man. "I told you I'd return to check on Nellie."

"Yes, sir, I know dat, but, well . . . I guess I didn' really 'spect you'd come back. What with the weather bein' so cold and all."

"And the fact that most white folks haven't kept their word to you in the past?"

"I s'pose that, too." There was an awkward pause before the colored man asked, "This here your daughter?"

"Yes. Macia, this is Calvin Harris and that's his wife, Nellie. And if memory serves me correctly, this young lady is Jarena Harban. Am I correct?"

The attractive young lady with bright chocolate brown eyes smiled. "That's correct. Pleased to meet you, Miss Boyle."

Macia smiled in return. "Why don't we dispense with formality and use our given names? After all, we are out here in the middle of nowhere. Please call me Macia."

"Thank you. I'm Jarena, and this is

Nathan." She proudly held the baby up for examination.

Miss Hattie cleared her throat and leaned forward with a twinkle in her eye. "And I's Nellie's grandmammy, but ever'one calls me Miss Hattie—you can do the same. Take your coat off and set a spell."

Macia removed her coat and handed it to Calvin, who hung it on one of the pegs along the wall. The interior of the soddy was as dank and dark as Macia had imagined, but so far as she could tell, no one seemed to notice or care. Of course, she had no idea of what kind of homes they'd lived in before coming to Kansas. Perhaps they had lived in even worse, she decided.

Dr. Boyle approached Nellie's bedside. "I can see that young Nathan is doing well, but I've come to check on how you're faring, Nellie. Any problems that need attention?"

"I been doing perty good," she said brightly. "My milk come in and Nathan's been nursin' real good. Granny and Mrs. Kemble been watching after me and say everything looks fine. And Jarena's been comin' over every day to help out."

"You had a rough time of it, so you

shouldn't try to do too much for at least a few more days. I'm glad to hear you've been helping, Jarena."

"Does me more good than Nellie. I don't mind helping with the chores when I take a peek at this sweet baby every few minutes. Seeing his pretty little face sure helps to make the days go by."

"Dat and the pleasure of talking with two women 'stead of being cooped up all day with the twins," Miss Hattie said with a chuckle.

Jarena laughed. "That's true enough!"

Macia's eyebrows arched. "You have twins?"

"Twin *sisters.* They're fifteen, but sometimes they act much younger."

" 'Cause you spoilt 'em when your mama died. You shoulda took a switch to 'em instead of all the time coddlin' 'em," Miss Hattie said. "They'd be more responsible."

"Look who's talkin' about using a switch," Calvin said with a laugh. "You talk rough, but you got the softest heart I ever seen."

"Can I fetch you a cup of coffee, Dr. Boyle?" Miss Hattie asked. "Ain't the real thing, but rye coffee's better'n nothing at all."

"No, thank you. If you're certain Nellie and Nathan don't need any medical assistance, I promised I would check on others who might be in need of my care. And I want to stop and see Mr. Harban, also. Do you want to come along with me, Macia?"

Macia glanced at Nellie and Jarena. "Would it be inconvenient if I stayed here until my father is ready to leave for Hill City?"

"Course not," Miss Hattie replied, answering for the group. "Go on 'bout your business, Dr. Boyle. Your daughter will be jest fine with us. We may even put her to work," she said with a jovial laugh.

"I almost forgot. My mother sent gifts for the baby—and some Christmas gifts, also. Did you bring them in with you, Father?"

"Indeed." Her father retrieved a basket he'd placed near the door and handed it to Nellie. "I insisted my wife be practical. Of course, with only the general store, it's difficult for her to be impractical. I think she would have much preferred to send an engraved silver rattle, but I believe these items will be of greater use."

"Thank you." Nellie self-consciously accepted the beribboned basket, but her face soon shone with joy. Inside she discovered yards of flannel toweling from which to make diapers, two safety pins, four soft blankets with satin edging, and two gowns, which had completely depleted Mrs. Johnson's inventory of baby goods from the general store.

"These items are Christmas gifts for your family. However, my wife insisted I tell you that you need not wait until Christmas to open the packages." Samuel carried several additional bundles from beside the small entrance and placed them on the rough-hewn table. "Now, I believe I should take my leave and go visit Mr. Harban. Do you want to come along, Calvin?"

"Believe I will. The womenfolk will likely enjoy themselves more if there ain't no man sittin' around listenin' to 'em."

While the men donned their coats and Calvin bid Nellie good-bye, Macia stared at the pile of beribboned packages resting on the dilapidated table. Their gifts seemed strangely out of place in these stark surroundings.

Nellie rubbed her fingers over the soft flannel. "Tell your mama we is mighty thankful for her kindness."

Macia forced her gaze away from the table and smiled at Nellie. "Mother had hoped to have sufficient time to cut and hem the diapers, but she couldn't manage to complete them and the blankets, as well. She wanted the satin binding stitched perfectly. And, of course, my ability to sew would have served only to ruin either of the projects," Macia admitted with a sheepish grin.

Miss Hattie thumped a thick branch onto the hard dirt floor. "Only way to learn is by doing."

Macia shrugged her shoulders. "Oh, I've tried on occasion, but I seem to stick myself more than anything, and Mother grows upset when I bleed on the expensive fabric."

"Ain't no time like the present. We can work on these here diapers while we's talkin'," Miss Hattie said. "Jarena, put that chil' down. He don' need to be held every minute. Fetch my sewing supplies from that box over there, and you can commence to cutting. I'll give Macia here a lesson or two, and then all of us can begin hemmin' the diapers."

Macia cringed at the thought and wondered if she should have gone along with her father. Miss Hattie would soon realize she had spoken the truth: any diapers she hemmed would need a good soaking in cold water to remove the blood left by her pricked fingers.

"Thread you a needle." Miss Hattie issued the order with the authority of a general taking command of his troops.

Macia placed the thread between her lips and wet it before attempting to hit the eye of the needle. It took several attempts in the semi-dark room, but she finally succeeded. She gave Miss Hattie a triumphant smile.

"Well, put a knot in da end," Miss Hattie coached.

Macia did so and held the threaded needle in front of Miss Hattie's face. "How's that?"

She didn't look up. "If it's threaded and knotted, it's fine. Now watch how I double over this edge. Put it on the table and den press it down with yer finger so it holds. Otherwise, you can heat up the sadiron and press the edges down."

Macia truly did not want to iron, so she did as she was told. "Now what?"

"Stick the needle down underneath so the knot doesn't show when you take your first stitch, and then you's gonna whipstitch all the way up the edge, jest like this. And don' you dare be stickin' that needle in your finger and bleedin' on that there diaper. I ain't got time to be doing no extra washin'."

Both Nellie and Jarena were grinning at Miss Hattie, but Macia was certain the old woman meant every word she'd spoken. And so she watched closely as Miss Hattie made exaggerated movements with her needle and thread, carefully instructing Macia exactly where she should place the needle in order to catch the cloth while properly hiding her stitches beneath the folded edge of fabric.

She gave Macia's hand a slight push and urged her into action. "Now, you's a smart gal, and I figure you's gonna do jest fine. Go on, now. Get started with your own."

With each stitch, Macia gave Miss Hattie a sidelong glance and wondered what would happen if she stuck herself and bled upon the fabric, though she truly didn't want to find out. Perhaps some conversation would help divert Miss Hattie's attention.

Macia kept her eyes fixed upon her stitching, fearful of a reprimand from Miss Hattie. "Tell me, when you aren't sewing or tending to a newborn baby, how do you pass your time on these long winter days?"

Jarena glanced up from her stitching. "When there's no snow on the ground and it's not overly cold, we go out and gather buffalo bones as well as sunflower stalks and buffalo chips for our fires. Seems as though there's never enough fuel to keep our fires burning warm. Of course, there's always the cooking and laundry—and I enjoy reading when time permits. As for the men keeping busy, my pappy has been working on digging a well. He and Thomas were careful to dig deep enough before the ground froze so they could continue their digging once winter set in—same with some of the other families."

Macia stared at Jarena, both bewildered and fascinated. "The buffalo bones you mentioned—you burn those in your fires, also?"

Jarena shook her head. "No. A storekeeper in Ellis told us that buffalo bones are shipped back east to make fertilizer, so we've begun to collect them—it's one way the women and children can help to earn money."

Macia nearly swooned at the notion.

Traipsing out on the cold open prairie to retrieve animal bones was certainly not *her*
idea of a suitable pastime.

Suddenly Miss Hattie pointed a finger at
the diaper Macia was stitching. "Let me see
what you got done."

Macia immediately held up the cloth for
Miss Hattie's inspection.

The older woman nodded her approval.
"See there? I knowed you could do it.
Sewing is like everything else—you jest
gotta decide you's gonna learn how and
then have someone like me to spur you on
by using jest the right tool."

"A needle?" Macia asked, confused by
the remark.

"Course not, chil'. Fear! Ain't nothin' like a
good dose of fear to make a person realize
they's able to do more'n they ever thought
possible. I learnt that lesson back in the
days afore we was freed from bondage."

Nellie grimaced. "Now, Granny, don't let's
talk about the old days. This here's a whole
new life."

"Dis may be a new life, but we ain't livin'
no better than back in dem days," Miss Hattie muttered.

"I didn't want to move out here, either, but

Father insisted," Macia said, hoping to find some common ground with the old woman.

"I did!" Nellie hastened to reply.

Miss Hattie folded the diaper and placed it on the bed. "You's the *only* one that thought this would be one fine place to set down roots."

"Am not—Calvin wanted to move out here, too."

Miss Hattie snorted. "We ain't talkin' 'bout no menfolk—we's talkin' 'bout the women. Everyone knows what them men is thinking—they's got to own them a piece of land."

Jarena broke off another piece of thread. "I didn't want to come out here."

"But now that Charles done moved out here, she's not so unhappy," Nellie teased.

"Is Charles your beau?" Macia asked.

"We're not betrothed. . . ."

Nellie giggled. "But she's hopin'."

Macia directed a soulful look at Jarena. "I left my beau back in Kentucky, too, but I haven't been as fortunate as you. He made it quite clear he had no intention of leaving—not that I would ever expect him to. Instead, I prefer to return home, but I would be most happy if he would at least come for a visit."

"That *would* be nice," Jarena said, bobbing her head in agreement. "And perhaps if he saw what it was like out here, he'd be inclined to propose more quickly and take you back to Kentucky. Have you asked him to come and visit for a spell?"

"Oh yes. And I continue to hope he will soon write and tell me that he'll arrive at the first sign of spring. I thought it would be lovely to return for the holidays, but of course Father sold our house, and he wouldn't consider remaining overnight with Jackson's family—in fact, I doubt he'd consider spending any time at all with them. Besides, he says it's foolish to consider traveling in the middle of winter."

Miss Hattie inspected Macia's stitching. "Um, hmm. Now, jest look what you's been able to learn today. You's doin' a fine job. Jest knot off the thread and get started on the other side."

Macia breathed a sigh of relief. She had completed one edge without pricking her finger, and apparently the stitches met Miss Hattie's exacting standards. Though she would have preferred to cease sewing, she realized that wouldn't be an option—not with Miss Hattie watching her every move.

Jarena placed the scissors back in the box and picked up a needle and thread. "Your father doesn't approve of your beau?"

"He's not overly fond of him, but he doesn't hold any member of the Kincaid family in high esteem."

Macia thought the women appeared surprised by the admission, particularly Jarena. Perhaps they were more surprised by the fact that she was permitted to continue seeing a man for whom her father had little respect than by the admission of her father's dislike of the Kincaid family.

"And why does your father dislike this family?" Jarena asked.

Macia hesitated, hoping her words wouldn't cast Jackson in an unfair light. "My father was born and reared in the North. He has always opposed slavery and was vocal about his beliefs. Needless to say, he found himself at odds with most folks living in the South, including the Kincaid family."

"Ouch!" Jarena quickly shoved her finger into her mouth.

Miss Hattie gave Jarena a look of surprise. "You stick yerself?"

She nodded. "My finger will be fine—and I didn't get any blood on the diaper. Do go on with what you were telling us, Macia. I believe you were saying something about the *Kincaid* family, weren't you?"

"Yes. Father says that because the Kincaids owned one of the few large plantations in Kentucky, they could have led by example after the war. Instead, they chose to maintain their hemp fields by using sharecropping tactics that continue to hold the former slaves in bondage. Of course, I don't know if that's true. . . ."

"If you knew it were true, would it make a difference in how you feel about your beau?" Jarena softly inquired.

"I'm not certain—I've never given the matter any thought. Does it bother you to talk about it?"

"Oh, I can *talk* 'bout such things all day long," Miss Hattie said. "That don' bother me even a whit. But livin' in dem conditions—now, *that's* what's troublin' to the soul. Ain't so easy to push them thoughts aside if you's ever been on the receivin' end of a bullwhip or been the one held down in a sharecropper's shack."

"Well, at least all of you seem to have

fared well. Jarena speaks quite eloquently. I know there were freed men living in George-town even before the war who owned small businesses and learned to read and write. Did you attend school, Jarena?"

Jarena's focus remained on her sewing. "You might say I was blessed with a private tutor. For a time, I worked for an elderly woman who had a vast library. In exchange for a portion of my salary, my parents asked that she assist me with my education. She was a fine lady, and though she spent more time teaching me than I did cleaning her house, she never withheld any money from my wages. Then when my mother became ill, she would loan me books from her library. After I read each one, I wrote a report for her, and then we would discuss the book. She died several years ago, but she directed many of her books be given to me."

"There now—isn't that a pleasant story?" Macia commented.

Miss Hattie shook her head vigorously and grunted. "It may be a pleasant story, but dat's all it is. Jarena never got them books. When Missus Clardy's daughter found out, she packed up all dem books and shipped 'em off to her house in Georgia. Weren't nobody said a word 'bout the fact dat Jarena got cheated out of dem books, neither."

CHAPTER

22

Samuel pulled his collar tight under his chin and walked alongside Calvin, glad the Harban dugout wasn't far off. He hoped to enlist the assistance of Calvin and one or two of the other young men to unload the remaining supplies from his sleigh while he spoke with Ezekiel Harban. They approached the residence and the two of them turned their backs to the wind as Calvin knocked on the door.

The door inched open a crack, and Thomas Grayson peeked through the narrow gap before pulling back on the leather handle and permitting the two men entry. "Come in!"

Ezekiel's shoulders remained slightly stooped, but he stood as tall as the roof of the dugout would permit. Samuel noted that neither Ezekiel nor Thomas could stand completely upright unless they were directly in the center of the dwelling. His earlier visit with Thomas had revealed the Harris dugout had been built first, when they'd been less pressured for time. But as winter had approached they'd been forced to move more quickly—and they'd been able to locate even less wood to use for the rafters needed to shore up their roofs. He wondered how frequently the two men banged their heads each day.

"Good to see ya, Dr. Boyle," Ezekiel greeted as he accepted Samuel's outstretched hand in a hearty handshake. "We wasn't fer certain you'd come back—what with the weather bein' so cold, but I'm pleased to see you's a man of your word. I reckon you been over to see Nellie and Calvin's young'un."

"Yes, and he's a fine-looking boy. I've been worried about all of you and wondering how I might help. I did manage to bring a few supplies that I hope will assist to some degree. However, I fear it's not enough to do a great deal of good. The small general store in Hill City is low on supplies, but I brought what they could spare. How are you folks going to make it through the remainder of the winter? Have you come up with a plan?"

Ezekiel sat at the table near the fire and motioned for his guests to join him. "I ain't in charge of things 'round here, Dr. Boyle. We did take a vote a while back and sent Wilbur Rawlins back to the eastern part of the state."

Samuel sat down opposite Ezekiel, anxious for more details.

"He and Ivan Lovejoy had differin' ideas 'bout what was best fer the town," Ezekiel continued. "Wilbur's plan got the most votes."

"Exactly what is Mr. Rawlins hoping to accomplish on his trip?"

"He was plannin' ta ask for aid—either money or goods, whichever he could get. We'd about given up thinkin' he was gonna send anything when, lo and behold, he sent ten dollars via the post office in Ellis. Weren't much, but it was a beginnin'."

Calvin's face contorted in a look of frustration as he dropped onto the chair beside Ezekiel. "At least we was *hopin'* it was only the beginning. But it's startin' to look like dat paltry amount was the beginning, the middle, an' the end."

"Now, Calvin, we don' know that fer certain. Ain't fair to be judgin' him too harshly afore we know the facts. Wilbur coulda met up with some kind of trouble."

"Or he could be gettin' money and then keepin' it for hisself," Thomas put in as he joined them.

Samuel leaned forward and rested his forearms on the table. "Tell me, Ezekiel, what was Mr. Lovejoy's plan for surviving the winter?"

Ezekiel wrapped his large hand around a tin coffee cup. "Well, he wanted to go to the governor and then to the Congress and ask for help, if the governor agreed to the idea. I didn' unnerstand all he was saying, but I do know most folks don' like the idea of gettin' the government involved. Ivan got a couple letters from Walt Tuttle—Walt come from Georgetown with us, but den he decided to stay in Topeka. Walt wrote that Wilbur's been collectin' large sums of money. So Ivan decided Wilbur must be keepin' the money for hisself. Ever since Ivan heard that news, he's been pushin' to go to the governor again."

"I see no reason why he shouldn't," Samuel said. "It's obvious the community needs assistance. The more people you have working to foster the town's cause, the better. Why don't you and I go and talk with Mr. Lovejoy while Thomas and Calvin unload my sleigh?"

Ezekiel hunched over the table. "No disrespect, Doctor, but my people ain't so quick to believe that them in power will always do what they say. Ownin' this here land means more to us than you's likely to understand. Folks ain't wantin' to take any chances of losin' it."

Samuel reached across the table to pat Ezekiel's shoulder. "I wouldn't suggest anything that might jeopardize ownership of your land. However, at this point, I think the probability of starvation is more worrisome than the slight prospect of losing your land."

Ezekiel slowly rose from his chair. "I s'pose you's right about that."

While Thomas and Calvin began unloading the provisions from the sleigh, Ezekiel and Samuel walked toward the Lovejoy dugout. A light snow had begun to fall, and Samuel looked off to the north, where a bank of darker clouds was slowly moving in their direction. He hoped the weather would hold off until he and Macia made it back home. He didn't know how his daughter would cope should they be forced to remain overnight in one of the dugouts.

Ezekiel followed Samuel's gaze. "Looks like we's in for some more snow."

As they approached the Lovejoy dugout, Samuel shrank into his turned-up collar like a turtle retreating into its shell. "I hope I can make it back to Hill City before those clouds dump any more snow."

Ivan Lovejoy opened the door. "What you doin' out in this cold weather, Ezekiel?" he asked as he stepped aside to permit the two men entry.

"Dr. Boyle here says maybe you's right 'bout gettin' help from the government. I still ain't so sure, but we's here 'cause he wanted to hear what you was plannin'. I done tol' him 'bout the money we got from Wilbur."

Ivan immediately launched into the particulars of the earlier meeting, detailing the settlers' unwillingness to place their trust in his plan. "And so we now finds us in a even worse condition. Wilbur has one team of horses an' a wagon, and he's likely sold dem, too. If Wilbur don' send any more funds by the end of December, I could make the trip to Topeka and meet with the governor."

"I'd be willing to accompany you to Topeka, if you'd like," Samuel said.

Ivan glanced at the floor for a moment. "I 'preciate your offer, Dr. Boyle, but we need to take charge of our future without dependin' on others speakin' fer us."

"Perhaps I could at least write a letter setting forth my concerns for the health of the residents. You could leave it with the governor as additional support for your position, if you think it might help."

Ivan smiled broadly. "I agree that a letter from you could be helpful. I 'preciate dat."

Samuel penned a letter at the Harban dugout before going to the Harris place to collect his daughter. "What have you done with Macia?" he joked when his eyes adjusted to the darkness of the dugout.

The women gave him a strange look and Hattie pointed at Macia. "That right there's your gal."

"But that girl is sewing. Macia can't sew. You must have replaced her while I was gone," he teased.

Miss Hattie chuckled in delight. "That chil' can learn anythin' she sets her mind to. Ain't dat right, Macia?"

"Yes, Miss Hattie."

"Show your pappy all dem diapers you hemmed," Nellie encouraged.

When Macia hesitated, Miss Hattie tapped her on the arm. "Go on now, show 'im."

"I finished all of these." She held up the pieces of flannel that had been neatly edged.

Her father examined the stitches as though he were checking a healing incision rather than a piece of cloth.

"Didn't she do a nice job?" Jarena asked as she folded the diaper she had just completed.

"I would say so. I'm very proud of you. I wish we could stay longer so you could help complete all of the diapers, but we must be on our way home."

"This here gal shows promise," Miss Hattie told the doctor. "With a little nudgin', she gonna turn out jest fine."

Macia's cheeks flushed at the praise as she handed the partially hemmed diaper to Miss Hattie. "Thank you for teaching me," she said shyly. "It's been an enjoyable visit, and I hope you'll come to Hill City and call on us sometime in the future."

"I don' think we'll be comin' any time soon, but we thank you for the invite," Miss Hattie replied with a broad grin. The old woman turned her gaze to Dr. Boyle and nodded.

Samuel smiled at his daughter and knew she did not grasp the import of her invitation. When they were finally on their way home, Samuel patted Macia's hand. "I'm proud of you for actually inviting people of color into our home."

The corners of Macia's lips turned up. "It is truly strange how you forget the color of someone's skin once you become acquainted, don't you think?"

"Indeed. Unfortunately, most people won't take that first step."

"If Jackson knew of my invitation, he'd likely think I've gone mad out here on the prairie. But I suppose there's no need to worry on that account, for I doubt either Jackson or the folks in Nicodemus will be visiting Hill City any time soon."

Samuel flicked the reins and urged the team onward. He, too, doubted whether there would be any visitors in the near future. Yet he enjoyed the thought of having the residents of Nicodemus come calling while Jackson Kincaid was at their home. What would Jackson think of such an occurrence? He grinned, relishing the notion.

CHAPTER

23

Nicodemus, Kansas • January 1878

Jarena peeked from under the covers. A light skiff of snow had blown under the ill-fitting door, and bitter cold now seeped through every crevice in the dugout. She snuggled deeper under the blankets, longing for the warm days of summer. There was no reason to jump up from her bed. The ground had been frozen for nearly a week, and little could be accomplished in such weather—at least nothing that required her to rise and prepare an early breakfast. Her sisters and Thomas were sleeping soundly, though she imagined her father had been awake for at least an hour. At least his snoring had ceased some time ago. Likely he found no compelling reason to leave his bed, either.

Jarena turned on her side, wishing for another blanket. Perhaps she should get up and add fuel to the waning fire. Her father and Thomas would likely want a cup of coffee. Her stomach growled as she thought about breakfast. How long had it been since they'd eaten enough to satisfy their hunger? Jarena could barely remember what it was like to sit down and eat her fill. Instead, they now counted themselves fortunate if there was enough food to ward off the hunger pangs. Their daily fare of corn mush thinned to a watery gruel had taken its toll on all of them. She had watched her sisters' fleshy arms and legs slowly diminish to little more than twiglike appendages and her father's thickset body turn much too lean. If help didn't arrive, they'd be no more than skeletons by winter's end.

Jarena sat up in the bed and forced her feet into the cold shoes beside her bed. Might as well get up. If these troublesome thoughts of hunger were going to plague her, she'd not get any sleep. Wrapping one of the thin blankets around her shoulders, she tossed several buffalo chips and a handful of dried sunflower stalks onto the banked fire. Thankful for the pail of water Thomas had fetched for her last night, Jarena broke the thin layer of ice and filled the coffeepot. The coffee would be weak, but no matter—the men wouldn't complain. They knew she was doing her best to make do. She moved silently about the room, but the others were soon awake and ready to begin another day.

They had gathered near the fire for Bible reading when a loud commotion came from outside. Certain it was nothing more than children playing in the snow, her father motioned for Jarena to continue reading. She focused on the passage, trying to ignore the noise as it escalated to extraordinary heights. Jarena read more stridently, but when pounding fists sounded at their front door, the Bible reading came to an abrupt halt.

Truth hurried off to answer the door and was immediately greeted by several of the Beyer children. "Come quick! There's Indians out here, and we don' know what they's sayin'."

Truth peered around the doorway. Without a word, she yanked the children inside the dugout and turned to her family, her eyes filled with fear and her mouth gaping. "There truly is Injuns out there. What are we gonna do, Pappy?"

Ezekiel rose to his feet and grabbed his coat from a peg. Thomas and Jarena followed suit, and Jarena immediately issued instructions to the twins to keep the Beyer children indoors. She sent up a silent prayer that the little ruffians wouldn't completely destroy the dugout before they returned. Several other children were watching the Indians from what Jarena hoped was a safe distance. Ezekiel shooed them off toward home as the three adults approached the group of Indians. Though they appeared friendly enough, Jarena thought her father should have a weapon of some kind—what if they needed protection? There were at least twenty Indians standing around. Perhaps there were even more of them lurking nearby. A nervous giggle stuck in her throat like a wad of cotton.

She stared at the fearsome group. All of them were tall and muscular. Their heads were completely shaved—except for a scalp lock that extended from their foreheads to the back of their necks. Tattoos emblazoned their chests and arms, and they wore beaded ear ornaments and armbands of intricate design and beauty. Robes of buffalo or bearskin draped their shoulders. Jarena marveled at their apparent comfort standing outdoors in the frigid January weather. They appeared stately, and she hoped it was kindness she saw in the eyes of the warrior who stepped forward.

He rubbed his belly and pointed toward the dugouts. "Food!"

Jarena took a step backward and nearly laughed aloud at the request. If only they knew how little food there was in this tiny settlement. Overcome by the absurdity of the request, Jarena motioned the man to follow her.

Ezekiel shot a warning glance in her direction. "Jarena!"

"No, Pappy, let them see we have no food."

She trudged forward, occasionally glancing back over her shoulder and motioning the man forward. The remainder of the entourage followed at a distance while watching the apprehensive faces that peered from behind partially open doors. Jarena pushed open the dugout door and told her sisters and the Beyer children to sit on the bed. The visitor bent down as he entered the hovel. Jarena lifted the near empty sack of cornmeal and opened the other crates and sacks, as well, showing him what little they had.

"No food. We have no food." She pulled on her dress to emphasize she'd grown thin from lack of nutrition. She wanted to make him understand they were starving.

He looked at her and frowned. "Food!"

She hurried to her sisters and tugged on their too-large clothing. How could she make him understand? She held out her empty hands. "No food."

"Food!" The Indian grabbed her by the wrist and pulled her outside of the dugout. Motioning to Thomas and Ezekiel to follow, he walked to the edge of the settlement and pointed to their tethered horses and supplies a number of yards away. Still holding Jarena by the arm, he continued toward the horses with Ezekiel and Thomas following on his heels.

As they drew nearer, Thomas said, "They been on a winter hunt. I heard tell in Topeka 'bout the Osage Indians comin' through and goin' to the mountains on their winter hunts. Looks like they was mighty successful, too."

The leader looked at Jarena and walked toward a dead antelope. "Food!"

Jarena pointed back and forth between the animal and the settlement. "For us? We can have this antelope? You're giving it to us?"

The leader grunted an affirmation and then spoke to several of his men. A short time later the animal had been deposited outside the Harban residence and Jarena was attempting to thank the leader for his kindness. She quickly grew frustrated, doubting he'd understood any of her rambling words.

Without warning, he tugged on the side of her loose-fitting dress and then pretended to eat. "Food." He nodded encouragingly.

She smiled and agreed. "Yes. Food will help my dress to once again fit. Thank you."

The Osage left the settlement as silently as they'd entered. There had been no reason for the small band of hunters to stop and share their food in Nicodemus—no reason, save the prayers of God's starving people.

————

The bright February sun glistened with an intensity that belied the ice- and snow-covered ground outside Samuel's window. He wondered how the folks in Nicodemus were faring and if Ivan Lovejoy's visit with the governor had resulted in any assistance for the fledgling community. Though Christmas had been somewhat bleak in the Boyle household, he was certain the folks in Nicodemus would have gladly exchanged places. Samuel had hoped to make another journey to the settlement on several occasions, but his plans had been thwarted each time, either by the weather or his wife's sickly condition. Today, however, he was determined to succeed. No threat of a storm loomed on the horizon, and there were no patients waiting for medical attention, save his wife. He prayed this journey to Nicodemus would resolve some of her worries so that she would finally stay abed and regain her strength.

Macia walked into the parlor with a pleading look upon her face. "Please may I go with you, Father? I do long to get out of this house for a short time—and I would so like to see how much little Nathan has grown."

"And I would enjoy your company, my dear. But someone needs to remain at home with your mother. I think you can lend her more comfort than Harvey. I'll do all in my power to take you with me the next time. The weather will be much more pleasant by early spring."

Macia wrinkled her nose and plopped down in the chair opposite him. "We don't know that for certain. The snow may remain on the ground until May or June."

His daughter was correct. They didn't know when the cold weather would disappear. He'd heard varying reports from the folks in Ellis, Stockton, and other outlying areas. Even those living in Hill City gave conflicting accounts, and Samuel wasn't sure whom to believe. Besides, the weather could change dramatically from year to year. He doubted if anyone could accurately predict when spring would finally arrive in Kansas.

"Be certain you heat some soup for your mother's noonday meal and take it to her in our room, Macia. She needs to remain in bed. If she's awake, you could read to her. I received a newspaper from Georgetown the other day—better yet, read from one of those books of poetry she enjoys."

"Yes, Father. And where is Harvey? Is he going with you?" There was a hint of jealousy in her voice.

"No. He's helping Jeb Malone down at the livery."

She sniggered. "Harvey is helping Jeb? It's more likely Harvey is sitting by the fire avoiding any work here at home while Jeb takes care of his own tasks at the livery, don't you think?"

"Jeb came and asked for your brother's assistance. That being the case, I must assume he's helping in one way or another. Besides, there's not much he can do here at home right now. The wood is piled high and the animals are cared for. Was there something you wanted him to do?"

"I suppose not. You had best be on your

way if you're going to get back before night-fall."

Samuel leaned down and kissed Macia's cheek. He realized she was lonely, and a visit with Betsy Turnbull, Ada Johnson, or Louise Kramer did little to allay his daughter's feelings of isolation. Truth be told, young Lucy Malone provided more company than any of the married women. When he went to the livery for his sleigh, he would ask Jeb if Lucy could visit Macia this afternoon.

By the time Samuel arrived in Nicodemus, the sun was overhead. The journey had taken longer than he'd anticipated with the snow slowing the horses considerably. He realized the unfortunate delays would limit his time in Nicodemus. Along the way, he decided to stop first at the Harban dugout. Ezekiel could likely give him any news regarding the success of Mr. Lovejoy's visit with the governor. That fact aside, Samuel found a warmth and sincerity in Ezekiel, a camaraderie that drew him to the man. Certainly there were others in the community who were more educated and of greater means than Ezekiel Harban, but none of finer character—at least not in Samuel's mind.

The door to the Harban dugout opened, and Samuel was greeted with Ezekiel's welcoming smile. "Come in. Come in. Ain't this a good surprise. Look who's come to see us," he said to the three girls who were gathered around the fading fire.

Truth jumped up. "Dr. Boyle! How nice to see ya. I'll pour you a cup of coffee."

Samuel waved for her to sit down. "No. You save that coffee for yourselves."

"You sho' you don' want some?" She remained standing beside her chair. "Don't nobody drink it 'cept Pappy and Thomas."

Jarena emitted an exasperated sigh. "Nobody drinks it except Pappy and Thomas."

"Dat's what I said." Truth's eyes twinkled with mischief.

"No, but I thank you for the kind offer." Samuel glanced about the small room before returning his gaze to Ezekiel. "Where is Thomas?"

"Seems to think he's gonna find him some critter out there in the snow to trap and bring us for supper. Tol' him the only thing he's gonna get out there is cold hands and feet, but he don' listen no better'n the rest of these young'uns. He goes out there ever' day and checks them traps."

Leaning forward, Jarena directed her full attention on their visitor. "What brings you out in this frigid weather, Dr. Boyle?"

"Several matters, but first tell me how you folks have been faring through these last months."

"It's been a true test of faith, but the Lord has provided—not a lot, mind you, but we's getting by," Ezekiel answered. "About the middle of January, when we thought we wouldn't make it no longer, we had us a prayer meetin' led by the reverend. The next day—the very next day—there was a band of Indians come through here. What kind was they, Jarena?"

"Osage."

"That's it. Osage Indians. Anyway, Thomas said he heard tell they come through this way on their hunts from time to time."

Samuel listened as the small family related the details of the Indians' visit and other occurrences of the past month; he marveled at their thankful spirits. He doubted he or his family would have remained so stalwart. In fact, after hearing their story, he considered leaving the dugout without putting voice to his primary cause for coming.

"And what about you and your family?" Ezekiel asked.

The question gave him the needed opportunity to make his appeal. He hesitated a moment, worried the small family might find his request insensitive after all they had been forced to endure. However, Margaret's need won out. "My wife is ill and she needs to remain in bed or she isn't going to get well. However, she feels obligated to get up every day and complete her housework, cook meals, and perform all of her household duties. Jarena, I'm sure you'll remember that Macia is ill-equipped to be of much assistance."

Jarena smiled. "As I recall, she didn't seem to have much training with housework, though Miss Hattie was able to improve her sewing skills."

Samuel laughed. "Indeed. However, I fear that her mother hasn't been able to do the same. I was wondering if one of you girls, or perhaps someone else here in Nicodemus, might be willing to come and live with us in Hill City—take care of Mrs. Boyle's duties so that she'd be willing to remain abed. Of course, there would be room and board as well as wages."

"Well?" Ezekiel arched his bushy eyebrows and looked at his daughters. "Any of you wantin' to go and earn some money?"

"I'd be pleased to assist you, Dr. Boyle, but—" Jarena started.

Truth giggled and winked at Grace. "But she ain't willing to leave Charlie Francis back here in Nicodemus."

"I don't need you speaking for me," she said, directing a frown at her younger sister.

Grace wrapped her arms tight around her waist and seemed to shrivel into a small child. "I don't think I want to leave the rest of my family," Grace meekly replied.

"I'll go," Truth said bravely. "The money will help, won't it, Pappy?"

"Of course it will help, but you don't need to be goin' 'less that's what you want to do. You needs to be sure, 'cause the doctor can't be bringin' you back here every time you's missin' me or your sisters. Ain't you gonna miss havin' Grace ta keep ya company?"

"Course I will, but I ain't gonna be gone

forever. Once the missus gets better, I'll be back home. Ain't that right, Dr. Boyle?"

"Yes, if that's what you decide. And I'm in hopes my wife's health will be restored very soon."

"You's gonna have to work, gal," Ezekiel said. "Ain't gonna be like livin' here where you depend on Jarena to do things when you's wantin' to slack off. When you's workin' for someone, you's got to give your very best. You understan' that?"

"Yes, Pappy."

"You knows when it's washday or time to be fixin' a meal, so don' you be waitin' 'round fer someone to tell you to get to movin'. Jarena done trained you ta do things proper, and you need to make us proud."

"I know, Pappy. I only do that at home 'cause it makes Jarena get all upset," she said with a quick chuckle. "Only thing is, I don' know if I can cook the fancy kind of food your missus might want. I only learned to cook simple fare."

"I'm certain we'll be pleased with whatever you prepare. However, if she wants something special, she can give you some instruction. Besides, she has cookbooks.

Even she must use those from time to time. She didn't do much cooking before we moved to Hill City. Can you read, Truth?"

"Oh yes. Jarena's been teachin' us to read since we was little."

A frown creased Jarena's soft features. "I do worry Truth won't be receiving her school lessons once she leaves home."

"Set your mind at ease, Jarena. I'll be certain to have Macia assist in that regard. In fact, Macia has quite a library of books, and she also helps one of the young girls in Hill City with lessons. I'm certain she'd be pleased to do the same for Truth."

Truth shot her sister a disgusted look. "You're determined to keep my nose in a book, ain't you?"

"*Aren't* you! Obviously you need additional lessons since you refuse to use proper English. And we'll expect to receive letters from you, also," Jarena added.

"No doubt you'll be goin' over each one lookin' for mistakes."

Jarena gave her sister a hug. "Only because I want you to always do your best."

"Your sister's right, Truth," their father said. "You need to be learnin' to read and write real good. Don' want you growin' up like me: not able to read or write ceptin' to sign my name. I's good at signin' my name."

"Yes, Pappy."

Ezekiel slapped his palm on the table. "Guess we's settled, then. Best get busy and pack your clothes while me and Dr. Boyle visit fer a while."

"Tell me, Ezekiel, has there been any word since Ivan Lovejoy made his visit to Topeka? I've been anxious to know if the governor has notified Ivan of any efforts made on behalf of the community."

"Seems as though the governor don' think he can do nothing on his own 'less there's been some of them politicians come to look at things fer themselves. Guess they need to see if it's as bad as Ivan tol' 'em. He says if things is bad, he'll seek aid fer us. Course, we could all be dead by the time they gets here." There was sadness in his eyes as he spoke.

"Did Ivan think the governor was sincere in his commitment to investigate?"

"I don' think Ivan was too pleased." Ezekiel motioned to Jarena. "You thought Ivan was upset 'bout his visit with the governor, didn' you?"

She nodded. "Mr. Lovejoy doesn't think

the governor was sincere, but there's little chance of getting our message to Congress without the man's support. Mr. Lovejoy thought there was little else he could do, so he agreed to wait for the arrival of the senators. Unfortunately, the governor didn't set a date for the visit, so we have no way of knowing when help may arrive."

Samuel rubbed his jaw and thought for a moment. "Any word from Wilbur Rawlins?"

Ezekiel shook his head. "Nothin'. Ivan stopped at several businesses in Topeka and asked if they'd donate food or money. Seems Wilbur had already gone to most of the stores askin' for aid. Wilbur done tol' one of them storeowners he was comin' back to Nicodemus weeks ago. Course, we know that ain't the truth."

"So Ivan didn't have success gathering any supplies to bring back?"

Jarena poured her father a cup of coffee and set it before him. "Once Mr. Lovejoy learned that most of the business owners had already been approached to contribute, he decided any further efforts would be futile. He returned home with nothing more than his hope that the governor will soon send a few of his senators."

Ezekiel took a swallow of the coffee. "Hard to believe Wilbur would do such a thing. Sure is sad to see how gettin' hold of money tests the honor of a man. But I'm still prayin' that Wilbur's gonna return with the money or supplies and prove he's da man I thought he was."

CHAPTER

24

Truth snuggled under the heavy sleigh blankets and enjoyed the jingling of the sleigh bells and whooshing sound of the runners cutting through the snow. She wondered if Mrs. Boyle would be as kind as her husband was and if their daughter, Macia, would like her. Jarena had said Macia was nice, but Jarena had spent only one afternoon with Dr. Boyle's daughter. Truth hoped her sister was correct, but anyone could act pleasant for a little while—especially among strangers.

What if they didn't like her cooking or the way she made the beds? Would they slap her like the Kincaids had the help at their mansion? After all, Macia was looking to marry one of the Kincaids—leastwise, that's what Jarena said, along with the fact that Truth shouldn't let on like she'd ever heard of the Kincaids. However, Truth wasn't certain what difference it made if she told the Boyles that her father had sharecropped for the Kincaids. But she had promised her sister, and if there was one thing Truth could do, it was keep her word. She could keep her mouth shut and bite her tongue along with the best of them. No, she wouldn't say a word, but she might just try to find out why Macia would want to marry into the Kincaid family.

"What if your family don't—doesn't like the way I cook and clean?" she ventured, careful to correct her English. Jarena had cautioned that she'd be expected to use her best grammar.

Dr. Boyle patted her hand. "I believe you'll find we're not hard to please. As I said, Mrs. Boyle has cookbooks, and she'll answer your questions. Please don't concern yourself. My wife has likely already made a list of chores that she'll explain once we get you settled in your room."

Truth stared in disbelief. "I get to have my own room?"

He laughed. "Yes, of course. It's certainly

nothing elegant, but it's private. Of course, *none* of the house would be considered elegant—especially by my wife's standards."

"My friend Dovie's living in Topeka and workin' as a housekeeper. Her family was gonna move to Nicodemus, but when we got to Topeka, they decided to stay there. I had one letter from her since we got to Nicodemus. There may be more waitin' at the post office down in Ellis. . . ."

"You must write her and tell her to address her letters to you in Hill City. Levi Turnbull goes down to Ellis and picks up the mail when the weather permits. He's the postmaster for Hill City."

"Now that I'm workin', I'll be able to pay for postage so I can write to Dovie. Pappy said we needed to use our money fer food instead of stamps. I know he was right, but I sure didn't want Dovie thinking I'd forgotten 'bout her already."

"And how does she like working in Topeka?"

"She likes it real good. Both her and her mama are working for a rich man who works in the capitol. A congressman or something like that."

"I'm afraid our house will bear little resemblance to the house where your friend Dovie is working. However, I've promised my wife that we will build a new home as soon as the weather turns warm."

"She don't like your house?"

"No, and I understand her complaints. Our home in Kentucky was far superior. However, compared to other homes in Hill City or Ellis, it's quite nice."

The two of them settled into a comfortable silence until Truth spied the semblance of a small town not far in the distance. "Is that Hill City?"

"Yes. Not long now."

In no time, Dr. Boyle was reining the team of horses to a halt in front of a large frame house. Truth looked back and forth between the house and Dr. Boyle. "Is this *your* house?"

"This is it. I'll get your bag and we'll go inside. I'll have Harvey take the horses and sleigh to the livery."

Truth's stomach began to turn like cream being churned into butter. As she followed Dr. Boyle up the front steps, she said a silent prayer that the Boyle family would find her acceptable. Though she told herself there was nothing to fear, she still wasn't completely convinced.

"I'm home!" Dr. Boyle called as they entered the hallway.

"Did you find someone to—" Macia stopped short when Truth stepped out from behind her father. "Oh, good! I was worried you'd come home without help." She grasped Truth by the hand. "Do take off your coat and come and help me in the kitchen. I have no idea what I'm doing, and Mother insists upon chicken for supper. You can cook chicken, can't you?"

"Macia! Where are your manners? You've not even been properly introduced."

"I'm sorry, Father," Macia replied, her cheeks now crimson. "Mother has been unwavering about supper preparations. She insisted upon chicken even though she knows such preparation goes well beyond my culinary expertise. I'm Macia Boyle." She smiled brightly.

"My name is Truth Harban. Pleased to meet you."

"Jarena's sister?"

"One of them. I have a twin sister, too. Her name is Grace."

"Truth and Grace—interesting names."

She nodded. "My mama said our names was good principles to live by—straight outta the Bible."

"And so they are," Dr. Boyle said. "You may hang your coat here in the hallway or in your room, whichever you choose. I'll take you upstairs and show you the room where you'll be staying."

"Why don't I help Macia with supper first? There'll be plenty of time to see my room later."

"Thank you," Macia whispered as they walked down the hallway to the kitchen. "I haven't any idea how to cut up a chicken, much less fry it."

Truth sighed with relief. She was thankful Mrs. Boyle didn't want some fancy recipe like Dovie helped fix for that congressman in Topeka. Maybe things wouldn't be so bad after all. The house was much finer than she'd expected, and she reveled in the warmth. The Boyles obviously had enough fuel to keep their fires burning throughout the house. Truth tried to imagine Macia out hunting for buffalo chips to fuel the fires and almost laughed aloud.

"If you'll show me where your mama keeps her kitchenwares, I kin get started."

Macia quickly removed her apron and handed it to Truth as she pointed out what little she knew about the kitchen. "If you can't find something, just begin looking until you find it. I'll set the table."

Before Macia could flee from the kitchen, Truth grasped her by the hand. "Wait. What else were you s'posed to fix with this chicken?"

"Whatever you want to fix. There are some sweet potatoes and some white potatoes in the root cellar. Mama said she'd like some green beans. Just fix whatever you think would be good."

Truth stared at the chicken and wondered who had killed and plucked the bird. She was sure it hadn't been Macia Boyle. "You pluck this chicken?"

Macia shivered. "No. We buy our chickens from Mrs. Johnson. We brought a couple when we first came here and she's taking care of them for us. She kills and plucks them for Mama when we need one."

As she surveyed the kitchen, Truth was thankful for the hours of cooking instructions Jarena had forced upon her throughout the years—even if she had attempted to avoid using the skills while living at home.

Although preparations had taken longer than she expected, Truth hoped that the final product would meet with Mrs. Boyle's approval. Despite the fact that Truth longed for the taste of sweet potatoes, she prepared the white potatoes instead. After adding a lump of butter and several dollops of cream, she mashed the potatoes until her arm ached. The gravy was nice and thick, just the way her own pappy loved it, and she thought of him sitting down to this fine meal and how he would savor each bite. She'd let the fire get too low and the biscuits hadn't browned the way they should have, but she hoped the family would allow for the fact that she hadn't ever cooked on a stove quite so nice as the one in their kitchen. Once she'd prepared a few more meals on the cast-iron cookstove, she'd do better.

When Macia finally peeked into the kitchen, Truth beckoned her forward. "Should I fix a tray for your mama, or can she come to the table for her meals?"

"She'll come down and join us, though

she'll go back upstairs if she becomes over-tired during the meal."

Truth wanted to ask what ailed Mrs. Boyle but knew such a question would be considered improper. Perhaps Dr. Boyle or Macia would volunteer the information. Truth stood near the sideboard, prepared to serve as the family entered the dining room.

Dr. Boyle entered the room with his wife firmly clutching his arm. "My dear, this is Truth Harban."

Truth gave a slight curtsy and smiled. "Pleased to meet you, Mrs. Boyle. I hope supper is to your liking."

Mrs. Boyle smiled in return. "We're all very pleased to have you here with us—especially Macia."

"And I'm Harvey," a younger version of Dr. Boyle said as he entered the dining room. "You can disregard Mother's last statement. I'm even more pleased to have you. Eating Macia's cooking was difficult on my digestive system." He chortled as he looked in Macia's direction.

Once the family was seated and Dr. Boyle had offered thanks, Truth began to serve the meal. "I don't have no experience serving,

Mrs. Boyle, so please tell me when I do something wrong."

Harvey chewed a bite of chicken. "So long as the food tastes this good, you can't do anything wrong around this place."

When the dishes had finally been washed and put away, Macia accompanied Truth upstairs to her room. "This house is truly awful. You must be very careful or you'll trip on the loose floorboards. I've fallen down any number of times since moving here. I can't wait until I can leave this horrid place."

Truth thought the house quite wonderful, but she didn't dispute Macia's opinion. "Your father said he's buildin' a new house this spring. You must be very happy."

The brown silk fringe that trimmed Macia's cream wool day dress swayed in a gentle rhythm as she walked down the hallway. "It is my hope that I'll be living in Kentucky by the time construction is completed on such a house. If good fortune is with me, Jackson Kincaid will ask for my hand, and we'll return to live at his home in Georgetown."

Truth snapped to attention at the mention of the Kincaid name. So Jarena had been correct: Macia Boyle *was* planning to marry Jackson Kincaid. How could someone who treated colored folks so kindly be smitten with the likes of such a man? And how could her father permit such a thing? Dr. Boyle and old Mr. Kincaid were as different as daylight and dark.

"Father mentioned Jarena is concerned about your schooling. If you'd like, I'd be happy to take over with your lessons. Jarena mentioned her love of reading. If you share her interest, you might enjoy my large library of books. You may borrow any of them."

"Thank you. I'm not so interested in education as my sister, but I better not get behind on my lessons. If I do, Jarena will tell Pappy I need to return home."

"Well, I don't want that to occur, so we best begin your lessons tomorrow. Besides, it will give us time to become better acquainted."

"Does your father cotton to the idea of you marryin' that Kincaid fellow you mentioned earlier?"

Macia giggled nervously. "Father doesn't particularly like any of the Kincaids. In fact, I believe that's one of the reasons he moved to Hill City—to keep me away from Jackson, though I doubt he'd ever admit that fact to me."

"You'd marry 'im without your father's approval?"

"If Jackson and I decide to wed, Father will eventually give his blessing. He wouldn't want to see me unhappy. Here we are—this is your room."

The room was more than Truth had imagined, and her eyes widened at the sight. There was a bedstead topped by a mattress that looked soft and a coverlet that looked warm, there were pictures on the wall, and there was even a slat-backed rocker in one corner. The single window facing the rear yard was flanked by lacy white curtains. After eating a supper of fried chicken, biscuits, and gravy, she was in a room the likes of which she could never have imagined for her own. She wondered what Jarena and Grace would think of having such a place for themselves. A part of her longed to have them see it, yet a sense of guilt crept in and captured a piece of her joy. While her family huddled around a tiny fire struggling to keep warm, she was cozy and well fed in this lovely house—it seemed completely improper.

———

Ezekiel pulled his coat tight and ducked his head against the wind as he made his way back to his dugout. He had spent the afternoon visiting with Ivan Lovejoy. Even though he knew no one could have made it to Ellis for the mail, Ezekiel had hoped Ivan might have something positive to say about their situation. Making do had become an all-consuming task. Folks had scrimped and borrowed until there was little left among any of them. Ezekiel had portioned out the cornmeal, flour, beans, and rice delivered by Dr. Boyle. However, each family's portion had been small, and it wouldn't be long until those few rations were gone. Thomas had occasional good fortune at a small fishing hole in the river, but none of the others seemed to have his knack for fishing through a hole in the ice.

He'd be pleased to see spring arrive so he could begin working his own piece of land. Even though he knew the plowing and planting would prove a challenge, he longed to begin farming in earnest. Without tools and horses, they'd likely be unable to sow many fields. But even if he had to use an axe to chop out the rows, Ezekiel vowed he'd put in a crop—it would be his first order of business. Certainly, he wanted to build a house on his own land, but his crops would come first. They would provide a means to support his family. At least he prayed they would.

"Ho! Ezekiel!"

Ezekiel lifted his gaze and was met by a blast of icy wind. "Charles! What you doin' out in this weather?"

"Thought I'd come and spend a little time with Jarena, if that's all right with you."

"Course it is. Time gets heavy when we's indoors all the time. How's your mama and pappy doin'?"

"Mama's wishing she was back in Kentucky, and she doesn't miss any opportunity to tell me, but other than that, I guess they're fine. Like everyone else, they're wondering if we're going to have enough food to make it through the rest of the winter."

Ezekiel nodded knowingly as he opened the door for Charles. "Come on in." Charles stopped short at the sight that greeted him.

Jarena and Thomas sat at the small wooden table with their heads close together. They obviously were expecting only Ezekiel to enter the room, for they didn't look up until he cleared his throat.

Jarena jumped to her feet and sent her chair crashing to the dirt floor. "Charles! What a pleasant surprise. I wasn't expecting you."

Charles clenched his jaw and glowered at Thomas. "I can see that."

Thomas grinned and shook his head. "Don't go gettin' yourself all riled up. Ain't what ya think."

"You have no idea what I'm thinking," Charles shot back.

Thomas picked up Jarena's chair. "Ain't much doubt—all I gotta do is look at all that anger you're sending my way. You think I'm tryin' to steal Jarena's affections."

"Pretty easy to see that's exactly what you're doing," Charles grumbled, continuing to glare at Thomas. "The two of you sitting there side by side, all cozy."

"Stop it, Charles! I'm helping Thomas learn to read and write—nothing more. You seem to be condemning both of us for acting dishonorably. I don't appreciate such accusations, nor do I take them lightly. Do you think so little of me that you believe I would behave in such a manner?"

Charles's pleading look reminded Ezekiel of a drowning man longing to reach shore, but this wasn't Ezekiel's quarrel. "You got into this on your own, and I guess you's gonna have to get out the same way."

"I apologize, Jarena. I wasn't meaning to cast doubt on your behavior, but I figure Thomas is going to use any time alone with you to his advantage—what with you being so pretty and all."

Grace giggled at the final remark.

"Are you implyin' I'd act less than honorable toward anyone in this house?" Thomas pressed.

"I'm saying I think you'll do whatever you can to win Jarena's heart. I see the way you look at her when you think I'm not watching," Charles countered vehemently.

"This is foolishness. Thomas isn't interested in me. He only wants to develop his reading and penmanship skills. Isn't that right?" Jarena looked to Thomas for confirmation.

He shrugged. "Guess if he wants to believe I'm tryin' to court you, then that's up to him. I ain't gonna say nothin' more."

"You see?" Charles scowled. "He all but admitted I'm right."

"Enough!" Ezekiel interrupted. "Ain't gonna spend the rest of the evenin' listenin' to this arguing back and forth. Either make your peace or I'm gonna have to ask you to leave, Charles. Not that I'm holdin' nothin' against you, but Thomas lives here, too, so I sure can't be askin' him to leave."

"May I ask permission to have Jarena come and visit over at our dugout? If she wants to, that is." Charles gave Jarena a sidelong glance as he made the request.

"I don't see why not," Ezekiel said. "You wanna go over and visit with Charles and his folks, Jarena?"

"Sure is cold out there. You might wanna stay here by the fire," Thomas said, raising a questioning eyebrow toward Jarena.

"I think I can manage to keep her warm," Charles said with an icy stare.

CHAPTER

25

Hill City, Kansas • February 1878

Truth donned the heavy woolen cape Macia had given her and decided she should check with Mrs. Boyle one final time before heading off to the general store. She silently padded upstairs and quietly entered the bedroom. Should Mrs. Boyle be napping, she didn't want to disturb her. Truth remained still, waiting to be acknowledged.

"Yes, Truth?"

"I'm leaving for the general store, Mrs. Boyle. I have your list with me. Is there anything you need afore I go?"

"No, thank you. I finished my tea, and I

believe I'll go back to sleep for a while. Close the door as you leave, please."

"Yes, ma'am." Truth backed out of the door and carefully pulled the door handle until she heard the now-familiar click.

Grasping the basket with one hand, she trudged through the crusted snow toward the Johnsons' general store. The world was silent save the crunching of snow beneath her feet, and she wondered if this quiet was anything like the vast silence that had surrounded God before He created the animals and mankind. The thought of such ongoing stillness caused her to shiver.

The tiny bell over the front door of the store announced her arrival, and Mrs. Johnson fluttered from their living quarters. "Truth! It's mighty cold to be out walking."

She shrugged. "It's not so bad."

"How's Margaret doing today?"

"Not well," she said as she pulled the grocery list from her pocket, "but she was up and about earlier in the week. I've got a list of supplies I need to purchase. Hope you got everything on hand."

"I should be able to help you. Mr. Johnson was down to Ellis on Saturday and made it through the snow in fine order, thanks to the good waxing job he did on the runners before leaving. At least that's what he says." She started scurrying around, gathering the items on the list. "I think it's the horses that should be receiving thanks for hauling that load of goods through the snow."

"Either way, it's a blessing he was able to make it. I know your supplies were running low, and Dr. Boyle's been hankerin' for some real coffee."

"I can sure help you with that. We got coffee and tea in our shipment. Mr. Johnson picked up the mail, too. There's several letters for the Boyles you can take with you. And I believe there's one for you and another for your father."

"One for me? I hope it's from my friend Dovie. I can't figure who'd be writing to my pappy, though," she commented with a thoughtful frown. She examined the envelopes and nearly squealed with delight when she saw Dovie's familiar handwriting on the envelope addressed to her. She didn't recognize the awkward script on her father's letter, but the name in the upper corner was familiar: Lilly Verdue—her mother's half-sister, who lived in Louisiana. Why would she be writing to her father?

"Looks important," Mrs. Johnson said while examining a piece of mail addressed to Dr. Boyle.

Truth took the letter with an official-appearing seal imprinted on the envelope. "It does look important." She carefully tucked the missive among the supplies in her basket. "I suppose I best be on my way. Don't want Mrs. Boyle worrying."

Mrs. Johnson tapped her finger on the counter. "You need to sign the ledger."

"Sorry," Truth mumbled. She always had to be reminded to sign the Boyles's page in Mrs. Johnson's ledger book.

The walk home wasn't nearly so enjoyable as her earlier journey. The basket was heavy and soon cut into the flesh along the inside of her arm. Just when she'd comfortably positioned the basket, the wind increased and swirled a continuous blast of stinging snow into her face. By the time she arrived home, she wished for nothing more than the warmth of a fire, a cup of something warm to drink, and a few moments alone to read Dovie's letter.

Dr. Boyle opened the door as she arrived

and quickly took the overflowing container from her arm. "What are you doing walking about in this cold weather?"

"We needed the supplies, and the wind wasn't blowing when I left the house. In fact, it didn't seem cold in the least as I walked to the mercantile."

Truth fidgeted excitedly. "I received a letter from my friend Dovie, who's living in Topeka. And I brought letters for you, too."

"Then you must sit down and read yours while I read mine." Dr. Boyle pulled one of the kitchen chairs away from the worktable.

"I'll make you a cup of coffee before—"

"Sit, sit. My coffee can wait," he instructed.

Truth sat down opposite Dr. Boyle and began reading Dovie's carefully formed words, smiling at her friend's funny stories about keeping house and tending the two sons of a legislator and his wife. From all accounts, Dovie was plenty busy with all of her duties, and her mistress didn't sound nearly so nice as Mrs. Boyle. However, she was off duty each Sunday and allowed to attend church services and visit with her family until sundown. In that regard, Truth thought Dovie quite fortunate. She wished that she could visit her family once a week. However, both distance and weather prohibited any such arrangement for her.

Dr. Boyle slapped his letter on the table with a resounding whack. "That man infuriates me!"

Truth flinched and immediately dropped her letter onto the table. Dr. Boyle's face was twisted in anger. "What man?" Her voice warbled with fear.

He glanced up, and his countenance softened. "I've frightened you. I'm terribly sorry. It's just that this letter angered me."

"I noticed." She wondered exactly what had caused Dr. Boyle's rage but hesitated to inquire further. She'd bide her time. If he wanted to tell her, so be it.

He folded the letter, tucked it back into the envelope, and stood up. "I'll be in my library."

"But your coffee . . ."

He gazed at her absentmindedly. "When it's ready, I'll come back and fetch a cup."

Macia entered the kitchen in yet another dress Truth had never seen. She wondered how many clothes were stuffed into the two wardrobes in Macia's room. "I thought I heard Father down here."

Truth nodded. "He was—but he's gone off to his library. He closed the door."

"I went over your lessons while you were at the store. I noticed them on the chest in your room as I passed down the hallway. I've corrected them for you."

Truth startled at Macia's comment. "You went through all of the papers on my chest?"

"As I said, I corrected your lessons." Macia glanced at the ceiling. "I believe I hear mother stirring about upstairs. I best go check on her."

Long after Macia had departed the room, Truth remained rooted to her chair. What if Macia had read the letter she'd begun writing to Jarena? Truth trembled, but she willed herself to remain calm. She must begin supper preparations. Forcing herself into action, she counted out enough potatoes for the evening meal. Her hands shook as she began to peel. She tightened her fingers around the handle of the paring knife and hoped she wouldn't cut herself. Why hadn't she tucked the half-finished letter into the chest of drawers before leaving for the store? She tried to remember Macia's exact reply. It had been elusive—which meant she'd surely read Truth's remarks to Jarena regarding the Kincaids. Now Macia would know her father had been a share-cropper for the Kincaids. This wasn't good—not good at all. Yet what could she do? Confront Macia? No. Best to remain silent and wait. If Macia didn't mention the letter, neither would she.

There was little time to think about the let-ter during supper, for it was then that Truth discovered the contents of Dr. Boyle's letter. He'd obviously spent the remainder of the afternoon fretting about it, for it was the first thing he mentioned once the family had seated themselves for supper. Surprisingly, Mrs. Boyle decided to join them, and as Truth hurried to set another place at the table, the doctor told about the correspon-dence.

"I've had a letter from Governor Anthony. Truth picked it up at the mercantile when she was shopping today."

Margaret arched her eyebrows. "The gov-ernor? And why is he writing to *you,* my dear?"

"Seems he's sending a delegation of leg-islators from Topeka. He wants them to ob-serve firsthand the conditions in Nicodemus. He says he's received conflicting reports and needs accurate information so he can make an informed decision."

"But why come to Hill City if it's Nicodemus he's investigating?" Mrs. Boyle said, frowning.

"They can't possibly conclude their journey in one day, and it seems that Mr. Hill told the governor I would be willing to make arrangements for an overnight stay for the gentlemen."

She gasped. "Here? In Hill City? At that primitive sod hotel? Whatever will those men think?"

"I'm certain they'll be mortified," Macia offered.

Dr. Boyle spread a thick layer of jam on his biscuit. "Just because you'd be affronted doesn't mean they'll feel the same. I'm certain these men know what to expect out here on the prairie. I plan to register them at the hotel unless you'd prefer to host them."

Margaret clutched her bodice as though she might faint at the suggestion. "Have you taken leave of your senses, Samuel? I wouldn't consider entertaining overnight guests in this house."

"Then I suppose the issue of their accommodations is settled. In addition to the governor's missive, I also received a letter from Mr. Hill—one that truly caused my blood to boil. Had Mr. Hill been standing in front of me, I do believe I would have given him a tongue-lashing that he'd not soon forget."

Harvey leaned back in his chair. "A letter from Mr. Hill? So the lost has been found. What did he have to say, Father?"

"He asked that I escort the group of delegates to Nicodemus and give the men a good report concerning the two communities. A *good* report. Can you believe he'd ask such a thing? He went on to say he'd be in my debt if I would explain that he's had difficulty meeting the completion dates because of his other commitments. Then he asked that I tell the legislators he did everything possible to fulfill his promises."

"From his request, I surmise he's hoping your principles are no better than his own, which proves he does not know you at all, my dear—after all, you spent little time with him in Georgetown. He likely believes you have no personal knowledge of the difficult circumstances in Nicodemus." Margaret lifted her cup to her lips and then hesitated.

"I suppose we should at least extend a supper invitation, though I abhor the thought of entertaining dignitaries in this excuse of a house. When will the delegation arrive?"

Samuel unfolded the letter, scanned the contents, and gave his wife a wry smile. "If I calculate correctly, they should arrive in Ellis next week and in Hill City shortly thereafter, weather permitting."

Margaret frowned as she set her coffee cup back on the matching saucer with a loud clank. "They certainly didn't allow much time to prepare for their visit. I suppose we could all pray for a snowstorm."

"I've never known a time when you weren't prepared to entertain," Samuel said with a smile.

The next week was a blur, the days fading in and out at a rapid pace as Truth worked to complete Mrs. Boyle's list of preparations. The older woman was up and about for long periods each day, apparently feeling well enough to plan a dinner party. Though Truth had gone to her room late last night, she remained awake long enough to complete her letter to Jarena and pen a brief letter to her father and one to Grace.

Dr. Boyle had agreed to deliver her missives along with the mail Mr. Johnson had picked up in Ellis for the Nicodemus settlers. Even though Dr. Boyle and the other delegates would be in Nicodemus for only a few hours, Truth hoped Jarena or Grace would have time to send a reply with Dr. Boyle. She longed to hear how her family had been faring and perhaps receive a word of praise for the money she enclosed with her letter. But mostly she wanted to know why Aunt Lilly had written to her father.

CHAPTER

26

Supper would be served at seven o'clock, and as the hour drew closer, Truth began listening for the sound of voices in the outer rooms. She feared Mrs. Boyle would be upset if the guests were late and even more distressed if the meal didn't proceed exactly as planned. Truth hoped she could meet the older woman's expectations. She hadn't even heard of some of the dishes she was expected to prepare, nor had she been aware of the finer points of setting a "proper" table for eight. She now knew that the napkins must be folded to resemble fans and placed in the exact center of each dinner plate. Pure nonsense so far as Truth was concerned, yet Mrs. Boyle found these minute details to be of extreme importance.

Truth had just begun to whisk cream into the soup when she heard the front door open. Soon thereafter, the sounds of animated chatter and laughter floated into the kitchen. When she heard the tinkling of a small bell, she quickly donned the white apron Mrs. Boyle had instructed her to wear when serving.

The four guests and the Boyle family settled into their chairs as Truth delivered the platters and bowls to the dining room. When she was sure she had brought everything, she stood near the buffet, preparing to refill dishes and fill empty glasses and cups while the family and guests partook of the meal.

"I can't tell you how much we appreciate your invitation to supper, Mrs. Boyle." Senator Pomeroy helped himself to yet another piece of the succulent chicken as he spoke. "I must say, this is the first bite of decent food I've had since leaving Topeka."

"Thank you, Senator. Back in Kentucky, we would have truly entertained you. We left a lovely home with magnificent gardens back in Georgetown."

"You sound much like my wife. She's still

longing for her home in Vermont. However, the future of our country is in the frontier."

Dr. Boyle nodded his agreement. "Settling any new area takes time and frequently requires the assistance of others. After viewing the conditions in Nicodemus, I feel certain you men will encourage the governor to seek immediate aid for the town."

Senator Pomeroy wiggled his neck and then gently tugged at his nooselike collar. "I don't believe Governor Anthony was completely forthright in his letter to you, Dr. Boyle. He sent this delegation primarily because he had promised Mr. Hill that he would do so. However, the governor is of the strong opinion it wouldn't be in the best interest of the state to send out a plea for help."

Dr. Boyle frowned. "Why not? Surely there are those who would be willing to help. If not those living in Kansas, then surely in the surrounding states—or even back east."

"You must remember that we're still attempting to live down the grasshopper plague of 1874."

"We sent out a cry for help after that disaster," Senator Dwyer remarked. "However, our appeal proved to be a mistake."

"When folks heard of that catastrophic event," Pomeroy continued, "they decided against settling on the plains. We are now beginning to recover from that misconception. Once again, we've begun to increase our citizenry by convincing people that Kansas is the granary of the West." He sprinkled pepper on his baked potato. "If we send a representative to Washington stating that our western communities are failing and need assistance, it will be the ruination of populating the high plains."

"And do the rest of you concur with Senator Pomeroy?" Dr. Boyle asked the others at the table.

Senator Eustis speared several green beans with his fork. "There's no denying that the settlers in Nicodemus have a genuine need."

"Oh, that fact goes without saying," Senator Dwyer agreed. "None of us believes their request is unjustified."

Senator Pomeroy shifted in his chair. "However, the fact remains that the governor and other members of the legislature have grave concerns over the tactics being employed to attract more coloreds to the state. Unless they have the proper resources to sustain themselves, they'll become a burden upon the government. They'll be expecting handouts all the time. Surely you agree that such ongoing requests will place an unfair burden on the remaining citizenry."

Dr. Boyle sighed. "I believe that argument should be directed toward the governor's friend and colleague Mr. Hill. He's the one who actively wooed coloreds from Kentucky with promises of an existing town—false promises, I might add."

"It is patently clear that Mr. Hill made false assertions, but nothing can be done to change what has occurred in Nicodemus." Senator Dwyer stroked his graying beard as he spoke.

Dr. Boyle leaned forward and gazed directly into Dwyer's intense blue eyes. "I must heartily disagree, Senator Dwyer. The legislature can set things aright by granting aid to the families in Nicodemus who were enticed to Kansas under false pretenses."

"For the record, Dr. Boyle, we have had numerous reports that Wilbur Rawlins, one of the Nicodemus settlers, has been send-

ing out pleas for help that extend throughout eastern Kansas and even into other
states. In addition," Pomeroy continued, "I
believe you'll find that he has received food,
supplies, *and* money from private sources.
I'm told he even traveled to the Michigan
state fair and gave an impassioned plea for
his poor, starving Negro brothers. Supposedly, the audience was so moved that several boxcars of supplies were sent. We can
only hope Mr. Rawlins will cease this activ-
ity." Pomeroy pointed his fork at Dr. Boyle.
"Immigrants who plan to settle on the high
plains will be deterred should they hear
these disparaging reports!"

The young man who had been introduced
as Senator Eustis's son suddenly leaned
forward in his chair. "Then the land promoters must paint a clear picture of what awaits
these settlers. Instead, they create chaos
with half truths; the settlers will continue to
come ill-prepared to build new lives when
they believe civilization already exists in this
vast wilderness."

Everyone at the table turned to stare at
Martin Eustis. From all appearances, they
were surprised he'd entered into the conversation and even more taken aback by his

pronouncement. Senator Pomeroy's look of surprise soon turned to irritation.

"It is my understanding that you accompanied our delegation because you wanted to write a piece for the Topeka newspaper encouraging folks to settle in western Kansas." The senator's voice was tinged with anger.

"Let's don't forget that my father extended the invitation." Martin directed an amiable smile toward his father.

"Indeed. And the governor concurred that Martin would make a fine addition to our number." There was a note of pride in the senator's voice as he spoke.

"However, I made no agreement to write an article that upheld your opinions, Senator Pomeroy. I'll report the facts as I see them. The newspaper owes that to its readers; don't you agree?" Martin's unwavering stare required a response.

Senator Pomeroy cleared his throat. "Yes, of course. I wasn't implying you should write a misleading story. However, I do hope you'll grant me the courtesy of reading your article before it's submitted to your editor— especially since you're traveling at the pleasure of the governor and the legislature."

"Quite the contrary, sir. My employer is paying the cost of my train ticket and accommodations. As for reading the article before it's submitted, I'd need to seek my editor's permission."

Macia gave the young newspaper reporter a look of admiration. "I agree with Mr. Eustis. I don't believe my father would have purchased land and moved us into these primitive conditions had Mr. Hill honestly presented the existing state of affairs in Hill City."

A gentle smile curved Dr. Boyle's lips as he watched the exchange between the two young people.

Martin turned his attention to the doctor. "Is that true, Dr. Boyle?"

"It's true that I was somewhat misled. I did expect to see a larger community and better living conditions."

"But you've remained in Hill City," Senator Pomeroy asserted, "and you've not looked to others for financial aid. As I see things, the land agents should immediately cease beating the drum for the coloreds—they must issue their appeals to white immigrants who have the money and intelligence to establish themselves without begging from others." There was a hint of triumph in his statement.

"The land promoters are doing exactly what the legislature expected of them: bringing in new homesteaders to settle the plains," Senator Dwyer said. "It only makes good sense to reach out to those most in need of a new beginning."

"You mark my words," Pomeroy said, clenching his jaw, "the coloreds will be the ruination of the West."

Angered by Senator Pomeroy's remarks, Truth thought to take up the argument, but she stopped short when Dr. Boyle slapped his hand on the table with a resounding *whap.*

"I am completely disgusted by such attitudes. I've visited with every member of the Nicodemus community, and I have absolutely no doubt that those fine folks will make exceptional contributions to this state. They are a dedicated, industrious group of people who are intent upon carving out a good life for their families. In spite of their dire circumstances, they remain enthusiastic and anxious to begin planting crops, building new homes, and establishing businesses. And they'll be able to do all of that if they are given the same assistance and treated with the same kindnesses as their white brothers receive."

Senator Eustis took a drink of water and nodded. "I'm certain the governor will give credence to your words."

Samuel directed a wry smile at Senator Eustis. "Only if he actually hears them."

———

"Are you certain you wouldn't prefer joining the men in my father's library?" Macia asked Martin Eustis as they walked into the parlor.

"I'm absolutely certain. Since leaving Topeka, my days have been filled with political discussions. I long to talk about something other than the Kansas legislature and the problems they are attempting to solve. Spending time with you and Harvey will be a welcome change." Martin sat down opposite Macia.

"I'm afraid you'll have to settle for a visit with Macia," Harvey said as he shrugged into his coat. "I promised our local blacksmith I'd return to assist him after supper. I don't expect I'll be home until late." He buttoned the last button. "It was a pleasure meeting you. I'm certain Macia will do her best to entertain you." Harvey gave his sister an exaggerated wink, shook hands with Martin, and then hurried out the front door.

Martin leaned back in his chair. "I'm thankful you're not going to send me off to a smoke-filled room of legislators who are likely belaboring their strategies for settling the West."

"You mentioned an article you're writing for the newspaper. Do your readers in Topeka find western settlement a topic of interest?"

He nodded. "Growth in population and settlement of the high plains is a matter of importance to many folks, though I'm sure there are those who find the topic dull. However, tales of the grasshopper infestation several years ago have caused many to reconsider moving to the plains. There remains a sense of doubt that farmers will ever be self-sufficient in this part of the state. And while I don't think I can alleviate all of their doubts, I do want to give an honest report of what I find."

"That's admirable of you. However, I don't believe that even an honest report would have prepared me for life in this region. I long for the day when I'll return to make my home in Kentucky."

"I'm surprised to hear that. From all that your father said, I believed he was going to remain in Kansas. I must say I'm truly disappointed by your revelation—especially since I planned to draw upon his relocation to illustrate the caliber of men who are choosing to move west with their families."

"Oh, Father doesn't plan to leave, only me," she corrected.

Deep wrinkles creased Martin's forehead. "Your father is more progressive than I realized."

"Why, whatever do you mean by that remark, Mr. Eustis?"

"Allowing his daughter to move away and live by herself is rather unusual, wouldn't you agree?"

She smiled as she shook her head. "Dear me, you completely misunderstood. My beau, Jackson Kincaid, lives in Georgetown. My heart tells me Jackson and I will marry within a year. Of course, we would live on his father's plantation—Jackson would never consider leaving Kentucky."

"Since you're intent upon leaving Kansas, I suppose that's reason enough to marry Mr.

Kincaid, though I must admit I'm sorry to hear you'll be departing."

Macia tucked an errant curl behind one ear. "Oh? And why is that, Mr. Eustis?"

"I had hoped for the opportunity to have you visit Topeka—with your family, of course," he said. "Though I realize Topeka isn't as modern as some of the large eastern cities, I find it quite agreeable."

At the moment, any place larger than Hill City sounded agreeable. Besides, Jackson might not arrive for many months. A journey to Topeka could prove a pleasant diversion in the near future—something to amuse her until Jackson arrived.

CHAPTER

27

Ellis, Kansas • March 1878

Dawn hadn't arrived any too soon for members of the Boyle family. Macia decided the only thing that would have been more exciting than meeting Carlisle's train in Ellis would be the arrival of Jackson Kincaid. However, the thought of seeing her older brother was reason enough for her to rise at daybreak. And even Harvey, who detested the early morning, had hurried off to retrieve the team of horses and wagon before first light.

Mrs. Boyle stepped onto the porch and

shaded her eyes as the wagon approached. "I thought we would take the carriage."

Dr. Boyle took his wife by the arm and patiently urged her forward. "If we're to bring back supplies as well as Carlisle and his baggage, we'll need something larger than the carriage, my dear."

Harvey rushed forward. "Father had Jeb and me replace the wooden bench with a cushioned seat with a back support so you could comfortably rest your back. Jeb even used his blacksmith tools and fashioned some springs to cradle the seat. I'm certain you'll find it more comfortable."

Margaret aimed a benevolent smile at her son. "How thoughtful of you boys to try and help."

Macia grinned at her brother as she climbed into the wagon. The reply made Jeb and Harvey sound as though they were ten-year-olds. "I see you and Jeb put seats along the sides of the wagon, also."

Harvey nodded. "They can be removed easily enough, if need be. Jeb thought you'd find the ride more enjoyable if you didn't have to sit in the wagon bed."

"Did he? I didn't realize Jeb worried so

much about the Boyle women," Macia commented as they rode out of town.

"Only you. Though I tell him to give up. He's truly a nice fellow."

"What is *that* supposed to mean? That I don't deserve a nice fellow? Jackson Kincaid is a nice fellow, also!"

Harvey grunted. "Jackson is pompous and self-indulgent; he cares little for anyone other than himself. When are you going to see that?"

Macia tilted her chin up and folded her arms across her waist. She almost *hmmph*ed but decided not to give Harvey the satisfaction of knowing he'd gotten to her.

Harvey pulled his hat forward to cover his eyes. Minutes later he was slouched on the seat, sleeping soundly as the wagon bounced toward Ellis.

A train whistle sounded in the distance as they neared the town of Ellis. Harvey pushed himself upright and peered toward the east.

"Did I hear a train whistle?"

Macia shot her brother a look of annoyance. "Yes. If you'd stay awake, you'd know what was going on about you. I believe the only time I've seen you awake is when we stopped to water the horses."

"Come on, I'll help you down." He jumped from the wagon and offered his hand.

"You two go on ahead while I assist your mother," Dr. Boyle instructed.

Macia and Harvey didn't need any further encouragement. The two of them hurried through the doors of the train station. Though the train had arrived, the passengers had not yet begun to disembark.

Harvey grasped Macia's hand and strutted toward the rear doors of the station. "Let's go wait on the platform."

She glanced over her shoulder. "Wait, Harvey. Mother and Father are coming in now. Let's all go out together. It will be nice for Carlisle to see the entire family waiting for him when he gets off the train."

The four of them gathered near the passenger cars, all straining to catch a glimpse of Carlisle through the sooty windows.

Macia pointed at a cluster of passengers inside the train waiting to disembark. "There he is!"

A tear rolled down her mother's cheek, and Macia embraced the older woman's shoulder. "Don't cry, Mother. This is a time for rejoicing. Carlisle is going to be here for a nice long visit."

"But then he's off to Fort Sill in the Indian Territory." She sighed and looked heavenward.

"Let's enjoy the time we have with him, my dear. There he is now." Samuel pointed at two men striding toward them. "I wonder if the fellow with him is in the military, too."

"Father! Mother!" Carlisle greeted as he hugged his parents and then turned his attention to Macia and Harvey. "You all look wonderful," he said before turning to pull his companion forward. "I'd like all of you to meet Moses Wyman. We met on the train, and Moses explained that he's going to settle here in Kansas."

"Good for you, young man." Dr. Boyle grasped Moses's hand in a firm handshake. "Have you decided which town?"

The man smiled broadly. "Yes. In a town known as Nicodemus. Have you heard of it?"

Dr. Boyle hesitated. "Yes. We live in Hill City, not far from Nicodemus. I've visited Nicodemus on a number of occasions, but I don't think it's where you'll want to make your home. Why don't we get your baggage and you can accompany us to Hill City."

"I don't want to inconvenience you. I was planning on renting a wagon and going directly to Nicodemus."

"We would truly be delighted to have you accompany us to Hill City," Mrs. Boyle said. "After my husband explains the circumstances in Nicodemus, you can then make an informed decision about your future."

Carlisle gently slapped Moses on the shoulder and laughed. "I told you they would be determined to have you visit Hill City first."

Moses shrugged amiably. "If you insist— I'm not on a schedule."

After the family was situated in the wagon, Macia asked Moses some polite questions about his trip. "However did you hear about Nicodemus, Mr. Wyman?"

He shifted on the wagon seat. "I've lived in Boston for a number of years now and decided it was time to get out and explore some new frontiers. Our newspaper recently printed several articles about Kansas settlements, and I decided Nicodemus might appeal to me."

"Apparently your local newspaper didn't

investigate very well. You see, Nicodemus is for *coloreds.* Both Hill City and Nicodemus were organized by the same men. They set up one town for whites and one for coloreds."

"Well, Miss Boyle, I was the editor of the newspaper, and I always insist my reporters gain accurate information before submitting a story."

Macia could feel the heat rise in her cheeks. "I didn't realize you were a newspaper editor. And you want to sacrifice living in Boston to come west and live in a soddy or a dugout? I can't imagine anyone willingly doing such a thing. Had your reporter actually visited Nicodemus?"

"No. However, he did interview Mr. Hill. I believe your fair city is named after him, isn't it?"

She giggled. "Our city isn't fair—in fact, it isn't even a city. However, it does bear Mr. Hill's name. I fear you will be sadly disappointed if you believed Mr. Hill's commentary on Hill City—or Nicodemus."

"No need to discourage Moses before he's even arrived," Carlisle said. "Your assessment may be tainted by your over-

whelming desire to be living in Georgetown."

"Just because you're excited over the
prospect of living in tents or in a frontier military outpost doesn't mean such a life appeals to others, Carlisle. Nicodemus is truly
in dire straits, isn't it, Father?"

"Macia isn't exaggerating the plight that
has befallen the fine folks in Nicodemus.
They arrived to pitiable circumstances. You
see, Mr. Hill did not fulfill his many promises
regarding the organization of the city. The
Nicodemus settlers came expecting to find
an established town. Instead, they were
greeted by the same open prairie they'd tra-
versed since leaving the Flint Hills in eastern
Kansas. They're a strong and determined
group, but they've been forced to live in
harsh circumstances."

"Is nobody willing to help them?" he
asked with a frown.

The wind began to blow harder, and Macia held one hand atop her bonnet. "Father
has given them limited assistance and medical treatment, as funds and weather permit."

Her father waved his right hand. "I've
been able to accomplish very little, though

it's not for lack of trying. And the residents have made valiant attempts themselves, but thus far nothing of substance has been forthcoming."

Moses leaned forward and rested his arms across his thighs. "Perhaps a plea to the state legislature or to the Congress should be considered, Dr. Boyle."

Samuel nodded in agreement. "We entertained a delegation from the Kansas legislature not long ago, but there are divisive opinions. When they departed, I didn't have a clear-cut feeling that anything had been accomplished. Even though land promoters actively pursued these settlers, there are men in the legislature who believe coloreds have nothing of value to offer Kansas. A sad commentary upon some of those who hold positions of power in this state."

"When Carlisle said his family hailed from Kentucky, I didn't expect such a tolerant attitude toward coloreds."

Samuel laughed. "Though I've lived many years in Kentucky, I was reared in the North. I was never a proponent of slavery, a position that didn't endear me to most Kentuckians. Unfortunately, my attempts to influence them against slavery weren't particularly successful, either."

"Seems as though you did a fine job with Carlisle. He tells me he's going to be a chaplain for our colored soldiers."

Mrs. Boyle flapped her hands in a dismissive wave. "I'd be pleased if he would avoid the military entirely."

"You're worrying needlessly, Mother. I'm doing the work God has called me to, and I'm going to be fine. I'm certain you'll be pleased to hear that Moses is hoping he can continue his newspaper work out here in the West."

Macia almost giggled. Carlisle obviously hoped to direct the conversation away from his military assignment.

"Now, that's a wonderful piece of information," Dr. Boyle said excitedly. "Hill City had a newspaper for a short time. Unfortunately, the owner printed only four editions of the paper before succumbing to a heart attack. We could certainly use a man of your talents in Hill City."

"To be honest, my plan was to set up my newspaper in Nicodemus. Like Carlisle, I had hoped to work and live with the colored folks."

"I think you've both taken leave of your senses," Macia said with a sigh.

"There's an old printing press and some other newspaper equipment in Hill City. Widow Jacoby took the train back to Ohio and left everything just as it was the day her husband died."

Moses's eyes glowed with excitement. "Do you think she might be interested in selling the equipment?"

Samuel nodded enthusiastically. "I'm certain she'd be delighted to accept any offer. She left the matter in Walt Johnson's hands—he owns the general store."

Moses and the family gathered around the dining table that had been elegantly set with fine china and silver in anticipation of Carlisle's homecoming supper. Both sweet potatoes and white potatoes surrounded the loin of pork that had been roasted to perfection. Mrs. Boyle's corn relish, pickled beets, and apple butter, which she said had been carefully packed in straw and transported from Georgetown, were served in fancy china bowls. Slices of lightly browned homemade bread were neatly arranged on

a silver bread plate that matched the other
pieces of glistening silver service that be-
decked the table. Moses couldn't remember when he'd eaten a meal quite so well
prepared and beautifully served.

The conversation was lively and enjoyable, yet Moses found himself watching
Truth Harban as she moved in and out of
the room, anticipating every need before a
word was spoken. At one point she noticed
him scrutinizing her and she frowned, but
he was unable to keep his gaze off of her.

Mrs. Boyle's face contorted into a scowl
as she placed her fork on her empty plate.
"I don't think I shall ever speak to William
Wheeler again!"

The woman's remark interrupted Moses's
thoughts, and he turned toward her. "Why is
that, Mrs. Boyle?"

The hostess stared at him in disbelief.
"Why, because he used his influence as
vice-president to procure Carlisle's appoint-
ment as an officer in the Army even though
Carlisle never attended West Point."

"And that displeases you?"

"Indeed! It makes me sorry we have
friends of influence when something of
this nature occurs. I doubt Vice-President

Wheeler would want *his* son entering the military and going off to the hinterlands to be killed by savages."

"Do have a little faith, Mother. I may surprise you and come back alive."

Mrs. Boyle looked at Carlisle from the sides of her eyes. "The truth is, you haven't had the proper military training to prepare yourself for the harsh conditions you're going to experience living in the wilderness and fighting Indians. I doubt you'd raise a hand even if one of those savages attacked you."

Dr. Boyle patted his wife's arm. "Now, my dear, I don't believe you need to work yourself into a state of apoplexy. We want to enjoy our time with Carlisle."

"If you would excuse me for a moment"— Moses wiped his mouth with the linen napkin and pushed back his chair—"I believe I'll fetch a glass of water."

Mrs. Boyle lifted a small bell. "Sit still, Mr. Wyman. I'll ring for Truth."

"No, please don't do that. I need to stretch my legs, and I'm certain she's busy with her other duties."

"As you wish."

Moses walked down the hallway and into

the kitchen. He stood quietly in the doorway, observing Truth as she bent over a pan of steamy water washing the supper dishes. She seemed to sense his presence and glanced over her shoulder.

As Moses moved farther into the kitchen, Truth spun around. "Is there something you need?"

"I told the family I wanted a glass of water, but what I truly wanted was a few moments to visit with you."

Her brow puckered and she narrowed her eyes. "Why?"

"Because I find you interesting."

She stared deep into his eyes before turning back to the dirty dishes. "I think you best go find some white gal to interest you, Mr. Wyman."

"I mean you no harm. I was merely going to question you a bit about Nicodemus and your family."

"You likely already heard all there is to hear about Nicodemus. As for my family, my mama's dead. It's just Pappy, Jarena, and Grace—she's my twin sister. Isn't much more to tell you, so I'm thinking you best go back and join the others before Mrs. Boyle wonders why you're dallying out here in the kitchen."

"I suppose you're right. Thank you for an excellent meal. Your cooking is exceptional."

"Thank you." Truth watched until he was out of the kitchen. She didn't want him hanging around her causing any trouble!

CHAPTER

28

Nicodemus, Kansas • March 1878

Shouts of excitement echoed throughout the small town as word spread from dugout to dugout that the long-awaited boxcar of supplies procured by Wilbur Rawlins had finally arrived in Ellis and awaited transport to Nicodemus. Harvey Boyle had delivered the message along with an offer to use his father's wagon and team. An offer that was enthusiastically accepted.

"We's gonna be doing real fine soon as dose supplies get here." Ezekiel was delighted to spread encouragement to those who had gathered to celebrate the good news.

Charles folded his arms across his chest and glowered at Jarena. "You're not going to do as I asked, are you?"

Jarena avoided his intimidating glare. "I've already told you I'm going. You could reconsider and come along."

"There's no reason for me to waste time going to Ellis when there's land here in Nicodemus that needs to be plowed and planted."

"The other young men are going to investigate the possibility of seasonal work with the railroad. You could do the same. Besides, it's too early for planting. I think the only reason you won't go is because of Thomas."

"And what if it is?" He pulled her aside so the others couldn't hear their conversation. "I'm beginning to think I should have been keeping company with Belle Harris instead of you. At least she made it clear she wasn't interested in anyone except me."

Jarena bristled at the response. "If you think Belle's a better choice, perhaps you need to go back to Georgetown and marry her. I've told you over and over that I have no romantic interest in Thomas. He has always been a gentleman. However, I do have an interest in helping with the supplies so folks will have some food to fill their empty bellies. Staying here and chopping on a plot of frozen ground isn't going to put food in anyone's mouth."

Charles glowered. "That little bit of food you're going to get isn't going to feed folks for long. We need this ground prepared for planting come spring—that's what will provide food later on."

"Not if we all starve to death first!" Jarena pulled away from him and stepped up into the wagon, her lips tightened into a firm line. She was *not* going to yield to Charles's exasperating influence. Nothing she said or did alleviated his suspicions regarding Thomas, and she had tired of his childish behavior.

As the horses stepped out, Jarena glanced over her shoulder. Seeing Charles staring after them, she slid closer to Thomas in one final defiant act. She knew that her behavior was childish—even cruel. But his words about Belle Harris had cut her to the quick, and she wanted to hurt him in return.

Obviously surprised by her action, Thomas edged farther down the seat. "Don't be using me to get that fella of yours jealous. I don't want no trouble with him or nobody else."

"Don't worry. He wouldn't attempt to hurt anyone, especially someone of your size."

"I ain't worried about gettin' hurt. I just don't want to be gettin' in the middle of your squabble. I heard you two fussin' at each other. Doesn't bode well for marriage when a man and woman are havin' spats afore they ever jump the broom," he observed.

Jarena folded her arms tightly across her chest and stared straight ahead. "From what Charles said, it appears as if he thinks Belle Harris might be a better choice for a wife."

"I don't know nothing 'bout Belle Harris, but I think Charles would be a fool if he let you get away."

She peeked at Thomas from beneath her thick lashes. "Thank you."

The two of them rode in silence, listening as the others chattered excitedly about the contents of the anticipated boxcar of supplies. Percy Sharp and Henry Ralston, the other two single men who had joined them in Topeka, sat across from Jarena and Thomas. Mary Fowler had claimed the spot beside her husband, Robert, on the wagon's high seat. Jarena leaned against the side of the wagon with a tiny smile playing on her lips as she considered Thomas's words. Did he genuinely consider Charles fortunate to have her, or was he merely attempting to salve her wounded feelings? Never, in all the time he'd lived with her family, had he said anything to make her think he found her pleasing. Oh, he had complimented her on her cooking and her intelligence and skills as she assisted him with his reading and writing, but he'd never uttered any admiration for her as a woman.

Her gaze settled on his large, callused hands. There was little doubt Thomas had spent his years much as her father had—working hard with little reward. However, her attempts to learn the secrets of his past remained unsuccessful. Now that he'd spoken in a forthcoming manner, perhaps she would finally be able to get him to open up.

"The other two single men said they were going to seek employment with the railroad. Were you planning to do the same?"

Thomas pushed his wide-brimmed hat

back on his head and squinted against the bright sunlight. "I sure don't have any know-how 'bout working fer the railroad, but if what they're needin' is someone to swing a pick or hammer, they might hire me. Doc Boyle said the railroad pays better'n most jobs, so I'm thinkin' to check on working there. If not, I guess I'll see Mr. Horton. I owe him a couple days of work for loanin' me the breaking plow."

"What kind of work have you done in the past—before you came to Nicodemus?"

He gave her a sidelong glance. "Nothin' that took much thought. Muscle was the only thing needed for any of the work I ever done."

She bit her lower lip and thought for a moment. "How does Kansas compare to the other places you've lived, Thomas?"

"Kansas is the only place where I ever had a chance to own land, so I'd say it's the best place to be. Other'n that, one place has been as good as the other."

She knew he was attempting to avoid her questions, but Jarena was undeterred. "Are you planning to bring any of your family to Kansas once you get established?"

"Nope. Told you my folks is dead—ain't

got nobody else, and the only plans I've got is to get my land plowed and planted."

Although Thomas didn't appear agitated by her interrogation, he didn't seem to want to divulge any further information about his past. "I should just give up," she muttered.

"Excuse me?" he said, leaning closer.

She forced a smile. "Nothing. I was just saying I might as well try to take a nap. We'll be arriving in an hour or so."

He nodded, pulled his hat down over his eyes, and stretched his lanky legs across the wagon bed. Jarena stared at his sleeping form until the horses came to a halt in front of the Ellis train station.

Percy Sharp was first to jump down. "Guess we better check inside and see about the boxcar and if we're gonna be able to load all them goods in this wagon."

"I'm hopin' Wilbur sent some money along, too," Thomas said as he assisted Jarena from the wagon. "Sure would help if we could buy us another team and wagon—and I'm surely prayin' there's a plow in that boxcar."

His remark surprised Jarena. "I didn't know you were a praying man, Thomas."

"Seems to help sometimes—leastways I

figure prayer is what got me out of that blizzard alive."

———

Thomas surveyed the crowded depot, hoping he might find someone who could direct them to the waiting boxcar. Passengers swarmed in all directions as he continued to peer about the room. The unexpected sound of shouting children caused him to turn toward the doorway. With his eyes widened in startled disbelief, Thomas quickly positioned himself behind one of the supporting pilasters located throughout the building.

Using extraordinary caution, he peered at several men lingering near the rear doorway and swallowed hard to push down the rising lump in his throat. His breath came in wrenching shallow gasps as rivulets of perspiration inched downward from his brow. He leaned back against the pillar. A chill seeped through the loosely woven fibers of his shirt and sent a shiver rushing down his spine. How had they found him? And how was he going to explain his reluctance to move away from the hiding place that now separated him from certain death?

As each new question exploded in his mind, the men began to walk in his direction. Clutching the column to steady his quaking body, he shifted ever so slightly. A finger jabbed his shoulder. He could almost feel a noose tightening around his neck as he turned with a start.

"Jarena," he gasped in a sigh of relief. Without thinking, he pulled her into a tight embrace, careful to turn his face away from the approaching men.

"Whatever are you doing?" She pushed against his chest with more force than he had imagined she could muster.

If he didn't do something soon, her protests were going to attract the men's attention. Without further deliberation, he tightened his hold and covered her mouth with an ardent kiss and was surprised when Jarena relaxed in his arms. Suddenly aware the kiss was lasting much too long, he abruptly loosened his hold. Jarena stumbled backward but still clung to his shirt, a look of bewilderment filling her eyes. He steadied her, almost forgetting what had caused his daring behavior, but soon the remembrance of his pursuers returned with a vengeance.

After a furtive glance toward the door, he surveyed the entire depot. "Please accept my apologies. I don' know what came over me."

She continued to hold his shirtsleeve. "Did you think because of my argument with Charles . . ."

"No. You didn't do nothin' to encourage my rude manners—it was all my fault and I'm sorry. I'll talk to your pappy and tell him what I did. If he wants me to move out, I will." His words tumbled out in a rush as he continued to watch both doors leading in and out of the train station. "I ain't got time to talk right now, Jarena, but I need your help. I gotta leave this place right now. Promise me that if any strangers ask if you know me or my whereabouts, you'll say you never heard of me—ask the others to do the same. I ain't got time to explain, but my life depends on it—there's a posse after me. Will you do that?"

She slowly nodded as she stared at him, obviously struck speechless by his request.

Thomas unclasped her shaking fingers from his shirt. "I'm sorry, Jarena," he whispered before hurrying out of the depot.

He heard Percy Sharp shout after him and

silently prayed that Jarena would soon quiet the man. Otherwise, he might as well stand in the middle of the dirt street and wait for the posse to come and get him. None of the men was in plain sight as Thomas ran across the street, giving momentary thought to requesting Will Southard's assistance. The young tow-headed lad would likely let him hide in the livery until the posse left town. Yet those very men might be in the livery looking to rent horses and get information. Besides, he didn't want to bring any danger to Will or Chester Goddard. And knowing the temperament of the men following him, Thomas was certain they would do harm to anyone helping him.

Keeping out of sight would be difficult, but if he remained undetected until the wagon passed by on its return to Nicodemus, perhaps he would be safe and the men would give up their search. Making his way to the outskirts of town, he prayed he could find a place to hide.

———

Jarena watched Thomas flee from the depot with a mixture of fear and excitement coursing through her body. Obviously, he had done something terrible or a posse wouldn't be searching for him. Yet as she touched her lips, she couldn't imagine him doing anything to bring such wrath upon himself. Even her father, who was a good judge of character, had concluded that Thomas was a fine young man.

She wondered if his troubles were why he had joined their group in Topeka. Her stomach swirled as though a million butterflies had taken up residence inside. Clutching one hand to her midsection, she searched the depot for the others. She spotted Percy outside the rear of the depot and then saw the others join him.

"Where you been?" Mary Fowler waved Jarena forward while her husband, Robert, jumped up into a boxcar.

"Is that our goods?" Jarena asked.

"Course it is. Robert wouldn't be unloading 'em if it wasn't. Where's Thomas? Just when we're needin' everyone to help, the two of you disappear." Her words were filled with disapproval.

"We didn't disappear. I was in the train station the entire time."

Mary glanced about. "And where's Thomas? Percy an' Robert need his help."

Their horses and wagon had been strategically moved beside the boxcar that was located on a small spur of track near the railroad station. Percy and Robert stood in the opening of the boxcar awaiting her response.

With a surreptitious glance over her shoulder, Jarena moved closer to Mary and the others and began to speak in a hushed voice. "There are men looking for Thomas. He asked that we keep his identity a secret if anyone should ask if we know him."

Mary frowned. "What kind of men?"

"I think it's a posse. We'll need to get unloaded and on our way without his assistance."

Percy wiped his sleeve across his forehead. "Without his help, it's gonna take us longer to get done. Ain't gonna be time to do no lookin' for jobs, Robert."

"Think you two can stand in the back of da wagon and take dese boxes as we hand 'em over to ya?" Robert asked Jarena and Mary.

Jarena nodded and hoisted herself into the wagon before giving Mary a hand up. The horses shifted, and Jarena looked toward Robert Fowler. "Are the horses tied?"

He smiled. "They ain't going nowhere."

Mary took a box of goods from her husband and wedged it into a corner of the wagon. "What you think Thomas done that he's got a posse lookin' for him?"

Jarena shrugged as she continued working. "I don't know. He didn't go into detail. Looks like there's quite a supply of goods, don't you think?"

"Not near what we're needin'."

Unfortunately, Mary was correct. The boxcar had been a little less than a third full, and it didn't appear the supplies were going to eliminate the desperate need within their small community. Jarena hoped there would be enough to keep them going until another boxcar arrived.

"Guess we didn' need to worry 'bout needin' extra wagons to haul the supplies back home." Mary's voice was edged with bitterness as the group settled on the benches.

Robert flicked the reins and the horses stepped out. "We best be thankful we got anything. You need to quit lookin' at the bad instead of the good."

Mary gave her husband a look of disdain. "No need for me to look fer the good in ever'thing when you're always anxious to do it. 'Sides, we wouldn't be in this place if it weren't for you insistin' on how we could trust everyone and how owning land was gonna be the answer to all our problems."

Robert's jaw tightened, and he focused on the horses.

A slight chill remained in the early spring air, yet the sun beat down on them with a surprising warmth. Jarena pulled off her jacket and carefully formed it into a head-rest while contemplating Thomas's safety and whereabouts. She'd watched for him as they unloaded the boxcar, hoping he might reappear yet worried he'd be caught if he showed himself. If only she'd seen the men who were looking for him, she could have watched to see if they had left town. But she couldn't identify any of them. At the moment they had passed her in the depot, she had been enveloped in Thomas's warm embrace.

The thought of his kiss caused a return of the butterflies she'd experienced when he had kissed her. She'd never felt that way when Charles had kissed her. Though, truth be told, Charles had never kissed her in the same way. There had never been any urgency or fervor in his brief kisses. She wondered how other women felt when they were kissed. If only her mother were alive, she would certainly explain. Perhaps she would ask Nellie when they arrived home. Mary would not be a good choice, she decided. The mere thought of asking the dour woman about kisses caused her to grin as the wagon lumbered off toward Nicodemus.

"What's that up there?" Robert pointed into the distance.

Percy leaned forward. "Can't tell. Looks like it might be a man."

Shifting up onto her knees, Jarena shaded her eyes with one hand. "It's Thomas!"

"I just got to sleep," Mary complained as she lifted up onto one elbow. "What's all the commotion?"

Robert glanced back at his wife. "You been sleepin' ever since you got in da wagon. Looks like Thomas is up ahead— behind dem rocks and off to the left."

"Best leave him there if there's a posse hunting 'im. Last thing we need is men totin' guns and chasin' after us."

"No! We can't leave him," Jarena cried.

Robert waved one hand at Jarena. "Settle down, gal. I ain't gonna leave him stranded out here."

Mary wagged her left index finger back and forth like the pendulum of a grandfather clock. "You mark my words—that fella ain't gonna bring us nothin' but trouble."

Jarena felt the need to defend Thomas against Mary's angry remarks. "He's the one who got us the plow."

"Don't matter none—he's got trouble written all over him. I can always tell. And how come *you's* so set on defending him? You's acting like a lovesick calf when you's s'posed to be promised to someone else. Charles know about this?"

Thomas hurried toward them and jumped into the wagon. "Keep moving, Robert. I'm gonna stay down outta sight in case them men come this way."

Mary scowled at Thomas. "And what we gonna do if they show up? We s'pose to say, 'Don' you pay no attention to that big lump laying dere in the wagon. That ain't nobody you's interested in'? You's puttin' us all in danger, Thomas. Why they lookin' for you, anyway? What you done to have the law comin' after you?"

"I don't wanna cause no trouble, Mary," he said. "If we see them comin', I'll jump outta the wagon."

"Be too late then. They'll still come after us for helpin' you."

"We's takin' him with us," Robert told his wife. "Ain't no more gonna be said 'bout it. Now hush, woman."

Mary scooted away and turned her face to the side of the wagon. Jarena wasn't certain if Mary was attempting to distance herself from Thomas or if she was embarrassed by her husband's response. Though there was little doubt Mary's tongue would be wagging the moment they reached Nicodemus, she remained blessedly silent and brooding for the remainder of the journey.

CHAPTER

29

Hill City, Kansas • April 1878

Samuel Boyle hadn't lost any time contacting Walt Johnson at the general store. The morning after Moses's arrival, Samuel had slipped out before breakfast, anxious to gather details about the newspaper office. And Walt had proven helpful. The price sounded reasonable, and the equipment was in good condition. In fact, Walt had even been keeping the printing press lubricated according to the handwritten specifications he'd found in Mr. Jacoby's desk.

Later that same morning, Samuel had led Moses into the mercantile, feeling confident the young man would immediately agree to purchase the equipment. But he was disappointed. Although Moses agreed that both the price and equipment were acceptable, he didn't give a final answer. In a surprisingly self-assured manner, he told Dr. Boyle he would commit the matter to prayer. And so he waited for an answer, but thankfully not for long.

Once the decision was made, Moses ensconced himself in the newspaper office, intent upon familiarizing himself with Mr. Jacoby's operation. Harvey soon became his constant companion, for the young man was excited by the notion of setting type and learning to use the Washington handpress.

Moses had patiently taught him the process, and the entire family had been surprised by Harvey's continued interest.

"So you truly think you'd like to work in a newspaper office?" The family was seated around the Boyles's dining table when Moses asked the question.

"I do," Harvey said as he slathered butter onto a flaky biscuit. "It's exciting to see a blank piece of paper turn into printed words."

Moses laughed and agreed. "Yes, but I fear you'll grow weary of setting type. It becomes a tiresome task once you've done it for a while. And a newspaper requires dedication to duty. You can't run off to fish or picnic on warm spring days or sit at home by the fire when a snowstorm is swirling outdoors. Men who work in the newspaper business must be reliable. Then, too, your father tells me you'll soon need to begin plowing his acreage."

Harvey grimaced and looked at the head of the table. "You know I have no interest in farming, Father. I haven't told you previously, but you need to know I've entered into an agreement with Thomas Grayson and several other fellows in Nicodemus. In exchange for the use of the farm implements, they've agreed to work our land. I never did plan to spend my time tilling the land—that was always *your* plan for my life."

Samuel took a sip of coffee and then placed the cup back onto the china saucer. "My hope has always been that you would find a vocation that captured your interest. If you believe the newspaper business is what you'd like to try, then I won't stop you. As for the acreage, I'm sorry to hear you made an agreement that was completely self-serving. I'll let the men use the equipment and team, but I'd prefer to *hire* them to perform the work."

Harvey chuckled. "I did tell them they wouldn't have to work very hard in our fields, as you wouldn't expect me to make much progress."

Samuel joined his son's laughter. "You see what you'll have to contend with, Moses?"

"*I* can always fire him, Dr. Boyle." Moses smiled broadly. "*You* don't have that advantage. I'll be busy seeking advertisers and writing copy for him to typeset and print. He'll work hard and do as he's told, or he'll find himself behind that plow after all."

Samuel didn't doubt for a moment that Moses was speaking the truth. His youngest son would follow orders; otherwise he'd be out of work.

When they'd finished supper, Macia pushed her chair away from the table. "If you'll excuse me, I told Truth I'd take Mother's supper up to her. She hasn't been willing to eat a thing today."

Samuel's smile disappeared at the news. "I'll join you momentarily, Macia. Carlisle, why don't you come along? Your mother would like to spend some time with you before you leave."

―――――

"Good evening."

Truth startled, and the pan of dishwater tipped, spilling sudsy water down the front of her apron and onto the floor. When she turned around, there was a look of exasperation on her face.

"Do you *always* sneak up on folks?" She bent down to sop the pooling water from the floor.

"Let me do that." Moses squatted down to help her and attempted to take the rag from her hand.

She looked up and stared directly into his brown eyes and was reminded of a large bear she'd once seen traveling through Georgetown in a circus cage. She wondered what this refined gentleman would think of her comparison and almost giggled aloud.

"I'll take care of it. Wouldn't want you to get that fine suit of yours all wet." She stood up when she had finished wiping the floor. "Something you're needin'?"

"Everyone's busy elsewhere and I thought I'd come out and visit with you, but all I've succeeded in doing is creating more work for you. I'm terribly sorry."

She shrugged. "The floor has to be scrubbed anyway—you just gave me an early start on getting it done."

"I must say you have an excellent attitude about your work. Do you like being in the Boyles's employ?"

"Dr. Boyle is a good man. He freely gives medical attention to the folks over in Nicodemus, and he truly believes in equality," she told him as she wiped down the counters. "Some folks say the words, but they don't really mean them in here," she said, touching her chest. "But not Dr. Boyle—he's honest. Why, he even stood up to a bunch of congressmen that came out here from Topeka." Without encouragement, she related the details of Dr. Boyle's disagreement with Senator Pomeroy. "He told those congressmen exactly what he thought."

"He does appear to be a fine man—as does his son Carlisle. They both put their faith into practice. And even Harvey shows promise. He's going to work for me at the newspaper office."

"So you decided to stay in Hill City after all."

He nodded. "You gave me some sound advice. Folks who can't buy food can't buy newspapers. However, I do plan to print a free monthly newspaper for the folks in Nicodemus once I get established."

"That's right nice of you."

"Seems like we're a lot alike."

She looked skeptical at his remark. "How's that?"

"For one thing, we've both decided we're going to live in Hill City rather than Nicodemus. And we both like the Boyle family. You did say you enjoyed working for the Boyles, didn't you?"

"I'd say those are about the *only* things we got in common, Mr. Wyman. As far as working for the Boyles, how could I *not* like it? I'm living in better conditions than I ever had in my life. The Boyles are kind; I have my own room with a soft bed and good food to eat. But you shouldn't be askin' me questions like that. I already said you should find you a white gal."

"But it's *you* I find interesting and attractive."

Truth picked up a towel and wiped her hands. "I'm not that kind of girl, Mr. Wyman. If you're looking for someone to warm your bed, you've come to the wrong person."

The air escaped Moses's lungs in a giant heave. "I am so sorry. So very, very sorry. I'm not attempting any such thing."

"Come on, now, Mr. Wyman. What else does a white man want with a colored girl?" She hung the towel on a hook. "I think you better leave."

————

Thomas scanned the horizon, certain he heard horses approaching in the distance. Perspiration began to form across his upper lip as he strained to listen. He had been fervently praying the posse would give up and return back east, yet it was too soon to rest easy. He doubted whether they would admit defeat this soon, especially after following him all this distance.

Jarena stood by the kettle of boiling water near the dugout, dropping small pieces of soap into the caldron of dirty clothes. She'd been most pleased with the lye soap she'd gotten from the boxcar of goods sent by Wilbur Rawlins. Thomas drew near and gave her a brief smile before fixing his gaze to the south. "Do you hear horses comin' our way?" Surprised by the tremor in his voice, he broadened his smile and awaited her reply.

With a tilt of her head, she listened for a moment and then nodded. "Yes. Do you think it's the posse?"

"I did, but now that they's closer, I think that looks like Dr. Boyle." He pointed to the west.

Jarena smiled as the horses and carriage came into view. "Oh, it is. I do hope he brought Truth with him."

The two of them stood transfixed as the carriage neared. However, Thomas noted Jarena's smile slowly disappear when she realized Truth had not accompanied the doctor.

Dr. Boyle brought the horses to a halt. "Good morning!" He jumped down from the carriage and was followed by two men they'd never seen before.

Thomas remained cautious, uncertain if the strangers with Dr. Boyle had some connection to the posse. He greeted them from a safe distance. He disliked the idea, but if matters took a turn for the worse, he would steal Dr. Boyle's carriage and run for his life.

Dr. Boyle strode toward them and motioned the other men forward. "This is my son Carlisle. He's a lieutenant in the Army—a chaplain who will soon be heading off to serve with a group of colored soldiers at Fort Sill in the Indian Territory. And this is Moses Wyman. He's recently moved west to start a newspaper, and I've convinced him to remain in Hill City." The men removed their hats as they were introduced. "This is Thomas Grayson," he told his companions, "and this is Jarena Harban, one of Ezekiel's other daughters."

"Truth's sister?" Moses asked.

Jarena nodded and smiled, and Moses noticed the family resemblance was evident. "I was hoping Truth would be with you."

Dr. Boyle looked apologetic. "I had planned to bring her, but my wife has taken a turn for the worse. She hasn't been eating, and I fear leaving her alone. Both Harvey and Macia were otherwise occupied," he explained.

"Ain't no need for no apology, Dr. Boyle," Ezekiel said as he came out of the dugout. "Truth's being paid to help out, and we's mighty pleased you give her the work. Ain't we, Jarena?"

"Yes, Pappy. I wasn't saying . . ."

Ezekiel nodded. "Who is these young men?"

Dr. Boyle smiled broadly as he introduced the two men and then excused himself to go check on several of the patients he'd been treating. "I won't be too long. Perhaps Thomas and Jarena would be willing to show you about the town and introduce you to a few of the folks."

Thomas chuckled softly. "Don' think there's much here to show you 'cept what you're lookin' at and maybe the inside of the dugouts. But I'd be glad to show you where me an' Ezekiel are beginning our permanent homes and gettin' ready to plant our crops. Our acreage starts a couple miles past the edge of town," he said as he pointed. "We's close enough it don't take us too long to walk back to town. Some folks, like Robert, ain't so lucky—their land is farther out in the township—ain't so easy for them gettin' back and forth what with no horses and such. I tilled the land with a borrowed plow last year, and I'm using a hatchet to work on it now—leastways until Harvey..." He stopped short, suddenly realizing he was betraying his arrangement with the younger Boyle son.

Carlisle laughed. "No need to worry, Thomas. Harvey's come clean and told us of his arrangement. In fact, Father plans to talk to you about working his land."

"Harvey is coming to work for me at the newspaper office," Moses said, "so he's no longer interested in bartering the tools in exchange for your labor. Instead, Dr. Boyle plans to hire several willing laborers to work his land."

Ezekiel immediately stepped forward. "I kin work as hard as any of dese younger fellows, so I hope he'll count me among that number."

Carlisle smiled and clapped Ezekiel on the shoulder. "I'm certain he will."

While Jarena engaged Moses in conversation about her sister, Thomas pulled Lieutenant Boyle aside. "I heard your pappy say you was gonna lead a regiment of coloreds down in the Indian Territory. I'd be mighty interested to hear more about that—I just might consider joinin' up."

Carlisle chuckled. "First of all, I won't be leading anyone. This is my first assignment, and I'll be serving as a chaplain, but if you're interested, there's always a place for new recruits. The pay is steady and life can't be any harder than it is here—unless we get into skirmishes with the Indians. Then your life could be in danger. If you truly want to join up, you could come along with me to Fort Sill."

"Don' sound so bad. I already know 'bout bein' in danger."

"Why don't you give it some time and prayer before making a decision?"

Thomas had expected questions from Mr. Harban, so he wasn't surprised when Ezekiel asked Grace to go outside and help her sister so he and Thomas could talk in private.

Ezekiel faced him with a stern expression. "There's been lots of talk flying 'round town ever since you got back from Ellis last month. Folks is wonderin' about a posse that was lookin' for ya down there. Jarena tells me she don't know nothin' more than that, and I believe her. I ain't pried into your business afore, and I done give you plenty of time to come talk to me since that trip down to Ellis. But now—after hearing you's planning to join the Army, I think it's time you come clean with me."

Thomas wrung his hands together and met the older man's questioning eyes. "Ain't no denying you been good to me, but I'm not gonna tell you nothin' except this: I been accused of somethin' terrible. It ain't true, but it comes down to my word against a white man's, and who you think folks is gonna believe?"

Ezekiel leaned forward until only inches separated them. "Just tell me what it is, boy. Iffen I know what we's fightin', maybe I can help."

"Ain't nobody that can help me with this one, ceptin' maybe the good Lord. Best thing I can do is get outta Nicodemus so's I'm not putting everyone else in danger. That posse won't look kindly on folks they think been givin' me shelter."

"I figure I've fought off worse than any of

them men that's lookin' for you, and I think if you'll just tell us what happened, folks will rally around and help. I don't believe you got a mean bone in your body, and if you tell me you's innocent, then I believe you and I'm willin' to fight for you. I reckon that posse woulda already been here if they was coming."

"I pray you're right, Ezekiel. But I didn' think they'd follow me to Kansas, and they did. I shouldn't have come back here when we left Ellis, but I didn't know what else to do. I've been worried ever since that somethin' was gonna happen and folks would be hurt." He stood and started pacing in the small space. "But after hearing Dr. Boyle's son talk about these buffalo soldiers down in Indian Territory, I got me a place to go. I've been prayin' about what to do over these last few days since he was here, and I think this is God's answer."

"I ain't one to argue with God *or* His plans, but ya need to be sure. Headin' off for Indian Territory, now that don't sound like something that's gonna solve your problems. Get ya killed, maybe." There was a glint in Ezekiel's eyes.

The older man's ploy to frighten him

wasn't going to work. "I want you to make me a promise—if that posse shows up, don't tell them I was livin' with you or that we was gonna farm together. Don't tell them nothing that would make them think you know me at all. I've made up my mind—joining the Army is the best thing for everyone in Nicodemus. I'm gonna ride over to Hill City tomorrow and tell Lieutenant Boyle I'm gonna enlist and find out when he's leaving for Fort Sill," Thomas said as he pushed back from the table. "Believe I'll go and work on the acreage for a while." He picked up the axe and hurried out the door before Ezekiel could argue any further.

———

Jarena kissed her father's leathery cheek. "Thank you," she whispered before turning to Grace. "I know you were hoping to go along and see Truth. I hope you aren't too angry with me."

"Pappy said I can go next time." Grace pulled a letter from her apron pocket. "Will you give this to Truth?"

"Of course. Perhaps she'll have time to pen you a reply before our return." She carefully tucked the letter away.

Ezekiel patted Grace's shoulder and then addressed Jarena and Thomas. "You two go on, now. You got a long day ahead if you's gonna get back here afore nightfall."

A splash of melon red smeared the horizon and forecast a bright morning sun would soon lighten the sky. As the horses clopped out of the beleaguered town, Jarena settled against the wooden wagon seat and silently uttered a prayer that the gaunt animals would not suffer from the rigors of their journey.

"A good day to travel."

Jarena nodded. "Pappy seemed evasive when I asked why you decided to travel to Hill City today."

Thomas clucked at the horses and slapped the reins. "I'm gonna borrow some tools from the doctor."

She gave him a sidelong glance. There were more causes for this journey than borrowing tools, but she wouldn't press the issue. For some reason, Thomas didn't plan to be forthright, yet Jarena was certain her father knew the true motivation for Thomas's journey.

"Ain't seen much of Charles lately."

"Do you need to talk to him about something in particular?" Jarena decided she, too, could be vague.

Thomas grinned and shook his head. "No. Jest wonderin' why he ain't been calling on you like he did when his family first arrived in Nicodemus."

The thought of being kissed by Thomas at the train station in Ellis drifted through Jarena's mind, and she peeked at him from under the rim of her bonnet. His air of nonchalance left her wondering what he might be thinking.

"Is your concern that I will become an old maid—or perhaps you believe me already to be a member of that vilified group of women?" She batted her lashes in an exaggerated fashion.

He gave a hearty laugh, and she soon joined him in his amusement. Once their laughter ebbed, he warily smiled. "You sure don' need to worry about that—you're far too pretty."

A rush of heat flooded Jarena's cheeks; the flattering remark both surprised and pleased her. Though dire circumstances had caused Thomas to kiss her at the railroad station, she had been stirred by his touch. However, since that day, he'd kept his distance. Now she wondered if Thomas had experienced that same delightful feeling.

"Thank you." She didn't know what else to say.

He scratched the back of his head. "You still ain't told me 'bout Charles. You two still makin' plans to jump the broom? 'Cause I was thinking I'd sure be pleased for the opportunity to win your hand—if you and Charles ain't made no final decision. I'd talk to your pappy first."

His words pleased her, and she couldn't squelch the nervous giggle that escaped her lips. "Charles has been distant of late, keeping to himself mostly. We seem to argue when we're together, and I think both he and his parents blame me for their circumstances. I used to think he was the man I'd marry, but now . . ."

"Could you ever be interested in me?"

It was quiet as Jarena took a couple of deep breaths. "I think . . . oh, I don't know, Thomas. You're always so evasive when I ask about your past. And then there were those men looking for you. . . ."

"Would ya give me a chance to explain all that?"

She nodded.

He straightened his back and shifted on the seat. "You already know the law is after me. I hope you believe I'm innocent. I didn' run 'cause I did anything wrong, but I knew no one would believe me. There was a murder." His voice was very soft.

Jarena shivered. "Was it self-defense?"

"Didn't you hear me? I didn't do it!" His jaw tightened and his eyes were clouded with pain.

"I believe you, Thomas," she said, touching his arm. Her voice was but a mere whisper in the prairie wind, but his body relaxed, and she knew he'd heard her words.

"The less anyone knows, the better. I ain't believin' for one minute that them men has finally given up findin' me, and I don't wanna bring harm to anyone in Nicodemus. Gonna be best if I leave for a while. The Army's a good place to hide, and Lieutenant Boyle said I could go with him. That posse ain't gonna follow me into Indian Territory."

"You might die in some Indian skirmish if you join the Army."

"I hope not, but I'd rather serve in the

Army than be strung up by vigilantes for something I didn' do. If Lieutenant Boyle thinks the Army'll take me, then I think it's best for the town if I leave Nicodemus. Will you write to me if I go?"

"Surely there's another answer. Once those men are convinced you're not in Kansas, maybe they'll leave."

"They ain't gonna be easily convinced, Jarena. They're mean, and they'll do what it takes to find me. It's best if I'm gone, and I gotta have me some way to earn money. I can save my Army pay and maybe have a little money to get my farm started when I return. I'm hoping you'll write me, but I don't expect you to make no promises 'bout your future. You're a fine woman, and I can't expect you to wait and take your chances with the likes of me."

"So you didn't truly mean it when you said you wanted to win my hand?"

"Course I meant it, but it wouldn't be right to ask you to wait around—'specially on the likes of me. I shouldn'ta ever mentioned courtin' you afore I was certain 'bout my future. Guess I was over-anxious, but I wanted to state my case if you and Charles was gonna lay aside your plans to marry."

Jarena listened to his befuddled explanation. There was little doubt Thomas was living in a state of fear. Yet through the chaos, he was attempting to plan his future—with her.

"I appreciate your honesty, Thomas, and if you decide to join the Army, I'll be honored to write to you—no matter what happens between Charles and me."

His broad smile and sparkling eyes revealed his pleasure. "You gotta remember my writin' ain't all that good—and don't be writin' me no long words I ain't learned yet."

"Let's wait and see what Lieutenant Boyle has to say before worrying about your ability to read my letters." Her smile wavered as she thought about Thomas going off to join the colored regiment in Indian Territory. As the wagon slowed to a halt in front of the Boyle home, she prayed Lieutenant Boyle would discourage Thomas's enlistment.

Jarena thought the substantial frame house was an overpowering presence among the soddies and other ramshackle buildings within her sight. And to think Dr. Boyle was constructing a new home even grander than this one—one that would suit his wife's desires. How could she be unhappy living in such a fine home while others around her were starving to death and living in dreadful conditions?

The front door swung open, and Truth stood in the doorway. Jarena's mouth opened in a wide oval. Her sister appeared to have grown at least two inches, and she looked like a young woman rather than the playful girl who had left them only a short time ago. "Truth! You look wonderful," she cried, running to her sister and wrapping her in a warm embrace.

They chattered loudly until they were joined by Dr. Boyle and his children. "I'm sorry my wife isn't here to greet you," Dr. Boyle said. "She's upstairs resting, but perhaps she can join us later."

"I apologize. I hope our boisterous behavior hasn't disturbed her." Jarena cast a quick glance in her sister's direction.

"No apology needed. I'm pleased your father permitted you to accompany Thomas on his visit. I know Truth is excited to see you."

"And Grace? Didn't she want to come along?" The disappointment was evident in Truth's voice.

"Most certainly. But Pappy thought it best

we visit one at a time. He said Grace can come next time. I think he wanted to make certain someone would be at home to fix his supper." Noting the sadness in her sister's eyes, she now regretted her decision to accompany Thomas. She'd put her own selfish desires above those of her sister. After all, she knew the twins hadn't previously been separated for any length of time.

As though she knew what Jarena was thinking, Truth grasped her sister's hand and said, "I'm very glad you came. Would you like to see the rest of the house?"

"Yes, of course. If you've no duties to which you must attend."

"You go and visit with your sister, Truth," Dr. Boyle encouraged. "There's nothing we can't manage for ourselves during the next few hours."

"Thank you, Dr. Boyle," Truth replied before leading Jarena from the room. "Come this way. I'll show you the kitchen, and we can have a cup of tea," she whispered as they walked down the hallway. "Do watch the floorboards. I don't want you to trip." Truth pointed to one of the uneven boards.

"I remember Macia commenting about

the warped flooring. What a luxury to have something other than dirt under your feet."

"It took me only a few days to find all of the rippled boards. Now I know where they are without even looking. But Macia still trips over them occasionally, and then she becomes very angry." Truth giggled as they entered the kitchen.

"My! Look at the stove you have to prepare the meals. And the pantry! And all that food!" Jarena turned to her sister. "Are you happy, Truth?"

"Mostly, though I miss Grace somethin' awful—you and Pappy, too." She put the teakettle on the stove and sat with Jarena at the table.

"I understand. It's only natural you'd miss Grace very much. She misses you, also. In fact, she asked me to deliver this." Jarena pulled Grace's letter from her pocket.

"Oh, a letter. Thank you." Truth gave a contented sigh. "Did Dr. Boyle deliver the letter to Pappy?"

Jarena nodded. "It was from Aunt Lilly. She said she had gotten word from some distant relative in Georgetown that we moved to Kansas, and she asked Pappy to let her know about life on the frontier.

Pappy's afraid she might want to move out here, so he said when I write to her, I'm supposed to tell her what a hard life we're having."

"Doesn't he want her to come visit?" Truth asked. "I'd like to meet her."

"Pappy says we're not going to be in any hurry to write back—says Aunt Lilly is filled with the devil."

"What's that mean?" Truth whispered.

"Voodoo and witchcraft. He said he doesn't want anyone around who believes in such things—kinfolk or not."

Truth shivered. "I don't think folks would take kindly to someone practicing voodoo in Nicodemus. I'm having enough trouble just trying to figure out the white folks here in Hill City. Did you meet Mr. Wyman when they came to Nicodemus?"

"Yes. We didn't talk much, but he seemed nice enough. He appeared particularly pleased when he discovered I was your sister. I must admit that for a man of obvious means, he seemed quite contented among our scraggly group. And he talked to Pappy with an ease that surprised me."

"What'd they talk about?" Truth's insistent tone surprised Jarena.

"I didn't hear all of it, but Pappy said he liked him and that he was a well-spoken young man, though I do recall Pappy saying there was something about Mr. Wyman— something he couldn't quite figure out. I did hear Mr. Wyman mention he was setting up his newspaper in Hill City and that he was planning to print a paper for Nicodemus, too."

"He's up to something, Jarena. That man has something on his mind besides a news-paper. He's always coming into the kitchen and talking to me. He even asked me if I would be interested in writing some articles for the paper."

Jarena swelled with pride. "You see? Your education is going to help you more than you ever anticipated. And I must admit your grammar has improved immensely since you've been living with the Boyle family."

"Jarena, you're not hearing me." Truth scooted her chair across the plank floor un-til there wasn't enough space to force a piece of paper between them. She kept her voice to a whisper. "He's been making ad-vances toward me."

"Advances? You mean . . ."

Truth bobbed her head up and down, her

features creased into a tight frown. "But I put him in his place the other day when he came out here to the kitchen with his sweet-talk. Told him I knew what he had in mind, and I wasn't going to be a part of it. I said he best stay out of the kitchen, but I don't know if he's going to heed my words."

"Have you told the Boyles about his behavior?"

"I'm scared to tell them. What if Mr. Wyman says I'm lying and Dr. Boyle believes him? They might send me back home. Pappy needs every cent of the money I'm earning here. I don't want to lose my job."

Jarena grasped her sister's hand. "Do you want me to talk with Dr. Boyle—or Pappy? You know Pappy would never forgive himself if something happened to you, Truth."

"No. I shouldn't have said anything. Now that Mr. Wyman's started up his newspaper, he's not around much, and I heard him tell Dr. Boyle he's making arrangements to stay at the hotel until he can build a house for himself. I'll be fine. Promise you won't say anything."

Jarena hesitated for a moment. "If you're

certain that's what you want, but I'm not sure remaining silent is best."

"I am. Please don't make me regret I told you. Now, let's talk about something else— tell me about things at home. What's Grace been doing? And you? And why didn't Charles come along with you instead of Thomas?"

"Actually, *I* came with Thomas. He wanted to talk to Lieutenant Boyle, and I asked if I could ride along with him. I haven't seen much of Charles lately. Each time we're together, we seem to have a disagreement."

"I never did think you two were suited. Thomas would be a better match." Truth gave her sister a broad grin. "How come Thomas is talking to Lieutenant Boyle?"

"He's considering joining the Army."

Truth rocked back in her chair. "Then I guess you best not plan on jumping the broom with *him.*"

Jarena shook her head slowly. "No, I suppose not."

The sound of the men's voices drifted down the hallway. Jarena held a finger to her pursed lips to silence Truth. When she heard Thomas agree to depart for Indian

Territory in two days, fear gripped her with an intensity she'd not known since their mother lay gasping for breath on her deathbed.

CHAPTER

30

Streaks of orange and pink splashed the morning sky in a welcoming design as Jarena walked out to greet the new day. Taking only a moment to rub warmth into her arms, she added a mound of buffalo chips to the waning fire in the limestone pit outside their dugout. With winter now behind them, she'd taken to cooking outdoors, yet this morning the colder temperatures of March had returned. After settling a pot of water atop the grate, Jarena quickly poured a batch of cornmeal mush into a skillet and sighed. She had long ago wearied of preparing the same dull fare each day.

Ezekiel chuckled softly as he walked outdoors. "I see you 'cided to shiver out here in the cold rather than put up with the stink of them buffalo chips burnin' inside the dug-out."

Jarena wiped the sleep from her eyes and nodded. She hadn't taken the time to wash up before starting the fire, deciding to wait until it was a little warmer. Besides, Pappy would fuss if his breakfast wasn't ready on time, and nowadays he wanted to start work mighty early. "I've got your food ready for nooning," she said, handing him a folded cloth containing last night's leftover corn-bread and a jug of water that would stave off his hunger until he returned home.

When they heard the clomping of ap-proaching horses, her father peered off to the south. "Wonder who that could be."

Jarena squinted and cupped one hand above her eyes. "They're white—all of them."

Jarena waved at a few of their neighbors emerging from their hillside dwellings. The small group of settlers gathered together in the center of town and watched as the horses trotted between the dugouts and then encircled them. The riders sat atop their fine-looking animals and stared down at the tattered half-starved residents with an air of authority.

"We're looking for a man—he's colored like all of you." The rider's words were filled with the same disgust that shone in his eyes. Rising in his stirrups, he searched their faces. "I know he's here. I give you my word that there won't be any trouble if you just turn him over to us. We're looking for Thomas Grayson."

Jarena's blood chilled as she heard the man say the name. Now she knew who they were! These were the men from the railroad station. Because of Thomas's unexpected kiss, she'd not gotten a good look at any of them, but these must be the same men. Thomas had been correct. They'd not given up their search, though she wondered why they hadn't appeared in Nicodemus long ago.

Her father approached the men with a surprising calmness. "Ain't nobody by that name livin' in Nicodemus. Why don' you fellas be on your way? We don' want no trouble. We's just tryin' to make a life fer ourselves out here on the prairie. Ain't nothin' here you's looking fer."

The man tugged on his expensive jacket until the fabric aligned to perfection. "You think I'm going to believe you, old man? You think that because you tell me Thomas Grayson isn't here, I'm going to nod my head and ride out of town?"

Ezekiel folded his arms across his chest. "Might as well, 'cause it's the truth. You ain't gonna find nobody by that name living in this here town." The other settlers murmured their agreement.

With lightning speed, the man tugged his foot from the stirrup and kicked Ezekiel with a force that sent the older man reeling. Jarena shrieked as her father fell with blood dripping from his forehead.

Jarena knelt by her father as the other settlers raced to their homes. She pulled a cloth from her pocket and dabbed at the blood. Her father rolled up onto his elbow but still looked dazed.

The leader leaned over from his horse, grabbed a clump of dry sunflower stalks, and shoved the ends into the fire outside the Harban dugout. "Search these dugouts!" The leader used the flaming stalks to set fire to several nearby dwellings as his cohorts followed his instructions.

The frightened townspeople huddled in small groups as they watched in terror.

The men emerged from one of the

dwellings a short time later. "He's not in any of those miserable holes. We been in all of them."

Their leader pointed at the nearby Francis dugout. "You didn't check that one."

As the rider neared the Francis dwelling, Charles emerged from the doorway with his father's rifle in hand. He stood in the morning light, transfixed by the brightness and sights that assailed him. Disbelief filled his dark eyes as he took in the flames blazing from the dugout roofs. His eyes darted about, and as he lifted his rifle, a shot cracked through the morning air and met its mark.

Jarena gasped in horror as a pool of red colored Charles's shirtfront and he slowly dropped to the ground. His mother rushed up and fell to her knees beside him as the gunman rode past them and shot another bullet into the air, startling a team of horses attached to one of the wagons.

"The wagon! My little William's in there!" Effie Beyer's screams echoed across the prairie as she raced after the frightened team of horses. The wagon careened perilously, and William's cries for help matched his mother's frantic shouts. She screamed at the boy to sit down so he wouldn't fall out. The riders laughed as they watched the young boy's terror and his mother's maniacal attempts to intercept the frightened team of horses.

"That crazy woman thinks she's gonna catch up with that wagon," one of the men hooted.

"Grayson ain't in this town. Let's get out of here." Their leader waved his gun and turned his horse toward the east. "Wyatt! Where you going?" he yelled as one of his men rode off after the runaway team. "Get on back here. We're not gonna wait on you!" He fired another shot and then watched Wyatt for a moment before he turned to the other men. "Let's go—far as I'm concerned, he's on his own."

Jarena grasped her father by the shoulders. "Let me help you to your feet."

"I's all right. Go see 'bout Charles. Don't look good, and Lula ain't in no shape to be carin' for him."

Jarena hesitated when she noticed blood now soaked the cloth she'd applied to his forehead. "Hold this tight on the wound. Are you certain you'll be all right?"

The plaintive cries of Lula Francis and

Effie Beyer assaulted Jarena's ears as her father shooed her away to care for Charles. "I'm fine. Go on now."

———

Ezekiel followed Effie and John Beyer toward the approaching horseman. Their young son sat in front of the man who'd chased after the frightened team of horses. The broad-shouldered man handed the boy down to Effie, who sobbed her thanks before promptly turning to scold her wayward child for playing in the wagon.

The man swung down from his horse and handed over the team of horses to Ezekiel. "The hitch broke. Wagon's likely going to need repair. I'm terrible sorry about what happened here."

Ezekiel handed the reins to John Beyer and then turned his attention back to the rider. "Iffen you're truly sorry, would you at least tell me what this is all about? We're all thankful for the boy's safe return. Ain't nobody gonna do you no harm." Ezekiel extended his right hand, still holding the cloth to his head with his left. "My name's Ezekiel Harban."

"Wyatt Pell." The man shook Ezekiel's

hand and then followed along until they were inside the Harban dwelling.

Ezekiel pointed to one of the log chairs in the dugout. "Just what was it you fellas was thinkin' to accomplish by yer actions?"

"Clifton Mowry—he's the fellow that was riding the black mount—he's determined to find Thomas and return him to Louisiana." Wyatt's voice was laced with a deep southern drawl.

"Sounds as though you might be from Louisiana, too," Ezekiel ventured.

The man nodded. "We're all from Louisiana—known each other since we were young boys. All the same, I don't hold with what's going on. Clifton's gone too far this time."

"What you mean, gone too far?"

"Shooting innocent people and setting homes on fire. It's crazy, but he's afraid the truth is going to come out and *he'll* be charged with murder. That's why he's determined to find Thomas."

Ezekiel removed the bloody cloth from his head and replaced it with a clean one. "I still don' understand."

Wyatt pressed the brim of his hat back and forth through his fingers. "It's a long story, but I'll try to explain. You see, Clifton is an only child and his mother died years ago. His father was wealthy. He owned a large cotton plantation that mostly escaped the perils of the war. Sharecroppers who once were slaves continue working the plantation, and Thomas was one of those sharecroppers. It was Thomas who found old Mr. Mowry's dead body—I'm talking about Clifton's father—and delivered it to Clifton at the big house. Thomas said he found the body along the riverbank where he'd gone to fish. That was his first mistake."

Ezekiel leaned back in his chair. "Hard to fault a man for doin' a good thing, but I know you's right. He shoulda jest left the body laying on the riverbank."

"Clifton immediately went to the authorities and told them Thomas was the killer and that his father's gold watch and money were missing. He said he'd seen Thomas with the watch. Of course, the authorities believed Clifton, and they brought out the dogs to help find Thomas. Someone must have told Thomas he had been accused, because he was already gone by the time the posse got to his place. After a few days

I think everyone knew Thomas wasn't the killer, but we didn't want to call Clifton a liar. He's one mean fella. Your life is much easier if you just go along with him."

"I surely knows that fer a fact," Ezekiel said, pulling the cloth from his forehead to see if the bleeding had stopped. "But how come you decided Thomas was innocent?"

Wyatt stared at the floor. "Old Mr. Mowry was tightfisted with his money, and Clifton always had to fight for every cent he got from the old man. He complained incessantly about his father's miserly ways and was always saying he didn't think the old man would ever die."

"But that don't 'splain what made you decide Thomas didn' do it."

Wyatt looked up and met Ezekiel's eyes. "No, it doesn't. From the beginning, I said Thomas could have just taken the watch when he found the old man dead along the riverbank, but nobody listened. After all, Thomas was colored and had been a slave on the plantation—Clifton told the sheriff Thomas was likely attempting to get back at his father for the years he'd lived in slavery."

"Why didn't Clifton jest let the law take

care of matters? Why's he out here chasing down someone so far from home?"

"Clifton and his father fought all the time over money, and I guess the old man thought his son might kill him. He put a clause in his will providing that if he died under strange circumstances, Clifton was not to inherit his estate unless someone else was convicted of the crime."

"So that's why he's so determined."

Wyatt nodded. "Clifton promised all of us a large amount of money to help him bring Thomas to justice. When we first started out, I truly believed Thomas might be guilty. Later, when I saw Clifton in possession of his father's pocket watch, I confronted him. He said the watch was one he'd recently purchased—not the one that had belonged to his father. But I knew he was lying—it wasn't a new watch. I think he knew I didn't believe him, but I was afraid to argue any further. Guess the truth is, I wanted the money he was offering, too. My family lost everything in the war—we were burned out. I thought the money would be enough to begin a new life. Not a good reason, but the only one I've got."

"How'd you ever think you could trust a man that would kill his own pappy?"

The Southerner shrugged. "Didn't give it much thought. I figured he'd be afraid we'd turn on him."

Ezekiel arched his eyebrows. "And you weren't afraid he'd kill you, too?"

"Not too smart, I guess."

"You's right about that," Ezekiel agreed. "One more question."

"What's that?"

"What took you so long to get here? You was seen down in Ellis over a month ago."

Wyatt appeared startled by Ezekiel's remark. "How'd you know that? Thomas is here, isn't he?"

Ezekiel wagged his head back and forth. "No. He's not, but I'm not gonna lie to you. He was here, and we expected you long ago. He never told me what dis was about, but I figured you gave up the search weeks ago."

Wyatt nodded. "We met a young fellow at the livery. Clifton asked if he knew Thomas and told the fellow Thomas was wanted for murder. The boy said he didn't believe Clifton. That Thomas wouldn't kill anyone. Clifton threatened to pistol-whip the fellow if he didn't tell us where Thomas was living. The boy relented and said Thomas told him he was heading for Colorado. We followed and made inquiry at every little town or way station along the route we figured he would have taken. Finally, after three weeks of looking, we turned back. We happened upon a farmstead outside of Ellis owned by Jeremiah Horton. He told us Thomas had worked for him and that he was living in Nicodemus. We tried to talk Clifton into going back home, but he's like a man possessed. He won't rest until he's found Thomas. I figure he'll come back to Nicodemus since Mr. Horton told him he knew for a fact that Thomas lived here."

"You can search this place. Like I told you, Thomas lived here, but he's gone and not expected to return."

Ezekiel walked Wyatt Pell back to his horse and made sure his neighbors allowed the man to leave town safely.

When Wyatt's form was just a tiny spot on the horizon, Lula Francis's scream echoed from inside the Francis dugout.

Jarena appeared in the Francises' doorway, looking harried and stunned. "He's dead, Pappy. Charles is dead!"

CHAPTER

31

Jarena glanced at the soft gray clouds and hoped the showers would wait until the laundry dried. *Selfish girl,* she chided. After all, hadn't her father and Thomas worked diligently with the breaking plow for this very purpose? Hadn't they hoped and prayed to take advantage of the spring rains? Certainly rain for the fields was more important than a tub of laundry. With a flick of her wrists, Jarena snapped her father's wet shirt and draped it over the rope. There was nothing to do but hang the clothes and trust God for the rest.

The lack of sunshine did little to improve Jarena's spirits. Though she had begun adapting to life in their small community, she longed for the joyful chatter of her sisters, a good book to read, enough food to prepare for their meals, or a letter from Thomas—oh yes, a letter from Thomas would be most welcome. A twinge of guilt invaded her thoughts as one of the Beyer boys raced by her with his younger brother following on his heels. Instead of plump youthful faces, their prominent cheekbones reinforced their thin features. Shirts and pants hung on their emaciated frames. The boys reminded Jarena of a scarecrow her mother had dressed years ago and placed in their vegetable garden to fend off the birds. Yet these two were fortunate. Their youngest brother had died a few weeks back, and though some said it was the fever, most knew it was from lack of nutritious food. Effie and John had buried the boy near Charles and declared the area to be a cemetery—the Nicodemus cemetery.

The thought stirred a chill, and Jarena rubbed her hands together. She remained numb over Charles's death, for though her romantic feelings for him had cooled, she missed his friendship and banter, and grieved deeply for his parents, who had now suffered the loss of two sons.

She pushed away thoughts of Charles

and told herself she had little to complain about. Hadn't Truth's employment with the Boyles benefited their entire family? And though there was never enough to go around, her father had always shared with others. Of course, she couldn't forget Dr. Boyle. He had certainly been a stalwart friend to their small group. She remembered fondly the many acts of kindness he'd performed during the past months. Amid the hardships there had been many blessings.

Even Grace's love for the outdoors had become an invaluable asset. Nowadays she worked alongside their father in the fields like a seasoned hand, reveling in the pleasure of turning the soil.

Indeed there were small things for which to give thanks—and Jarena would dwell upon those.

Swiping damp hands down her apron, Jarena hurried off to the Francis dugout, keeping a watchful eye on the bowl of thin soup she carried. Although she doubted Mrs. Francis would partake of more than a few spoonfuls, Jarena continued to encourage the woman to eat—sometimes with success, sometimes not. The distant sound of whooping men and screaming women caused her to look away from the dish.

Wagons! A multitude of wagons—filled with people—were moving toward Nicodemus! Her heart quickened at the sight.

She rushed into the Francis dugout and shouted the news. "Another wagon train of folks is arriving. Come see!" In her excitement, she nearly dropped the bowl.

In the month since Charles's death, Mrs. Francis had languished in pain. Now a flicker of light shone in her eyes.

"You sure, girl?" Mr. Francis asked as he reached for his hat.

Jarena leaned down and crooked an arm around his wife's shoulders to help her up. "Oh, I'm sure, Mr. Francis. Come see for yourself."

The column of wagons was drawing ever closer when the trio finally exited the dugout. Mrs. Francis leaned heavily on Jarena and her husband as they joined the other townsfolk gathering to welcome the new arrivals.

"Isn't it wonderful? Appears they've come with supplies," Jarena exclaimed. "I can even make out some cows following alongside them."

Mrs. Francis pushed a strand of hair from her face. "I hope at least one of dem will wanna purchase some land."

"So you're still determined to leave?"

Richard Francis gave a resolute nod. "Only thing that's been holdin' us back is the lack of money to get home. Maybe this here's the answer to our prayers, Lula."

Jarena looked down at the grieving woman. "I don't think your wife is strong enough to make the journey, Mr. Francis. She's barely eaten since . . . since . . ."

"Since Charles was gunned down? You's right on dat account. But I believe this is all she'll need to regain her strength—ain't it, Lula?"

A faint smile curved the older woman's lips. "I'll be strong enough to leave here. Don' you doubt me for even a minute. The only regret I'll have when I leave dis place is that I'll be leavin' Charles behind."

"Ain't nothin' we can do 'bout that, Lula, but it looks like we's gonna be able to go back home, and that there's a blessing in itself."

Jarena stayed beside Mrs. Francis while her husband and the others rushed to greet the newcomers. Children had hurried off to spread the word to those working their fields, and some of them were now gathering in town to see the new arrivals.

"I ain't taking nothing back to Kentucky ceptin' the clothes I need for traveling," Mrs. Francis said. "Don't want no memories of this place going back to Kentucky with us, so iffen you want any of our goods, you can have 'em."

Jarena's eyes were filled with warmth, and she patted the older woman's hand. "We don't have any money to purchase them, Mrs. Francis. But thank you kindly for the offer. Besides, we don't know for certain that anyone's going to have money to buy your land."

Before Mrs. Francis could rebut Jarena's words, Mr. Francis came hurrying back, flailing his arms above his head. "The Lemmonses from back home is in this group! George Lemmons says he'll buy our place! We got money enough to leave, Lula."

Her husband's announcement brought a deeper smile to Mrs. Francis's lips. "Looks like you're wrong, Jarena. Richard has done gone and found us a buyer already. Why don't you come inside and see what ya'd like to have. Ain't askin' for no money.

Charles would want me to treat you kindly. I know you doubted his love for you, and truth be told, so did I—thought he and Belle Harris was better suited."

Mrs. Francis's words nearly mimicked what Charles had said before Jarena had gone off to Ellis. What was it? *"I'm beginning to think I should have been keeping company with Belle Harris."* If only he *had* begun courting Belle Harris! He'd likely still be alive!

Mrs. Francis settled into a rickety chair with a faraway look in her eyes. "I know it wasn't you that lured him out to this desolate place, Jarena. He told me he would have come even if you wasn't here. I'm telling you all this so you won't go on blamin' yo'self. I know it ain't your fault, gal. My boy is dead and ain't nothing gonna bring him back, but ain't right for you to spend the rest of your life thinkin' you was the cause. It's God's timing, not ours."

"That's what Miss Hattie said, too."

The woman wiped a tear from her cheek and grasped Jarena's hand. "You wanna come back to Georgetown with us? We'll have enough money to buy you a train ticket, and you could pay us back once you found work."

Last fall Jarena would have seized the opportunity, but now she amazed even herself as she declined the invitation. "Thank you, Mrs. Francis, but I couldn't leave. Not now—probably not ever. Our home isn't in Georgetown anymore—it's out here on these plains."

"If you ever change your mind . . ."

Jarena leaned down and placed a kiss on the woman's tear-stained cheek. "Thank you, Mrs. Francis."

Charles's mother nodded and brushed a wisp of hair from her forehead. "Now get busy and pack up dese things. The faster you tote 'em out of here, the sooner we kin be on our way."

Jarena eagerly began to fill a crate. The Francises didn't have much, but it would help.

———

Moses folded his hands and met Dr. Boyle's warm gaze. "Thank you for agreeing to see me on short notice."

Dr. Boyle laughed as he glanced about the room. "As you can see, there are no patients awaiting my care so I'm not causing anyone undue hardship. However, I must admit I'm intrigued by your request."

Beads of perspiration had formed along Moses's upper lip, and he pulled out his handerchief. "What I have to tell you is difficult—especially since I've waited until now."

"What can I do to help?"

Moses wiped his face and slowly tucked the handkerchief back into his pocket. He had hoped the perfect words would come to mind. There was no denying he needed a compelling explanation for his regretful behavior. He was, after all, a wordsmith—a man who made his living crafting words into stories that would sell newspapers. Yet at this moment, language failed him. There was no explanation—persuasive or otherwise.

"I'm colored." The words whizzed through the air like two arrows aimed at a bull's-eye.

Dr. Boyle rocked back in his chair. "Colored? Whatever are you talking about? Have you lost your senses?"

"I'm not white—not like you." Moses shifted in his chair. "Oh, I appear as white as most, and I've as many white ancestors as colored, perhaps more. However, we both know that if any Negro blood runs through my veins, I'm not considered a white man. And I don't want to be considered white. I'm not ashamed of my people. In fact, you'll recall I had planned to make my home in Nicodemus when I first arrived."

Dr. Boyle nodded. "I do remember."

"Everything else you know about me is true. My background, education, work at the various newspapers—all of that information is accurate. When I met Carlisle on the train, I should have told him."

The doctor looked wary. "Why didn't you?"

"Honestly? I wanted to see if he was genuine in his desire to go off and serve with colored soldiers. At first I thought he was just another sanctimonious white man seeking to fulfill himself in the name of God. By the time I learned that wasn't true, I was already passing as white. With each day, it grew more difficult to speak the truth. But I can no longer live this lie."

"Something in particular bring you to this point or merely a guilty conscience?"

"I know you're angry, and you have a right

to be. What I did was completely inappropriate and unacceptable. If you never speak to me again, I couldn't fault you."

Dr. Boyle's countenance softened. "And what good would such behavior accomplish? Besides, what you perceive as my anger is actually pain—pain that you didn't believe you could trust me or my son enough to speak the truth. But now you have, and for that I am thankful. However, I'm curious why you've decided to tell me at this juncture."

"To clear my conscience, but also because I've deeply offended Truth. You see, on several occasions I've tried to talk to her. In fact, I attempted to convince her to write news articles for the paper. However, she mistook my interest in her. She thinks I'm a white man endeavoring to . . . to . . . get her in my bed."

"Ah, I see." He leaned back in his chair. "You're interested in courting Truth, and you want her to know you're an acceptable suitor?"

"Exactly. What has caused my honesty is a guilty conscience and my selfish—but honorable, I assure you—interest in a woman. You see, Dr. Boyle, I was hoping you might speak to her on my behalf."

"*Were* you, now?"

"Rather presumptuous of me, I know—especially in light of the circumstances."

Dr. Boyle gave a hearty laugh. "I think *you* should be the one who reveals your true heritage to Truth. I'm willing to confirm that you've told me these facts, but beyond that—well, I'd say that you're on your own." He rubbed his hand along his jaw. "What if she doesn't believe you? Have you planned for that event?"

"I have papers that show my lineage, but I fear she'll think me a man ashamed of his race. An unforgivable fraud. If so, I doubt she'll ever consider me as a suitor, but I must at least try. I do care for her very much."

"Then why don't you come over this evening? I'll explain that you want to talk to her and that she has nothing to fear. The two of you can visit in the parlor. She'll likely feel more relaxed if she knows I'm aware of your presence and that someone is nearby should you attempt to . . . uh, accost her," he said with a lopsided grin.

Moses stood suddenly and grasped Dr.

Boyle's hand. "Would eight o'clock be acceptable?"

He nodded. "We'll expect you."

———

The day was warm, and there was a lightness to his step as Samuel contemplated exactly what he would say to Truth that evening. He didn't want to alarm the girl, yet if she was already fearful of Moses, his announcement of the visit might cause her undue concern. Waiting until shortly before Moses's arrival would likely be best, he decided while sauntering past the general store. He tipped his hat at Mrs. Johnson before turning his attention to a horse galloping into town.

"Slow down, young fellow!" Dr. Boyle hollered as the man reined his horse to an abrupt halt. "You've got that horse in quite a lather."

The young man yanked his wide-brimmed hat from his head. "Dr. Boyle! I was hoping to see a familiar face when I arrived."

"Jackson! What are *you* doing in Hill City?" Samuel could feel the blood drain from his face. Was Macia making secret plans? He'd heard no mention of Jackson in weeks. Jackson dismounted and stood before him with a wide smirk on his face.

"I can see you're surprised. I imagine Macia will be taken aback, also."

Samuel clenched his jaw. "So she wasn't expecting you?"

"No." The smug grin remained on Jackson's lips. "I didn't answer her letters. It's been quite some time since she's corresponded."

"And *that's* why you've come? Because Macia ceased writing to you?"

Jackson looked down the street and curled his upper lip with disdain. "Not exactly. There are some other matters that have come to my attention. But let's not discuss them here. I'm anxious to see your new home and the . . . well, this poor excuse for a town."

Samuel led the way into the livery. "Jeb! Come meet Jackson Kincaid."

Jeb rounded the corner of a stall and ambled toward the two men.

"This young fellow is from back in Georgetown. Jackson, this is Jeb Malone."

Jeb nodded at Jackson and glanced at the sorrel. "You rent that horse from Chester

Goddard down in Ellis?" Without waiting for an answer, Jeb began to assess the animal. "Chester don't take kindly to having his animals mistreated, Mr. Kincaid."

"What he doesn't know won't hurt him. I was anxious to arrive and rode the animal hard. He'll survive without problem."

Jeb directed an icy stare at Jackson. "You Macia's beau?"

"I wouldn't go quite that far." He tugged at his collar and looked uncomfortably from one man to the other. "We kept company when she lived in Georgetown, but I don't think I could be considered her beau. I believe there are too many miles between us for such an arrangement."

"Then what brought you all the way to Hill City?" Jeb's voice was full of suspicion.

"I'd say what brings me to Hill City is none of your business. I find your behavior offensive, Mr. Malone." He examined the bottom of his boot and wiped it on the straw. "Are all of the locals as brash and rude as this man?" he asked Dr. Boyle.

"I find Jeb neither brash nor rude," Samuel answered. "He is, in my opinion, a refreshingly forthright, hardworking young man."

Jeb's chest swelled at the accolades. "Why, thank you, Dr. Boyle."

Turning on his heel, Jackson angrily strode toward the doorway. "Since Mr. Goddard is your friend, I assume you know how to care for his horse."

"That I do," Jeb yelled back. "Nice to see you, Dr. Boyle," he said as Samuel followed Jackson. "Give my regards to Macia."

Jackson winced, but Samuel smiled and waved, delighted Jeb Malone had held his ground against the likes of Jackson Kincaid.

"Is that you, Samuel?"

Margaret's voice came from the kitchen as the two entered the house. He wondered if she was assisting Truth with some new dish for supper. "Indeed it is, my dear. Do come join me. We have a visitor."

Margaret emerged from the kitchen and removed her soiled apron as she approached them.

"Who is it, Mother?" Macia called from the kitchen.

Samuel placed a finger to his lips and cautioned his wife to remain silent. "Don't spoil the surprise for Macia." Jackson grinned at Margaret and stepped behind Samuel to add to the surprise.

"Oh, Samuel, I don't think this is a good idea. Macia isn't dressed to receive . . ."

Before his wife could complete her sentence, Macia appeared in the hallway, wearing a print dress soiled with flour. Her damp and disheveled curls were drooping like a bouquet of wilted flowers. As she drew near, Jackson stepped from behind her father. His smile vanished when he saw her.

"Macia! What has happened to you? You've changed into a common housewife."

Macia's eyes shone with anger, and she clenched her flour-dusted fists. "That's hardly possible, since I'm a *single* woman. Notice of your arrival would have prevented this catastrophic event." She tucked a wisp of hair behind one ear, looking like she was about to break into sobs.

"My dear," Samuel said, "I didn't expect to find you in such a state of disarray." As soon as he'd spoken, he wished he could snatch back the words, for he'd only made matters worse. "We could leave and return in an hour or so."

"The damage is already done." Macia pushed Jackson aside and raced up the stairs.

"Do come into the parlor and have a

seat," Margaret invited. "I'm certain Macia will return once she's had an opportunity to properly prepare herself."

She edged to her husband's side and stood on tiptoe, her lips pressed close to Samuel's ear. "Did you not even *think* before bringing him here unannounced?"

Samuel had offered to leave and return at a later time. So far as he was concerned, there was little else that could be done to change the awkward circumstances. He shrugged apologetically and directed a disheartened smile at his wife. "Perhaps Truth could bring us a glass of lemonade."

Margaret frowned at her husband as they sat down in the parlor. "Truth isn't here. That's why Macia and I were in the kitchen preparing supper. Harvey came rushing home a short time ago with word that a large group of settlers arrived in Nicodemus. Walt Johnson heard the news in Ellis and stopped by the newspaper office to give Moses the information. Harvey said Moses had a previous engagement scheduled this evening—though I still can't imagine what it would be. In any event, Moses asked Harvey to go to Nicodemus and gather information for the newspaper. Of course, Truth was excited to hear that there were new arrivals and asked if she could accompany him. I gave her permission to go along."

Samuel massaged his forehead. "So Truth went to Nicodemus with Harvey? She's spending the night with her family?"

"Yes. Is something wrong, Samuel?"

"No, no. I . . . well . . . I had planned . . ." He jumped up from the settee. "I . . . uh, there's a matter that needs my immediate attention. I'll be back in a few moments."

The bell above the door rattled a pathetic clink as Samuel entered the newspaper office. Moses stood searching through type cases with a metal composing stick in his hand.

"Seems as though our plans for this evening have gone awry," Samuel told him.

Moses laid the composing stick across the cabinet. "How so?"

"My wife tells me you sent Harvey to Nicodemus."

He nodded. "A difficult decision. I truly wanted to go and visit with the new settlers, but I knew if I didn't talk with Truth tonight, I might lose courage."

"Truth went to Nicodemus with Harvey.

She wanted to visit her family, and my wife thought it a fine opportunity."

Moses's face was filled with disbelief. "Truth traveled to Nicodemus with Harvey? So I can't talk with her this evening?"

"I'm afraid not. And to make matters even worse, Macia's beau from back in Kentucky arrived unexpectedly."

He grinned. "And Truth isn't there to prepare supper."

"It's going to be a long evening." Samuel ran his hand over his face and sighed.

Moses looked like he was trying to contain his laughter. "I guess I'm glad I won't be there, then. I'll make arrangements with you when Truth returns."

"And you'll tell the others your secret, too?"

"And the others. Everyone should know the truth."

CHAPTER

32

Supper was less than perfection. Margaret insisted upon completing the preparations and serving the meal while Macia and Samuel entertained Jackson. Samuel briefly gave thought to offering his services in the kitchen rather than keeping company with Jackson, but then he remembered his lack of cooking skills. Perhaps he would take the opportunity to see if Jackson Kincaid had changed for the better in the last few months.

When Margaret scurried off to check something in the kitchen, Samuel turned his full attention to their guest. "So what is the news from Georgetown?"

Jackson folded his arms across his chest and groaned. "There's been a mass migration of coloreds moving out of Georgetown and the surrounding area. In fact, we've lost a number of our sharecroppers. You can imagine the impact upon our crops this year if we don't resolve this matter."

Samuel couldn't stop a wry grin from crossing his lips. "If you expect to turn a profit, you may be required to work in the fields yourself."

"Or force the return of those who had no right to flee," Jackson countered.

"Have you forgotten the war, Jackson? Slavery has been outlawed. Everyone now possesses the right to come and go at will—even your colored sharecroppers." Beside him, Samuel heard Macia gasp at his harsh tone.

"Not if they owe my family money," Jackson grunted. "And I have papers with me proving all those who left have outstanding debts with my family."

Samuel stroked his jaw. "That's hard to believe, Jackson. I never knew your father to be a man who would loan money to any of his sharecroppers."

"Well, he did!" Jackson jumped to his feet. "Are you calling me a *liar,* Dr. Boyle?"

Before Samuel could reply, his wife

walked into the room carrying a perfectly browned apple pie on a tray. "I apologize for my delay." She met Samuel's stern gaze. "Is something amiss?"

"Father is attempting to malign Jackson and his family," Macia accused.

Samuel laughed. "I'm doing no such thing. Do sit down, my dear."

Margaret placed a thick slice of pie on each of the four china plates. "Is your mother in good health, Jackson?"

"She's become overwrought with these recent events," he said as he forked a bite of the pie. "Our sharecroppers and even some of our household servants decided to come west and try their hand at homesteading. We've been told a goodly number were coming to Kansas."

Samuel dropped his fork. "So *that's* why you're here! You believe your sharecroppers have come west to settle in Nicodemus!"

"Jackson came to Hill City to see *me*. Isn't that correct?" Macia's voice was unusually high-pitched.

Jackson cleared his throat and shifted in his chair. "It's true I planned to see you. . . ." He hesitated.

Samuel hunched forward. "But visiting Macia isn't what precipitated this visit, is it?"

"I need to get those sharecroppers back or we'll lose our crops, our income. Someone has to work the fields. They never should have outlawed slavery—"

Macia gasped and clasped a hand to her chest. "Jackson!"

Samuel was on his feet now. "You're no longer welcome in my home, Jackson." He pointed at the front door.

Jackson turned a pleading gaze on Mrs. Boyle. "But . . . I haven't made any arrangements. . . ."

A wicked gleam shone in Macia's eyes. "There's a nice little sod hotel right down the street. Watch out for snakes."

After Jackson had stormed out and Margaret had returned to the kitchen, Macia sat down next to Samuel. "I must tell you something, Father."

"You look serious. What's all this secretive business?"

"The Harbans—Truth's family. They were sharecroppers at the Kincaid plantation."

Samuel reeled back as though he'd been

punched in the midsection. "Ezekiel never mentioned the Kincaids. Are you certain? How do you know?"

"I read the information in a letter Truth wrote to Jarena."

"You read Truth's private mail? I can't believe—"

Macia grasped her father's arm. "It wasn't intentional. I picked up her lessons to correct them. The letter to Jarena was at the bottom of the stack. I truly didn't realize what it was until I'd begun to examine the contents. When I saw she was writing about the Kincaids, I continued to read. I know my behavior was improper."

Samuel nodded. " 'Tis true your behavior was distasteful, but what's done can't now be changed. Does Truth know you read the letter?"

"We've never discussed the matter, though I'm certain she believes I perused the contents. From what I read, I don't believe Mr. Harban owes money to the Kincaids. But if they worked on their plantation . . ."

"Jackson may *allege* that Ezekiel owes him money."

"Yes," Macia whispered. "Jackson has proved to be everything you thought. I fear I'm a terrible judge of character."

Her father pulled her into a comforting embrace. "We all make mistakes, some more painful than others. You were impressed by Jackson's worldly possessions and let his wealth blind you. Now that you see him clearly, you realize your error. The next step is to learn from your mistake so that you don't experience the same pain again."

She smiled. "I don't think I'll be blinded by anyone's wealth or power so long as we're living in Hill City."

"Jackson's the one who's blind, my dear. He doesn't even realize he's permitting a lovely young woman to slip through his fingers. In fact, you've matured immeasurably since moving to Hill City. However, I'll not be the one to tell him!"

———

Samuel maneuvered the buggy close to the end of the field where Ezekiel was working. Hat in hand, Samuel waved wildly before jumping down. "Ezekiel! I need to talk with you."

The two men walked toward each other, their feet sinking into the soft black loam.

Ezekiel extended his large hand. "This here's an unexpected surprise. You come to Nicodemus to meet all our new arrivals?"

He shook his head. "While I'm eager to get acquainted with the new folks, there's another matter that brings me to Nicodemus. A matter that could spell trouble for you as well as some other residents. We need to talk."

"Sounds serious. Let's sit down over dere—that's usually where I eat my dinner. That lone tree provides me a bit of shade."

A short time later, the two men sat facing each other in the meager shade provided by the sprawling bush that Ezekiel had munificently described as a tree. There was little time for elaborate explanation. With quick precision, Samuel presented Jackson's allegations of his sharecroppers owing money and then awaited Ezekiel's response.

Ezekiel took a long swallow from the earthen water jug Jarena had sent. "I don't owe no man money, Dr. Boyle. I worked hard to save the money I used to buy this here land, and ain't no man, Kincaid or otherwise, gonna prove no different."

"I've not seen them, but Jackson tells me he's in possession of signed notes for the debts owed to his family."

Ezekiel frowned. "I ain't never signed no paper. Kincaid treated us bad as slaves, Dr. Boyle, and he didn't do no better when we was sharecropping. Didn't much of nothin' change ceptin' we had to pay rent for them same rundown quarters we was livin' in. By the time ol' Mr. Kincaid held out his rent money, we didn't have hardly nothin' left to buy food. But afore she died, my wife, Jennie, was mighty careful with the money. She made sure we saved—maybe not much, but we saved. And that's what I used to buy this here land."

"I believe you, Ezekiel, but you're likely correct. The only way to get Jackson Kincaid out of Nicodemus is to prove his claims are nothing but lies."

"Iffen you think it's best, I'll go back with you and talk with the Kincaid young'un."

Samuel nodded. They left Ezekiel's hoe in the field where he'd dropped it a short time ago and made their way to the buggy, stepping over the blue-eyed prairie grass, which had begun to blossom only a few weeks earlier. They rode in silence, and as they neared the center of Nicodemus, Samuel spied Harvey. Then he saw Jackson Kincaid outside the Harris dugout. Miss Hattie was following behind Jackson, slapping her parasol on his shoulder none too gently.

The old woman waved the parasol over her head when she spied the buggy. "Get on over here, Ezekiel. Dis here Kincaid fella's been tellin' us a pack of lies 'bout you and some of the other settlers that just arrived." Miss Hattie pointed her parasol at the horizon. "Now who's that comin'?"

In the distance, a horse was galloping toward the town.

"It's Moses Wyman," Ezekiel said as the rider came closer.

Jackson ignored the horseman and glowered at Samuel. "I can prove that these people owe me money." He pulled a sheaf of paper from his horse's saddlebags. "Come look at this—signed by Ezekiel Harban. There's his mark." Jackson tapped his finger on an *X* at the bottom of the page.

Harvey waved his employer forward as the horse approached. "Sure am glad to see you, Moses. I think we've got a news story here that's way too complicated for me to write. Jackson Kincaid has come from Kentucky claiming some of the settlers were sharecroppers on his place and they left owing him money."

Moses dismounted and handed the reins to Harvey before stepping forward. "Jeb Malone told me you were on your way to Nicodemus, Mr. Kincaid. I'm Moses Wyman, owner of the Hill City newspaper."

"I believe I'll need a lawman more than a newspaper reporter," Jackson tersely stated before turning back to Ezekiel. "Do you deny this is your mark?"

Ezekiel took a good look. "I do."

Moses stepped closer to Ezekiel. "He's accused you of owing him money, Mr. Harban?"

Ezekiel nodded as his daughters joined the group. Truth grasped her father's arm and looked up into his eyes. "What's going on, Pappy?"

"Mr. Kincaid is accusing your father of owing him money," Moses said.

"We're wasting time," Jackson snapped. "How many times must I explain? I have a paper here that says the Kincaid family loaned money to Ezekiel Harban. He has never repaid the loan, and I've come to take him back to Kentucky until he's met his obligation. And I see others around here that sharecropped our land. I have papers on them, also. No use trying to hide!" Jackson stretched a finger toward some of the onlookers huddled in the distance.

Rushing forward, Jarena grasped the paper from Jackson's hand. "Let me see what you're offering as evidence against my father."

Jackson quickly retrieved the paper and pointed to the bottom of the page. "Right there—that's his mark."

"You're wrong. My father didn't make that mark." There was finality in her voice.

"You can't prove that—it's his *X*. I watched him make it," Jackson insisted.

Jarena's face was alight with pride as she met Jackson Kincaid's scowl straight on. "No one in our family signs with an *X*, Mr. Kincaid. My father can write his name as well as you—perhaps even more legibly."

"You're lying! None of our slaves . . . uh, sharecroppers can read or write."

Jarena laughed aloud. "How little you know, Mr. Kincaid. You've lost your workers, so you've come here with forged papers in an attempt to browbeat us into returning to your plantation. Well, it's not going to happen. We're landowners, just like you, Mr. Kincaid. We'll work our own land. I suggest you do the same."

Whoops of agreement filled the air, and Jackson looked pleadingly at Dr. Boyle.

"Don't expect any assistance from me, Jackson."

Moses seized the papers from Jackson and tossed them into a nearby fire. The bogus contracts flamed and quickly disintegrated into smoke and ash.

————

"He's done it again," Truth whispered to Jarena as they walked hand in hand back to the dugout. "How can I possibly avoid being alone with him?"

Jarena squeezed her sister's hand. "Why don't we talk to Pappy? He'll set things right. Once he knows you're afraid, he's not going to send you back to Hill City."

"Didn't you see how happy he was when I handed him my pay last evening? He's already planning to buy more seed, and he rushed to buy those chickens from Maribel Lemmons so you could have eggs to cook with. If I don't go back, the Boyles will find someone else to do their chores. I'm sure there's lots of folks among these new arrivals who would be happy for the work."

"No, Truth. The Boyles will understand—especially once Pappy talks to Dr. Boyle. They wouldn't want you to come to any harm. I doubt they have any idea what kind of man their son is working for."

Neither of the girls heard Moses approach, and they started at his words. "I'd like to speak to your father if he's around."

Truth could feel the heat rise in her cheeks. She wondered how long Moses had been listening to their conversation before he spoke. "Pappy's inside the dugout, but he's anxious to get back out to the fields."

"I'll try to be brief."

The girls waited outside while Moses went into the dugout. Truth leaned closer to Jarena and whispered, "Do you think he heard us talking and that's why he's gone in to talk to Pappy?"

"I don't think so, but I still believe you should talk to Pappy. If you don't, I'm going to."

Truth plopped down on a grassy spot not far from the doorway and hugged her arms to her chest. "Grace told me about Mr. and Mrs. Francis leaving early this morning."

Jarena nodded. "They never wanted to come here—it's best they're returning to Kentucky. My heart aches for them: first the death of their eldest son and now Charles. Mr. Francis was too frail to work their acreage, and George Lemmons was pleased to purchase it for his two older boys."

Truth looked at her sister. "The Lemmons family surely came prepared, didn't they? All that livestock and a wagon filled with more than all of us combined brought when we first arrived."

"From what I understand, Mrs. Lemmons and Caroline Holt had been corresponding. As a result, Maribel had a better idea of what to bring than the rest of us—and also the money to purchase their goods." Jarena plucked a prickle from the hem of her dress. "Mr. Lemmons sold his livestock, and Caroline said he turned a nice profit on everything he sold before coming out here. When they arrived in Ellis, they bought all those animals and supplies."

"And he had money to purchase the Francis acreage in addition to buying all those supplies?" Truth asked. "I'm surprised they wanted to leave Georgetown."

"Well, we managed to get a few chickens outta their comin'," Grace commented as she joined them. "I'm sure gonna enjoy having eggs, and Mrs. Lemmons said she'd be sellin' milk and butter, too."

"All it takes to purchase those items is money. I'll send my pay more often. Tell Mrs. Lemmons you want milk and butter every week."

"Harvey Boyle said Moses is writin' a newspaper article 'bout the posse comin' through Nicodemus and shooting Charles," Grace told her sisters. "He showed me the article. It says none of them claims about Thomas was true."

"Trouble is, Thomas was long gone by the time Wyatt Pell cleared his name," Jarena said. "Sure is hard to figure things out—Charles dead and now Thomas is off to Indian Territory. I do pray Thomas remains safe."

Truth's face wrinkled with confusion. "I'm confused, Jarena. Are you saying you truly care for Thomas?"

Grace bobbed her head up and down and giggled. "She won't admit it to us, but she's been writing him letters ever since he rode off with Lieutenant Boyle."

"Have you heard back from him?" Truth asked eagerly.

"No—not a word. That's why I fear something has happened."

Before Truth could respond, Moses stepped out of the dugout. "The three of you are looking mighty sad." His gaze finally settled on Truth. "Your father would like you to join us inside."

Truth couldn't move. "Me?"

Why did her father want to see both of them *together*? What had Moses said? Why wouldn't he just leave her alone?

She took a deep breath and walked inside to her father's side.

Ezekiel gestured to the chair beside him. "Sit down, daughter. We need ta talk, and it's gonna take a little while."

Truth shivered. She wanted to run from the dugout and away from Moses Wyman, but she did as her father bid.

"Moses come here to set a few things aright. I think it's best if I let him do the talkin'—but I want you to listen careful like. You's gonna find some of what he says hard to believe, but it's true."

"How do you know what he's saying is true?"

"I have documents to prove what I'm going to tell you," Moses stated quietly.

Truth chewed on the inside of her bottom lip. "Go ahead, then."

"I know you think I'm a white man who is making unseemly advances toward you." Truth wanted to run from the room. Moses had come here and convinced her father that his actions were justified. She narrowed her eyes and glared at him.

"I can see you're rushing to judgment— but please wait until I've finished. You see, it's true that I feel affection toward you. However, I am not what I seem." He took a deep breath. "Just like you, I am colored."

Truth jumped up from her chair. "I don't believe you! Pappy! You don't believe this lie, do you? Why, he's as white as the Boyles. Everyone in Hill City knows he's a white man."

"He's been passing," Ezekiel said quietly.

"I don't believe him. He's white, Pappy. White! He's telling you these lies to try and get me in his bed. Can't you see what he's doing?"

"Show her the letters, Moses. I couldn't

read them letters, but you can. And Moses tol' me what's in 'em."

"Read the letters, Truth." Moses gave her the folded documents that had been on the table. "If you still have doubt after you've read them, you can write to any of these people and confirm that I am truly the same as you. I've had a much easier life—of that there's no doubt. I was raised in privilege and given education and training from an early age, but none of that changes the fact that I am a Negro—just like you."

Truth sat down and unfolded one of the letters. The missive was penned on fine linen stationery and released a faint scent of jasmine. Likely written by one of his white lady friends, she surmised before gazing into his deep brown eyes.

"You ashamed of being one of us? Is that why you're passing? Or is it because you want the life only the whites can have?"

"Why don't you read the letter? We'll talk when you've finished," he replied unflinchingly.

Truth pressed the pages open and carefully read each one, glancing at Moses from time to time. When she had completed the letters, she refolded them and handed them back to him. "And why should I believe what these people say? Like this Spencer Houston? You could have had anyone write a letter such as this for you."

"But why would I? If my desire is to pass for white, why would I carry something identifying myself as colored—a man born to a slave on a cotton plantation in Louisiana? I can explain all of this on our journey back to Hill City, but I think your father will vouch for me—as will Dr. Boyle."

"You've told Dr. Boyle?"

"Yes. It was never my intention to pass as white when I moved west. I've never before done such a thing. From the start, my plan had been to settle in Nicodemus, but then I met Carlisle Boyle on the train, and it seemed as though matters quickly got out of hand. Everyone assumed I was white and discouraged my move to Nicodemus; then when Dr. Boyle told me there was a newspaper for sale . . ." His voice faltered and then faded completely.

"I'll ride back to Hill City with you, but that doesn't mean I completely believe you. I still have a lot of questions."

Moses smiled broadly. "And I'll answer *all* of them. I won't be happy until you're completely satisfied your questions have all been answered. However, we truly do need to be on our way back to Hill City," he said as he rose from his chair.

Truth followed suit and leaned down to place a kiss on her father's cheek before hurrying outside, where her sisters were still seated on the grass. "Moses is *colored,*" she told them in a loud whisper. "Have Pappy tell you about him once we leave for Hill City. He says his parents were slaves."

Grace stared at her twin as though she'd gone daft. "He's as white as any white man I ever did see."

"But he has dark eyes and dark hair—and it is wavy," Jarena haltingly stated as she stared at Moses, who was bidding her father goodbye. "He just might be. When you look at him real close, there's a possibility he might be one of us."

Truth hugged her twin. "I best be on my way. Don't forget you promised to come and spend the night, Grace. Mrs. Boyle said it would be fine for you to come whenever Pappy says."

Truth hugged Jarena and then scurried off, waving her handkerchief in the air. For their return to Hill City, she rode with Moses in the buggy while Harvey raced off on Moses's chestnut mare. She hoped Moses Wyman was prepared to talk, for she had already formulated a mental list of questions that would surely take him hours to answer!

CHAPTER

33

Macia and Lucy Malone presented a picture of solidarity as they sat side-by-side on the front porch of the Boyle home. The younger girl shivered as a late afternoon breeze swept across the porch. Clucking like a mother hen, Macia grasped her knit shawl and carefully wrapped it around Lucy's thin shoulders. Pleased when the girl snuggled closer, Macia smiled and then nodded for Lucy to continue reading from the primer.

As Lucy completed another page, Macia heard the sound of an approaching buggy, and they both glanced up from the book. Lucy began to wave with childlike enthusiasm as Dr. Boyle brought the horse and buggy to a halt a short distance from the house.

Macia remained seated as her father slowly ascended the steps. He swooped his hat in a grand gesture. "Good afternoon, ladies. I trust you're enjoying your after-noon."

Lucy giggled at his antics. "I'm reading to Macia."

"And I trust you're doing a good job?" Dr. Boyle responded with mock seriousness.

"I think so." The child looked up at Macia.

"Her reading skills have improved im-mensely. In fact, we were just completing our lesson. I believe Lucy's expected home very soon, aren't you?"

Lucy placed the fringed bookmark Macia had given her between the pages. "Can I come back tomorrow?"

" '*May* I come back tomorrow' is the proper question. And the answer is yes. Shall I expect you at the regular time?"

Lucy bobbed her head up and down as she carefully removed Macia's shawl from around her shoulders. "Good-bye, Dr. Boyle. See you tomorrow, Macia—and thank you."

"You're welcome." Macia smiled and waved.

Her father watched the child skip down the street. "Engaging little girl, isn't she?"

"She is quite lovable," Macia agreed. "What happened in Nicodemus?"

"All of Jackson's allegations were proven to be lies. He's quite fortunate the residents of Nicodemus didn't take the law into their own hands."

Her father sat down beside her. "I know all of this is painful for you, Macia. You left little doubt in any of our minds that you had planned to make your home in Kentucky with Jackson. Though it's difficult right now, I do hope that you'll eventually realize this is truly a blessing in disguise. Better to know in advance that the man is unscrupulous. He would never be the husband you deserve."

"Oh, Father," she lamented, her lips quivering, "am I doomed to be an old maid?"

He patted her hand. "Don't be impatient, Macia. I believe God has someone exactly right for you—someone who will make you very happy."

Macia remained on the porch while her father walked toward the livery to thank Jeb for warning Moses that Jackson was headed to Nicodemus. She'd likely never see Jackson Kincaid again, but that was all right. She no longer cared for him as she once had. Perhaps she should discuss a journey to Topeka with her parents. She hadn't yet taken up Martin Eustis on his offer to show her the sights in the capital city, even though he'd sent a formal invitation after his visit to Hill City. Yes, a visit to Topeka just might be in order, she decided.

Macia looked up as her mother stepped out onto the porch a short time later. "Looks like Lucy's returning for another lesson."

The sun was dropping from sight, and Macia squinted as she looked down the street. "Is that Jeb with her? I wonder what he's up to."

"I don't know, my dear, but I'd venture to guess that he's not coming to see me."

"Or me!" Macia jumped up from the wooden bench and firmly planted a hand on each hip. She could now see that her father was accompanying the Malones.

"You dare not rush off, Macia. You'll hurt poor Lucy's feelings. Do sit down and be civil."

"Look who I convinced to come and visit," her father said enthusiastically as he pushed Jeb ahead of him and toward the porch.

Her father's tone was a bit too cheerful,

and Macia sent a warning look in his direction. Surely he wasn't thinking she could ever have *any* interest in the likes of Jeb Malone! She nodded politely before turning her attention toward Lucy.

"I thought perhaps you were returning for another reading lesson, Lucy."

"We are—well, at least that's what we've come to ask you. Jeb never did learn to read real good, and I told him you're a mighty good teacher. You think you could teach him to read as good as me?"

"I'm guessing Jeb can read just fine. He's been operating that blacksmith business, and I have a feeling your mother probably taught him how to read when he was a little boy." She met Jeb's unwavering stare and dared him to defy her.

"I believe I'm going to go inside and have a slice of pie if I can convince your mother to cut one for me," Dr. Boyle said. "Lucy, would you care for a piece of pie?"

The girl didn't hesitate. She was inside waiting in the hallway before Dr. Boyle had taken his first step. "That must mean she'd like some pie," he said to his wife with a chuckle.

Jeb sat down beside Macia, careful to

maintain a wide gap between his dusty pant leg and her fancy floral print skirt. The air was thick with tension. Macia knew he was uncomfortable. She hesitated, contemplating how to handle his obvious embarrassment. She considered offering him a book to test his reading skills, but stopped herself. *Treat him as you would want to be treated.*

She gave him a sidelong glance while contemplating the idea. She didn't want to be like Jackson Kincaid, believing she deserved more than others because of her father's income or position in society. She almost laughed aloud at her last thought. *There is no society in western Kansas.*

She turned to face Jeb. "You didn't come here for reading lessons, did you?"

"No. I can read just fine. But my sister thought that if I told you I needed reading lessons, we could spend time together— and you'd get to know me."

She gave him a gentle smile. "And to know you is to love you?"

"Lucy thinks so, but she doesn't have much basis for comparison."

Macia nodded. "She's a bright child. Perhaps she's right. You never did take me fishing."

"You just say the word," he said, his eyes bright. "How 'bout we take a picnic and go after meetin' next Sunday?"

She hesitated a moment and contemplated his invitation. An afternoon picnic could prove a relaxing diversion, but she didn't want Jeb to build false hope.

"No obligation," he continued, "we'll just have fun. And if you never want to go again, I'll honor your request. I promise. And folks around here can tell you I'm a man of my word." He watched her eagerly.

"I'm sure you are, Jeb. Sunday sounds fine." She stood. "Now, why don't we join the others and have a piece of that apple pie before they eat it all without us?"

Long after the rest of the family had gone to bed, Macia pulled a chair near her open bedroom window and stared out into the starlit night. The air was filled with the scents of springtime—honeysuckle and lilacs and irises—the promise of a new beginning. A new beginning with no plans and few prospects. Her father had often said she needed to trust God and always attempt to place the welfare of others before her own. . . . Perhaps she should consider a teaching position for the area children.

She lit the small lamp on her bedside table and lifted her Bible from the table. Flipping open to the book of Psalms, she gazed in wonderment at the words she read: *Trust in the Lord, and do good. . . .*

Macia sucked in a deep breath and slowly exhaled. Apparently her father and God were like-minded—they both thought a good portion of trust and a few selfless deeds were in order. She closed her Bible, snuffed the light, and once again stared into the starlit sky.

"I'll try," she whispered. She hesitated and then nodded her head. "I'll try!" This time the words were filled with determination.

———

Each day Jarena listened as her father lauded the fact that his seeds had begun to sprout. But emerging weeds accompanied the new crop, and the battle for control quickly ensued. The hoeing and chopping were endless, and Grace now spent more time in the fields than at the dugout with Jarena. While their father worked his acreage, Grace hoed the sprouting crop in Thomas's fields. Jarena longed to be the one pulling weeds and nurturing Thomas's fledgling crop, but her father had quickly opposed that idea. He cited several reasons, but mostly it was Grace's inept cooking that had influenced his decision. "That chil' does real good out there workin' in the fields, but she scorches everything she tries to cook," her father had remarked. "We ain't got us enough food to be burnin' it up, and that chil's cookin' ain't fit for man or beast."

Jarena hadn't argued, for it would do no good. Though she attempted to find pleasure in each day, she grew weary of performing the same monotonous chores without anything to break the daily routine. One morning she spied Miss Hattie sitting outside the Harris dugout and motioned to the older woman. "Come on over and have a cup of coffee, Miss Hattie."

Miss Hattie waved in return and soon made her way to Jarena's side, with her sewing basket in one hand and her ever-present parasol in the other. The tattered lace edging of the sunshade flapped lazily in the afternoon breeze. "Gettin' kinda warm, ain't it?"

Jarena nodded and smiled. Everything about Miss Hattie made Jarena smile. In fact, Jarena believed Miss Hattie to be one of the wisest people she'd ever met. "I thought you'd be tending to Nathan while Calvin and Nellie were out in the fields hoeing."

"You ferget Calvin went to Ellis yesterday for the supplies and mail? Ain't expectin' him back 'til a little later this afternoon. I tol' Nellie she needed to spend some time with her young'un whilst Calvin's down to Ellis. Chil' needs more time with Nellie 'stead of all the time bouncin' on my knee. Dat boy's beginnin' to think *I's* his mama." She positioned her ample body on a chair Jarena had carried outdoors and rested her folded parasol against her side. "Calvin says your pappy's gonna have the best crop of anybody in Nicodemus township."

"I wouldn't doubt it. Except for attending Sunday morning meeting, he's out there from sunup to sundown. If it's only determination that counts, he'll have a fine crop— and Grace, too. She's working on Thomas's claim from dawn to dusk. Both of them think the land is going to produce just fine, but this ground isn't the rich black loam promised in those broadsides, and it definitely doesn't compare to the fertile soil back in Kentucky. Wouldn't surprise me if nobody has much of a crop come harvest time. I keep wondering if I'll ever get used to this flat, unpleasant prairie."

"This here place got a beauty all its own, Jarena. You gotta learn to enjoy what's in front of you. God created this here countryside, same as he created the hills and valleys in Kentucky. There's beauty in all of what He made for us."

"You must admit the beauty's a little more difficult to find out here in Kansas," Jarena quipped.

"I ain't so sure that's true. There's a kind of beauty out here on dese plains you can't find in Kentucky. I figure God must like variety. When you gets to thinkin' about it, He made all His people look different. And the animals, they's all got their own special look, too—same with the countryside. Don't mean one place is prettier than the other—just different. Why, I never did see me none of dem pretty little star-shaped blue blossoms or dem big yellow sunflowers or even a buffalo until I come to Kansas. Course, I don't reckon we could count them beasts as beautiful, but dey sure is a mighty creation. Truth is, gal, contentment don't come from the outside—it comes from in here." She tapped a finger over her heart. "It's time you made your peace 'bout all that anger you been storin' up since you left home. Now, don't misunderstand—I been seein' good changes in you. But the truth is, you still got a ways to go if you're gonna find the inner peace that's gonna set you free."

"I've been trying, Miss Hattie. I pray and pray, but my prayers seem like a vapor that rises up and dissolves before reaching God. It's as though I never uttered the words—I don't think God hears me. Do you ever wonder about God, about where He is?" Jarena's words were a mere whisper.

Miss Hattie automatically lifted her eyes heavenward. "He's right where He's always been, chil'. He hears your prayers and He cares about you, but you gotta have some trust. The Bible says God knows how many hairs you got on your head. I always did figure that if God's keepin' count of each strand of hair growin' on this old head, He cares 'bout all the rest of my life. Now, dat don't mean I understand everything that happens. Just means I know God's got it under control, and I ain't got to be tryin' to take charge." She fanned herself with the apron she wore over her dress. "Instead of always holdin' on and thinkin' you know best, you gotta let Him take control. God knows what's good for you, Jarena, but you keep tryin' to make your own plans without Him. You's a smart girl. I *know* you's able to understand what I'm sayin'."

"I've asked God to forgive me."

"Forgive you for *what*? Being such a headstrong gal?" The older woman looked straight into Jarena's eyes. "You ain't blamin' yourself 'bout Charles comin' out here and getting hisself killed, are you?"

"No, though I did at first. Now I've accepted the fact that Charles didn't come to Kansas because of his love for me. After talking to his mother, I understand he wanted to move out here as much as Pappy did—Charles believed he needed to prove himself. Trouble is, I didn't understand a lot of things about Charles until after his death. There wasn't much time between Pappy giving Charles permission to come calling and our departure for Kansas. Given enough time back in Kentucky, I think I would have realized we weren't a good match. He likely should have married Belle Harris—they were better suited."

"So what you done that needs God's forgiveness?"

"I've been terribly angry since Mama died. Then when Pappy said we were leaving Georgetown, that only made matters worse. I made it hard on him. Oh, I did what he asked, but not without grumbling and making sure he knew of my unhappiness at every turn. I never once considered his feelings or what he and the twins wanted. Before my mama died, she said she prayed I would grow up to be a righteous woman. I haven't done that, Miss Hattie. I've been selfish and angry."

The older woman threaded a needle and began to darn a hole in one of Calvin's socks. "And so you asked God to forgive yer foolish ways, but you don' think He's heard you, is dat right?"

"Um-hum." Jarena gazed off into the distance.

Miss Hattie took a stitch and pulled the thread tight. "How come you think God ain't heard your prayers and forgiven you?"

She shrugged. "Because nothing's changed."

"What you mean, chil'? Was you expectin' the earth to tremble 'cause you finally asked God to forgive you?" Miss Hattie asked playfully.

"No, but I thought things would get better. Instead, they've become worse. Pappy and Grace are out in the fields all day long, leaving me alone most days. I still miss Mama. Then, too, Thomas is gone, and I haven't heard a word from him since he left. . . ."

"Now we's getting somewhere. Problem is, you's all confused about forgiveness. Jest 'cause you don't get what you want, that don't mean God ain't forgiven you. Dem two things ain't connected, Jarena. God's forgiveness ain't tied to nothing else. You's wantin' God to *prove* His forgiveness by providin' you with a reward—something *you* think you deserve." Miss Hattie cackled. "God ain't in the bartering business. You's still tryin' to keep control."

"I suppose you're right."

"You *s'pose*? You *knows* I'm right, gal! Now, you quit tryin' to take charge of everything and give the good Lord control. He's gonna do a better job than you can even imagine." She tucked the mended sock into her basket. "And if you's lonely all day long, you could tend to a few of Effie's young'uns from time to time. Poor woman still ain't got used to life out here on the prairie."

"That's what I'm talking about, Miss Hattie. Why didn't God let my mama live when I prayed? Why doesn't God deliver Effie Beyer from her misery?"

"God don't always answer our prayers the way we want, Jarena. Ain't nothing in the Bible what promises He's gonna give us whatever we pray for, but that's where trust comes in—you gotta trust God knows better than you."

Jarena frowned. "I still don't understand all the suffering and misery He allows."

"You can't blame God for the evil and misery in the world, Jarena—you got to give the devil his due on that account. Evil and misery goes way back to the Garden of Eden. Man wasn't content to enjoy what God give him. Don't you make that mistake, Jarena. You trust God and do like the Bible says—count it as joy when you face hard times. It's during them hard times when we's got the chance to draw close to Jesus, 'cause during the good times—"

"We forget about God?"

She nodded. "*Now* you's beginnin' to understand. You see, when we believe in Jesus, we can make it through the hard times 'cause we got Him to lean on. How you think our people come through slavery?"

Without giving an opportunity for a reply, the leathery-skinned old woman pointed her darning needle in Jarena's direction. "Dem slaves wasn't able to make it on their own strength—they knew Jesus was their strength and salvation. It was Jesus that was gonna deliver them out of bondage. Don' mean a lot of 'em didn't die afore freedom come to our people, but God was watchin' and waitin' for the right time. And only He knows when the time is right, Jarena. But ooh my—when God moves, He stirs with a swiftness and power dat's beyond compare."

"I wish I had your faith, Miss Hattie," Jarena whispered.

"Wishin' don' do no good—wishin' is for fools. *Prayer!* That's what grow your faith, gal. And you need to open the Good Book and read what God's got to say. You's blessed you know how to read, Jarena. I think your pappy would be right pleased if you read to him from the Bible every evenin' when he gets back from the fields." She pulled another sock from her basket and examined it. "Now I could do with a cup of coffee if you's got some."

"I'll go inside and get you a cup."

Jarena felt every word Miss Hattie had spoken to the core of her being. She'd been pulling away from God ever since her mother died. Oh, she prayed from time to time and occasionally read the Bible, but mostly she thought about God only at Sunday meetings or when some problem arose. She stood inside the dugout, with the smell of the Kansas soil filling her nostrils, and she closed her eyes.

"Forgive me," she whispered. "You already know trust is a hard thing for me, but I'm going to try—and with your help, I believe I'll succeed."

The sunlight momentarily blinded Jarena as she walked back outdoors with Miss Hattie's cup of coffee. "Is that Calvin coming in this direction?"

"Sure 'nuff. It looks like he's got somethin' in his hand. Maybe a letter. Maybe I done heard from my sister. You can read it to me."

Jarena handed the cup of coffee to the older woman. "I'd be pleased to do that, Miss Hattie."

"What you got there, Calvin?" she called, waving her sewing basket.

His face lit up with a toothy grin. "Letter for Jarena. Looks like it come from Indian Territory!"

Miss Hattie whooped with glee. "Dat's even better than a letter from my sister! Is it from *him*?"

Jarena's eyes filled with happy tears as she took the envelope from Calvin. She recognized Thomas's uneven script. "It's from Thomas! Oh, thank you." She looked up toward heaven. "Thank you, Lord!"

Long after Miss Hattie had returned to her dugout, Jarena contemplated the changes in her life. She was much like this Kansas prairie—tough and uncompromising. But with proper care and tending, even the prairie had begun to show promise. With God's help, perhaps she would demonstrate that same potential. Green shoots had already begun to sprout in the rows of planted fields. Instead of dwelling upon the weeds, she should be giving thanks for new growth. Come summer, there would be abundant crops to gather—and with the arrival of the recent homesteaders, the harvest would be made easier.

Indeed, there would be much to celebrate come summer. They should plan an Emancipation Celebration much like the ones they'd always celebrated back home. There was no reason not to observe emancipation of the West Indian slaves from Britain here in Kansas the same as they had back in Kentucky. Surely the entire community would support the idea of a summer festival.

Her untamed thoughts stirred with an excitement she'd not experienced in much too long. Jarena's enthusiasm continued to grow as she warmed to the idea of the celebration. The men could set up tables down in one of the groves near the river, where the children could play games and swim, and the adults could eat and visit and rejoice. They would commemorate the emancipation, but they would also celebrate the enduring effort it had taken to survive their first winter on this untamed prairie. And they would celebrate their future. With God's help, the town would continue to grow, and their farms would prosper. Yes, she would talk to the others come morning. Together, they would begin their own traditions in this new land they now called home.

ACKNOWLEDGMENTS

Special thanks to:

My husband, Jim—for everything
The stalwart pioneers who willingly
    sacrificed to settle the Kansas prairie
The staff of the National Park Service,
    Nicodemus Historic Site
The staff of the Kansas State Historical
    Society
Angela Bates-Tompkins
Deletria Nash

Books by Judith Miller

BELLS OF LOWELL*
Daughter of the Loom
A Fragile Design
These Tangled Threads

LIGHTS OF LOWELL*
A Tapestry of Hope
A Love Woven True
The Pattern of Her Heart

FREEDOM'S PATH
First Dawn

*with Tracie Peterson